M.A.I.A.

W.D. SHIPLEY

First Edition

PAGE PUBLISHING, INC.
New York, NY

First originally published by Page Publishing, Inc. 2016

ISBN 978-1-68289-406-4 (pbk)
ISBN 978-1-68289-407-1 (digital)

Printed in the United States of America

DEDICATION

"To not just following your dreams, but catching them too."

For artists everywhere that never stop dreaming.

"Special thanks to Heather for support and encouragement."
-W.D. Shipley

MAIA
(MANUFACTURING ARTIFICIAL INTELLIGENCE AGENCY)

Production Floor

I pinched the clear chip and brought it up to the light. I squinted through my glasses and read the number out loud and scribbled down the digits. "Okay." I pressed my thumb to the fingerprint scanner, and a tray slid out from the tablet. I placed the nanochip into the tray. A hologram keyboard beamed out from the bottom of the tablet. I hovered my hands over it to the traditional keyboard next to it. I pitter-pattered on the keys and found the boy's sperm donor's profile—Social Security numbers, although useless in today's society, effective serialization.

I poked at the screen and swiped the digital outline of the chip swiveling around in a full 360-degree motion. I clicked on the main segments. "Okay..." I cracked my fingers. "Infantry. Good to switch it up, I've been programming female chip's all morning. Basic skills. Yada-yada-yada, all right. Got that. And that..." My fingers banged on the keys. I scrolled down the line, all the basic math skills, science, logic—everything you could learn in years of high school and college in my day, done in a programmer's ill attempt at milking an hour. I checked off basic programming for syncing to the MAIA monitors much like the flat screen computer overlooking the white room. "And done. Okay, just military programming left."

Binary code filled the lower half of the screen before me, and the upper half of the screen a series of equations and a color coded helix of DNA twirling boxes. I loaded in basic military logic for an infantryman. Thousands of years of military strategy crammed into one upload. "Another drone for MAIA. He'll be counting his kills eventually." I pressed the finger pad, and the tray slid out. I placed the chip into what could be an electronic engagement ring box and checked off the social security. "Ah, one more for the day."

I pinched the clear chip. I squinted in the light to read the next number.

"You know, they have these harmless procedures for vision," the doors slid shut behind Albert, and he placed my cup of coffee right under my arms. "Doesn't hurt a bit, see better than the eyes you were born with. Been around for, I don't know, fifty years or so. You might want to try it."

"Al, if I dropped this chip in my coffee, you would owe me a year's worth of rations, because guess what? They take it out of mine." I placed the chip onto the tray and opened the donor's profile. I sipped my coffee.

"You should owe me at least a week's pay for all the sludge you make me walk down the hall with." Al nibbled on a ration, a bitter brown cube. "This is all I need to make it through a day."

"Al, I'm sixty years old. I need more than a candy bar to keep me going."

"Candy bar, when's the last time you had a candy bar? This doesn't taste like anything, and it gives you half a days nutrients, carbs, and vitamins in less than thirty seconds. I'm around the same age as you, Tom."

"And I still wonder what's wrong with you on a day-to-day basis." The tray ate my chip. "The answer is right in front of me the whole time, you're cranky because you haven't eaten in over ten years."

I read the serial number, or Social Security, of the sperm donor. A number that was issued to someone at birth if you were born even "here" at one point, as a promise of life, liberty, freedom, and the pursuit of happiness, a number people use to strive to receive just to be considered part of the greatest nation the world history has ever known, a number that sealed *my* identity as an American citizen at one point, a number that turned my stomach and swished my insides, because I couldn't tell you the last time I saw it. The blood drained from my hands. My brain boiled, but my face felt frozen.

"Tom, you alright?" Al's neck craned forward. "I was just kidding about your watch."

I looked down at my watch, A Rolex my father gave me the last time I saw him on the last day of his life. The diamond for the five spot had been missing for years, maybe even before he gave it to me. I did feel like I had missed an hour. I looked at the Social Security number again. "Al, can you read me this number? My eyes are getting tired, I think. It's the end of the day."

Al confirmed. The chip that lay before me could very well, biologically, be considered my child. My child, in the MAIA army being trained as a—I fluttered the documents—sniper. I thought of all the files for the sniper, all the advanced math that had to be done on the fly to make a shot nearly from two miles away. I began working, but taking my time, programming this chip.

"Tom, are you sure you're feeling well?"

My fingers spread across the keyboard. "I just have this last chip to program, to meet my quota for the day, and I really want to get out of here. The coffee is upsetting my stomach."

"Should just switch to strips." Al turned around in his glass desk facing the opposite way.

I scanned through the programs checking anything I thought might be necessary to the extreme success of a young sniper. My throat itched. The list seemed extensive. Not too extensive it might be put aside for audit, but did a sniper really need to understand four languages?

My fingers paused. I read the last program. The flat screen overlooked Rob and my hologram cockpit. I stared down at the tray only large enough to hold the day's quota's worth of programmable mind chips. A blue wave flowed across the screen. Were they watching? If I had one of these chips in my head, could they really read my mind or control what I knew or thought I knew? I started down at the keys. This is the first time I've ever questioned it.

Program number 19-84, the vanishing sequence. The ability for MAIA, the central supercomputer, to dictate what I know. I stared at the protocol, and then at the monitor, back at the protocol, and then at the little chip that would be put into my boy's head. Minds are not meant for controlling. Delete 19-84, do not allow access for the vanishing sequence.

1

NINETEEN YEARS LATER

Alix Basil stared down at his hand. The helicopter jolted and shook, but his hand remained still; his body pulsated and his mind raced, but his hand remained still, a picture of stiffness. His other hand gripped his rifle, a series of deadly mechanics covered in computer implements all molded for perfect accuracy.

"Atten-tion!" Captain Milligan's steel studded boots scraped on the metal panel beneath his feet, and he yelled over the deafening hum of the engines and propellers. A Smith and Wesson revolver hung from his hip. "Listen, boys! First attack, you're all green, and none of you have a story to tell! Today it starts! Right here! Right Now! Your first day on the field! Now, strap up! ETA two minutes! No fucking around now, ladies!"

The eight soldiers strapped on their gray camouflage vests, tightened their black boots, clicks and clinks, pistols hung by their thigh, knives by their ankle, primary weapons from their shoulders, and secondary semiautomatic guns on their backs.

Alix held his back straight and his neck back. His eyes locked on Hayden across the helicopter. Hayden's jaw clenched, and the muscle on his shaved head tightened. "This is what we live for, Alix." Hayden lifted his chin. "Why the dim eyes?"

"I'm thinking."

Hayden shook his head. "No time for that, brother, it's already been thought up."

Alix smirked and pulled his mask over his face, the world brightened through the yellow lenses, and he inhaled his first audible bitter breath.

Captain Milligan held the support straps dangling from the ceiling, overlooking each pair of yellow eyes. His forearms tightened to hold him in place from jerking back and forth. His orange beard glowed, his freckles beamed. "ETA thirty seconds! Hayden, Wes, Phil, Eli, Matt, and Adam, you're Team Mantis. Alix and Victor, you're Team Engine. Don't forget your training! Keep your masks on! And remember, if you find yourself out of contact of MAIA and surrounded by them, do yourself a favor and turn the gun on yourself after taking a few of those bastards down with you."

The top of a pine tree scrapped under the steel floor. Snow and ash puffed into a swirling cloud of jet fuel and exhaust. The captain spun and caught his balance.

"Sorry, Captain!" A girl's voice over the intercom. "Closing in."

Sweat dripped under Alix's vest, and the helicopter vibrated.

The intercom bellowed. "Ready for deployment maneuver!" The helicopter jolted. The small flying machine banked backward. Eli and Phil closed their eyes and held in their stomachs as the chopper dropped. Matt and Adam pressed their feet to the floor and their heads back into the seat. Victor hung his head low, but the straps held him up. Alix stared forward and let his eyes blur in an unfocusing laziness, and the chopper descended faster than gravity. Metal pings engulfed the small armored cabin, and anxieties filled it to the ceiling.

Bullets.

The soldier's shaky hands released their shoulder straps.

"Three!" The pilot's voice stuttered. "Two!"

The straps tangled Matt in. He broke a strap to get loose. The helicopter hovered over the ground, their bodies all forced forward.

Captain caught himself hanging off a strap. "Deploy!"

The plated door flopped open, and the heavy steel rattle echoed in their helmets. The floor shook. Hayden lifted his assault rifle, screamed, and barreled out of the chopper's cabin. Hayden's gun spat to the left. Like a sneeze, the helicopter emptied. The earth vibrated beneath their boots.

Gravity pulled harder here. Smoke lifted in twisters from surrounding burning fallen buildings, overlooking white-tipped mountains in the background. The smell of decay clogged the air. Remains of disintegrating structures leaned, tilted, and shook as they ran.

Machinegun sputter hogged the sound in the air aside from Hayden's scream. Blood pelted out of the back of Hayden's vest. Bullets thudded into his body, drew him back, down and screaming.

Suddenly there was silence.

The helicopter lifted. Pebbles mushroomed out and sandblasted the nearby broken stone walls. The smoldering chopper shrank behind the pines. A small missile launched from over the burning horizon and left a streak of smoke across the sky. Their heads all followed the missile over the tips of pines in pursuit of the chopper.

Wes dropped his eyes first. "To the wall!"

Everybody veered after him to the left and slammed against the crumbling stone wall. Anxiety and fear tugged their boiling hearts back and forth across their chests. Alix watched a wave of dust crawl over Hayden's dead body and drown him into the shredded street, just another piece of debris amongst the broken boards and glass, loose trash, dead carcasses, and rusting cars.

"Don't look at him!" Wes slugged Alix's vest and drew a finger to his face. "Don't!" He grabbed Alix by the strap and pulled him down as a wave of bullets poured over them. Bits of rock rained down.

Alix stared into yellow metallic bubbles that were the eyes of Wes's mask, his breaths filtered and robotic. "Focus." He angled his rifle over the wall and stared through the video display built into his helmet. "Infrared scan the building across the street. We might have a shot at this guy." A burst of bullets skimmed the top of the wall. Wes swiped his rifle back.

Adam pointed his rifle at the building and scanned it for any heat created by a living body. "One possible on second floor. I'll keep him tagged if he moves, you'll know about it."

Wes turned to Adam. "Keep it in your sights." He turned to the rest. "We're going to provide cover fire. Alix and Victor go over to that old coffee shop across the street, clear the top floor, and take out that gunner!"

Wes swiveled, tossed his gun over the wall. "Suppressing fire!"

The sound of a million bags of popcorn amplified and moved Alix's legs for him. He slung his massive rifle over his shoulder and stumbled. Victor clasped Alix's arm and shoved him forward into the disheveled street.

Alix and Victor hauled ass across the devoured road. Bullets sputtered the concrete behind them. Holes the size of grapefruits trailed them across the pavement in a game of connect the dots neither wanted to finish. Victor aimed his pistol at the wooden door of the shop midstride. His gun spat. The door splintered around the knob. Alix and Victor split the door in two, crashed into the room, and slid into the counter and a busted cash register. Machinegun rounds sprayed the doorway, wooden walls, and shelves. The room fell to pieces around them as coffee beans, utensils, pieces of the porcelain, glass, wooden shards, and shredded paper floated from the shop. Alix lifted his head and shook the dust and debris off his helmet. He checked left. Victor checked right.

Victor hunched against the counter, breaths sifting hard through his mask, and drew his assault rifle. "Adam, how's that body looking?"

"All clear. Hasn't moved yet."

Alix's radio rang. "Engine, take 'em out! We're pinned!"

Alix pulled his sidearm out his side hostler. They hopped the sticky counter, cleared the small rooms behind it, and rushed up creaking old stairs in six heartbeats. In times like this, Alix counted time as such. Victor kicked the door off its hinges, veered left, and checked his corners searching for the section of heat radiating in Adam's infrared scanner.

Alix pulled right, checked his corners, nothing. Victor pointed his gun down at a mixed ball of two people. A white partial halo of hair circled the man's head, and he clutched the quivering bulk under him. White lace trimmed the outside of her blue dress. It poured out from under the old man. "Please, allow me to live. Por favor. Por favor!"

"Shut the fuck up!" Victor kicked the man in the ribs.

"Por favor. Por favor!"

Victor stomped on him Again.

"Ah, por favor!"

And again.

And again.

The quivering smothered girl yelped and tears hit the floor.

Alix twitched, closed his eyes lightly to the yellow-lit world.

Victor lowered his assault rifle. His bullets tore through the man's arched body and into the dress beneath him. The man's scream blended into the thick purple blooming of the dress. Blood sifted through the cracks of the splintering planks.

Alix opened his eyes, shook his head. "Room clear!"

Victor shoved two cups of dirty water and the checkerboard off the table. Red and black pieces skidded across the floor, rolled into the blood, stalled on the dress, and clinked down the stairs. Alix dragged the table toward the broken window. He propped up his rifle on its bipod and prepared to fire. He aimed from the shadows of the room to the clamoring of machine gun.

Victor tossed the motion detector down the stairs. Invisible beams sprung up, and when broken it would ring in their ears. Victor drew his scope, a mirror image to Alix's. He focused on the gunner, a human figure, but only human in its animal form. He breathed hard between words. "Target, gunner, .50 cal. Distance, one hundred-fifty meters. Wind…" Victor checked his embedded screen on his wrist. "Ten kilometers per hour south, southeast." He dug his eyes back into his scope.

Alix zoomed in on the gunner, cranked his scope two clicks counterclockwise, and set the crosshairs over the target's forehead. The gunner's ripped, raggedy clothes hung off his shoulders. His goggles glowed red. His teeth gritted in the nest of beard. His arms jiggled from a massive machine gun strapped to the back of a broken down pickup truck.

Victor whispered. "Fire. Shoot."

Alix exhaled and squeezed the trigger. The gun kicked. Air and sound got sucked from the room.

Blood sprayed the brick wall behind the gunner, and he disappeared behind the truck. Victor didn't pull the bubble eyes away from the scope. "Engine to Mantis, target down. Clear to advance."

"Copy that! Mantis advancing. Cover us until we get to the end of the street." Wes's voice trailed in Alix's ear. He lifted his eye from the scope to watch Wes led the team parallel down the narrow road, crouched and hugging the outside embankment.

Alix returned his eye to the scope and spotted her. Dark hair fluttered out from the grill of the truck. She stood, and Alix used the crosshairs to explore her body. She wore a dirty smock over a tank top and ripped denim pants. Smudges of ash and dirt smeared her smooth face and high cheek bones. She stepped over the body behind the truck, and her head veered down dropping tears onto the dead man. The streams cleared clean paths down her cheek. Her skinny body sprang up for the gun.

Victor spotted her. "Engine to Mantis, not clear. I repeat it is not clear to advance!" The girl climbed onto the bed of the truck.

"Too late, Engine! Cover us!"

Victor glared through his binoculars. "Target gunner, distance same, wind same, fire, shoot. Fire, shoot dammit!"

Alix zoomed in on the girl's face. He felt his pulse increase, the difference between perfection and a total miss lay in the pulse rate. All the training in the world can't substitute for that.

She grabbed the gun like her arms weren't hers anymore, but robotic add-ons; her face froze in fright and shock, but her arms drove from instinct. Alix shifted the crosshairs across her cheek and to her forehead. "Her eyes are brown," Alix whispered.

Through the scope of his rifle continuing on forever into the girl's brown outlined pupil, Alix allowed hundreds of distorted instances to click into one vague image, an image that answered unasked questions but formed new ones exponentially in its place. In the back of Alix's mind, a struggle to find reason to shoot consumed him like a storm hovering over a port. A storm smashing bound sailboats back into the barge, but casting one unhooked boat into the dead of night. Reason and emotion mixed into an unpredictable vortex of unthinkable distortion, and the weight and intensity of his rifle overpowered him.

With this rifle, Alix played judge in a court of preexisting, unhindered laws MAIA forced him to enforce. Guilty or not, a question holding no clear distinction, shifted across his eyes and forced him to enjoin at gunpoint; only Alix held the gun, and he had to squeeze the suddenly stiff trigger. But he couldn't; he couldn't decide guilty or not because it wasn't that easy. It wasn't that defined for this girl. Unfortunately, there is no partially guilty like there was no partially defending MAIA, or partially blowing a hole in a girl's face. But what about the grey area Alix felt suspended in from that moment and on, what are the laws there, what is guilty, and where was everybody else?

"Anna?" Alix's whisper focused him.

"What! Alix!" Victor shouldered Alix without pulling his eyes out of the binoculars. "Alix! Fire, shoot!"

The girl pulled the trigger on the mounted gun.

Alix held his breath.

Victor watched the bullets tear through team Mantis, their regiment torn apart, ripped open by smoldering metal, and pile on top of one another like dominos. Their dead mouths still screamed, their dead hands still held the triggers of their weapons, and their dead eyes held a dark haze in its beginning phase of perish.

Victor chucked his binoculars to the side, gripped Alix by the throat, and thrust him backward. Victor set the gun into his shoulder and aimed.

Alix leaned back on his elbows. He eyes followed the trail of blood, his hand soaked in blue dress, and found himself there again—there in the middle of nowhere, a place he didn't know, doing things for reasons he couldn't understand or realize. He attempted to pull his eyes away from the dress and the man's blank eyes, but a dead face never looked so alive. The man's mouth hung open. Alix couldn't figure whether his ears didn't hear the man's scream or if sound wasn't just coming out. His eyes shined like a dolls, but his skin already lost its complexion.

The shot erupted in Alix's ear. He pictured the girl, the blood splatter, her toppling over, her loose limbs bouncing off the dirt, the red and black hole in her dirty face, and her eyes, her brown eyes, wasted, sunken in and lost forever.

Victor turned and pulled back his fist, and he fell into Alix. Victor ripped Alix's helmet off and the first muffle breath of shit air clogged Alix's lungs. Alix's face burst into fire, and his head thumped off the floorboard after the third punch. Alix felt the smoldering blood oozing out the crack in the back of his head. He saw sounds, swirling blue and yellow, and heard colors, birds screeching and bellowing thunder. His vision sprinkled back. Victor raised his fist again.

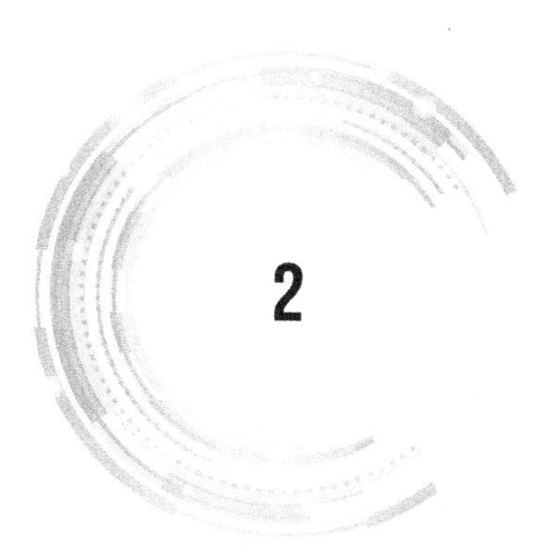

2

"Enough! Turn the simulator off!" Captain Milligan's voice congealed from a dreamlike place—far away, yet loud enough to hear the echo in your own head.

Alix lifted the shield to his helmet. The desolate world he just existed from glitched and disappeared. The florescent lights on the rounded ceiling above him flickered, and the door alarm cranked and echoed. Alix squinted. His pupils shrank fast. He undid the chinstrap and lifted his helmet. The battle simulator powered down to a low hum. The hard pads inside the helmet stuck a checkered pattern of red irritated regions on his shaved head.

"What the fuck happened, Alix?" Hayden ripped the Velcro strap off his arm and plucked the sensors from his elbow.

"You didn't see?" Victor tossed his helmet. It rolled and twisted on the metal floor at the foot of his simulator lounge chair.

Hayden shook his head. "Nah. All I saw was my leg barely on. I could move my toes though."

Alix sat up in the chair. He anticipated the bombardment, felt the humility squeeze his balls and run up his spine. He clenched his teeth and ripped a strap off.

Wes pulled his feet from the boots in the chair and rubbed his heel. "Alix blew it! He's fried. His chip's tapped."

"He fell in love with that little brunette behind the gun." Victor smirked.

Alix's head snapped sideways. "Fuck you! It had nothing to do with the girl."

"Here, take my helmet and go ahead back in. We'll leave you two alone." Victor reached for his helmet.

Laughs from the rest of the team swirled around the round room.

Victor dropped his helmet at Alix's feet. "She's dead now, but at least now there are two holes in her face to stick it in."

Snickers and small laughter filled the egg-shaped room; Phil's deep laugh held over the others.

Alix boiled and leaned forward.

"Shut up!" Captain entered the room outlined in simulator beds.

Alix swallowed his acidic words.

Captain scratched his orange frizz. "You all suck!"

Victor pulled a strap off.

"Do not interrupt me!" He pointed at Victor. "My office! All of you in two hours. Victor, five miles before coming to my office." The room hushed. He left, but his presence lingered like an excretion of ass gas, and in his wake echoed the stomping of his boots.

Silence assumed. Victor jerked the rest of the straps off and stood. "Alix gets nearly all of us killed, and I get five miles. This is bullshit!" He approached Alix. "You got a virus in that little chip of yours or what? Next time shoot, citi!"

The word burned. To be called a citi, as in citizen of what country lay in desolate condition hundreds of feet above them.

Alix sprung up and shoved Victor back. "I'm no citi!" The room jumbled, Phil pushed Alix back into the white chair and leaned on him. Adam hooked Victor's arms and pulled them behind his head. Matt shoved Adam and Victor forward. Eli tripped over a simulator and cut his forearm. Helmets skidded and twirled.

Victor looked back. "I won't spot for a citi! Find another spotter!" Adam shoved him again.

Phil held Alix's shoulder. Alix hung his shaved head, kept his eyes straight, and his lips and jaw tight. He ran his hand over his bristles feeling the heat leak out the pores on his face.

Phil's eyes weighed down on Alix. "You good?"

Alix met his glance full force. "Yeah, I'm good. What's that suppose to mean?"

Phil pursed his lips and shook his head.

* * *

Alix walked into the common room. Four squads and a unit of infantry looked up from billiards, darts, military video games, and the weight benches, and the eyes of each soldier followed him. Alix passed by the billiard table, and a large cadet smirked, eyed his partner, and nodded toward Alix. Insulting glances. He felt his squad's eyes on him most heavily.

Alix leaned back in a chair. Ancient pool balls cracked. Five chairs surrounded the large screen embedded in the wall, a faint blue wave rippled as the background. Alix sat alone, the whispers of the squads blew on the back of his neck, his failing a spreading virus throughout the regiment. He focused on the flat screen. He couldn't stop thinking about Anna. He'd looked for her during the walk from the simulator, passed by the worker's quarters, passed by the vehicle bunkers full of tanks, armored all-terrain vehicles, passed by the weapons bunker, passed by the hallway leading to the programmer's offices—even when standing within the impossibility of actually seeing her, Alix still looked. MAIA didn't make mistakes, like letting the boy and girl cadets mingle.

Everyone's face turned toward the screen at the same time before a woman appeared behind a glass desk in white attire. Her MAIA badge shined. She shifted her hologram tablet in her arms and held it to her chest. She looked up at the camera. "Good evening. As always, I'm Maia, bringing your the latest information on our progress and goals. I have determined there to only be about two weeks before we start seeing efficient sunlight in Sector 320 E for possible conservation of the city. The increase in sunlight will provide the energy needed to power the other half of the island. Reader Albert Rankin predicts our entering the mainland for conserving before the autumn. With 92 percent efficiency against the citizens on the mainland, I only predict 500 deaths in the first week and only 1,300 deaths in the first six months with complete control of the islands within a 5-mile radius."

"Can we vote who goes and who lives? Ha." Chuckles are heard from over Alix's shoulder.

"I also intend on introducing the first trainings on *new* military technology. Security of the main land is inevitable. Anyone captured will have the ability to have a new updated level 3 chip installed and would later join you at the front lines."

"I wonder what that is." Eli leaned over Alix. "The level 3 chip" He raised his eyebrows.

Alix looked away. Eli smiled. Alix leaned his chin back on his palm. "Probably just another crazy ability for the computer to get in your head." Alix spoke through his jaw he leaned on. "Like we don't have enough power already to take the world over five times."

Eli sat down, held his pool stick in between his legs, and stared at Alix. He spun his stick. "What happened today?"

Alix checked over the chair to Hayden and Wes in the corner, exchanging words without pulling their eyes away from the monitor.

"I don't know. I didn't shoot."

Eli's eyes didn't falter. "Alix, I gathered that. We got to do this. If you don't…"

"I know." Alix sighed, banged his wrist lightly on the end of the chair, and pursed his lips. "Next time."

Eli looked away and scratched his dark stubbles on his head. "You better hope there is a next time. Captain was pretty pissed."

Alix looked at Eli's freckle above his lip in the form of a grin. Alix sighed. "Yeah. I haven't even heard it yet."

The woman on the screen smiled. A picture of an bald old man appeared in the corner of the screen. "In other news, lead programmer Dr. Thomas Ethex died yesterday at the age of eighty. Dr. Ethex was born in the state of Massachusetts, from the former United States of America, at the time when MAIA was just a Fortune 500 company working on top of this very island formerly known as Governor's Island. Tom served in the most top secret technology production center. Dr. Ethex remained programming for MAIA even after the riots after the political implements on oil, gasoline, and travel itself.

Dr. Ethex programmed cerebral MAIA chips for mostly military personnel since the failure of the United States of America until the end of his life. His cerebral chip and memory has been requested to be stored in the archives. I predict and statistically hold Doc-Prog Robert Davis in highest ranking and experience to take over the position as head of the Manufacturing Artificial Intelligence Agency facility's cerebral chips."

Eli smiled. "I hope my chip is stored after I die."

"Humph." Alix shrugged.

Eli watched Alix's eyes and the wonder in them. It swirled around in his iris in a spiral of curiosity and conspiracy and wonder.

"Alix, when we get back, and we are genetically paired up with the medics and pilots, who would you hope to be conjoined with?"

Alix's face flushed. "I don't know. We don't really have a say in who we are genetically comparable to. Maia makes that decision. She puts us all into a pool and matches us up based on compatibility."

"Come on though, if you *could* choose."

"I really don't know, Eli." Oh, the name burned under Alix's eyes. Anna! And if Eli only knew.

Eli leaned in closer. "Come on, I can't talk to any of the other guys about this stuff. They look at me crazy. Like I got a virus or something."

"We don't have a choice anyway. What does it matter? Besides we've only ever seen them in simulation. How do you know how they really are?" Alix looked at his embedded screen on his wrist.

"Alix? Come on? Who would it be? If it could be anybody? Sid? Beth? Anna? They have to be the three best looking in the regiment. We've had the most time in simulation with them."

Alix's eyes wandered, but twitched.

"I knew it!"

Alix melted into his chair as Eli squirmed in his and popped out, sat on the edge, pumped his fists lightly and laughed.

"What are you talking about?" Alix smirked.

Alix looked over his chair. Hayden's lips moved. Wes laughed, leaned over on the table, aimed his stick, and took his shot. The eight ball sank into the corner pocket, Wes stood and looked over to Alix. Alix looked away.

Eli's grin dug deeper into Alix. "You were about to say Anna?"

Alix shrugged. "What? I seriously don't…I wasn't, no…Why do you want to know?"

Eli's teeth gleamed. "If you don't think you'd be conjoined with Anna, that's good, because I think I'd like to be." Eli folded his fingers.

Alix's smile shattered. "I didn't say I wouldn't be compatible with Anna!" Alix's face froze.

Eli leaned in, dropped his pool stick, retrieved it, and leaned in closer. "Why's that?"

"Maia decides, that's why?" Alix held eye contact.

"And because Anna is who you would like to be conjoined with. Just admit it. I'm telling you now, I'm going to hope Sid and I are paired so hard that Maia is going to have a migraine if she tries to access my head. Anna would be my second choice though. She is soo voluptuous. Umph. You lucky man you."

Alix locked eyes with the woman on the TV. "And good luck, new cadets. Our technology is now far more superior than the citizens since the last attempted conserving mission. This siege should be the end of the citizens and the beginning of a new era. Remember, I promises a bright future for all employees and soldiers conserving the mainland. Thank you, have a good night and remember, train hard." The screen flicked off and hummed for a moment.

"Ah! I hate that." Eli bowed his head and squeezed his temples.

"What?" Alix angled his eyebrows.

Eli squinted. "What do you mean what? That low humming before and after the screen prompts? It's stronger if you miss a broadcast."

"Oh, yeah. I hate that too." Alix's forehead wrinkled. "What were you doing this morning anyway? You almost missed Captain's briefing."

Eli pushed the pool stick back and forth between his hands. "Shh." Eli checked over his shoulder. "I didn't get too far, but I was trying to use the simulator on one of those nonmilitary scenes. I heard when you graduate and pass, you can use rations to create your own time in the simulator, for whatever you want."

Alix smirked and leaned farther back in his chair. "You're lucky you didn't get caught. You remember what happened to the last guy, right?"

"No."

"You don't remember?" Alix gestured.

"No. Who?"

"I forget his name, Who knows?"

Eli leaned in. "I'm going to do it though. I can't wait. I wanted to see the sun, Alix. Aren't you curious how it feels?" Eli's eyes trailed off. "Or used to feel? Imagine a bright sun over the ocean, a burning star so big it could eat the largest planet in our solar system. Imagine how powerful it must be and the colors it creates over a blue ocean with more water than you could ever think to drink."

"You can't drink the water."

"That's not the point! Imagine how amazing it must feel to actually have wind tickle your neck. I can't wait to surface for the conservation, I bet the mainland is unbelievable. It can't be as bad and toxic as they say."

Alix pursed his lips together and glanced at him. "They say it's pretty bad. I heard the smell is unbearable. The bombs did a number on the ozone around this part of the world."

The gleam in Eli's eyes diminished. "You have to believe there is more to life than down here."

Alix pictured Anna and knew more lay beyond his living. Life went on for so long under different circumstance, lives where people had freedom to do what they wished. He knew what Eli was saying held truth. Alix knew in Eli's twisted little way, he was right, and that someday Alix and the rest of the MAIA community just might think in the context he does, in a strange case where a single deranged man's ways becomes the norm. But until then, Alix also knew somehow to keep his mouth shut and his thoughts to himself if he could help it. He hoped Eli was right, but would do the same...for his sake.

Alix checked his wrist. He wondered about the time, and the time appeared in the blue hazy screen on his skin: 19:55:38. "We should get going, Captain's already ready to scrap us all. We're going to get stuck below in the gun cages."

* * *

Captain Milligan stared into the eight pairs of eyes. The cadets stood frozen, suspended in a tiny room. Milligan glanced at the screen hovering on the wall behind his cadets. A gentle blue wave was on the screen.

He leaned over his desk. A hologram map of Sector 320 E lay out before him. His elbows planted firmly on the desk, he rubbed his eyes. "Gentlemen." The room enclosed the eight cadets and somehow shrank, and Captain Milligan's thick voice added to the unwelcoming addition of volume. "We had a problem today, didn't we?"

Victor raised his chin. "Permission to speak, Captain."

"Denied. Shut up and listen." The Captain eyed Victor.

Victor clenched his jaw.

The captain swiveled in his chair and pulled his boot up to his knee. He swirled his finger around a small glass globe on the desk. "You see, some of you believe that there is one person in this room responsible for your deaths today. That, by the way, gentlemen"—the captain raised a finger and leaned forward—"is on your military record for the rest of your lives. Today was when you were supposed to take all that you've learned in your ten years of schooling, all the strength and physical ability of your training, and then apply all the tactical maneuvering you've learned and combine it all into one perfect symphony of a perfectly executed extensive mission."

Eight pairs of eyes fell.

The captain gripped the small glass globe. "Now, the problem today was not just your sniper and spotter. Hayden, how long were you alive in simulation?"

Silence.

"Hayden! You with us?" Captain snapped his fingers. "I asked you a question, boy."

Hayden raised his chin. "One minute, sir."

"You were in *simulation* for one minute, how long were you on the field?"

"Seconds, sir."

"How long!" Captain slammed his fist over the eastern seaboard on the map and stole all the breath in the room.

Hayden's throat thinned. "Approximately three seconds, sir."

"You charged out of the helicopter with no suppression fire. The covering fire from the chopper couldn't have been sufficient enough. There is one of two things wrong with this scenario, boys." The captain held his fingers in the shape of a gun and pointed at Hayden. "Either you charged out too quick, or your team didn't come out fast enough." Captain dropped his hand. "What was the first thing I told you about this squad?"

No one responded.

"What was the first fucking thing I told you!?"

Phil gulped. "Move as a unit, sir!"

"You don't take a damn breath if the person next to you isn't ready for it." Captain sat back. "Victor…"

"Yes, sir."

Alix held his breath in the firing line. He felt the blindfold coming over his eyes. He was next. He felt the blade on his neck practically.

The captain's eyes glowed a soggy red. His thick worn finger aimed at Victor. "The man in the building that you executed. Do you know who he was?"

Victor's eyes shot sideways and he thought. "No, sir."

"Of course not. May I ask you, what in that little chip of yours says that beating down this eighty-year-old man and his daughter and killing them is more important than taking out the gunner that has your team pinned?"

Captain held his breath in.

"What the fuck are you wasting time for! You see a man, you shoot. If you have time to realize he is not going to kill you, then you"—the captain slammed his hand down—"restrain the bastard and report it for cleanup crew so we can get some damn information out of the bastard and his bitch of a daughter! Your team is pinned, and you're worried about this old unarmed man. Stop dicking around and get it done!"

Victor snuffed out his nose and spoke through his teeth. "Yes, sir."

"The team after you guys secured him, took out the gunner and interrogated him. You know what they found out?"

Victor shook his head.

"Exactly! Because he was too dead to talk! He's eighty! Weigh your damned options, Victor. You're lucky I only gave you five miles for that."

The captain stopped and waved his hand. "Get out of here, all of you. Dismissed. I can't stand to look at you. You disappoint me. I'm going to go back to the Readers and listen to the reasons MAIA thinks you failed and how I could have prevented it."

Victor shot a glance at Alix, and then back to the Captain. "Sir?"

"I said get out of here, now get out of here! There's an old expression we used to use, and you guys weren't around to hear, and it's 'shit rolls down hill,' and right now, you're at the fucking bottom. Get ready for a double session tomorrow. Back to step one, boys. Learning how to work. And run. A lot. As a team. I don't want to see your faces. Get out." Captain studied his map.

The cadets turned to leave, but Victor held his footing. "Sir? Permission to—"

Alix tagged on the end of the line. Eli smirked. The captain dabbed the screen. The blood cooled in Alix's face. Eli looked over his shoulder and whispered, "Second chances."

Victor pursed his lips. "Sir?"

The captain whipped a pen at Victor. "Permission for nothing! Out or you'll be running until the conservation starts!" Victor dodged the pen. It missed, bounced off the wall, and rolled toward the doorway.

Silence followed Victor down the hall behind the pack.

"Alix," the captain's voice cooled to a rigid temperature, "get back here."

Victor smiled.

Alix stalled in the hall. He turned slowly back to the office, and Victor shouldered him on the way. The door swished shut behind Alix, narrowly missing him.

"Take a seat."

The captain pointed to the old computer chair in the corner. He did as he was told.

The captain stared at Alix for a moment, swaying back and forth in his chair with his leg pulled up onto his lap, and his fist pressed to his lips. "Alix, I have my theories about what happened today, but I want to know what you think happened today in simulation."

Stone became the medium of which Alix's lips were made, chiseled out of single piece of unmovable rock. He stared at the captain like he spoke an incomprehensible language. Alix couldn't find words in a jar of nothing.

"Alix?" He picked up the glass globe. Flickering sprinkles floated around weightlessly in the sphere. In the clear dome stood a miniature clock tower within a protective casing from the water and the flickering sprinkles. The second hand ticked within. "It's funny, you know they still call it a snow globe even though it's sparkles in it."

Alix swallowed.

"That's what they call these things, snow globes. It's some scene, usually something related to a holiday we used to celebrate, and then they would fill it with white stuff, and when you shook it"—the captain flicked his wrist, and the sparkles exploded within—"it looked like it was snowing inside the globe. But when it's replaced with sparkles, it's still called a snow globe. You might need one of these someday."

Alix's lips broke. "Sir, I froze."

The captain drummed his fingers on the top of the globe. His face said something, his expression said another. "And…"

Alix wiped the sweat in his palms on his knees. "Captain, before I pulled the trigger, I thought—"

"Correction, before you squeezed the trigger. And you can't think."

"Sir?"

Captain's stare ripped through Alix, dead eyes and pupils under dead lids and lashes. "Alix, you, more than anyone out there, can't think. The thinking is done for you. But for them"—Captain pointed toward the barracks—"it's easier. They shoot their enemy, and it's often a blind shot filled with adrenalin, a figure falls, and then they move to the next target. You on the other hand"—Captain leaned forward—"have to stay composed, don't you? You can't have adrenalin running through your veins. You are supposed to be completely still, hidden from the battle, accurate, steady, pulse rate, normal." Captain held his hand flat and still.

"Furthermore, you're often hundreds of meters away from the battle, but here's the hard part, Alix, and I think you know this, from all the way back there, from hundreds and hundreds of meters from the battlefield sometimes, you get to look into their eyes, don't you?"

Alix swallowed.

Captain Milligan closed in over the desk. "Something they don't have to do. You have to look into this thing's eyes and end its life. You get to see the grit on their face, their missing teeth, their fucking zits on the side of their cheek, and the missing pieces of ears and noses. You are like an assassin, you get to know them and then blow them away. Alix, you are the most important person on this team because you are far more dangerous to the enemy, and if you can't do this, if you can't shoot, you won't have the opportunity to.

"If you're going to be on this team, then you have to squeeze the trigger." Captain lifted the small glass globe off his desk and began twisting a knob on the bottom. "I don't care if you see *me* down there with a machine gun shooting at your team. You see someone threatening MAIA, you shoot. If you find yourself threatening MAIA, blow your own brains out. No matter what, defend the company, and Maia—that supercomputer thingy is your life." Captain finished twisting the knob. Twinkling music began to play from the globe. The screen above Alix flickered, and the blue wave stilled and faded into a still line.

Alix's mind rested to the music. He felt relaxed. Strange. Different. A breath of air before drowning, water before dehydration, flame before hypothermia—Alix felt alive. Free to the music.

The captain's eyes darkened, and his voice descended. "Alix, listen to me now more than ever, you don't see what happens to the one's who can't shoot, who can't conserve and defend MAIA, who *think*. It's just an empty bunk. People are forgotten overnight, Alix, existence can be erased for your generation. I made a promise to a man who just passed away, don't make me break it, so *conserve*

MAIA." The music stopped and the screen flickered and the blue wave continued.

Alix's head tightened, felt shriveled up when the music stopped. Dead. Drowned. Depleted. Burned. Alix stared at the globe and wondered of it's power. The second hand within the globe hit twelve.

"Dismissed."

Alix didn't check the room for more permission to leave.

"And, Alix."

Alix forced his head to the face captain's as if their faces were repelling ends of a magnet. "Who was the girl behind the gun?"

Alix didn't say anything, the flush of his face spoke for him.

The captain squeezed the globe and looked down at his blue outlined map. "Get to sleep. You're going to need every bit for tomorrow."

The captain's phone rang. He picked up the clunker rotary phone connected by a spiraling cord. "No, sir, everything is fine here. I think there was just a glitch."

Alix laid in his cold bunk. He listened to the electronic silent static of the screens. He watched the waving blue light through a helix of thin vertical bars holding bunks on top of bunks, just thick enough to hold Eli above Alix's bed.

He thought about the girl behind the gun, her brown hair and eyes, the curve of her hips and body, and her sad face. Alix recognized her, which wasn't the scary part. The true eeriness of it laid in the actual facts. Simulation is programmed. It could not have been just a mere coincidence. Anna was placed in that simulation for Alix to see, but how could anyone know about Anna and what they've been doing? For that reason alone, he could not meet her tonight. The thought of using the simulation tonight to see Anna brought a shocking wave of blackness to his stomach. Hopefully she would understand. Too risky tonight.

Instead he whispered to himself, "People can disappear overnight, *conserve* MAIA."

3

Anna lifted her head. She looked left to right, almost a senseless act in the darkness, but still reassuring. It's been days since she's seen him. Her heart bumped in her throat, and she felt her pulse in her ears, an anxiety cured only by the calmness of his clutch, her skin pressed against his, and his arms around her. Sweet surrender and tranquility. The door slammed shut an hour ago, and she couldn't wait any longer. She lifted her sheet.

Beth, in the bunk above Anna, breathed heavily when she slept and left no question in Anna's mind she lay in dreamland wondering about the first soldier she will get to patch up and drag off the battlefield.

Anna slid the sheets off. Her bare feet warmed the floor as she placed them softly in the blackened silence of the girls' barracks. The sound of her bare tiptoes leaving the coldness echoed in the boxed cave, and bounced off the faint reverberation of the friction of her clothes as she stalked through the barracks of musty smell and hushed sounds of sleep.

Twenty-two steps to the right, and she could barely make out the silhouette of the door to the hallway at her left. She didn't dare close her eyes again. Last time took what seemed like a half hour to orient herself and make it back to the barracks. One hundred and five steps towards the door, and she could make her move.

"Step back! Get back to where you were!" Sirens rang through the facility and breaking the darkness; the voice bellowed out from Anna's 3 o'clock. Anna's eyes heightened. Her blood became lava boiling through her veins. She stopped. Turned. Froze. Got caught. She pictured Sue storming down the hall and full spear and tackle and holding her down for a MAIA robot to come and seal her eyes shut, wipe her brain, and store her in a medical box until after the conservation.

The lights remained off. The alarms didn't sound. No Sue. No Tackle. No brain wiping.

"Shut up, Tracy! I can't fucking stand her. I can't believe she did it again."

"Jackie, stop."

"What? That bitch always screams in her sleep and wakes me up once a week. One more time she's going to need a medic."

Blackness ensued. Words became whispers and chased away the heightened alert. Anna felt her pulse calm. She smiled. She snuck to the door.

Through a small line of light she could see the booth. Two nurses talked and stared down at a boxed computer. Anna raised her wrist. The time appeared on her EED. Two minutes, thirty-five seconds. She and Alix ran this in simulation so many times; Anna knew how many times the nurse at the computer would blink before she signed out, and a replacement came in to provide Anna thirty-two seconds needed to slide down the hallway and skid into the solo simulation room.

* * *

Light filtered through his eyelids at the same time a horn pierced Alix's eardrums. Alix sprang up. He ripped his shorts and shirt off. The cool floor numbed his feet, and the chilly air licked his rear and his groin. He hoisted up his boxers and white camouflage pants, dove into a black shirt, zipped up his vest, and stood at attention at the end of his bed. He felt lighter, smaller. Alone. Two hundred and fifty steal-framed bunk beds held two cadets at the foot, but Alix felt alone in this container of cadets. Why was he the only one at the foot of the bed? He looked around. Two soldiers stood at the end of each bed. Except Alix's.

Captain Milligan trudged up the hall to Alix's area. "Squad 28, you ready to pay for your fuckup!"

"Sir, yes, sir!" The seven-man squad screamed as if they didn't have the attention of the whole brigade on them already.

"Good, take your tabs and let's go! The rest of you, because the whole brigade didn't pass the simulation, run six miles before your half day off."

The air sucked got out of the room. Alix felt the final stone lumped on the top of the pressing pallet, the last bit of weight compressing his lungs down and him not having the capacity or strength to breath any longer. Officially, Alix became the reason for the gallons of sweat over 6 miles, the reason of the 31,680 feet of hustle, because it wasn't just jogging, it was running for your life. Good fucking morning.

Milligan placed his hands behind his back and marched away. "Squad 28, Vomit Room at oh five hundred!"

Alix pulled two blue tabs and two red tabs from the column next to their bunk. The extra two red and blue tabs stood out. Alix squinted and checked over his shoulder. Extra tabs? Why would he, out of everyone in there, get extra tabs? He pulled them out and shoved them under his pillow.

"Alix, don't bail on us today." Victor zipped up his vest. "Can't have you forget how to run too."

Alix turned and stood stiff. He held Victor's gaze through the interludes of cadets crossing their path, shaved head after shaved head, breaking eye contact.

Alix smiled. "Hope you can keep up."

* * *

"Pick up the pace!" Captain Milligan's voice shook their brains from the loudspeaker above. He watched from a glassed room overlooking the vomit room, their legs churning gears, their pores pumping wells of sweat. Alix led the group around the track encircling above the beige painted room 401, a room where physical training anomalies cluttered the floor below, a room that pushed body and mind further than it ever wanted to go, a room that often lead to puking in midstride, but you kept going, kept pushing. It was a room that every time you finished, you just began because there was more your body could or had to do. There was no choice, no decision making, no regret, just the first step, first push, first thrust, then another and another until your body pleaded for mercy; but when it came, it came in the form of another physical challenge. This room deteriorated humans and created soldiers in their place. It erased the human mind's ability to object to your captain's demands if it meant personal sacrifice. Several have come to near death, but the room really only claimed one life that Alix knew of.

Alix felt Wes's strides behind him, Victor's and the other four behind him, same width, same burning, tingling, and straining of the muscles. Alix breathed through his nose, ignored the sweat streaming down his face, the numbness of his muscles, the strain in his legs, the ache in his knees, and tried to forget the amount of times they've circled the track—easily triple digits. He knew better than to wish captain would allow them to stop running because when you waited for the command, it seemed to take longer to come, like he knew what you were thinking.

"That's enough!" the captain's voice echoed. "For now."

Wes's hands planted to his knees. His breaths sputtered out of rhythm.

Alix breathed deep through his nose. He listened for his pulse, checked his EED and was correct.

"Why'd we let Alix lead?" Wes wiped the sweat from his forehead. "Who's dumb idea was that to have the fastest one out front?" He straightened his neck, his eyes widened, and he yawned.

"Mine." Phil squeezed his eyes together and breathed through his teeth.

Wes ran to the nearest pale and stuck his head in, and the echo of the splatter turned Alix's stomach.

Adam winced.

Victor sucked air and propped himself up on his knees. "Let's not forget he's the whole reason we're here." Victor's eyes stared through his eyebrows, and he slid off his knee.

Wes's voice echoed from deep inside the bucket, "Shut up, Victor."

"Where were you…the whole time anyway, Vick?" Alix asked between breaths.

"Don't call me Vick," Victor's face weighed down by sweat didn't change. He held up his middle finger.

The captain stormed through the swinging side doors. He grabbed Hayden and Matt's vests by the back of the neck and ripped them straight up. "Don't bow your damn heads! Stop feeling sorry for your damned selves!" He grabbed Wes's shoulders and pulled him up as brown strains dripped back into the pale and on the floor. "Stand up straight! Straighten the pipes! This is your own fault!" The captain looked in the seven pairs of eyes begging for mercy. "Look at you all. You're as sad as the first day we started physical training. You want to go back to education?"

They spoke together. "Sir, no, sir!"

"I'll be happy to put you boys back in the classroom. Want to sit through some more programming? Schooling? You want to watch those five-hour strategic videos again? Learn more about those savages outside?"

"Sir, no, sir!"

"You want to be first on the mainland?"

"Sir, yes, sir!"

"Well what the fuck are you waiting for? Eight more laps, go!" Captain kicked the pale from under Wes, the contents smearing the mats.

* * *

Alix reached for the thirty-pound dumbbells and stood in front of the stretched mirror. He raised them to his shoulders. Above a stampede of runners on the track pulled his attention off his own rubbery legs. Alix watched the younger cadets race around above them. He remembered the first time out of education and into training, running around the track and looking down at an older generation of soldiers wondering how amazing it would be to be so close to simulation. Alix set the bars down and waited for Matt to get out of the way and move ahead to the next station – bench-press.

Phil picked up the forty-five ounce dumbbells next to Alix; Phil's reflection inches taller than Alix's. "You may be able to run the best, but you don't have it here." His voice echoed from a distant lightning strike down his throat; his vocal box a deep, slow, rumbling thunder. "You don't have the goods." He laughed.

Alix began curling thirty-five pounds. "Lifting these weights isn't going keep you alive out there."

Veins strained out of Phil's arms, and they bulged every time he brought the iron to his pectoral. "And running will just get you shot in the ass." Phil gritted his teeth and ripped his cheeks back into a scary smile, breathing through his teeth. "Alix, what happened, arh, in simulation?"

Alix felt his arms ripping but kept bringing the dumbbell up. "It won't happen again."

Phil slammed the iron dumbbells down on the steel shelf. "You for real? 'Cause if I get shot again 'cause of you, bullet in the brain or not, I'm coming after you."

Alix dropped the weights. "*I'm for real.*"

"Good, 'cause I don't want to have to hurt you, Alix. I like you."

They walked over to the weight bench. Matt moved onto the next station, and Hayden took the dumbbells. They tossed two big plates on each end of the bar, and Alix lay down beneath it and began to press.

"Come on, boy, you got one more in ya, come on." Phil crossed his arms and watched the bar teeter back and forth. "Come on, a little more. I ain't helpin' you, you better put that up. Three more… and one more for getting me shot."

Alix grit his teeth and shoved the bar up onto the hooks. "Ar! Fuck!" He sat up.

Phil slapped him on the back. "There you go!"

Alix caught his breath and checked the mirrored office windows overlooking the room. He could feel the stares. He knew at least the captain watched them. "Phil, you feel like something's missing today?"

Phil added weights to each side. "Yeah, our day off."

Alix got up and spotted for Phil.

Phil leveled his grip, checking the length between his hands and the weights were equal. He hoisted the bar up above his chest.

Alix lowered his hands.

"Don't touch it. I got this."

Alix counted the weight. "No seriously, something's missing."

Phil pumped the weights twelve times. He tossed the bar up on the hooks. "I'll tell you what's missin'. It's the actual action. I'm sick of simulation. We are trained from the time we're born, and I don't think simulation is hacking it. You would have shot if we were really out there, you know? Like it's making us fucking soft. Let me put a notch on my belt for god's sake. You wouldn't have held your fire if it were real."

Alix looked back up the mirrors. "Yeah." Alix's eyes fell. "You're right."

* * *

Captain Milligan watched his team play musical chairs with the different lifting mechanisms. His mind faded, grey and humid, to a better place. He rubbed his beard and remembered his father surrounded by hay, driving a metal mallet down on a horseshoe an eternity ago, a mallet little Milligan needed all his strength to carry, let alone swing it. Each metal-on metal--clink blinked Robby's eyes for him, and he wondered how his father could see where he was hitting. How? His father stopped, stumbled the mallet down on the workbench, and wiped the sweat from his head on the bottom of his shirt. "A Virginian farm can cause you no harm." His father looked up at little Milligan sitting on the fence on the horse stall. "But the heat's only cured is Virginia's Beach."

"Where's Virginia Beach?" The horse stirred, neighed, and it looked toward little Captain Milligan.

"It's about a five hour's drive from here. I'll bring you again someday. Ya see, you were too little to remember the last time your mother and I brought you."

Milligan pushed the dirt beneath his feet into an arc spread before him.

"Why don't you run over to the house and get momma to get us some lemonade or iced tea or something?"

Milligan hopped the fence and pushed the heavy door aside, plowing dried hay from it's path. He stared across the field of the biggest farm in Virginia. The house appeared small and hazy, grown out of the rows and rows of corn, farther than what he wanted to run in this heat. Robby reached in his pocket and pulled out his small cell phone his mother got him. He dialed his mother with his tiny fingers and held the receiver to his ear.

"Robby hunny, where are you calling from?" Her voice sang to him. He watched as a curtain wrestled to the side in the kitchen window of the large colonial. The phone lifted from his hands and pulled up to the sky. He jumped up to grab it, but huge callus hands already fastened a steel grip around it. His father brought the cell phone over to the workbench faster than Milligan's lips could scream.

"Hello? Robby?" His mother's melody. "Robby, is everything okay?"

His father lifted the mallet and drove it down. Pieces of screen, plastic, and components erupted from the bench. The metal mallet came down again and again. Milligan's mouth hung open. His eyes locked on the destruction of his first cell phone.

"Close your mouth, Robby. No need to bother momma on the cellular phone just to bring us some drinks. Now, run over across the yard to momma and get us some lemonade."

"Yes, sir." Robby wiped the tears away from his little cheek.

A shadow cast over the captain and pulled him from his memory, a light reflection of himself in a one-sided mirror overlooking the gym.

"Captain Milligan, how's Squad 28 looking after the terrible performance yesterday?" Albert Rankin's voice lingered through the dimness of the office. Rankin floated into the room, arms connected at the wrists behind his back, his medals and badges decorated his long navy blue coat, his smile pulled far back, bald head shined, and his T-port set too high to pass through some centers of the facility without hunching. "At the last Maia reading, they *were* favorable to be the firsts deployed. Statistically, they had the best chance. I can't say that's still the case, Maia will have to do another analysis of the brigade. Did you see Squad 53?"

Captain Milligan stared down at the seven cadets lifting weights from the mirrored windowed office set on the above floor. "Yeah, they scored a 97.7. That's the new course record if I'm not mistaken. Isn't it, Mr. Rankin?"

"Uhm. I never would have thought your favored squad would get a 23.8 on their final battle simulation test. They've fared so well when in the past practice simulations. That Alix is quite a shot. Practically does the math in his head."

"I know. I'm not entirely sure what happened."

Rankin's T-port electronically whined around the stretched glass table and swiped one of the swivel chairs leaving the back connected to the table. He rolled up next to Milligan, still overlooking the vomit room. "How are they taking it? Not just the failing, I mean the recent change."

Captain Milligan looked down at his men and stiffened his jaw. "The physical reprimands they can take, the loss of team member if they really knew? Immeasurable. But, so far, no signs of psychological repercussions. Doesn't appear like any of them have any clue. "

Rankin's voice reciprocated. "Do you propose that the vanishing sequence of Private Eli Williams was not a sound decision, and that keeping him on the team was actually beneficial to the conservation of MAIA?"

Captain looked Rankin in the polished eyes. "That's a decision for Maia the computer, not an old man like myself," Captain looked away. "My expertise is in military strategy, not societal discipline."

"You know the crimes he committed, why can't you accept the punishment? I sensed your bitterness, but didn't think it would affect your judgment. We caught him in the simulators, MAIA property."

Captain shook his head and faced Rankin. "Don't give me that shit about MAIA property. Everything is MAIA property." Captain turned from Rankin and back to the glass. "This team was just starting to come together, sir."

"From my understanding, Captain," Rankin's voice hissed, "Squad 28 just failed simulation. I don't want my lead squad to be 'just coming together' just weeks before our commencement of the conservation of the mainland. They need to be ready. And quickly. Once we get enough sun to power—"

"Sir, with all due respect, I've already—"

The old man's face turned hot. "Keep your respect, Captain, and bite your tongue. Hold it until it bleeds, no matter. The boy snuck out of bed during system hibernation hours and used a two billion-dollar piece of equipment to run a simulation on how to swim in the ocean and run naked on the beach! Maia has configured—" Rankin coughed—"the most logical punishment. I've been on this planet for a hundred and three years. I've been on this island since the United States called this a underground military stronghold! Do you doubt Maia's analysis of the situation? Maia recommended reprimand was Required Action 644—to erase his cerebral chip and start over, repress old memories and create fabricated new ones—the vanishing sequence. We didn't kill him, Captain. Eli is not dead."

No, but his existence is, the captain wanted to say. The captain clenched his jaw instead. He looked down at the steel supports holding Rankin's knees locked and his boots in place. He wondered if Rankin's short little body could get out of the high T-port, and if the machine held his prick for him while he pissed too.

Rankin eyed the screen in the corner.

Captain sighed. "What about the girl they caught too?"

"Maia is going to decide later this evening. She's one of the best medics we have, I think that is why Maia is taking longer to decipher. The girl is none of your concern."

Captain cleared his throat. "Sir, requesting permission for Squad 28 to get another chance at battle simulation."

Rankin stared at Alix below. Alix looked up to the booth. He turned to Phil, said something, and looked back up at the mirrored office.

"What about Alix? How's he been after simulation? Did you discuss his performance?"

"I have, sir."

Rankin smiled. "I know, I watched the recordings, of simulation and of your meeting. You didn't go too hard on Private Alix did you? Well, that is until after the rest of the squad left, but even then it's hard to tell because your screen's signal got cut off. I found that peculiar." Rankin knotted his fingers in front of him, "I'll send someone in to check out your server."

"As you wish."

Rankin smiled. "We'll see what the other Readers think about giving your squad another chance, but as for first deployed, I don't see that happening." Rankin pulled away.

The captain listened to the electronic strain of the T-port, stopped to align the swivel chair back to a right angle to the glass table.

"And, Captain. Don't feel bad. Your team doesn't miss Eli. They don't even remember him." The door closed.

* * *

"Come on! Push yourselves!" Captain's voice chased them around the gym, but his body paced back and forth across the middle of the floor, wrists locked behind his back, and the rush of Squad 28 swished by him. They crouched down and touched the painted line, and the captain's voice pursued the stampeding legs back the way they came, only to return after touching another line, and they did it again and again.

Alix lopped over to touch the line, craned himself back up, and jogged across the court to the other line. Sweat leaked from his depleted body. He couldn't feel his knees; he long since accepted his toes might not be there, and his body overheated.

"Down!"

The team dropped to their hands, scattered throughout the floor, pushed up and continued running.

"All right! Stop and breathe!"

Alix held his breath. He heard his pulse. He felt his stomach heating up and rising to his chest. His knees throbbed and kept buckling under him. He strained to stand.

Victor's hands hit the court. His palms slapped the floor and left him on all fours. He spat. Strings of saliva dangled from his dry lips. He spat again. He stared into the floor for a resolution for his body dysfunction, as if laying his head down on the floor would fix all the muscle destruction.

The captain shook his head, listened to their huffing and wheezing—a symphony of weakness and depravity. Pathetic. "Must be a generational thing. If my captain could get his hands on you for two minutes, you'd be crying to these little sprints."

Deep body odor melted together and hovered over the group. The vomit room lay vacant. Only the teams huffing and puffing held volume by the room's beige walls. The rising heat in Alix's stomach fell. He held his shoulders up straight and let himself *breath*. Sweat rained down his face, and he stared at the captain through the stinging pain, doing what he was always taught not to—blame someone for his pain, someone else for technically his own folly, but it wasn't just that, it wasn't just the blame that for some reason everything didn't sit right. It wasn't his stinging eyes or his throbbing legs, his aching lungs or his water deprived body that left Alix feeling…dry. Alix felt a chill in this humid, hazy room, and it crawled up his spine and into his head. Something beyond the surface bothered Alix, and he couldn't put his finger on it.

The captain hung his own head and pinched the bridge of his nose. "Get up. You're embarrassing me."

A large thud. Phil collapsed.

Alix's body won over his conscious. Sweet gravity cupped Alix's neck and pulled him to the gym floor. Alix fell to his knees. Black dots sprinkled his vision, and sound pulsed in ways Alix didn't know sound could exist: colors were sounds, sounds were colors, deep blues waved in large slow arches, and reds radiated in little rapid ones. Alix began to breathe heavier. Matt fell next to him.

"Get up." The captain pinched the bridge of his nose harder. "Now!"

Alix planted his foot on the ground and pushed against his knee to stand. He wanted nothing more than to disappear.

The thought started a calm that began to rain into a storm. He wondered about the captain's words and what they really meant—not the words he spoke just today, but since the first day they began military intelligence, training, and awareness, all the words to the whole team and the few shared individually, but most importantly the most recent: "disappear." What did he really mean that people could disappear overnight? Forgotten? As in Alix could actually not exist tomorrow? Dying is dying, but the time of existence can't be taken away, can it?

The words rang in Alix's ear behind the throbbing pulse. Sweat covered Alix, seeped into his shirt, his vest, his pants, but Alix's body felt cold, abandoned. Alix's mind searched through his memory; school; Anna; training; simulation; a blood-soaked dress; checkers; his rifle; blood splatter; long dark hair; deep brown eyes; a stiff trigger; "People can disappear overnight. Conserve the MAIA," but something before that, something more than that. How can people disappear? Who disappears? Who disappeared? Flashes of scenes of his life became clear. His mind twisted and wrung out what energy he had left.

Alix's senses sharpened. His hair stood straight up. His eyes widened. Who the fuck disappeared!

"Eli," Alix whispered it.

The captain angled his eyebrows, sharpened his eyes, looked into Alix's hazy eyes. *Wait, what? Did he just say…*

Where's Eli? Alix's brain unraveled.

Alix looked around, his breaths spiraling down, oxygen deprivation, light-headed, hunched over and swaying before the captain. The room became small, the walls pushed in, the doors grew large. Color enzymes flicked on and off in his pupil. *Please help!* His brain became heavy along with his eyelids, and the world Alix saw swirled.

"Alix?" Wes gulped for air and grabbed Alix's shoulder. "Alix, you all right?"

The captain tilted his head to the side and watched Alix's wavering body. All eyes followed Captain's to the back of the group. Alix's eyes looked back at them, but somehow weren't there. His eyes circled around back into his head, and the color in his face fell the moment his eyes started flickering.

Hayden eased to catch him. "Alix?"

Alix looked at him, but his eyes glazed over and rolled back into the back of his head. His head tilted back, and he fell backwards. Wes's body strained to stop Alix's, but it was too much. Everyone gathered around Alix's sprawled-out body.

"Victor!" The captain's finger shot to the exit. "Go get a medic! His body's going into shock!"

Alix floated in a deep sea of a dream. His body felt a pressure like a giant fist squeezing him like a stress ball. A massive shadow floated in the distance and consumed his world. His ears popped over and over again, and a familiar voice echoed from under water.

"You better hope there is a next time. Captain was pretty pissed…I hope my chip is stored after I die…Come on. Beth? Anna? Sidney?"

The sentences formed from memory, like he'd heard them before, but something buzzed in Alix's head, in his mind or maybe his chip; and somehow, Alix believed the words never happened, like finding a downed tree and saying it never fell.

A face welded to the voice. A round male's face, a freckle above his lip, and dark stubbles on his head. He looked at Alix. "What do you mean *what*? That low humming before and after the screens prompts. It's stronger if you miss a broadcast…You were about to say Anna?"

Alix couldn't place the location of his own body. He couldn't feel his limbs, his chest or his face. Where is he? Alix thought about the question. Alix nodded his head. "I'm curious how it feels." He said out loud. How what feels though? The air? Love? Life? Alix angled his eyebrows at the face floating in the darkness of this dream.

Phil looked to the captain and furrowed his eyebrow.

"Imagine a bright sun over the ocean, a burning star so big it could eat the largest planet in our solar system. Imagine how powerful it must be and the colors it creates over a blue ocean with more water than you could ever think to drink."

A body began to take form. Alix felt he knew him, like someone you swore you knew, but couldn't place from where or how you met them, or even what their name was, almost like the relationship existed in a past life. The face got closer to Alix's view.

"You have to believe there is more to life than down here."

Alix felt his body leave the ground of the vomit room. He felt the hard pressure on his back of lying on wood and a floating sensation across a plane. Chatter in the distance that Alix couldn't identify swirled around his head. The background of Alix's vision became brighter, a dark polluted sunrise.

Alix recognized the face…Eli! Alix strained to piece it together. Where did he go? Where was he? Alix's mind and his chip struggled with facts, truth, and memory. This dream held certain facts and truths, but his memory denied them, his mind repelled him. Eli's face became transparent until the light overtook the apparition. "Eli!" Alix screamed after him, but the walls of the dream closed in and squeezed Alix out. "Eli! Wait!"

Eli's face vanished, but his voice trailed off down a large dark tunnel. "People can disappear overnight, Alix. I did. *Do not* defend MAIA."

4

The monitor lit up the room. "Good evening, Captain Milligan."

"Yes, Maia, run surveillance file on Alix from this morning to now." Captain sat in the dark booth of the security center. Maia's facial recognition allowed him in, a perk attached to his rank. Captain wondered how much longer. How much longer could he play this dangerous game of roulette? He did his job just the way he was supposed to until his first opportunity for action came mid-stream of a much-needed piss years ago. He's held it for the duration of three-hour meeting of all the higher-ranked officials and the twelve MAIA Readers going over developments and inquiries Maia deciphered would help the manufacturing section produce weapons and train soldiers faster.

An old programmer shuffled into the tiled restroom. He stood swaying on old legs and a limber back in front of the urinal. He used his index finger to hold his glasses on his face. What programmer still wore glasses? "Capt. Robert Milligan." The old man didn't break his aim of his weak stream for the statement.

Milligan's orange beard glowed in the white tile. "If I were Milligan, what would a programmer want with an officer? And who's asking?"

Their voice bounced off the empty walls.

"Dr. Thomas Ethex." He jiggled himself and stepped away from the urinal. It flushed.

"What brings the brains to the muscle? Seem to be quite a ways from your computer."

Ethex stepped, slowly catching his balance in each step toward the sink, and waved his swollen old knuckles under the motion sensor. The faucet started. "A man in his old age can't always regard the designated bathrooms. You'll find someday when your steps aren't so quick, and your bladder not so large sometimes leads to ignoring signs. You might find yourself shitting in the MAIA Reader's toilet."

"Someday." Captain laughed, jiggled, and zipped. "Imagine what Maia would recommend for punishment for shitting in a Reader's personal john." He approached the sink staring at the old man's reflection, his dying skin, wrinkled face, and old hands scrubbing under the water, clearly clean, but still being washed.

Ethex lifted his head and stared into the captain's eyes through the reflection.

The captain put his hands under the faucet.

"Are you going to report me?"

The captain smiled and focused on his hands. He rubbed them together under the water. "No. Can't report a man for pissing. It's not like you wandered into the ladies' room."

The captain looked at him. The sweat in his creases of forehead. An anxious look in his eye, a puzzling stare of judgment, weighing the captain and the type of man he was—whether or not Captain remained one of those men who thought that there wasn't a statistically perfect person for a job, that women were better at something than men or vise versa, and that it came down to an individual and his or her own mind that made them what they were…like in the good old days. Was Milligan a free thinker?

Ethex swallowed. "Private Alix Basil."

The captain angled his brows. "Yeah?" He stopped washing his hands.

Water outlined Ethex's eyes. "He's on your list of cadets coming from education to training next week. He's a sniper. Say he could be one of the best."

"I know, I read his file. Why, have you?"

"He's different."

The captain shrugged, put his wet hands on the side of the sink. "His programming is special ops. Of course he's going to be a bit different from the rest, Dr. Ethex. One out of ten take the time to be programmed for special ops. You should know that, you could have programmed him."

"I did program him. Are you familiar with the new program? Number 19-84?"

Captain's eyes flickered to the corners and searched them for a monitor. Yeah, a number that lit a fire under the captain's eyes years ago when the thought of that humanity stealing number fell upon the board of MAIA Readers, and only one opposed it before giving in, a number that took away what made being humans human, the number that took away what made us greater than any other animal on planet earth, program 19-84.

"You'll find Alix a bit different in that regard."

The memory of the bathroom on that day felt like a haze—far away yet so close. The computer blinked and flickered. The captain squinted in the dark to see the bright screen. The thought of that day dissembled time, and the captain shook his head and pinched his eyebrows to stay awake.

"One moment, please."

Alix appeared on the screen before his bunk standing next to no one, a place where Eli should have been.

"Computer run speed times two."

The footage sped up and flicked between camera angles following Alix and the team to the vomit room. Alix and the team zoomed around the track, then around the weight room, then back to the court where they did sprints.

"Computer, slow speed to real time."

The captain watched as Alix began to sway. What caused it? Alix collapsed. The captain watched himself fall to a knee and hold Alix's head up. The captain felt younger than he looked. He pointed and yelled for a medic. Two medics came running, Wes and Phil grabbed Alix's hands and feet and hoisted him onto a stretcher. The medics raised it. They wheeled it out through the double doors.

The monitor's view switched to a view from up above the entrance of the vomit room. Alix shook his head back and forth on the stretcher. He tried to break free from the straps. The view switched. As the stretcher progressed over a long stretch of hallway, the floor reflecting the long florescent bulbs, Alix screamed and mumble incoherent craziness. The view switched.

"Computer, increase volume."

"Eli! No, Eli! Eli?" Alix's screams echoed down the hallway. The medics pushed him passed the sign Manufacturing Artificial Intelligence Agency. Two men in black suits emerged from the elevator, took the stretcher from the medics, and pulled Alix in. The medic watched the doors close, and the monitor prompted them to turn around and return to work.

The screen blackened. "Data not receivable."

Milligan stood. "Computer, where is Alix Basil?"

The message blinked. "Data not receivable."

"Maia, my credentials grant me access to these files. Where is Alix Basil?"

"Data not receivable."

A drop of sweat ran down the side of the captain's face. He paused and looked down to the right. He looked up. "Computer, where is Private Matthew Stine?"

The monitor blinked and brought a live view overlooking the barracks and bunk that Matt slept in.

"Private Phillip Heins."

The computer switched angles to a massive lump under a sheet.

Captain thought, angled his head down. He lifted his head. "Private Eli Williams?"

"Data not receivable."

"Private Alix Basil."

"Data not receivable."

"Come on!" Captain Milligan slammed his fist down on the armrest, stood, and punched the screen. His knuckles clinked against the glass.

* * *

Eleven MAIA Readers sat around a polished oak meeting table, their blurring reflections in the wood a paint stroke of their felt intelligence, a smear portion of their normal everyday confidence in technology and science. How can this happen? It's physically impossible. They pondered in engulfing large leather recliners. They scratched their heads, pinched their chins, and stared off into space, and explored the depth of possibilities for improbability.

The door swished open. Rankin rolled in on the whine of the T-port and circled the table. He sat at the end.

The room hummed. "MAIA reading number 7841 commencing." A blue hologram screen sprung up and opened like a book in front of each reader.

Rankin cleared his throat. "Okay, gentlemen, we all know why we're here. Let's get to it," his words sprang up on the screen in front of them as record to what was discussed. "As you all know, earlier today a cadet had collapsed in the midst of a drill. Although not all that uncommon, it is what happened after his collapse that is what brings us back to this table so soon.

"Private Alix Basil, in a delusional state, has relinquished some past memories that according to MAIA reading number 7839 should not exist. As stated by the vanishing sequence section 19 line 13, 'All memory of a cadet that is vanished by the MAIA Central Computer is to be erased from absolutely all cerebral chips. Additionally, the chip is to work as a suppressant against any other acknowledgment of the individual from which the memories are vanished.' But somehow, gentlemen, as you've seen in recent surveillance, Alix at 17:47 has, in a dreamlike state, spoken the name of a vanished individual.

"This is violation of code 645, section 8, line 3 stating as such, "Any cadet that is subject under required action of vanishing sequence must not return to existence in any shape or form, including, but not limited to, speech both in written and vocal, photography, videography, media of any kind, thoughts, memories, or gestures of any kind leading to the thought of the vanished." It says on line 4 that 'any cadet in violation of remembrance of any sort of the latter shall be in itself subject to the vanishing sequence.' Any initial questions before we get started?" Rankin sniffed.

A blinking box appeared on the screen. The message inside reading "Are we going to vanish another one of our boys?"

The text on the screen never held a label, name, or an attachment. Anybody in the room thinking that could have posed that question or even Maia itself suggesting topics.

Rankin looked over at Reader Elmer Washington and his white hair parted to one side. Ranking stared at the screen. The glare from the screen entered his eyes, a direct route to his brain, where his cerebral chip congregated. He pictured the words, and they began appearing on the screen through a silent debate: "We are going to do exactly what Maia statistically says is orthodox."

Washington's eye wandered the screen: "*Statically*, at this rate we will not have a fighting force against the citizens. Two cadets in a week? Does anyone else think this could potentially be too much?"

The room ticked. A chair squeaked, and no one's eyes moved. Everyone held the power for debate, the key to the answer, but all but one had the stomach to turn the knob, to question the questions and answer to the answers.

Rankin watched everybody's eyes. "Let's leave it up to Maia. Like we have been all along. Shall we?"

Washington's face hardened. The words appeared on the screen. "It's too soon to tell. The question raised here should be whether or not Alix can remain in the armed forces or not. We can not determine the extent of Alix's condition yet until after further analysis. I think Maia and the rest of the Readers will agree."

The screen and chat box became green. Maia highlighted Washington's sentence in agreement. Maia agreed, it was too soon to tell about vanishing Alix or not. The true question was whether he could return to battle for the conservation at all, and if yes, when? Statistically, Alix remained one of their best fighters.

Rankin eyed the screen. The sentence appeared: "We will determine today if it is worth having Alix fight for MAIA or if he's a threat to it. We'll notify his officers and return in twenty-four hours for a re-reading of the Alix situation and possible vanishing sequence. End of meeting. Dismissed."

5

Susan stared up into his old eyes. "You just got back from an MAIA reading about erasing another boy's memory and existence, but you want to cover this up? I don't understand. How do you expect to stand behind that decision? Everyone is going to find out." Susan fell into the computer seat.

Rankin looked down at her from his T-port. He checked over the cubicle walls. "You don't have to understand this, Susan, but you have to take direction that I'm given from Maia. There is something about Anna that the computer does not seem fit to go to reading yet, that's what I'm sticking to if it comes up. Maia does not want her to be discussed yet. I don't always understand my orders either, but I have to abide by them."

"What do you want to tell the other girls?"

"Whatever you need to. You're the head of our medic department. You don't have to explain yourself to them, Susan. They are cadets."

"They are children, Albert." Sue crossed her arms. Her shoulders fell. She looked around for the nearest monitor. None in sight. These kids...I don't know, Al.

Rankin reached down and brushed her shoulder. "They aren't kids, Sue! They're damn near twenty years of age. And don't refer to me in public as Al. Remember your rank. If Maia heard that..."

She sighed. "Whatever, Albert Ranking, MAIA Reader, supercomputer genius, head of the department and company. Don't go blowing your own horn, Al."

"I'm sick and tired of being cooped up down here like animals while those savage Citi fight over streets because they have one semi-automatic weapon. They fight over cans of beans up there while we sit here and breathe pumped oxygen from hundreds of feet below! We will take over the island in less than and week and then reestablish and hold it down."

Sue rolled her eyes. "Rankin. Don't talk to me casually. I only have one conversation for you. Anna. You know why. That's it. I don't care about your other problems."

Rankin grabbed her arm and looked side to side. "Just tell the girls she was hand- selected to take care of our new situation. Tell them that Alix has a sickness that we can't explain, and we needed our top-producing medic to help understand his diagnosis. That will buy us some time, and if it doesn't all work out then we will do a reset of the whole system, and none of them will know who Eli, Alix or Anna was."

"But we would, Al."

His eyes narrowed.

"Albert Rankin, sir." She looked away. "Our own daughter? A vanishing sequence?"

"Don't push me. I'm doing everything I can. We should have just programmed her correctly. She wouldn't be sneaking out like that. I thought you had it under control?"

* * *

Crusted gook and old tears sealed Alix's eyes together. He forced them open. A dim monitor severed the blurry darkness. Alix blinked to break some of the crust and lifted his hand to dig it out of the corners. His arm was stopped short by a metal clank. Alix lifted both arms and both stopped short. He looked around. Several boxes glowed green in the dark. Jagged lines slow and steady beeps. Old courier green font print brought forth by the blackness. Old computers surrounded him and flowed a dim aquatic light over the room.

Alix twitched his nose. The smell of plastic tubes and pure oxygen restricted his nasal movement. He followed tubes to glimmer of a reflection on the metallic oxygen tank. From his wrist to a bag of clear fluid clung to the side of his bed. His eyes didn't focus, the label a blur of possibilities. Where? Why? What happened?

The name and face stood vividly in his mind now. Eli. Alix felt he couldn't talk about him, like the word alone held a knife to his throat. The back of his head tingled, his chip worked overtime to repress the thoughts and words, and failed miserably.

The door opened. A silhouetted slender figure stepped into the room in a white overcoat. "Alix?" She entered and went to the nook next to the bed, opened some drawers, and pulled out two rubber gloves and a stethoscope. "This is all I have to work with?" Her voice intended for herself. "Studies for the future with instruments of the past." She picked up some medicine plugs for his intravenous port.

"What's going on?" Alix lifted a restrained arm.

Her hands never stopped moving. Her brown hair never stopped swaying. She pulled the plug out of his intravenous tube, snapped another in place. A squirt of blood hit the back of the test tube. She lifted the sample to the ceiling and squinted.

Alix strained to make out her features.

"You caused quite the fuss today, do you remember anything?" The medic pulled Alix's gown down to his waist. Alix realized the difference from his light battle gear to the gown and his pure nakedness beneath it. He felt cold. She pressed the cool stethoscope to his chest.

Alix clenched his teeth and sucked in. "No."

"Okay, breathe for me."

Alix inhaled and let it out slow. "I remember getting dizzy after sprints."

"You came in a violent rage you know. Breathe again for me, please. You've wounded a couple medics."

"What do you mean wounded?" Alix strained his ears.

"Breathe one more time for me. I mean a bloody nose for one and a black eye for another. Several bruises throughout."

She unlatched his armband on her side and leaned over to unlatch the other. "You should try and go to the bathroom, this could be your only chance for the next twelve hours." She undid his ankle restraints.

Alix swiveled to the side of the bed, pulled the gown up over his shoulders and hung his head. He cupped the back of his neck and rubbed. His head felt top heavy. "What did you give me...What'd you say your name was?"

"I didn't, I'm not at liberty to discuss my name or what we've given you for medications at this time. I'm sorry. Your information has been classified exclusively to the Maia, the three medics here."

Alix turned to the shaded figure. "Are you serious? What is this? Did I die or something?" Alix checked his embedded screen and thought "Analyze blood."

"No, Alix, I can assure you you're very much alive."

Alix tapped his wrist. "What's wrong with my EED?"

"Your embedded electronic device has been temporarily disabled."

"Temporarily disabled! Is that possible?" Alix stood. The cold floor bit his toes. He swayed back and fourth. "What's going on here! Who are you!?" Alix stepped toward the nurse.

The nurse straightened her shoulder and raised a small hand-held device.

Alix eyed the small piece of metal in her hand. A blue light. He slapped her arm away. "I could kill you in—"

The nurse held the button. Alix's knees buckled, and he flopped to the floor, smacked his cheek hard to the coldness. He couldn't move his fingers. He couldn't move his toes. His eyes and ears worked, but drool trickled out the corner of his lips.

She released the button. Alix's body softened, and his muscles worked again. "Every nurse down here has one of these. It's a paralyzer. If any of the buttons are pressed, you hit the floor. There is an armed agent at the end of the hall. You gave him a bloody lip too. I wouldn't try anything, I'm sure he'd love the chance to return the favor."

Alix picked himself up to one knee, wiped the drool, and breathed. "Fuck! Fucking impossible! Ahr!"

"Use the restroom if you need to." The nurse pointed to the thin door. "You have two minutes."

Alix hoist himself and stumbled into the door. He looked around the ceiling of the dark room waiting for lighting, waiting for motion sensors, or heat sensors, or something to light the room. Nothing came.

The medic glanced above the labels she read on the intravenous plugs. "You have to turn on the light. There's a switch to your right."

Alix reached for the dongle and fingered it until the light flickered on. *This room is old*, Alix thought, staring at the grit between the cracks of ancient tiles. It smelled of damp copper and musty porcelain. He pissed and swayed back and forth. He walked away from the toilet, but it didn't flush. He looked back. Condensation dripped from the metal handle spouting off the pipes of the toilet. Alix stared awkwardly. He cranked it, the toilet flushed, and Alix wiped his hand off on his gown.

Alix checked himself in the mirror. His pale skin appeared stretched over his face, eyes dilated almost the width of his pupil, and under them hung sacks of tiredness regardless of what felt like days of sleeping. He stared into the reflection, into his own eyes, until it seemed to him that the person in front of him was more him than the person seeing him, more of a figure in a window than a reflection. He watched his reflection's pupil grow and shrink inside the hazel iris. The toilet stopped wallowing in its flush. He listened to the sudden silence.

He turned the nozzle on the old sink. The black water cleansed shortly after. He smelled metal in the water, sipped it, spit out the metallic tasting fluid, and just wet his face instead. The tops of his bangs darkened with water and dripped down in the sink, and he watched a drop roll down his forehead, sink into his eyebrows, slide to his eyelids, and dangle on his reflection's eyelashes. He blinked. The drop fell.

Alix enjoyed simplicity for a moment—breathing, blinking. He enjoyed the flow of his blood and the bumping of his heart. Alix felt his forehead strain. He felt his cerebral chip become background for what is naturally figured and thought. He found reason to challenge his programmed chip. The gears in Alix's mind churned out the ideas that simply provided *answers* to life without letting him see the enigma with his own eyes. His chip, it seemed, lacked efficiency. Being told what is, is not knowing what there is to be told, and he had to be the judge to his own judgment, the finder of his own find, and that Eli's philosophy, although twisted and different, had some sort of truth, and he was right. Alix wondered about how the sunlight looked over the ocean, how the sun felt on bare skin, and why it still appears to go around the earth when we all know what it truly doesn't.

The medic rapped on the door. "Okay, Alix."

Alix rolled his eyes, returned to his side of the mirror, and exited the bathroom. Two figures remained in the room. A shorter medic read the labels to the intravenous plugs.

Alix lay back down. His eyes traced her curvy silhouette, a windy path of natural attraction. He looked to what would be her eyes if sufficient light filled the room. The taller medic grabbed his wrist and pulled it to the side.

Alix withdrew. "Is this necessary?"

She held down his wrist and clasped the buckles. "Unfortunately, yes. I don't want another black eye in the morning." She looked over to the shorter medic. "Can you do his legs?"

Alix lay back and held back the impulse to kick both medic's asses and bolt for the door. *That little thing they had.* He lay limp instead. He glared at the dark ceiling. Her delicate hands clasp around his ankle. He looked down at her. The white hallway light painted one side of her body from the waist up. The light illuminated her shoulder, skidded across the wrinkles of her lab coat, brushed her breasts, glowed on her face, reflected a small glimmer in her eye, highlighted her eyelashes and thin eyebrows, and individually coated the brown strains straying away from the rest of her thin hair. Alix felt his pores tighten, his hair straighten. Her familiar profile. It can't be her.

The taller medic leaned over Alix and reached for the other strap. Her dark hair hung in the way. He felt his toe grabbed and twisted gently. Alix shifted right to see through thick, dark hair but couldn't see the other medic until both Alix's arms became latched.

The taller medic attached three medicine plugs to the intravenous ports. She pointed "Are those buckled tight?"

"Yes." She looked down at Alix.

Alix felt it excite his body. His senses heightened and searched for more confirmation. Is it really Anna? That was her voice, or could have been her voice? Alix homed in on the shorter medic for another glance, another something, something more to confirm her existence in the same room.

The taller medic tossed the empty medicine plugs into the barrel labeled Hazardous and left. The head medic turned her back toward the trainee. She tugged on Alix's leg hair. She turned in the doorway, her hair a swish of light brown and white light. She ran her finger up Alix's bare foot. Alix's toes curled. He jerked his leg against the chain, and the door closed. It was, it had to be her. Who else would have... It has to be. Alix slammed his head down... "Anna..."

His body became heavy. It sank into the sheets. Medicine grabbed him. First his fingers, and then his toes started to feel the paralyzing wave taking over his body. The steady advancing of the medicine crawled into his kneecaps and elbows and inserted the sinking, immobilizing feeling like a thousand pounds held him there in place. His hips became numb, and in his chest a heaviness set into each organ at a time. He lost control of his shoulders and neck and felt his head sink inches deeper into the pillow, and in his mind a question mark hung over Anna's and Eli's faces.

* * *

"Good job, Anna." Susan didn't look from her paperwork. How could she?

"Thanks." Her heart sank. Her broken breaths sputtered in every pull of air she made, a building up of energy in her chest. She's never been caught. She leaned her head in her hands.

"Anna?" Susan lifted her eyes and watched a tear drop onto the paper underneath the little girl.

"I'm sorry, Ms. Susan. I just..."

Sue stood and approached her.

Anna stiffened, pulled her shoulders in, and clenched her teeth ready for her lashing.

Sue put her hand on Anna's shoulder and squeezed.

Anna stiffened more, expecting her neck to twist off or Sue to ram her through the desk.

"I'm not going to hurt you, Anna."

Anna's sobs broke through. Her shoulders bobbed up and down. Her arms wrapped around Sue. "What are they going to do to me! Sue, I'm sorry. I'm so scared. Am I going to be able to return to the barracks?"

"Shhh," Sue rubbed her back and wrapped her arms around her daughter for the second time since birth when Rankin submitted Anna into the program. "You'll be fine. For right now, help me in this special assignment, and we'll wait for an answer. What were you doing sneaking around? This is the most secure facility in existence. You can't be deviant. You are one of our best medics and pilots. What are you thinking jeopardizing that?"

"I just wanted to use the simulator. I think I could have done better in the last simulation." Anna wiped her nose and sniffed. "What are we doing with this cadet?"

Sue sighed and rubbed her shoulders back and forth until warmth radiated beneath her palms. "It's complicated, hunny." Sue smirked. *Clever girl.*

Anna's heart busted. Hunny? Who is this woman and who killed Sue? Sue the drill sergeant, screaming at us to fix wounds faster, diagnose quicker, think greater, fly more efficient. Anna remembered the smack in the back of the head delivered from this same woman from clipping a tree in simulation once, and here Anna had her arms wrapped around the woman, drenching her tears into Susan's overcoat.

Sue looked up at the monitor overlooking the room. She pursed her lips.

6

Alix cracked his eyes open. A fluorescent white bulb glared above, but a tall bald figure blotted out a portion. The bright light, the only rays of light that have hit Alix's eyes since the vomit room, burned, and his pupils strained to get smaller than they could.

"Alix, feeling better today?"

Alix squinted to the towering man miles above his bed. The light reflected off his head, and his few strains of white hair and dust that circled the room. Alix's lips felt heavy, his words heavier. "Where am I? What are you doing to me?"

"We just need to run a few more tests." An electronic whine crawled around the bed side, and the figure let the light pass his silhouette. "This may sting a little." The man stood above Alix, withdrew a silver-bullet-looking object that beamed a red light into Alix's EED.

"Ah!" Alix's eyes burst open. He jerked on the chain, a boiling stream floating up his arm and into his shoulder. "What are you doing! Stop! It burns!" Electrical charges spider-webbed their way up his arm.

"Hold still! This will only take a minute!" The man clasped Alix's forearm, the chain pulled tight, and held the device to the small embedded screen. His T-port rolled back and forth.

"What are you doing to me? Stop!" A burning circle of pain encompassed Alix's wrist and followed the initial shot of hurt under his skin, to his elbow, his shoulder, and up the back of his neck. "Ahh! Fucking—" Alix gritted his teeth, and the muscles from his neck to his jaw tightened and pushed through the skin. He jerked his other arm in a clenched fist toward the man, but stopped short after reaching full speed, like a leashed mutt at the end of its chain.

A monitor next to Alix's bed wailed, a flatline whine crying for Alix. Beeping and malfunctioning computers filled the room. A brunette medic appeared in the doorway. "Is everything—"

The old man's head snapped towards the door. His eyes narrowed. "Leave us! I'm almost done!" The man brought the beam closer to Alix's EED. His cheeks pulled back. His teeth gritted. His old eyes widened.

"No! You're hurting him!" An arm sucked Anna back outside the door.

Alix's eyes rolled up into his forehead. "Arr." His tense jaw popped open, his tongue protruding out, a wild scream swirling off its caked dryness and foam forming at his lips. "Stoooop! Ah ah ah ah, fucking stoooooop!" Alix jerked his knee up. The chains tightened. He tried his other. The chains tightened. He tried twisting, but the old man's hands held him steady as the beam jumbled around his brain. His ears popped like a semiautomatic gun. "Ahr! Fucking STOP!" Alix slammed his head back. Tried shaking the pain from his ears.

"There!" Rankin dropped Alix's arm.

Alix's breath sputtered in and out, tears streaming around his face, down his nose and across his cheek. He looked down to his wrist as the pain retreated toward his EED. A receding tide of torture. The red finger imprints faded on his wrist like memory foam regaining its form. Sweat matted Alix's back, arms, forehead, and legs. He shook his head and glared at the man. "What the"—he breathed—"was that?"

"I just got a program analysis, that's all. I need to see what's on your chip to best treat you. I'm very sorry. I know how much that hurts." He dropped the silver bullet into a pouch and shoved that in his pocket.

"The fuck you do, let me shove that thing in your EED! What is going on? Where's Captain Milligan?" Alix jerked on his restraints over and over. "Let me out of here!"

"In time, Alix. In time." He rolled to the exit.

"In time? In time I'm going to kick your old ass! You moth—" Alix's body went limp. Paralysis. The device the nurse had. Alix caught a glance at his T-port as the old man ducked to exit the room. Alix scanned the black suit, the ranking, the medals. Alix's stomach twisted. He slammed back. A MAIA Supreme Reader. Great. His body turned on.

Albert Rankin rolled out of the room and approached the desk. Sue stared into her older monitor. Anna looked away as she released the button in her pocket. Alix would appreciate that later.

Rankin showed his fake pearly teeth. "Make sure the monitor is properly functioning. Play one of the educational documentaries on the civilians and their way of life, and track his emotional and thought patterns. I want the readings in the morning. I'm retiring for the night. Have Doctor Harrison send the records to me himself."

"Yes, sir." Sue looked over to Anna. "May I make a request?"

Rankin stopped and turned to her.

"Could we transfer him to the hospital on level U25. I feel like they have more proficient equipment than this—"

"Negative. I put Alix here for matters of discretion. He'll remain here until he's diagnosed, then we'll register his visit at the hospital on U30 from the day he got in here."

"I just can't remember the last time we used this facility, and to get it running for one patient—"

"Enough, Susan. We just used this site for Eli yesterday. Get to work. Stick to the privacy protocol. Don't tell him anything. He could be a threat to MAIA."

Susan's eyes hated him fully. She gazed at his pocket where the data from Alix's chip was uploaded to.

He felt it. His shoulder dipped. "I know there are easier ways to obtain a list of the programs, but we don't have the time to deal with this. This problem is my number one concern right now. I need to see what is on this boy's chip, and for some reason we can't upload it wirelessly."

Susan looked at her screen at a live feed of Alix.

Rankin smirked. "Put in the video. Get it done."

"Sure."

* * *

Alix looked down at the small patches connected to his fingertips, arms, chest, stomach, legs, feet and head. Black, red, and yellow thin wires ran from Alix's head, over his body from each patch to a single thicker black wire fastened to the wall console. Susan worked diligently shaving the thin hair in the spots for the sensors. She sighed each new spot, again ancient practices. She would have this done in minutes if they were allowed to bring him up top where she could put on a helmet, and using MAIA sensors track everything in his body. Rankin insisted, no MAIA equipment and no transporting him.

Alix sighed. "Are these even real? What the hell are these things going to do?"

"This is the older way of tracking emotional patterns of the brain and your body," Susan replied without taking her eyes off the screen. "These are just sensors, they just give us information about your body. That's all. These won't hurt."

Alix stared at the broken and stained ceiling tile above him. "I didn't think psycho was going to electronically rape my EED either."

Sue sighed.

"What?" Alix raised his head. "I've been blown up, shot, stabbed and even hit by a truck in simulation, and I could never imagine anything more painful than what that guy did to me. And for what? I've never seen that guy in my life."

"He wasn't supposed to do that."

"I'm not supposed to be here either. Is this what happened to Eli?"

Sue stopped her mouth, and she hid behind her blonde hair and fiddled with the wires around Alix's feet.

"Is it? Do you know Eli? What happened?"

"I'm not at liberty to discuss patient files with other patients."

Alix let his head fall back. "Patients. We are fucking patients now."

Sue finished wiring him up. A dark stillness set into Alix's body. Alix felt loneliness sink into his bones. He didn't even know where *here* was, or how long he's been here. But he knew now that Anna probably wasn't here, Eli was definitely not here, the captain and his team weren't here, and wherever here was, wasn't good, wasn't where he thought he should be.

Sue turned to him before she left. "We understand how boring it is in here, so on your monitor we're going to run some sort of footage for you to watch, okay."

"Oh, thanks that's going to make me forget all about these restraints and wires on body I'm sure."

The medic's head fell, and her pulled-back hair slid over her shoulders. She sighed and flicked the lights off. She left, but her small fingers held on to the old notched-out doorframe a second longer and elegantly let go. Alix watched her fingernails unhinge.

The monitor flickered. The video started. The camera panned high in the air above a snowy city surrounded by water. A deep apologetic man's voice came from behind the screen to a gentle instrumental jingle. "Manufacturing Artificial Intelligence Agency was not always the great, strong, advanced company we know it as today." The camera zoomed in over the island. "This world changing organization we know as the MAIA owes its life and birth to the once great nation formerly known as the United States of America." A map of the world appeared on the screen and the country highlighted. It flicked to programmers in lab coats checking their clipboards in the foreground, and two black-suited men standing at the door in the background.

"Before the war, the island we now reside deeply under used to be referred to as Governor's Island, outside of Manhattan, and part of New York City, home to nearly 9.5 million civilians before the invasion."

Alix sighed. He let the images and voice roll through him for the second time, remembering the exact video from his youth. Instead of watching, he gazed into the screen and wished he knew whether Anna resided close enough to be the one that touched his leg earlier.

He wanted nothing more than to meet her in simulation. Hopefully he wasn't letting her down. The thought of her in simulation alone at night waiting for Alix burned more than the silver bullet the Reader pulled on him. He remembered his favorite time in simulation.

Alix stared at the ceiling. He remembered a night like this. He checked his three and nine o'clock after hearing Eli's deep breaths above him. Alix lifted the sheets in the pure darkness. He'd stop, listen to the nothingness like antimatter danced in the air, absolute zero in a room of cadets. Three light steps forward and fifty steps toward his three, and the door latch could be cranked open perfectly. Too slow and it would squeak, a screeching tire in a silent street. Too quickly and slammed metal on metal, a sledgehammer on a tin can.

Alix closed his eyes and unlatched the door. In less than a breath, he swung the door open, entered, and closed the door. He latched it perfectly. Alix stared down the hall, slid down the hallway on the wall. His heart raced. He held his EED to the door to the simulator. It unlatched. The metal always echoed. Alix strapped up and attached his sensors and electronic equipment. He closed his eyes and hopped it was a night that Anna could make it out too.

He selected number thirteen. Whatever the simulation was. That was their method. No matter what thirteen was, no matter how gruesome or disgusting or difficult, they both entered in simulation thirteen and whatever revolving scenario lay. Alix checked the description and whispered it out loud. "MAIA intelligence detected Citi leader protected in the penthouse of an old hotel complex. Infiltrate the heavily patrolled infrastructure and take the terrorist leader dead or alive."

Alix shrugged. "Sure."

He pulled the shield over his eyes. "Please, Anna." The world zipped through a colorful wave of revolving shimmers, whooshed through vertical rainbow ocean held up by wind and sound vibrations. The world collated particles. First far, the sound of glass tinkered and shrank into a complete and solid tangible world. Alix dropped his binoculars. The dark hotel glowered back. He spotted yellow-lit rooms. White flakes drifted lightly from the sky. His breath was noticeable, a snipers nightmare. No long shots tonight.

He checked his six. A team of seven hunkered behind him, awaiting a plan. He searched each of their eyes and painted faces, all black clothes, none of them the sweet serenity that was his true love and passion and reason for living.

Alix returned his eyes to the binoculars, sighed, and went on with the mission. "Alright men, whelp. If we aren't meeting up tonight, might as well get some practice."

"Sorry, I'm late," Anna tucked in her shirt under her tactical vest.

Alix's body jolted in excitement. "Babe!" Alix stood.

"Shh." One of the men held his finger up to his lips.

"Shut up down there." Anna motioned to a computer version of a soldier.

Alix and Anna embraced, warm arms around each other like the rings of Saturn pulled tight. Their lips met.

Anna slouched down and snagged the binoculars. "What do we got?"

"We have a target in on the top-floor suite. It's cold, so we'd have to be careful if we try and get a shot. Other than that, my rifle won't be getting any use tonight."

"You're right." Anna's squinted face stared through the binoculars. "Plus, they know we're coming. Look at the guard at each doorway. Don't look like much, but by the bump in their jacket, I bet they have semiautos at least."

"Agreed. They would stand clear of the windows at least for sure."

Anna shouldered Alix. "Looks like we're getting a room."

Alix smiled. "Did you pack a dress, we could go undercover."

"Hold on, just let me pull a red dress and heels out of my ass, Alix. No, I don't have a dress. Did you bring a tux tucked in your rifle bag?"

"Actually, I did, but I won't need it now. First you're late, and now unprepared?"

"Bullshit you packed a tux, and if you did you forgot your shoes."

"That was one time."

"The only time we needed them."

"Okay." Alix smiled. "Let's try the back and see what that looks like."

"That's a waste of time. I say you and I flank left of the building, We can take out those two guards on the west side quietly, disable the elevators, and take the stairs to the top floor. When we are in position. Let's pull a full frontal assault with what we have from these guys. Leave one perched with a rifle to cover us."

"Not a bad plan." Alix huffed, a deep cool cloud left his lips. "Let's move."

Alix and Anna screwed on silencers and booked it down and around the left side of the building. The rest of the men less one went to the right to hijack a limousine. The rifleman watched Anna and Alix blend in like a chameleon to their surroundings and approach the east entrance like wolves.

The two guards heard something, drew guns, and approached Anna's position behind a bush. Anna appeared in a white tank top, no vest, no guns, no gear, just her main weapons pointed right at the men in the form of a low cut shirt and a well defined cleavage. She appeared disheveled as the two men stepped toward her. She fell to her knees with her hands up. Her lips moved and looked helplessly up toward the men, innocent and sexy through a long dark strand of hair. The rifleman placed his finger on the trigger. This is not how they planned it.

Alix hopped into frame from the right, behind the men, pulled a zipline around one's neck, and pulled him back and out of view. Anna sprung up, disarmed the other, bent his elbows in the wrong direction, and kicked his legs from under him. In the same motion, she drew a blade down into his throat. She dragged him out of view.

"Holy shit, that was close." Alix tossed the guard's body into a large trash bin and helped Anna lift hers in.

"I thought the night was going to end early. That would have sucked."

Alix smirked. "Don't try and get out this. I've missed you."

Anna pulled her gun and peeked around the corner. "The elevator controls are probably downstairs in the control room. I can't imagine they would post someone there. Let's move."

"All units! Checking in!" The radio from the bin bellowed in French.

"Shit. Let's go. No time to disable elevators. They are going to know what's happening in the next couple of minutes." Alix handed Anna her vest and took off his black overthrow, which left him in just a white tee, bulletproof vest and tactical pants.

"Agreed. Let's get in position." Anna kicked the door, her pistol checked each corner. Alix and Anna bolted down the rugged colorful hallway. Mirrors hung every ten paces, old paintings stood perfectly between doors, and little end tables held a single rose outside each decreasing room number. Classical music chimed throughout the facility.

"Foxtrot to Fairview, what is your position and possible ETA?" Alix held his microphone down on his shoulder as they entered the stairwell.

"Fairview to Foxtrot. Commandeered the bird waiting for signal to liftoff. ETA thirty seconds when given the signal."

"Roger that."

Anna and Alix bolted up the stairs. Anna watched his eyes scan the stairwell above, his pistol his focal point, his tricep a definitive accent, a walking, talking killing machine, a modern Achilles. So fucking hot. "Alix."

He stopped on the fourth floor platform, peeked out, and the echo subsided. "What?"

Anna approached him, nervous eyes. "You hear that?"

"No, hear what?" Only their whispers sank and rose through the stairwell.

Anna closed in on him. "Come here." She grabbed him by the V-neck and pulled him in.

Alix's teeth fought through his lips. "Anna…" He peaked through the thin, vertical glass, and peered down the hallway. "Here?"

Her teeth clamped around his earlobe, her nose breathed heavily in his ear. "Um-hum." She reached down and unbuckled her belt. He unsnapped his vest in the front as Anna pushed him hard into the corner of the stairwell. Alix eyed the long corridor through the thin glass window of the stairwell and shrugged.

Anna dug her nails into his white tee and separated the fabric; his hard stomach reflected the dim lit stairwell. Her pants dropped, a boot was kicked off. One pant leg released from her foot as Alix's pants lowered halfway down his butt, just enough to allow his hard self to plop out of the zipper. Alix spun and lifted her as her legs parted and wrapped around his waist.

Anna dragged her mouth along his neck and clung onto the back of his vest as he entered her wetness easily and they grinded. Her held back moans, and his light grunts bounced off the cement walls and stairs, tangled to their heavy, audible breathing. Her belt jingled like Christmas, and his elbows tapped the wall each thrust.

"Oh my god, Alix," She whispered in his ear, and her lips circled his entire lobe. "Oh my god."

He lifted his head off her shoulder and pressed his lips into her hard, and a loud groan from deep inside his body infused her. His hips revolved faster into her over and over, her insides bounced, her arms squeezed the straps on the back of his tactical vest as hard as her fingers would clasp. "Ohhhhh." She closed her eyes. Her body released, and a long high-pitched moan left her lips. Alix muffled her mouth hard and pushed her head in sideways to the corner. She lifted and shifted her head, nipped his palm hard.

"Ah!" Bite prints remained on the side of his hand.

His pushed his purlicue to her throat and shoved her deeper in the wall her head bounced. He revolved his hips heavier. She pulled him closer by the back of his head and mashed their lips together. He felt his pelvis twitch, his breaths became heavier. She smelt his sweat. She bit his lip hard and didn't release until he did. He grew inside her, his head bulged and exploded far within her. Her body released along with his and subsided. She tilted her head back and saw the black suit in the corner of her eye.

The door popped open. "What are you doing here!"

Anna, from her hoisted position against the wall and Alix still in her, pulled Alix's pistol out of his holster as both guns went off. A bullet smacked Alix in the back as the suited guard's head snapped back and revealed the blood spatter behind him.

Alix let Anna down, arched his back, and breathed through his teeth like he got stung by a bee. "Fuck that hurt." He snatched his pistol.

Anna scrambled to get dressed. "At least you got off first."

"Oh, my god that sucked."

"Excuse me!" Anna pulled her pants up.

"Not you, the fucking bullet in my back."

"Come here, you big baby. Turn around." Anna pulled the shell out of the back of his vest. "It's only a nine millimeter. Stop being a baby. Let's move." She tossed the shell haphazardly to the side. Ping.

"Here you go first. Let me shoot you in the back."

They raced up the stairs, "You shoot me in the back, Alix, you're going to be missing some body parts next time."

The computer sniper covering the whole scene watched as the building became crazy. Guests that pulled up were shooed away, guards ran in every direction, lights flickered on throughout the whole facility, gunfire and broken glass erupted throughout. A limo jolted in from the west and smashed through the front double wooden doors of the hotel. The sniper took fire at the sprinting suits after the scene. The team exited the limo and entered the building.

What seemed like seconds and the world stopped. "MISSION ACCOMPLISHED" Spread across Alix and Anna's world. Anna looked to Alix, who stood over the dead ambassador. She smiled. "We are good at this."

"We're great at this." He stood, approached her, and kissed her deeply. "I'll see you in three days?"

"Yeah. I'm going to miss you, babe." Anna kissed Alix.

"Me too. Be careful getting back into bed."

"Okay, you too."

Their worlds disintegrated.

Alix lay staring at the ceiling of the room as the video stopped. He wished it was that type of night. He wished he could sneak out and see Anna in simulation. He wished he was anywhere but there.

7

"At ease. Well you boys wanted to speak with me, so speak. Don't just stare at me like a bunch of idiots." Captain Milligan leaned back in his chair. He drummed on the top of the glass globe on his desk and looked at the six pairs of eyes looking down at him. Captain searched the men who called him to his own office for who had the sharpest stare, who was going to step up, grow a pair of balls and speak. Captain Milligan's dog-eat-dog mentality wondered if one of these dogs had the bite to step up.

Wes raised his chin. "Sir, we would like to be informed on the status of our sniper, sir. Where's Alix?"

Captain held one finger on the globe and glanced sideways. "So would I."

"Sir?"

Their faces twisted in a knot of confusion, their eyebrows narrow and lips pressed tight.

Captain Milligan glanced up at him and then looked away. He picked up his globe. He'd done it once recently with Alix, why not again? Captain pictured the night that a small mob of suited men would appear behind him while pissing and take him into the darkness for treason. He looked at the globe and the little clock inside, and he twisted the knob. Light twinkling music filled the room. The cadets looked at each other sideways, the music an odd unwelcoming uneasiness. "Let's assume there is no rank in this room, or even that the MAIA can't even hear what we are saying."

Their faces reddened. They felt the monitor behind them, like a second head peering over their shoulder listening and doing all the thinking for them. The globe put out an electromagnetic pulse and confused the MAIA systems.

No one spoke.

"Let's forget for an instant that there is any standard on behavior or language. It was just yesterday that Squad 28 seemed ready to lose their sniper. Why the sudden change in conception?"

Silence followed his question.

"Captain," Wes's eyes straightened, "a member of our squad fell. Fallen, in which way, we're not sure, but has fell nonetheless. We are trained to never leave a man behind. Without Alix, we're not Squad 28, and we're not going to be the first to set foot on the mainland. We've trained for this since we can remember remembering."

Captain's eyes dropped. First deployed? They had to know. Wasn't time to stomp their dreams out yet. "What about you, Victor? Where I grew up, we toss you and Alix a pair of gloves and say have it." Captain folded his hands in his lap and reclined back. "I'm surprised to see you here. I watched you shoulder him on your way out. I heard what you said to him. I'm just wondering, don't make that worried face. Stop trying to look over your shoulder, we're just simple men having a simple conversation. Now converse."

"Sir," Victor breathed, "Alix held his fire on my spot, but it shouldn't be enough to condemn a man into falling and being held back from his team."

Captain searched their eyes. The slow twinkling raised pressure, intensified the room. Awkward. Captain remembered the look on his father's face he shot at these boys right now. He remembered the television on porch and the hot and heavy Virginia air, and the story on the news about the first public cerebral chips being surgically implanted. His father sipped his brandy, slightly rocked in his rocking chair, a slight creek every time, and wrinkled his face under his dirty cowboy hat, one side more than the than other.

The captain remembered his father's southern tongue. "If God meant for human thought to be stored on a chip, he would have skipped the human part." He slurped his brandy.

The captain sipped his brandy and smelt the boiling ham lingering in the kitchen long after the men digested it. The faucet ran, dishes clanked, and captain thought his father was nuts. Why would a man refuse stored information? But then again, why would his mother clean the dishes by hand right next to the dishwasher?

His father that night said that every old man has the right to look at the next generation and feel sorry for them because a young man will never know the of way of life his father lived in which that individual was brought into this world. "It takes a long time to get to know life, Robert, and once you get to know it, you're nearly dead, so you try and explain it to young deaf ears. Because shit, when you're young, you have it all figured out until you figure yourself right into a hole and think 'Goddammit, I should have listened to my old man. And here we are." He looked at a mature Robert, mature enough to share a glass of brandy housing an ice cube. "So what the fuck do you want with a chip in your brain fo'?"

The captain's father's body knew fifty-three years of age on the porch that day in Virginia when he gave birth to those words. The captain felt much older than fifty-two remembering that day looking at these young men in his office and feeling bad for the next generation. He wished he'd never figure himself into this hole. He looked at these boys and thought like so many people in the past has, *This is going to be the generation that succeeds us...shit.* Only this time, the captain had a feeling he could change at least one of them.

Victor licked his lips. "If there's no sniper, there's no spotter. And I'm not all that good with a machine gun, Captain." A smile cracked along his lips.

"So all right. Fuck it. You won't remember me or anything I say anyway if this gets out of hand." Captain threw his hands behind his head. He checked the timer on the clock in the globe. The music played on. "Alix has been put down in a secret facility, because Reader Albert Rankin believes that his cerebral chip is defective. He believes that Alix knows stuff that he shouldn't because of things that Alix yelled in his sleep. That's all I can tell you. Ridiculous, I know, but I don't know when he'll be back or if he's all right. I haven't seen him nor spoke with him. That's all I can say, because that's all there is to say."

Everyone bowed their head. Matt raised his eyes. "So we're not going to be the first deployed, huh?"

Captain took a deep breath and looked above them to the monitor and then down at the globe tinkling its last notes of an electromagnetic-blocking song. "Depends."

"Depends on what, sir?" Matt stiffened.

Captain spoke softer. "Depends on what you consider deployed and which side you're on."

The cadets eyed each other. "Excuse me, sir?" Matt strained to hear correctly.

"Ah," Captain stopped his tongue. The globe strained for more power. "If you're willing to do anything, and I mean anything, you might have the chance to get Alix back and be first deployed on the mainland. You're all dismissed for now. We'll get back to this. For now, just regular training sessions. I'll see you in the morning."

They turned to the door. The music stopped.

"Gentlemen?" Their heads swiveled and shoulders facing the general. "Does the name Eli mean anything to you?"

They looked to one another. Their faces lost stones, solid and expressionless. Should they answer? What is truth? What is reality? And if they differ, which is correct? Their minds couldn't find it, couldn't place it, a burning diary of a distant version of ourselves.

Wes clenched his jaw and shrugged his shoulders. "Never heard of him, sir. A friend of yours? A cadet in a different division?"

"Never mind."

Phil turned to Wes down the hall. "Who's Eli?"

Captain pulled his drawer out from in front of him pulled out a picture of the boys before Eli's disappearance. A physical photograph could have been nearly impossible without knowing Dr. Harris. Captain pressed his fist against lips to the point he felt his bottom teeth pushing through. No amount of time measured how long the captain's eyes lived in that photo. His eyes welled up, and a tear fell over the little island on the digital map in front of him. Eli…

* * *

Susan Maynard leaned into her palms at the main desk. She rubbed her eyes and breathed deep. She's heard of the bottom facility on U40, forty stories below sea level, but never did she think they would have to use it, especially on this poor boy who only passed out during training. She never understood having a secretive hospital area. She got up to check on Alix. A message beeped on the screen from her e-mail. She looked over. "Anna, can you go just get the intravenous plugs ready, I'll be in there in a minute. Keep the lights off. You don't want this cadet to know your face. He's still considered highly dangerous."

"Sure." Anna opened the door.

Susan looked up and touched the monitor. The screen didn't react. She reached down for the mouse and clicked on the message sent from a guest log from level U21.

She read the message: "Anonymous U21 [Cadet's Media Center]: There's a boy being held in your detention center by means not ratified by the MAIA. The man in charge of the boy being held there is using unofficial means of treatment and overstepping protocol and his allotted power by the MAIA section 544:2. If you're in favor of dealing with Alix's sickness the correct way, respond. If not, this message was never sent."

Susan gazed at the monitor. She looked away. Her hands hovered over the keys.

* * *

Alix opened his eyes. The medic opened the door and stepped into the light from the hall. "You here to pump me with more drugs?"

She closed the door, appeared from the door to his side with no apparent in-between, and leaned over the bed. She pinned his shoulders and locked lips with him. She stopped and looked into his eyes. He knew. She pulled back and covered his mouth. Alix's senses sucked into a whirlwind.

"Shh, Alix. They have you on U40, a secret hospital area. It wasn't even running until we got here. The equipment is ancient. They were talking about what you said while you were dreaming, and they're concerned about your chip. I'm seeing what I can do to get your out of here. There's a lot of security. She kissed his cheek and whipped around.

Susan entered. Silence followed her in along with tension and uneasy stillness. "Undo his straps and allow him to go to the restroom, please."

Anna leaned over him to undo his strap, draping her hair in his face and tickling his nose. He got up and rubbed his wrists, stretched his back, and twisted each way. "You really know how to knock a guy out of shape."

"Go to the bathroom while you can. You get double rations tonight, but they're still only strips. Sorry." Susan pulled out a sheet of paper and checked over the stats.

Alix eyed the ancient ways before stepping into the bathroom. The door shut.

"Susan, permission to speak?" Anna whispered in the partially lit room.

"Granted."

"What's going on?"

"I'm not at liberty to discuss." Susan wiped her eyes. Being brave wasn't always being smart, and smart wasn't always right.

* * *

The captain rubbed his eyes and read the response from Susan one more time.

Susan Maynard U40: I understand Readers don't always read everything, and what they translate to us must not be the full truth. Yet, I still have to see to them and their wishes. Their decisions and wishes mirror my actions, their rules are my guidelines. I live for but one thing, MAIA. With that said, what happens beyond my control is just that, beyond my control. A door left ajar is not my fault if done on accident or ignorance, and it sounds like ignorance is bliss to you if my timing is good. Let me know when to be ignorant if it involves a young man getting out of harm's way.

Captain smiled under his red beard. She knew the consequences, and she still responded. She's a fucking loony—all those words about reflections and mirrors and all that shit, but she responded. He headed toward his quarters and longed for a large cup of water. Strips all day just didn't wet your throat, and the captain felt like he'd swallowed a roll of sandpaper. He just had to check the barracks, and he could try and sleep.

A light flickered in the hallway. Captain checked each way. The simulation room blinked. He edged down the hall, the lights brushing his face, the sounds a faint computer alert in the distance. *Who would…?* He checked his EED. Lights out was half hour ago. Not again.

Captain leaned his shoulder in the doorframe. Wes laid back in one of the recliners. Captain watched the small jolts and jitters of Wes's body under the influence of simulation, each bullet, each movement as if it really happened to the body. His helmet flickered, and the lights on the end of his sensors flashed. The captain entered the room on his heels and lowered his head into his palm. He rubbed his eyes and sat next to Wes in the simulator.

Wes crawled through wet grass engulfing his body. The sun beat down on his forty pounds of military gear, and tall conifers surrounded the hill they climbed. He heard a shuffle behind him. He stopped and held his fist up. The rustling bushes behind him seized. Black and green war paint caked Wes's face, his eyelids done black. He waved the men on. They crept farther up the green hill on their bellies, gripped their rifles, squeezed their rifles like a child with a teddy. An ache grew from his knees and his elbows to deeper in his legs and arms. He'll never lead men out in the open on foot again. He lost his head in the last simulation, a sniper some five hundred yards away.

Wes stopped them again and peered through the tall, sharp-edged grass through electronic binoculars. He panned the land below. Several citizens patrolled the encampment between the bank of the river and the thick woods of tall pines. Wes switched his binoculars to infrared and scanned the tents. Ten red figures glowed from each tent. A tank loomed by behind the tent. He signaled for the spotter.

It wasn't Victor who snaked his way next to Wes's location, but a computer version of him. It wasn't but an electrical version of his squad. Wes checked his embedded screen and pointed to the tank. He signaled for the spotter to call in an air strike for 1502 hours.

He turned to the rest and strategized in his head his sniper location and how they would approach this encampment. In his head this became a flex of muscle. His brain calculated positions, attack formations. Wes's mind understood each man is only as good as his team, and only a unit can penetrate an enemy, only a unit can become victorious. Like a single body, each man a limb, an organ, a function; like the human body, everything had to work to be alive. In Wes's head, he visualized attacks and approaches and calculated the greatest loss and success rate. He hasn't loss a game of chess since he was six.

Wes turned around to the upright green camouflaged ankle and black boot like the trunk of a tree before his nose and towered to the sky. Wes followed the leg up to a glowing red beard and an old Southern grin. "Captain? I…I…I…"

"Why are you in a simulation after lights out?"

Wes's digital spotter craned his head up from the binoculars and angled his eyebrows. His expression remained cemented in the black streaks across his face, but his programming couldn't figure the reason the captain stood without care of the enemy. He looked to Wes.

"He's fine."

The captain looked down at the spotter, kicked him lightly. "What are you looking at?" He pointed to the bottom of the hill. "Get back to work soldier."

Wes pushed himself up to his knees. His computer squad studied him, tried to read him. Wes pointed down the hill. "Proceed reconnaissance until my mark. Hold the air strike."

The digital spotter nodded. He texted for a hold on the location of the air strike.

Wes looked to captain. "Sir, I apologize. I, I mean we already passed this one as a team, I just wanted to get it perfect this time."

Captain laughed. "Trying to get it perfect, huh? That's funny, Wes." Captain looked down at the dark-haired, smooth-faced Wes. "You keep trying to get a mission perfect, you'll spend your whole life on this one simulation. And this simulation doesn't even matter, its just practice."

"Last time I got sniped, though. Alix got him once he gave his position up, but that didn't help me, Hayden still had to call for EMR. I hate having the medics come out on account of me, sir."

Captain crossed his arms. "Right now, Wes, you're sitting in an egg-shaped room next to me with a VR helmet on your head. There is no such thing as practice for the real thing. You say last time you got sniped. In real life, there's no saying last time because last time you got a hole in your head, and you're too fucking dead to say last time or next time or even this time."

Wes squinted in the sunlight. "Then why do we do it? Simulation, I mean."

"Well"— the captain kneeled and plucked a sharp blade of grass and popped it in his mouth—"so you at least believe you're ready for the real thing. So you don't freak out, hopefully, after the first man you kill or see dead. We used to call it shell shock or that other pussy technical name for it, um...post traumatic my dress is disordered or something or other."

Wes was stank faced.

"These simulations, Wes, these video games, as we used to call them, are just to desensitize you. That way there, you feel like you've been there before. America has trained it's civilians with videogames since the mid-2000s."

"Oh." Wes squished one side of his face in the sunlight.

"Don't get me wrong, Wes, they are good. *Statistically proven* to be effective by MAIA." The captain looked up at the sun and his embedded screen. "I hate when they are off, the sun and the time, I mean. I know this is simulation and all, but I used to be able to tell you what time it was from the tilt of the sun. I got that from my father. Working the farm, he'd tell you a minute before mama rung the dinner bell just by looking and holding his fingers to the horizon."

"I wouldn't know the difference." Wes checked the encampment through his binoculars and wondered why the captain hadn't gotten his head blown clear off yet just standing there chatting. "I've never had the real sun above my head, never mind a synced EED." Wes peered away from his binoculars. "So, if this is a joke to you, why do you have that ancient thing you call a pistol on your belt?"

Captain checked his revolver. "My father had one of these. I still have it, my father's, I mean bullets and all, but I never shot it though, well the real one." Captain drew his pistol, swung it on his finger, and whipped it back into his side holster. The brown holster strapped around his belt stood out from his green camouflage attire. "I just thought it'd mean a lot to him to shoot it one day." Captain looked down at the young man and followed his sight. Wes stared at his digital sniper, a computer player playing the part of Alix; it even kind of looked like him.

"Wes?"

"Yes, sir."

"If I told you I needed you within a moment's time to act possibly against your own judgment, and intuition, and against policy, would you be there, ready to go?"

Wes squinted toward the sun and looked back down the hill from the side he'd crawled all the way up from. He thought hard about what a question like that might mean. Wouldn't something he needed be an order? Wasn't he supposed to follow orders and not have judgment? Or did the order he had for them conflict with his orders from above, in which case its not really an order at all and for the first time in a soldiers life, Wes could decide? "Yes, sir. Locked and loaded."

"You think you could get the rest of the squad ready if it involved getting Alix out of trouble?"

Wes's face turned strict. "What kind of trouble is Alix in?"

"Do you?" Captain stared down at him.

"Yes, sir." Wes got the point and ripped some grass out from between his legs. "I believe it wouldn't take much to get the team on their toes, some would be faster than others against their own judgment, but they'd be there for you. And Alix. And for a chance to be first on the mainland."

"Good." Captain looked down at the patrolling men from the top of the hill. He sighed. "That's very good." He scanned the encampment. "Um, Wes."

"Yes, Captain."

"You shouldn't have canceled that air strike."

"Why?"

"You know that tank?"

"Yeah."

A thunderous rush of sound exploded from the barrel of the tank, but by the time it got to where they perched, red, yellow, and orange flowered in front of them, their bodies separated, and their view of flying through the sky ended when their heads crashed down in different parts of the terrain.

Wes watched a dirty hairy man approach from above what seemed like larger blades of grass. His torn uniform hung from his shoulders, and he held his rifle over his shoulder. He looked down at Wes's head. Wes's eyes looked back. The man smiled through crooked blackened teeth. The citizen's foot raised above Wes's head and stomped out Wes's vision. A glitch later, he sat back in the egg-shaped room. He looked over at the captain.

Captain pulled his helmet off. Static crackled in the air, in the dark and snapped when he lifted the helmet. He looked over at Wes. "I'm going to need you soon."

"Captain?" Wes held Captain's gaze. "Who's Eli?"

Captain looked away and plucked a sensor off his arm. "An old friend of yours."

"Of mine?" Wes shook his head and stared down at the ground before him.

"Yeah. You don't remember though, it was a long time ago. Get to your bunk. Stand by. I might need you sooner than you think."

8

Rankin checked over the shoulder of his dark blue suit. He rolled past the arrow leading down the hallway. He pointed the silver bullet controller into the fingerprint scanner, and the red light turned green and the door swished open.

Dim lights lined the hallway down to the security elevator. Rankin checked his EED, 04:36:03. One hour until power-up and MAIA will come to life; programmers will keep programming and surgically implanting chips into newborns; sperms for the new batch of military babies will be artificially inseminated into fit mothers; the military itself will continue simulations and training for the conservation in the weeks to follow; the manufacturers will manufacture weapons, materials for vehicles, clothes, utensils, and computer elements.

People, their voices, the scraping of their boots on the floor or the whine of their transportation devices will fill every hallway from the watchtowers on ground level to the nurses watching over Alix on U40—all moving in the same direction, for a common cause, like ants, to be that much closer to the conservation of the mainland and the birth of a new nation to cleanse itself of its horrendous old ways. It will be amazing to start taking ground back.

Rankin will wait for the other Readers back in the main hall on U21, and then he will use his thumb to open the doors, not his silver bullet remote bypassing the log book. The other Readers lack of faith in themselves and full reliance on Maia forced Rankin into programming the remote and its capabilities. Rankin thought about how no matter how hard humans tried, they always need an overseer, an innovator, whether it's creating imaginary gods and following their made-up religion and rules in books written and printed by humans themselves, or creating the MAIA to run the government they've created to take the power and accountability out of the hands of the individual. It makes them feel more comfortable that whatever happens, they can embrace the good and blame the bad on the higher power.

In early history, natural disasters and flooding used to be because the "gods" were angry; in Rankin's generation, they blamed life's problems on the "economy" or the government and their laws, all things that they, humans, have created to blame problems on, but live off their prosperities.

He shined his silver bullet remote into the finger pad at the elevator. He watched the top of the doors. They slid apart, and he rolled into its darkness. The small light attached to the transportation device flicked on. He pressed the bottom button, MAIA. The elevator screeched. It sucked more power out of the reserves, and somewhere in the complex, the lights dimmed. The elevator went down, down from U21, past the regular hospital facility on U25, passed the science and technology floor, U37, and down past U40, where Alix waited for the inevitable vanishing sequence, unless Rankin saw something he needed in this reading.

The elevator stopped, and Rankin followed the spread-out lights down the hall. He shined the red laser from his remote into two more scanners before stepping into the metallic room. Bolts the size of Rankin's fists lined the panels up and around the ceilings, the smell of tarnished tin filled the room, holes bigger than Rankin's head led thick wires in and out of the room surrounded by three feet of concrete deep within the island. This virtually indestructible one-entranced room held the super computer, a computer that ran on its own unreachable, untraceable frequency and its own nuclear generator. It could run for twenty years with no power and could coordinate a nation the size of the former United States politically, militarily, economically, and culturally—for twenty years without reprogramming or maintenance.

Rankin's eyes probed the machine, the two tall, bulky electronic towers connected by an entanglement of hundreds of fiber optical wires. The beeping, flickering, and altering lights from the MAIA sparkled in Rankin's pupils. "To think you could control all the traffic lights in a country for the most statistically efficient travel time, and that was only one trillionth of the recommended usage. Imagine what we could have done with you."

Rankin approached the console in the corner of the room and shined his light into the system. A white outlined monitor beamed up, and light filled the room. The computer automatically logged into a guest account in white font on the white background. Rankin highlighted the page to see his name and hit Enter. Three blinking blue buttons appeared: Law, Living, and Learning. Under the buttons a field with "Search" blinked. Rankin pressed Law. A blue spreadsheet spread out over the screen holding billions of governmental commands, controls, and inquiries.

He could enter anything, a proposition for a new law, a deletion of an old one, and the system would give a probability of the enhancement of the community with that law. He could enter the full circumstance of a criminal defendant and upload video the MAIA tracked at the time of the crime as evidence. It would scan the scene for DNA and it give back a statistic on the chances that it was that criminal that committed the crime.

Ranking clicked to the bottom of the scroll pad, and at the end put his silver bullet control to the computer screen. The outline of the screen switched to red. Miles of binary code filled the page and kept scrolling down and down in different patterns of zeros and ones. A box appeared on top of the binary code. Ranking began typing the implementing sequence, the same sequence he put in the night before tribunal reading 7839 for Private Eli. He entered in the scenario he'd built, implanted fake footage into MAIA. Alix's DNA and chip information he'd extracted through Alix's EED allowed him to recreate footage of Alix on tape doing anything Rankin wanted him to. When the MAIA found this data, it would make the best decision.

The MAIA had the statistical correct answer 100 and 95 percent of the time; that is, 100 percent of the readings when Readers needed answers for governmental reasons, and even made correct and effective decisions 95 percent of the time on its own, like automatically adjusting town wages or adjusting dams automatically due to the weather patterns it predicted. The days of a human predicting weather was limited to sticking your hand out the window. When a problem occurred and the MAIA read the situation and analyzed it, the outcome became based on the larger part of the statistic or the larger part of society; to inconvenience a minority within society statistically made sense to MAIA no matter the margin of error. It always correctly weighed statistics on matters such as raising the vanishing sequence on people. It gave the statistical chance an individual the Readers thought worthy of inquiry could harm the path of MAIA, and it also gave the percentage on the possibility they might not be a threat to the community, only Rankin couldn't control that.

What he could control is what is put into the system, therefore what the system knows and weighs. He couldn't enter all the information in front of the other Readers because they wouldn't sign off on such things being put in based on a validity and ethical problem. The problem concerning the other Readers, Rankin knew, was they forgot about personal judgment. Albert Einstein said, "Intellectuals can solve problems, a genius can prevent them." That's what the genius Albert Rankin intended, prevent future problems.

When Rankin looked at these kids, these out of control segments of this infidel generation, it made him sick to his stomach. These children, given the chance, would strip him of his position, blow up MAIA, and with their lack of intelligence be consumed into the lifestyle outside the limits of this island. Their minds are too weak, too two dimensional to work in a society as advanced and sophisticated as Maia the computer. Rankin made it his personal goal early in life to set the next generation and the future right, even if it meant going against the law abided by the MAIA and imputing false accusations about weak links in the system such as Eli or Alix, ones who started leaning backward in the direction of their ancestors, rejecting what they knew and wondering about something else, philosophers trying to be human in its most imperfect form. What good is a human if their minds are going to be wasted on menial processes and rejecting facts given to them? The mind, after all, is what sets us aside from all species, not wings, not claws, or teeth, but brains—the natural defense of the *Homo sapien*.

Rankin remembered the rest of his own generation before all this predicted violence happened. They watched television, reality TV, injecting sexual exploitation into the youth through seductive music videos, early pregnancies, and the talking on cellular phones for hours on end, tracking other's lives like celebrities enjoying life vicariously through them, always keeping in touch with the ugly arms of that consuming society, playing video games and sports, all just a waste of time, waste of brain power that could have been going toward something larger, something greater, something more advanced.

Rankin hit Enter after the files were uploaded to Alix's folder, and now he had an open door into Alix's mind to find out what makes him tick. What he thought. What he's been doing and why he knew about Eli.

9

"Sir, you said individual simulations today. Which would you have me do?"

The captain chewed the end of his pen and glared at the monitor above Phil's head, hating it every second it hung there, hated it for every potential word it heard and recorded, scanning for base words leading to conspiracy. "For the morning do hand-to-hand combat 530. I think that's…ah let me see." Captain pressed his screen spread out on his desk and dragged his finger across it, dabbed it here and there. "That's simulation 1397. Eat with the crew and do machine gunnery level 5. What gun do you prefer using if you had to fight right now? Close quarters?"

Phil smiled. "How close?"

"Close." Captain smiled. "Like hallways close. Say you were raiding a building or trying to get out of one."

Phil shrugged the bulk in his shoulders. "Probably the HK MG43."

"Why?"

"Classy, light, and still kicks some ass. Don't care if it's ancient. Don't need an accurate gun to send bullets straight down a hallway. The newer weapons don't punch you in the armpit for pulling their triggers. If it's not kicking back, it's not powerful enough to kick them back, you know what I mean, Captain?"

Captain smiled. At least someone around here has balls of steel still. "Sure do. They don't make them like they used to. Accuracy and sound suppression is no substitute for good old-fashioned hole in the chest. All right." The captain slapped his desk. "Level 5 simulation this afternoon with the HK MG43. After that, we're going to do a group simulation. Something new I've been working on."

"Yes, sir."

"Don't forget to consider the weight of that thing though, and you'll need two sidearms—a pistol and a submachine gun."

"Yes, sir."

"And send in Adam when you see him. I'll be here at 1700."

* * *

"Just let me see him, Dr. Harrison. It's the least you could do."

Dr. Harrison looked to either side, and his eyes became sincere—widened and brightened to the color of his lab coat. "It's protocol. I can't. You know I can't, Rob."

"The hell with your protocol at this point, you know this is wrong. There is nothing stopping you from opening that door. " He pointed toward the door. The captain could see just the reclined upper body of a young man through a gaping horizontal glass window. "I just want to see him. I've been working with him for several years now, and I feel somewhat responsible for what happened to him."

Dr. Harrison swallowed a water strip. "I'd have to report you. Regardless of our friendship."

"Then fucking report me." The captain pushed by Harrison and punched open the double swinging doors.

"Rob!" The doors creamed Harrison on their way back.

Two mirrored windows filled two of the eight walls the room had. A light blue glow circled the octagon at the bottom of each wall. Above the Captain's head hung thick and thin wires of every color, a predominant blue one led from the glassed window, on the ceiling, and dangled down above a chair. The blue wire ended at the back of the headrest and into the back of his head.

Eli lay back in the chair. His crystal blue eyes stared into the nest of wires above him. His eyes were opened, staring at the ceiling. A white cloth covered his body. The captain walked to the center of the octagon and put his hand on the top of the unconscious boy's head.

Harrison appeared by his side. "Life's not the same anymore, Rob. We had this discussion before. As a race we need to accept it. Darwin's theory is working against you right now, I'm afraid, and the fittest will survive. In the human world, intelligence is strength. Maia is the smartest it gets." He turned away.

The captain stared into Eli's eyes, a soulless jar, a carved fucking pumpkin and a new candle about to be implanted; just pop off the top and light a new one. "I used to fight for a country, Harry. A country that had balls. And heart…" A tear accumulated in the corner of Robert Milligan's eye. He was captain of Squad 28, but he felt feeling like a father who lost a son, his face twisted in emotion. His tear drifted down his cheek and into his orange beard. "This country used to stand for something. Stuck up for what was right, not what was logical."

"Rob…" Harrison's hand perched on the captain's shoulder.

"Don't touch me! We didn't have Maia when our patriots decided to become terrorists to the English throne and fight for our freedom. We didn't have Maia when our freedom became threatened by forces in Europe. We didn't have Maia when we policed the world and stuck up to bullies and tyrants! We had Maia when the United States collapsed…What the fuck makes her so amazing!"

Harrison looked through the glass, the reflection of him in his lab coat. "The day MAIA powered on, she answered the most complex questions advanced physicist had. She's the most valuable discovery since fire, Rob. She ended the theory of creationism and -"

Rob rolled his eyes. "I know what it did, Harry. It fucked everything up." The captain put his hand over Eli's head.

"Don't touch…" Dr. Harrison held out an arm. "You could—"

Captain held up his. "Okay, Harry. Relax. I'm done." He looked Eli in the eyes one last time. He wiped his river from his eye to his beard. He turned to Dr. Harrison. "What's the plan for him?"

Harrison sighed. "A cook."

The captain crossed his arms and shook his head. "He's a great soldier you know."

"I'm sure he was."

"A chef…" The captain choked up a boiling sadness and lifted his palm to smother his quivering lips. His eyes welled up. His face grew a shade close to his beard, and he had to look away for a moment.

The octagon grew quiet. A soothing quiet. The hum of the light cooled the captain's pulse. This poor boy. Curious about what he's never seen, a natural thing done every day years ago now gets your head erased, and you learn how to cook muck. Eli's chest barely took air, barely rose and fell. A vegetable until Dr. Harrison clapped his hands, and Eli became the best cook under sea level.

"Ah, look, Rob. I'm really am sorry about writing you up. It's just…"

The captain wiped his eyes. "I know, Harry."

"You haven't called me Harry in years."

"I know, Harry. Doctor Harold Harrison just sounds like a pussy that deserves to be shoved in a locker."

"Remember when we were friends then?"

"Yeah."

"You remember Virginia?"

"How could I forget? I sometimes wonder what it looks like now."

"More than likely just a smoking wasteland."

"You think? Sometimes I wonder if people would have been that bad after."

"Sickness and hunger will make people do some messed-up things, Rob."

The captain sighed. "I'm sorry we need to pretend not to know each other out there. I feel awful every time we pass each other. If the Readers knew any branch of science and military had any type of uncensored connections, they'd deem it treason, and we'd both be sitting in that chair."

"We're protected under…"

Captain's stare shot Harry's lips to silence. "You know our chips could be replaced with newer ones very easily."

"Yeah, but the laws—"

"Fuck your laws!" The captain's words echoed and transformed to silence. "So tell me, you lab monkeys have any word on Alix?"

Harrison's eyes widened. "They're taking another one of your guys? You're kidding me?"

Captain stared at Eli. "Nope. Is there any turning back or saving Eli now?"

"I haven't heard anything about Alix. I'll let you know if I get the chance. I'll keep an eye out. And no...Eli has been wiped completely."

"Listen, Harry, I got one more favor to ask." The captain turned to him. "You think you could hold that report for like, say fourteen hours or so?"

"Maybe. Why?" Harrison looked into Capt. Robert Milligan's eyes and made his biggest discovery of his career in that moment, just opened his wide eyes wide, "Oh my god."

The captain poked him in the chest. "You don't believe in God, remember."

"Rob, you're not thinking..."

Captain folded his arms again, bit his bottom lip hard, and nodded.

"You're fucking with me. Nobody's been out there in..."

The captain turned to him. "You don't use those words either, remember? There's other *intelligent* adjectives." The captain shot his glance. "And I am not fucking with you, my men and I leave in fourteen hours. Thanks for holding that report for me, Harry." The captain hit him on the back and walked back through the swinging doors.

"Wait! Here, I'll say you took it in, the report."

The captain looked at it. "You sure?"

"Yeah."

Captain turned away. "Harry, you're a good friend. And your little computer might have proved the Big Bang theory, but it could never destroy hope."

* * *

A gentle touch drifted over the tiny hairs on Alix's shoulder. The small spider rappelled from the ceiling and crawled up his neck and onto his forehead. He opened his eyes. Alix jerked at the straps to swat away the bug, but the strap caught his arm. He shook frantically in bed. The spider vanished.

"Ar!" Alix pulled harder on the strap until he felt the corner of the leather bindings cut into his wrists. "Ahr! Fuck! Let me out of here!" Alix jerked up on the leg restraints. "Let me go!" He forced his wrists up in a bench press motion, keeping the chains tight. "Fuck!" Alix panted, tried to wipe the sweat from his forehead and out of his eyes, but the chains straightened. Alix pounded the bed, sniffled, and slammed his head back into the pillow.

He stared at the monitor. In the bottom of the right hand corner of the screen blinked the message: "Reading in progress..." A sinking feeling rose when the three simple words appeared on the monitor. The feeling confirmed his next thought. He didn't know what the reading was about, but somehow knew it had something to do with him. *I need to get the fuck out of here.*

A shadow swept across the grid-glass window in the door. Alix's head snapped to the side. Anna?

Susan looked away from the window, her stomach a pit of guilt.

"Susan."

"Holy shit!" Susan's heart slapped the ceiling. "Al, you scared me."

"My T-port whines as I move. How did you not hear me? Never mind that, I don't have a lot of time. Where's Anna?"

Sue pointed in the side office where two beds lined each side of the room. "She's sleeping. Alix was too..."

"I don't care about Alix. Alix will be dead to me in time. I'm on my way to convince the MAIA Readers now for the Vanishing Sequence to be done on that little bastard. Do you know what our daughter has been doing?"

"Huh?" Susan's face twisted.

"She's been seeing Alix."

"What how? The boys and girls…" Sue's face played dumb, her brain a natural liar.

"In simulation!"

Susan's eyes bulged, and a smile almost broke out of her lips.

A vein grew from Rankin's eyebrow up and as high as Sue could see. "They've been sneaking around at night and meeting in simulation. I am going to put a stop to this. I will have Maia powered up 24/7 and monitoring everyone from now on." Rankin punched the wall.

Susan stepped back. "Al?"

"I'm going to put a monitor in every corner, every nick and cranny of this facility."

"Al, come on, how can you be sure?"

"I've seen it with my own eyes! She's had sex Sue! Your daughter has been fucking that little bastard soldier! I had to see it from his point of view from going through his files."

"Al, they weren't really having real sex, its fake, its simul—"

"It's my little girl! And that little shit in there is going to be my personal ass wiper and ball washer when he is reprogrammed."

Sue stared at Albert. "Quiet down! If anyone finds out Anna is our daughter, and she isn't fully programmed to Maia, we don't know what Maia will do to her. Don't let it happen, or so help me God, Al. I'll shove that ball you float around on so far up your fucking ass—"

Albert's backhand thrashed across Sue's face. "Watch your tongue you little bitch. I'll have you washing dishes tomorrow. I run this place. No one talks to me that way. I've looked out for you ever since you were dropped off because your family was too weak to protect you. You barely made the cutoff age, and I took you under my wing."

Sue held her cheek. "And to your bed chambers you sick fuck! Hence how your little daughter is here! You and the other board members run this facility, Al. Not just you. Don't ever hit me again, Al."

"We are MAIA Readers now, not board members." Rankin's pointer stabbed through Sue. "It's not just a company any longer. As for Anna, I haven't figured out what to do with that slut yet.

You though…I'll think of something to watch that temper." Rankin turned and whined down the hall, his screams echoing. "Weeks before the conservation and invasion of the mainland and everything goes wrong! Arhhh!"

Sue rubbed her cheek.

10

The light above the captain's desk dimmed. "So, be ready for even a moments notice to move. I mean it, gear and everything. This is for our division and our division only, you understand? Special orders from above. We're going in first."

"Yes, sir."

"All right. You're dismissed, Adam."

The captain rubbed his eyes and tapped his desk screen. He scanned the map of island, the old roads, and wondered about their condition—whether nature took its course and ridded the rocky rim of the asphalt lining the circumference of the old Governor's Island. He wondered the possibility of their vehicles traversing them far enough to the barge, getting an inflatable raft across the water. Or could they even chance just taking a raft from the far west bank around the island to the mainland? No. By the time the team got out, the Readers would be informed, and at the least Rankin would give the order for kill or capture. It wouldn't take long for them to gun the whole team down in a raft.

The captain ran his hand over his head. He rubbed the back of his neck and searched the ceiling for the reason he'd put himself in this predicament. How come it had to be him in the bathroom that day when Ethex sat lying in wait at the urinal for the next decorated officer to try and coax? Why him? It's the worst piss he'd ever taken aside for the one that got him scrubbing toilets for three months back in basic because he'd pissed out the barracks window at West Point. He remembered it being dark, but he guessed not dark enough to see the golden stream from his officer's window the captain only released for the fifty dollars bet. He never saw that fifty, but unlike Johnathan Dexter who bet him and didn't pay up, the captain still had his life.

He never thought of his career going from captain to *treason* walking out of military academy the day of graduation. How could his life come to this? But seeing how the world and its laws come to an even sicker state of anarchy to the point we now program the mind, maybe the captain didn't turn out *that* bad. Why can't people remain people? Why do we always have to find closer ways to monitor? Micromanage? Control? Govern?

Why?

Captain checked the monitor. "MAIA Reading Commenced" blinked in the bottom right-hand corner. They've already started deciding Alix's fate. First they would decide, and the captain would have only hours to execute. The upload to Maia would happen at midnight, and tomorrow no one in his generation would know who Alix was. The captain thought for a moment and hoped Alix's luck came through again, because somehow the little bastard managed to get this far; why not a little further?

Captain knew, Rankin and the other Readers would discover him—his chip wasn't his first thought process, that he could think for himself always, could decide for himself what to believe out of the MAIA broadcasts, could remember what Maia tried to block and control wirelessly. When the Readers found that, Alix was gone. He didn't fit in the "new generation."

The captain shook himself from his daydream, his casting away into nothing, wondering about life the way a child does while gazing at the stars. He found himself doing it more often lately and decided to stand. He looked over the map. Two ports stood a chance at having first a ferry or a barge large enough with enough fuel to get the trucks, gear, and all of them east over the Hudson River toward former Brooklyn. Pier 101 looked best. Captain measured it out. It will be the longest 1,500-foot traverse he'll have in his life. One missile and it all ends. They will have an army of about fourteen thousand chasing them, and another lord-knows-what waiting at the other end. But if they could get to the Brooklyn side of the Hudson River, they could fortify the night, get readings in the area, and so long as they brought enough rations, they could wait it out until the dim sun would power the Humvees 30 percent and growing every day. Hopefully, when they ran out of fuel, the sun would be, as Maia predicted, and able to power the Humvees. They could get away if the old roads held up.

The captain opened his center drawer. His dad's revolver stared back at him, and five bullets rounded each other.

"It's a Remington 1875 revolver." His father's words echoed, and the captain watched his father lift the sidearm straight out. "You don't fire a weapon like this, Robby. This is for gangsters and thugs. This means they don't know how to wield a weapon. Someone holds a gun like this to you, they probably never killed a man, and if they did, they did it on accident."

His father twirled the gun on his finger, and it slithered its way back into the holster, the Virginia sun glimmered off the hammer. "You want to kill a man, or scare him, you have to be quick."

In one hint of a motion, the gun snapped out of the holster, appeared in his fathers hand, and started popping. By the time the first can bailed off the rock wall, a second chased it. His father's other hand pulled the hammer while the gun blasted by his hip. The captain's little eyes closed every time the pistol stammered.

Two Pepsi cans scattered off the old disheveled rock wall, and Budweiser bottles disintegrated in seconds. His father waved the smoked away to check his aim. Spot on.

The blood rushed down the young Robby's body at the sight of the pistol. He stepped anyway. His hand shook. He left the room and walked down the hall still wondering where his legs intended on taking him. He was going to need a lot of help.

* * *

After signing in the video of Alix hitting the two medics, the Readers looked at each other from across the table outside the metal room of the MAIA. The old men around the table remembered the days of United States pride and unity, but were also old enough to know what happened when the country got too bold, too domineering and, ultimately, too powerful for its own good. And like the ways of their old country, they gathered in groups, representing the people in a government by the people, for the people, but with the guidance of supercomputer that didn't make mistakes.

Rankin smiled, standing next to his chair overlooking the stretched out oval sleek table. He looked into the other Reader's eyes feeling the advantage he had over them. "As we see here gentlemen, Private Alix Basil is obviously aware of the presence of the Private Eli Williams and the vanishing sequence that took place recently by Maia. According to the paragraph 6 in article 72 of the MAIA Law and Abidance Protocol, Alix poses a threat to MAIA and its probability for conservation of the mainland and getting off this island and to the surface."

Eight other MAIA Readers stared back at him. Eight men in powerful suits, sleek, black, and impressive, the most intimidating minds next to the largest supercomputer in the world. They were the ones who controlled what controlled. They oversaw what oversaw and put themselves below the system, the government, by choice, not subjected to it by birth.

"You know, Albert, if we keep running the vanishing sequence on these boys, we won't have an army to conserve the MAIA with." Elmer Washington's cheeks fell from his eyes in layers leading down to his double chin. His thick, bushy eyebrows hung over his eyes, robbing his face from most uplifting emotions.

"Elmer, this boy is a threat." Rankin stared down the large man solely in a sit-down T-port because of his weight, not his inability to move his legs. "There is no reason why we should allow this crazy boy to wield weapons that could put MAIA people at risk."

"So you're belief is to just erase his existence, along with every other MAIA person you believe is a threat?"

The other Readers bowed their heads and prepared themselves for the hours of debate in this verbal rematch of the last reading.

Rankin leaned on the table. "I believe that an ignorant, out-of-control child should not be in our military!"

"He's not a child! He's nineteen years old! You and I both fought in Iraq at eighteen! And what you call out of control, I call intelligence. And he's apparently not ignorant. If he's really intelligent enough to overlook Maia's decision about Eli, maybe we should move him to the military intelligence. You and I know about Eli! Does that put us in jeopardy of being risk?"

"You're going too far, Elmer!" Rankin placed his scarred old knuckles on the table.

"Maybe he should be up here with us discussing what's better for Maia if he's really that intelligent." Elmer grunted and his cheeks shook. "Before all this nonsense about wireless mind connection, monitoring, and altering, we used to praise people like this boy, award him." Elmer sat back seemingly defeated, but rose again out of his chair. "And for some reason Maia sees you favorable every time, and I don't believe that to be a coincidence, no, sir. I don't know what is going on, but Maia has never issued so many vanishing sequences out in one year as it has in this one thus far. Five in one year is unheard of. Isn't it, Frank?"

"Yes, El, I believe it is." Frank lifted his head and spoke through a dry, physically beaten expression.

Ranking waved his arm. "Well let's see what Maia seems to think. Shall we, gentlemen? Shall we resort to our actual form of government, the correct way of procedure? Maia controls MAIA right? We guide her along. Isn't that how it works?" Rankin grinned.

Rankin pushed the pad next to the chair he stood next to. He entered a number and waited for the others. They followed suit around the table entering their passwords and key codes for confirmation. All until Elmer. Elmer stared down at the button knowing the outcome. Regardless he entered his pin and push Access.

A loud rush came from the metal room, like a large release of steam, and the engines beneath hummed. MAIA searched through all its memory, all its video and audio recordings. It searched through expressed views, conversations, facial expressions by Alix and those around them. It searched through his whole life until that point, from the time his military mother gave birth to him and never saw him again, when the nurse pushed him into the room of cadets from military parents only to be mixed together.

Maia searched his mother and father's record for any odd behavior. It searched through his education, the questions he asked, the ideas he'd propose. It searched through all his recordable simulations, his actions, his hesitations, his recordable thoughts. It searched his life up until that point where it found a video from the night before.

Deep in Maia's memory it zoomed in on Alix in the mirror on U40. His eyes narrowed in the reflection. "You will be the one to bring down MAIA," Alix promised himself. He assured his reflection in the old dusty mirror that he would put an end to MAIA personally. Maia flagged this information and added it to the reasoning section. Maia stalled for a moment and realized within the last week, two cadets told themselves that same line, same quote, and same promise: "You will be the one to bring down MAIA." Eli Williams said that too only a weeks ago while curled up in a ball in a dark corner.

MAIA pulled together information that might be leading to these two boys both saying the same quote, both having the same mind frame. The searches lead to Albert Rankin traversing down the hallway to the Maia only one hour and twenty minutes ago. The computer searched for confirmation video and found that only an hour before Eli's vanishing sequence, Albert Rankin walked down the hall too. The computer stopped searching for Alix and Eli's connection to conspiracy and searched the correlation between Albert Rankin and the cadet's conspiracy.

Maia made a decision, drew up the percentages, and sent them back to the Readers. The Readers saw the binary code first, but not the verdict. Elmer held his breath as the answer came up across the screen. His mouth dropped.

* * *

Susan Maynard leaned on her palms. She checked the monitor. The "Reading in Progress" indicator still blinked. She'd watched it for an hour, dozed off debating if she should try and sleep and just leave Anna in charge. She knew sleep wouldn't come. Was she a medic or a prison guard?

Every time she set eyes on the boy, the urge to just fully comply with the messenger on U21 about getting Alix off this floor dug deeper, but like a softly spoken threat, she didn't know what to believe: the tone or the words? Would Alix be better off in this messenger's control? Maybe that's why she found herself staring at Alix throughout the night, waiting for her instinct to take over her chip's reasoning, let her and her human judgment decide whether or not to let him go, free him.

She wondered about "free" and what that might mean, what that word entailed these days. Free from MAIA, was there such thing still? Free from the cerebral chip or her EED? Life without Maia did exist, but Susan hadn't known anything since the day her mother left her on that side of the barge in Manhattan. She wondered how her mother could just do that, just leave her child, but MAIA only took children under sixteen years old, no adults after the first waves of attacks.

She was fifteen years and eleven months then. Her mother must have thought it safer to leave her daughter in the hands of a military intelligence company residing deep under Governor's Island than to try and survive the riots after the first attack. After all the riots and the collapsing buildings, maybe she was right. She remembered the chaos from the blackout, remembered her father saying how quickly everything can come crashing down when everything in life is done on the Internet, and suddenly it did.

Everything they knew and owned, everything they thought they had was gone. Vanished. The weird people who still kept cash in safes, still had the actual paperwork to their homes and talked on landline telephones weren't so weird—they were the only ones who had anything while anything was something.

"A classic example of leaving all your eggs in one basket," her father said two days before he died defending the home from the rioters. "Keep all money and 401K stored away in some computer and someday, and impossible somehow happened today."

She remembered his face, his thick mustache and the Louisville Slugger before the door slammed shut forever. She remembered the flames outside splattering the red and orange across the windows that night and the smell of smoke from her neighbors burning house. She remembered the screams and her mother's tears. Susan didn't know about the fighting, the looting, and burning taking place outside. She didn't know about her father knocking two young man's head in or the color of his bat after the assault, or the third boy and his pistol. She heard the bang outside her house but didn't know it was her father under the blast, didn't know she'd never see him again.

She remembered her mother dragging her teenage body too fast for her legs and Nike sneakers to keep up with. She remembered being hurled into the Jeep and jolting back and forth from her mother whipping the wheel left and right. She remembered the man's face that rolled up onto the hood and the screeching tires and roaring motor. She remembered not knowing the situation and why everyone became so crazy and remembered pretending a tornado ripped across the city to justify everybody's panic.

She remembered the talk on the car radio about what was left of the stock market and even the people who thought they might still have some money were now poor and fighting for food. She remembered her mother's Jeep sputtering out of gas because no one could have more than an eighth of a tank. The words of hope from the man on the radio blared from the open car door as they ran from the Jeep stuck in her head: "Please remain in doors, and God be with us."

A series of tall chain-link fence spread across the bridge. A man in a military suit met the crowd, megaphone in hand. Armored men in riot gear stretched shoulder to shoulder across the bridge four to five layers deep behind him. Machinegun fire spurt every few moments. Susan's mother fought the crowd to the font, at one point elbowed an older woman in the mouth. She reached the front of the line.

The military man received Susan and shoved her into the crowd of screaming children in the opposite direction after reading her birth certificate. The man didn't care about her skin like her father did. The general shoved her tiny body backward. He didn't run his callused hands over her arms and make it feel like silk, didn't lift her as delicately as her father had. She didn't scream like the rest of the crying children. She just held onto her mother's gaze as long as she could, watched her mother's lips scream her name into frosty breath. Susan watched her mother's face disappear behind the advancing crowd held back by the iron gates, and get washed away by a dirty fat man's face jeweled with two sapphire eyes and piggybacking a chubby-cheeked boy. When her mother's face disappeared forever, Susan turned around and watched pigeons fly across the morning sky.

Susan checked the screen. The blinking message disappeared, and she wondered about the verdict of the reading, but even the most curious person couldn't rejected the stronger impulse of sleep. The door swung open behind her to the medic's bunks. Susan turned around.

Anna held her hair back and wrapped it in a hair tie. "Susan, you look awful. Have you slept yet?"

"No." Susan yawned. She talked through it. "Keep watch over our patient for an hour. I'm going to take a nap. Wake me immediately if anything happens, anyone comes down, or if I get any other messages."

"Okay. I'll get him a water and food strip, and wait for you for anything else."

"Be careful, and remember to lock the door and bring your paralyzer."

11

"ERROR." The word blinked across their foreheads. Nine replicas of the same five- letter reflection labeled their faces as a reminder that even the most sophisticated supercomputer in the world wasn't perfect. Each time it flashed, all nine men wished for Maia to fix the problem itself, for it just reappear on a new screen displaying the numbers and percentages that rationalized why Alix should be subdued to the vanishing sequence. How were men supposed to judge whether or not to erase one's existence and replace it with a new one? How could men decided matters concerning men?

"Is this possible?" Elmer's fat arm flopped.

Perspiration filled the wrinkles in Rankin's face, and his teeth bent from the pressure under his jaw. Frank glanced at Elmer. Elmer scanned the table. The others' screens matched his, and their painted expressions paralleled his as well.

"What's this all about?" Frank slapped the table.

Eight men expressed eight different views about what they believed happened in a free-for-all inquiry, an eruption of noise, but Rankin stared at the screen, submerged in the debate. He felt the reason for the error well in his throat, the beat in his chest and pulse in his ear. Could it be discovered? Could *he* be discovered? Is it possible that Maia outsmarted *him*?

Elmer leaned on his forearm, the fat flattening against the table like rolling pin pressed to the dough. "So what do we do now?"

Rankin's voice cracked. He cleared his throat. "Maybe we should just try again tomorrow?"

"We can't leave the room until we have a decision. It's protocol!"

Rankin held his breath and his clenched fist.

"We have to make a decision ourselves."

Elmer exited out of the error screen. "Gentlemen, on your consoles would you kindly go to the MAIA Override/Manual Decision program and log in. This could take a while, we should get going."

Rankin stepped off his T-port and eased his achy body into the seat. He opened the program. It opened and, with it an opportunity for Rankin's plans to close.

* * *

Anna sat at the main desk. Her nails tapped against the old counter. There was something about Alix that just extracted her desire, a lump of burning evolution in her chest where the littlest simple memories would inflate and ignite again. It was in his eyes, something that dared her. Waiting until after conservation and submitting a request form for compatibility seemed an eternity away, and it existed only in limited conversation they were allowed to have during interaction sequences in simulations.

It didn't make sense to make them wait until after the conservation of the mainland. What would happen if Alix didn't make it back? She set her chin into her palm. It didn't occur to her until that point that it might be a possibility. It was possible that Alix could be taken from her. Killed. She realized something there. For a moment she realized that she would rather have Alix than have him sacrificed for the cause of her government. She checked over her shoulder. Susan's breaths didn't catch sleep yet.

She pictured the war and what it would be like, the insane civilians, one step above crazed monkeys, shooting at Alix, a bullet grazing his leg or shoulder and him going down screaming, pulling off his mask, sucking in the toxic air from manmade bombs dropped decades before. She pictured his face, the blood and dirt on it, and her body tensed when it wasn't her in her nightmare tending to Alix's wounds, but another medic, a blonde medic. The blonde medic, maybe Beth, ran to him and ripped off his vest, cut his shirt off down the middle exposing his chest to the dark sky. She pressed her hand over his body ahead of the portable X-ray scanner checking for breaks or fractures in his ribs. Over his legs. The inside of his hips. His chest. She pictured his bullet-riddled vest next to Beth. He stopped breathing. Anna couldn't stop the story she'd created even when Beth parted her lips wide, stuck them to Alix's mouth, blocked his nose, and blew air into his lungs. Beth leaned over him and pushed down on his chest. He coughs blood. She wipes his mouth. She bends down to blow more air in, and his eyes opened just as she started to blow air into his…

"Stop it!" Anna shook her head. I have to see him.

Her palm left small spots of sweat on the desk. Her body cooled. She took a deep breath. A message indicator blinked in the corner of the screen at the main desk: "Manual Reading in Progress." She checked over her shoulder into Susan's dark room again. She looked at the indicator. To get Alix out and be with him, she'd have to break rules.

12

"Maia, bring up anything regarding the vanishing sequence of Alix Basil." Elmer Washing pressed his forearm into the table and wiped his upper lip. The machine hummed.

Their screens in front of them all chimed, and a folder appeared in the middle of the screen. The electronic folder opened up and expanded into their faces. Hundreds of files.

"Maia, please extract any simulation folders that have no relevance on the vanishing sequence being done with him."

Files shot to the right of the screen and disappeared.

Rankin gritted his teeth. This could take forever.

* * *

"You're fucking insane."

"What do you want me to do? They're going to erase the kid's mind! His existence!"

"It's not the first, Rob. I've had two of my guys subjected to the vanish sequence. Christ, Milligan, what the fuck you thinking? Weeks before we are going to take the mainland. Would have a better shot at waiting and just going AWOL."

"I'm thinking you have a division of fifty men. I had eight. Besides, I'm thinking I've had enough. We've whispered it before..."

"Yeah, we've whispered it, we've yelled about it, but I've whispered about going to the moon, winning a billion dollars. We've all whispered shit. What you are talking about is insanity! Not to mention suicidal even if you make it off Governor's Island. You're talking with just a special forces team to take on a frontal assault of nearly what could be a hundred thousand men."

"Shh." The captain held his finger to his lips and looked over his shoulder. The lunch room lay vacant. "I'm going, Jack. It's too late. Either Maia catches up to me and charges me with conspiracy slash treason, or I'm out of here. We were born free men. Whatever the fuck we are now isn't cutting it. I'm calling in my favor, Jack. You owe me."

Jack looked at his longtime friend. The blood drained from Rob Milligan's face. The fight in his eyes had turned to rabid frustrations and violent lashings. Jack remembered meeting Milligan for the first time in the war, walking next to the Humvees; a packed military hearse meant no room for the living. The living walked because the dead couldn't and needed the ride back home. That was a day that the United States could *never* fall, *never* falter, was *never* wrong. Third-world countries and communist nations could *never* make their way here, the battle could *never* be brought to our front, our homes, our beaches, our towns, and our cities. Never. We were the *superpower* of the world, leader of a *free* world. All until one computer-hugging, backstabbing president named pro tempore couldn't refuse fifty years of presidential pay for three "accidental overlooks."

Rob and Jack walked four days through rubble. Cities burned. Cars exploded. People cried of sickness, hunger, pain, wounds, and many were dead. Dead-like-in-the-movies dead. Like this was all just one big movie that Jack and Rob walked through. Bullets popped in the distance, and everyone wondered, is it possible the whole United States is like this?

Craig was alive then. The kid was too quiet. Cleaned his gun constantly. "Can't shoot too straight, I always say." He was out of Missouri, one of the places hit the least. Why Missouri? Who the fuck knows. I think it was more like, why Boston? Why New York? Why Los Angeles? Why DC? Why Chicago, New Orleans, Tampa

Bay, San Diego, Las Vegas, and thirty other cities? Because a simultaneous technological attack on all our major cities and the sabotage of the supercomputer recently instated as a fourth branch of the United States government leaves the country vulnerable to a multi–nuclear attack and a full frontal invasion.

It was an explosion heard around the world. President pro tempore, the bitch, after doing her damage, disappeared. I guess anyone can be bought. Wonder what she thought when she watched her country fall into anarchy. Did the bitch even care?

The ambush came on Wall Street. The final trudge back to the barge at Battery Park. A small brigade waited in The Crest Building. After the Amex building came down on Broadway, they should have known about the diversion. Jack remembered the feeling of being stung in his leg and shoulder. The convoy scattered, and Jack lay in the middle of the road for thirty-five minutes until a grenade took out the front of the building and quieted the enemy long enough for Rob Milligan to charge the street, hurled a smoke grenade to the south side of the street, and drag Jack to the Humvee. That's when Jack made the promise.

Jack stared into Robs eyes across the lunch table and touched his scar on his shoulder over his shirt. He remembered a time before the chaos. He remembered his parents and his house, his little brother. Jack hoped at least his little brother made it, but they came so quick. The government didn't even know whom they were fighting at first. Took them two whole days to determine each corner of the map had a different opponent. A synchronized attack. How could this happen? Suburbia burned, cities fell, and the American Dream that took hundreds of years to build crumbled in days.

He pictured off the island, a boiling pit of death. It wouldn't be first major change. One or two more nuclear explosions, and the planet would have been toast. We're even lucky to be here. But is this much better?

Jack watched Rob stir his egg muck.

Would it be worth fighting the actual enemy again? Is there a chance the citizens weren't that animalistic and or were slaughtered by a superior enemy?

"Rob, getting off the island by yourself isn't a good idea."

"I'll have my team."

"I meant not alone. I'll have the Humvees ready. I'll have a few of my guys help. We have some good kids down here. You thinking sea or air?"

The captain slurped his muck. "It's got to be boat. They'd shoot us down in a second. Shit, if they gave a sniper nearly half as good as Alix a musket, he could shoot us down a hundred yards off the Island." Captain choked down the muck. "And you?"

"I'm staying."

"Okay." The captain tossed his spoon down. "You should come along though."

* * *

Alix heard the door latch. He kept his eyes shut. He heard her breath. He lifted his head. They soaked in a silent conversation, a conversation words couldn't have no more than a computer could have feelings, a conversation heard not with ears, but that small flutter beneath the tissues of the heart, a moving warmness, a flooding emotion, a slow flare from a small memory set back in time, in the back of their minds—only this was real. She sat on the side of the bed and put her hand on his chained arm. She swayed her fingertips along his wrist.

"It's amazing to feel your real skin for once." She bowed her head. She moved her hand up to his and tied their fingers together. "It's almost like the first time again, isn't it?"

Her words kissed his soul. His thin hairs stood on end, and his back tightened up. Alix squeezed her hand. "Remember the first time?" his voice broke into stuttering beats.

She remembered the smell of the land, the heat of the fire, the sound of destruction. She remembered the bombs in the distance lighting the sky over the smoldering buildings, the way the light burst through the holes in the infrastructure like blinking eyes, the black smoke mixed with clouds lurking on the horizon.

Neither made it to the helicopter. Alix's arm was slung around Anna's shoulder, and they watched it take off in front of them. The mission had gone wrong from the beginning. A missile from the lurking clouds screamed across the sky and landed around the base of the building Alix and Victor tried so valiantly to climb. Victor pushed his palms against the wall. Alix climbed up onto his shoulders, tossed their equipment up, and hoisted himself up, turned around and lowered his hand to grab Victor, both men up a fifteen-foot wall in fifteen seconds.

Victor stuck his eyes into his binoculars. "Bunker south west." He turned the nozzle. The view through his yellow mask and into the binoculars turned brighter, a rapidly increasing and decreasing number appeared. "Twenty hundred fifty-two meters. Wind northeast five kilometers per hour. Switch to .50 cal. Coriolis effect, one click up. Aim high. High capacity rounds, full metals. Difficulty, high. Percentage"—Victor checked his EED—"twelve percent."

Alix didn't look up. He checked his EED. "Forty-seven percent." His hands clicked in the magazine. His tossed his smaller rifle aside and set a pod next to Victor. He leaned down.

"Switch to night vision, brighten mask."

Alix lay down and pointed his rifle in the distance. He found his targets. He breathed audible breaths, his body adjusted to horizontal orientation, blood flowed across, not up and down. "Twenty hundred fifty-five meters."

"What?" Victor didn't pull his eyes away.

"Twenty hundred fifty-five meters."

"That's not what the system is saying, Alix. Adjust scope to twenty hundred fifty-three meters."

Alix looked down at his rifle. Hit three buttons on the side and looked back into the scope.

"Alix. What are you doing. My screen says you're projecting twenty hundred fifty-five, I'm telling you it's twenty hundred fifty-three."

"Fuck your system. I'm telling you, twenty hundred fifty-five meters. I'm taking the shot. Call out a target, count it down." Alix aimed at the oldest man out of the three. He adjusted his scope. Alix eyed the man's short brim. What expression would remain on his face if Alix just took off the brim of the hat?

"I hate you Alix. If we miss this shot, I'm shooting you in the leg before this simulation is over."

"If we make it, we're going home early. Chopper's waiting."

Alix didn't remove his eye from the glass.

Victor's jaw stiffened. "Target, ranking officer, arms behind his back, two thousand and…" Victor sighed. "Fifty-five meters. Heavy wind gusts, currently 1.5 kilometers north northwest. Counter wind"—Victor adjusted his scope—"1.8 kilometers south southeast. Coriolis effect, point two for vertical drift."

Alix steadied. His finger kissed the trigger. He breathed in and let it out slow. He visualized the shot.

"Fire. Shoot."

Alix pulled the trigger. The air was sucked out of the room and followed the bullet. Five long seconds of flight later, a slap from God smacked the ranking officer to the side and down. What was left over from below his shoulder followed the rest of the body over a bloody river to his comrade.

"Hit, target, gunner, two thousand and fifty-five meters."

Alix reloaded. *Click-click.* The shell hit the ground. *Ping-ping.*

"Wind same, fire shoot."

Alix's rifle exploded again. Neither of them could have predicted the missile that passed the bullet high above and rained down near their location. The whiz of the rocket perked their ears, but it was too late. The explosion took down the east side of the building. The floor below Victor and Alix shifted, tilted, and fell. They slid down the crashing floor, tons of broken desks, appliances, TVs, computers, shattered office glass poured down the three story slope after them. Alix's back slammed against a cement support to the car garage in the basement, his rifle hitting his stomach. The building toppled over.

Victor rolled down the splintering floor. His boots caught, sending him flipping in midair flopping on his back. The slope cracked, launching desks and most of the break room necessities of past life into the air and down on Victor. The building crashed around them in a roar no mind could imagine, for not too many minds made it out of a situation such as this.

Alix stared through his cracked face mask. He undid the straps and pulled his mask above his. The stale air tasted of dirty water and burnt birch. He rolled over to all fours and coughed, spat out a chunk of something he didn't think belonged in him, and looked over to Victor.

Victor's feet dangled out the bottom of a refrigerator. Alix hung his head and realized the shard of wood deep in his knee. He grasped it. Clenched his teeth. He ripped it out and screamed louder than the roaring fire and the bombs within meters of him surrounding the rubble.

He lit a medical flare and stuck the flame into his wound. The skin fused and the bleeding stopped, but pain increased. "Ahrr!" Alix leaned over on his side and screamed and clutched his sidearm. He squeezed his gun. The pain, a searing internal nastiness, floated up his leg, into his groin, showered all his internal organs, seized his neck, and attacked his brain.

"Alix!"

The voice stopped his screams and pain for a moment.

"Alix!"

"Over here!"

Anna appeared through the smoke. "What happened!"

"A missile took out the base of our position. Victor didn't make it. I'm going to have to bust his balls when we get back about getting killed by a refrigerator. Tell 'im to chill the fuck out."

"You guys are ridiculous!" Anna reached down and hoisted Alix up.

The door to the underground garage of the building kicked open.

"Get down!" Alix lashed Anna into the fridge and onto Victor's dead legs. "Anna, did you bring any backup?"

Alix put pressure on his wound and collapsed. He pointed the gun at the door, and fired three shots. A spray of bullets pinged behind them, hit the cement beam, and smacked the fridge. Alix fired three more rounds, and two men went down near the doorway. The air died for a moment. No fire, no bombs, no wind, no trickling rubble, just dead. From the side a sound of metal on metal rolled out. Alix turned. Too late. The gun pointed toward him. Alix's pistol raised. A flash from the citizens assault rifle. A sputter close to Alix's head and a roaring of fire from Alix's right. Anna held the trigger of Victor's machine gun, and the man went down.

"No! Let's go!"

Alix picked himself up and stumbled. "I can't walk."

"Let's go, we have to hurry." Anna threw Alix's arm over her shoulder. Alix raised his pistol and shot Victor in the leg as they hobbled by and toward the exit. "We don't have much time. It's getting too hot up there for the chopper."

Her radio buzzed. "Thirty seconds, Anna. You're going to regret this call if you don't bring someone back."

"We're trying."

"Try faster! We're taking fire!" Machine gun fire littered the background. "Sorry, you're on your own. We can't turn around! We're taking too much fire. Sorry."

Anna and Alix burst through the side door and hunched down behind a busted, shot- up car and fell to the ground after the helicopter lifted into the air. A missile emerged from the side, and a white trail led to the explosion of the red spinning flames that was their way out. The fire lit their faces, burning fuel singed their nose, and chopper going down reflected in their eyes. The propeller flung debris everywhere like a blooming onion.

Alix looked into her eyes. She wasn't wearing a mask. She didn't have time to prepare, so it hadn't been planned that she come out. They leaned back against the rusted car. His leg was elevated, her hand on his knee. "You okay?"

"I guess this means we all fail this time, huh?" Alix smirked and looked into the burning night. His head hung alongside his esteem.

Anna's desire burned. "You didn't fail. There was nothing you could have done. You hit your target." She couldn't take it anymore. They way they looked at each other, they way they talked. He had to know, and she believed he felt the same way. Anna grabbed his chin. She pressed her lips into his.

His body melted. He couldn't feel his leg. He wrapped his arm around the back of her neck, and he leaned on top of her. Her tongue drove into her mouth and clashed with his. He hoisted himself up, and her legs went to either side of him. He pressed into her, and their mouths clashed again.

Glass cracked and crushed under them. They jumped and while cornered on the ground, four citizens surrounded them, guns aimed down and screaming an Arabic dialect.

They moved slowly. Anna reached down for Alix's pistol.

They spun, and Alix scrambled for Victor's machine gun. Anna tossed her arm over Alix's shoulder and fired next to his ear. A citizen fell backward. Alix pulled the trigger, and the gun spurted. Another citizen flew back onto the car and slid back down over the hood. The bullets rained down on them from where they couldn't tell as pelt after pelt bullets tore their virtual sessions to threads, and their screens glitched out.

Alix opened his mask.

Matt looked at Alix. "So what happened?"

* * *

Anna touched the side of Alix's face after they reminisced about their first kiss. "That wasn't that long ago, but that simulation feels like an eternity ago. It was always just little flirty gestures before that day."

Alex nodded. "It wasn't even close to the last time either. We could have gotten caught so many times once we started sneaking out and using the simulators."

Anna smiled. "We said it would have been worth it." She put her hand on his stomach.

Alix moaned. "Remember the first time with just us? We planned which night and snuck in for the first time. I thought we were screwed."

Anna smiled bigger. "You mean like the time we snuck into a simulation?"

"Yeah. I've never been in simulation so long."

Anna laughed. "We just let the battle go on around us while we hunkered down in that abandoned bus."

Alix smiled. "I'm sure screaming people and blazing guns wasn't what you figured for your first time."

Anna's hand slid down his gown and grabbed his arousing self. "It wasn't my real first time."

A door slammed outside the room.

"Got to go. Love you." Anna disappeared out the door as silently as she came in.

13

"Gentlemen, I put a special simulation together for you guys." The captain paced back and forth in the egg-shaped room.

Squad 28 minus Eli and Alix looked back. Each stood in front of a simulator bed and held their helmet, chins up. Hayden clenched his jaw. Wes's chest expanded, his eyes a dead stare.

"I've got insight boys. I have a vision." Captain put his hands behind his back. "It's you, boys, on the mainland first. It's your whole team together once again on the battlefield like since you were six." Captain paced.

Phil flexed his shoulders and cracked his neck.

"It's even more than that, boys. I'm going to be glad to be there next you boys in the front of the fight." The captain stopped pacing and faced the boys, looked in each set of eyes for the fire. "No one has ever been where we are going. No one has ever fought the enemy that stands in our way, even in simulation."

Matt squinted. Adam saw, made eye contact and shrugged.

"So, boys, let's go there. Get into your simulation. I'll see you in there."

Everyone climbed onto the simulators and put on their helmets. They strapped on the sensors and lay back. They dropped their shields on their helmet and watched the world go colorful. Right before they entered simulation mode, and their senses forfeited to the artificial, virtual reality world, the captain's words echoed, "And, boys, enjoy your last simulation!"

The flash took them to wherever it was that they were going. Their toes went numb. Gravity pulled harder on their legs, and their kneecaps floated lightly. Their thighs became light, their hips submerged in uncontrollable sensations. Their fingers twitched, and their shoulders stiffened. Finally, their head fell back and their eyes closed. Their whole body fell into an abyss.

They landed. Their consciousness switched, and their world was now an alternate existence. Matt moved his fingers. He opened his eyes. He brought his hand to his head and wiped his eyes. He looked up, and the egg room stood before him. Not the trashed world outside the island, the nuclear wasteland that was former United States, not a sandy battlefield full of fire and bullets, not a forest of burning trees and enemies. It wasn't citizens lined up firing back at him, chucking grenades or rocks or whatever they had left over from the war. They weren't on a helicopter about to deploy; they weren't on a boat about to dock on enemy's beach. No. The captain had let them down. He had made some pretty intense simulations and even for Matt, being the tech dork he was, "a nerd with a gun," something was either wrong with the simulator or the captain went insane. "What the fuck!"

"What's going on here?" Phil stretched his legs and pulled off his simulator helmet. "Captain?"

Matt stood. "Anyone know what's going on here?"

"We're in simulation, dipshit, or did you get a virus?" Hayden stretched his arms.

"Are we? We're in the simulation room again?"

"Why would Captain make a simulation simulating the simulator?"

Phil's eyebrows narrowed; he looked to Wes. "Does that even make sense?"

Wes shrugged.

"No, you dipshit."

"What the fuck is going on?"

"Why is our equipment here?"

"Guys check this out! All our shit is in here."

"Shut up!" The echoes disappeared down the hall. The captain's boots scraped the metal grate. "Just shut up. We're wasting time."

"For what, Captain? Why are we here?" Adam rubbed his neck.

"Do you know who Alix is?" Captain stared.

"Yes." Victor's eyes became narrow.

"Well, by tomorrow morning, you might not." Captain promised each pair of eyes.

Silence responded.

"Captain, what do you mean?" Hayden crossed his arms.

"You boys are part of a generation of programmed chips that have the ability to be wirelessly controlled by Maia."

"Captain, with all do respect, sir." Wes straightened. "We are aware of our EED and our connection to Maia."

"You boys don't know the extent of these machines."

"What do you mean the *extent*?" Matt raised his voice.

"Do you know who Eli is?"

Phil cleared his throat. "You've asked this before like we should know the bastard. Was it someone in the brigade?"

Captain pulled the photograph and showed Phil. "Do you remember taking this photo?"

Phil stared at the picture of the boys. Everyone. Matt, Wes, Alix, Hayden, Adam, Victor and Phil all guns up in front of a Humvee. But a smaller guy knelt down in front of them all, a small mole above his lip, dark hair. A complete stranger. Phil thought hard. He remembered that day, seeing the real equipment, being out of the classes and stepping into real physical military work. No more pounding the books and watching videos of flanking strategies and assault and guerilla warfare and studying his opponent. He remembered posing for the picture. He tried to remember that boy. There was no one there. He pictured and pictured him. "That's a fancy trick. I'll bet my life on it, that that boy was never there that day."

The captain grabbed Phil by the jaw. "That is no trick!" The captain's lips launched fierce spurts of saliva. "This boy was one of you." Captain's eyes lit up as bright as his beard. "That boy is someone you will never see again. He was a great soldier and grew up with you! He fought with you! Next to you." The captain let his grip go.

A red pressure stain remained on his throat. Phil adjusted his neck and jaw.

"This boy"—the captain held up the photo—"would have died for any one of you on the battlefield, and you don't even know his name. You've had conversations with this boy, slept next to this boy! And you don't remember a god damn thing about him because of this fucked up society we live in! Maia has you boys so wired up you don't know your asshole from your elbow! You are free-thinking beings! That's how Maia got thought the fuck up! From free thinking humans." The captain stopped pacing. "This is about to happen again to you guys."

"To Alix?"

Captain nodded. And quieted. "To Alix." He sniffled. "I don't know why or how they do it, but Eli is no more as of yesterday. Alix will be gone tomorrow. You'll see this picture." He held it up. "And you'll wonder who they both are?"

"How do you know who they are?" Wes looked down.

"My chip is programmed level 1. I have knowledge and skill loaded on my chip. I can decipher between actual thought and programmed information. When I think"—the captain tapped on his temple—"I can feel the difference between actual thought and programmed information. My brain will not register programmed information Maia forces in when my brain remembers everything from before. You guys can't do this. The only one who can is Alix."

"What!" Victor's arms flared sideways.

"Alix doesn't have a level 2 chip. He has what I have. He can decipher actual and programmed thought. He knows who Eli is and remembers him well. That's why he's where he is right now. They're trying to figure out what I already know. That's why we have to move now." The captain knelt down and looked up at them. "When we get out of this simulation"— his eyebrows raised—"you will have a choice." The captain looked through their eyes. "A true choice. Your stuff will be laid out for you like this. Your weapons. Your gear. Everything you need to get away from all this mess. I'm gathering it all now as we speak. I'm not really in simulation with you. I'm leaving either way. I'm inviting you. I'm *not* giving programmed minds a command, I'm giving free-thinking men a decision to make. Make it."

The captain threw a black plate on the ground. An upside down blue pyramid appeared, and on the bottom face the captain outlined the screen. The boys hovered around it. "Our objective is to get to the lowest level of MAIA with or without force. We will be geared up, so Maia won't take long to figure we're in attack gear and send a team to stop us. I've bought us some time."

"Captain?"

"Yes."

"Wes's shoulders dropped. When you say Maia will send a team…"

"Boys, I realize how hard this will be. The men Maia might send could be your comrades."

"You expect us to shoot our brothers!" Victor stepped away from the demo.

"No. Gather around. I expect to use tranquilizers and taser darts…at first. Like I said I bought us some time. At precisely the moment we get out of simulation, a report is going to be filed, and a mock video feed is going to be submitted into Maia. It can take up to three hours for it to realize its validity, and we'll be long gone by then. It is a disturbance video of me bursting into the room where Eli is being held and stealing a key card from one of the doctors. I already have the keycard obtained earlier. That will send units up there while we run like hell to the elevators down bottom. I've got a card for this door.

"After getting down the elevator, we don't have access down there, and my guess is we are going to have to neutralize the guard here." The captain spun the hologram, and the small figure fell. "They are not one of us, they are strictly controlled by MAIA. These men in their suits answer to no one but MAIA and the Readers. They do not have free thinking minds like your own. They have level 3 chips and EEDs and are the next step down from a robot protecting only MAIA. They will kill you. Do not hesitate to fire on them. They are not completely human. They are programmed nightly.

"I have a connection to an open door down there, and we'll have access into the medical suite. If for some reason that door isn't open, Matt, you'll have about two minutes to open that door. Alix is being held here." The captain spun the hologram blueprint and marked the location. "I've been in contact with a nurse in this station. We will not be fired on once in these doors. Arms down. We'll have cover fire facing the elevators while myself, Wes, and Phil get Alix. Make sure we bring his gear. We'll need it for what's next.

"From here we'll take the elevator to the second to last floor." The hologram followed the men in the elevator up. "Honestly, we'll probably be taking fire the moment that door opens. So we are going to let Bravo out and take the stairs to the top floor. We'll have two breaking points. Here, and here where the elevator opens. We need Bravo standing by for covering fire and take out the snipers and machine gunners in the towers. We should have four Humvees waiting here for us full of equipment. Our exit strategy depends on your covering capability, but odds are we are going to exit here via Humvee, and take the main road, assuming it's in one piece to the barge. There's a 75 percent chance of having this older ferry boat waiting for us. Sorry, my intel is a little old, but if it isn't there, we're taking inflatable rafts. By then, the good news is, we'll be under the cover of night at least against any fire from the mainland. Citizens won't know we're coming, and if all according to plan, Maia won't know we're going until we're gone."

Silence filled the room.

"You're fucking joking, right?" Victor shook his head. "You're ordering us to launch a massive rescue mission, evacuation, sabotage, and treason against our very own military, the strongest known to the modern world, *and* launch a massive attack on the mainland—the most statistically failing approach since I don't know, Normandy against possibly half a million citizens from a raft?"

"No."

"What do you mean *no*? That's what you just described!"

"There should be at least another four of us from Squad 41."

"What's the percentage we're getting out?"

Captain's heart fell. "Do you think I ran this percentage through Maia?"

"You had the balls to make this simulation didn't you? We are supposed to decide our fate without knowing at least a percentage of our possibility of success?" Victor held out his arms.

Anxiety filled each member. Everyone eyed Victor. Talk about balls. No one stood up to anyone in MAIA. Their minds still swirled around a mission without Maia's approval or rating, percentage of survival, success rating, casualty rating.

Victor grimaced.

"Yes." The captain's face didn't flinch. "I'm giving you the choice, Victor, if you don't…"

Victor held up his hand. He thought of all the possibility, the shock of a different life from MAIA. His lips moved, and he didn't believe the words himself. "I'm not doing this simulation. I'm out. Fuck this." Victor reached down for his pistol cocked it back and put the barrel under his jaw.

"Victor, don't!"

Victor pulled the trigger. His blood splattered the ceiling.

"Fuck!" Matt wiped the sludge off and gagged a little.

The captain's eyes begged. "Free thinking men team. Don't worry about Victor. It just simulation this time."

Wes looked over at Victor's dead body. "Let's do this boys. For Alix. And for Eli."

The captain smiled.

* * *

The darkness of the room gave way to the blue and red of the hologram screens. Each Reader's eyes wiggled at the screens entering data, coding in their thoughts, searching through evidence. What evidence did MAIA have that Alix should be subjected to the Vanishing Sequence? Finally the video came up of Alix's unconscious screaming.

Each Reader stared at the video listening to him scream Eli's name. His chest flared up, his body convulsing, kicking, and screaming. He kept screaming his name.

Rankin clenched his jaw. "Gentlemen, isn't this in itself enough to convict Alix to vanishing sequence?"

Elmer Washington sighed. He wiped the sweat from his head. "I suppose this is our biggest piece of evidence. Let's submit it and see if the system will give us a percentage. Agreed?"

Silent nods surrounded the table. One by one they hit Submit.

14

Susan rubbed her eyes. She dug her numb fingers into the back of her neck. The world had changed yet again. Adjustment impossible, adapting a must, but this time, it was all or nothing. Getting caught meant death. Or at least death in the sense that she could understand. Taking away sanity is death, isn't it? What is left of you if your mind is gone? If your body is alive, fleshy and still functioning, but the brain doesn't have your memories, your past feelings, sensory reliving, are you alive? What is alive? What does dead mean? Only questions answered by Maia because even God is scratching his head at this point. What are we doing? Technology running our lives?

Susan watched Anna close the door gently, her back toward Susan quietly enough to muffle the click of the doorknob the way a mother would with a sleeping child.

"So why so secretive?"

"I'm not." Anna's eyes swished to the side.

Susan sat down at her computer. A message in the bottom right-hand corner from Anonymous: "Your accidental insubordination is going to be needed within the hour. Act fast to save a young man."

* * *

Maia stopped computing, stopped thinking. She came up with the decision. All the math added up. All the pieces fit. Maia worked backward. She had her goal and way of achieving it. What variables did Alix have on MAIA? His skill weighed. His ability measured. The timing of MAIA conservation, his impact, his accuracy...replaceable? His positive or negative? His relationship with Anna...beneficial to the success of the MAIA? Maia watched the young couple along with hundreds of other young cadets and workers of MAIA, waiting until it would hinder the MAIA's goals to interact. What about Anna's relation to Rankin and their potential effect on the MAIA?

On the contrary to Rankin believing he was outsmarting Maia, Maia knew of his every move, and if she didn't think his actions and aggressiveness would become a drive to get MAIA where it wanted to go, she would have stopped Rankin a long time ago. Instead Maia calculated the times she diverted Rankin away from Alix because she knew the potential of Alix having the chip he does outweighed the benefit of his level 2 controllable mind. She saw the damage in Alix remembering Eli after a vanishing sequence had been done, however. How could a cadet live in a different world as his fellow soldiers? Maia stopped. She weighed out the options, and with all the data, all the different combination of possible events, it made most statistical sense to MAIA if Alix became subject to the vanishing sequence. She prepared her answer for the Readers.

ALERT!

The room flashed red.

ALERT!

Everyone's head swiveled.

"What the..."

"What is all this!?" Elmer slammed his fist.

What's going on!"

"Alert!"

Before their eyes a video feed of Eli, his limp body in the surgical chair on their screens. A robotic arm stretched from the ceiling and pressed a new chip to the back of Eli's head through a hole in the headrest. A few drops of blood trickled down to the floor. The arm retracted, and blue light filled the room.

Captain Milligan approached Dr. Harrison, his face stern and frantic, his posture hunched and tired. Harris stepped in front of the captain, a monkey in front of an ape. Their lips moved, but sound didn't transmit.

Rankin squinted. "Computer, what's this all about!" he stood. "Continue vanishing sequence sentencing goddammit! What is the answer to Alix!?"

The video feed didn't divert. Dr. Harrison shook his head to Milligan's red stricken face. Milligan thrashed an elbow across the face of Harrison, forced his knee to his stomach and ripped a key-card from his belt all while twirling Harrison and forcing him to the ground – second nature tactics. Harrison coward in the corner and Milligan entered the room and stood before Eli.

The Readers watched helplessly. Captain looked up at the screen, the monitor and his knuckles flashed toward a dark screen where the footage stopped.

"Computer deploy strike force to contain Captain Milligan in the chip processing center! Assist the doctor and apprehend Milligan! Now!"

Maia froze. It thought, found Captain's real location in the simulator, with his team. The footage was authentic, seemingly real. Where did it come from? The readers said send them to Eli's room. Weighed the odds and the strategy. "Strike force sent."

* * *

The captain glanced at the monitor. By now the fake video feed had to be presented to Maia and shown to the Readers. That would buy him time to get the weapons loaded and everything in place. He even hoped it would delay the reading taking place to determine Alix's fate. One could hope.

He glanced at the monitor. Did it squint? The captain gave it a second glance. He turned. Down the hall in a full sprint, he headed to the weapons dock. He pressed his thumb to the scanner. The door cracked, and a cool air released into the corridor. He stepped into the dark room. The first long light snapped on and others following one after another. The lights extended down to the opposite side of a massive storage facility. The captain walked by the Humvees on top of Humvees in car racks, tanks of every size mirrored each other perfectly aligned, surface-to-air missile silos, stacks and stacks of expandable defense lines, riot shields stacked to the ceiling, gun racks just as high, ammunition bins the size of rooms, grenades piled in glass containers like gumballs for twenty-five cents, bins and bins of night vision goggles, magazines, everything needed for war.

He approached a bin as tall as he. A green light on top blinked. A note stuck to the side. "Here's to freedom. See you up top." Captain smiled. *Jack, you never let me down.*

The captain pushed the chest on wheels toward the door. He pushed his thumb against the scanner.

Whamp! The red light above the door flashed. *Whamp!* The door opened. Captain stepped into the corridor. People flooded into the hallways. The captain pushed his cart toward the simulator.

"Captain Milligan!"

He froze. The wheels on the cart turned sideways.

"You hear about the disturbance? Maia sent drones to the chip-processing center!"

Captain's face flushed. "No, I didn't hear. What for?"

Captain's equal in rank checked the weapons bin. "Where's that going?"

"Testing."

The larger man checked his EED for the answer for the disturbance.

"Chuck, I'm sorry." Captain looked both ways.

"For what?"

The captain shot his elbow to the side of Chuck's head. In the same motion he wrapped him up and pushed on a pressure point. Chuck's eyes rolled into the back of his head. The captain shoved the cart and ran down the hall as a woman holding linen dropped everything she had, screamed, and ran.

15

Six suited men hunched over, walked heel to toe, their backs against the wall, silent, their movement efficient, perfect, quiet, their dress shoes soundless. Their handguns up, they arrived at the chip-processing center and searched for the captain. Maia informed them about the unarmed Captain Milligan, but as long as he had nubs to swing, he was armed and considered extremely dangerous.

The leader looked back, a tattoo of a thirty-two on his neck. The others nodded, simultaneously revealing the different numbers on their necks and checked the man behind them. Thirty-two thought for forty-eight to take the other three across the double door and wait for entry. Forty-eight complied. No words exchanged. Thirty-two nodded. Forty-eight nodded. Shared thoughts between level 3 chips and Maia.

The lights kicked out. Maia complied to the thoughts of thirty-two. Their shades turned the corridor green in the dark. Thirty-two and forty-eight kicked in the doors, their guns darting and covering 180 of the room. The others followed covering all points of a clock, nine through three o'clock facing the room, a blooming flower of weapons at the entrance of the facility.

Desks lined the room perfectly. The doors remained sealed. The room stayed quiet after the echo of the slam simmered. No Dr. Harrison. No Milligan. The boy in the center of the chip processing center remained still.

A moan came from the corner. Six guns aimed at Dr. Harrison, sprawled out on the floor to the left of the room. He rubbed his neck. "He got away with my keycard." He stretched. "You're too late. He said he was going to kill the Readers. He has access to the room the Readers are in!"

The suits turned to each other and ran down the hallway thinking to all units there's been a mistake. Find Captain Milligan. He's on his way to the room where the Readers sat helplessly.

"Don't worry, I'll be fine." Dr. Harrison pushed himself up and brushed himself off. "No consideration for the older generation."

The lights flickered on, and Dr. Harrison did what he hadn't done since he was a child. Prayed. He prayed for the safety of Captain Milligan and his team. He prayed for their success and their chance for freedom, fighting once again for what he believed in. He envied him the captain for his courage, and even Dr. Harrison felt braver for simulating an attack and submitting it to Maia as a false feed to divert the suits toward this end of the facility. Hopefully, sending them to the other end where the Readers were would give Rob long enough to get Alix out. Good luck, Alix.

* * *

Sweat dripped down Wes's face inside the egged-shaped chair. That had to be the most confusing simulation ever in his life, the practice of breaking Alix out, one scrimmage before the game. They would wake and get right into actually breaking Alix out.

The bumpy digital ride paid off, and the ferry needed a little fuel but started right up. They drove their trucks right up onto the ferry and headed out the murky water. Wes still couldn't believe he actually shot at his own brothers at MAIA. Even in simulation… Three. Yeah, that was the number. There were three lives that Wes grew up with, schooled with, learned with, and now potentially, Wes had taken them away, his gunfire being the last thing they heard. He hoped Maia could nurse them back to health. With the nurses not too far, it's not impossible. The odds of surviving bullet wounds were in their favor at this point according to MAIA.

Fog and darkness hid the mainland and the ferry advanced into the mist. Wes hoped weather conditions were real in this simulation as to what they would be facing once they got out. Wes looked to Alix. Simulation Alix studied the dark island outline through his yellow mask, looking back at MAIA, back at home.

"Alix, thought you were gone back there and all this was just a waste of time." Wes's body drifted backward toward the mainland.

Alix tore his eyes away from the dark skyline. "It's just a flesh wound."

"You still shoot with that arm?"

"Better than before." Alix stretched it out.

Wes smiled. Even the simulated Alix was cocky. Wes studied the ones who made it through simulation. After breaking through the doors, the four towers, one at each corner of the landing pad on the top of the MAIA, sprayed bullets as fire from a dragon's mouth. Snipers manned each post. They somehow could pull it off. Wes nudged Phil, holding his machine gun over his shoulder and watching the smoldering stacks of smoke sink to the top of the sky.

Phil smiled. "I'm hoping that the two of Jack's men that didn't make it aren't really coming with us. I had to shoot over that bastards shoulder…"

Matt's head snapped to the side. Blood ran down his cheek, his eyes widened, and his body rag-dolled to the ground.

Wes ducked. "Sniper! Get down!"

The missile came from outer space. It tore ass through the sky and screeched like a hawk right before snagging its meal from the water. The explosion must have come because simulation statistically figured it so. Maia would have surface-to-air missiles that could be used to ultimately sink the ferry.

Water became the first explosion followed by a rain of fire and smoke. The ground that was the ferry deck became a seesaw launching the whole team sky high in a ball of dissolution and disorientation. The rest along with the Humvees were sucked down in the water after fire waved through their location on the ferry. Sound disappeared, traveling too fast to hear at the point of the explosion, or they were now deaf, seemingly weightless in a floating sea of smoke until the splash into the Hudson River from who knows how high, a slap from our creator, like all the atoms came together to form a palm and five fingers and slung it across Wes's body. Cold. A blizzard in a snow globe Alix and the captain shook and stuck Wes in. Then the cold water enveloping them and saturating their equipment. Their guns, ammo, grenades, packs, gear, pulled them deeper into the water until their masks started to fill. Water trickled above his view. He took his last breath; even in simulation, drowning sucked.

He lifted his shield from the simulation helmet, and the computer-generated world of drowning disappeared. Wes felt relieved to see the small egg-shaped room. He felt a pit in his stomach. Statistically, they don't make it out according to the simulation. He closed his eyes and shook his head.

The captain actually stood before them next to an ammo cart. "Got the gear. Let's do this. For real this time"

"Captain…" Victor lifted his shield from his helmet. "Count me in. I can't see what just happened actually happen to my team."

Captain looked at Wes. "What actually happened?"

Wes shook his head. "We drowned."

They all looked at the weapons bin.

Phil stood. "Well, the quicker we get to drowning, the faster I can get to sleep. Let's go, boys."

Everyone geared up. *Click, click, snap, snap, chick-ching.*

* * *

"Thirty-two, what is the status!" Rankin threw his fist through the hologram screen, the beams flickered.

"Infiltrated the holding room, sir. No sign of Captain Milligan." The words appeared on the screen.

The Readers shifted in their chairs, turned to each other looking for an answer, holding their arms up clueless.

Washington slammed his fist. "Maia, what the hell is going on here!"

"Captain Milligan is on the loose. Tactical team out to locate and destroy Captain Milligan. It is said that he is on his way to the Reader's Room."

"I know what is going on! Just fix it!" Washington slammed the table again. "Never in my life."

Rankin's throat tightened. Rankin thought of all the reasons why the captain would want to put a revolver to his head. He gulped.

* * *

Their hearts raced as they geared up. The real thing for the first real time, but nothing what they thought it would be—it was so…real. Wes felt the weight of his actual equipment. His assault rifle was a forbidden tool within these walls. Everything he believed in crumbled when he opened his eyes from the simulator. Everything drilled in his head, filled in, now unwound, shriveled, and placed with a mode of thinking that was logically incalculable. What if the captain was wrong? What if it isn't how it appears? Wes looked to the monitor across the room and squeezed his gun.

"I told you, boys, you would be the first on the island. Let's move out! Alix, where coming." The captain led the black stream of soldiers out the simulator. Full equipment weighed them down where they've always been through these halls in just white shirts and pants, shaved heads. In a double line, side by side in a single stride they jogged down the corridor.

Sweat dibbled down Phil's back. What is going to happen? Is this right? Going against everything he was ever told? A white coat heard the thunder and poked his body out the door. Matt's shoulder clipped the programmer, and he ping-ponged from each side of the doorframe to the floor. A group of young shave-headed cadets turned the corner and retracted back into the hall, their faces twisted. The black train whooshed by. Phil thought about the first MAIA soldier he shot in simulation minutes ago. He hoped the moment wouldn't come and wondered if he could really shoot what he wasn't sure was the enemy. Would he pull the trigger?

"Let's do this, boys!" Matt screamed.

Victor tightened his finger on the trigger.

* * *

"Captain Jack Silva, what brings you out on this fine evening? Coming to get some fresh air?" The soldier breathed deep through his mask and pointed outside the large garage doors. "Ah, evening air." He laughed and led three soldiers over in slow wide strides like cowboys entering a saloon, leaning on their assault rifles.

Jack eyed the young cadets. More training than they knew what to do with these guys near the surface, like trying to stuff a whole powder keg into a cannon and never lighting it. This generation, four to six years older than his guys, are ready for battle, have been ready for battle, and have been waiting and waiting and waiting. Three of his own guys lay hunkered in the front Humvee, still and quiet, ready to pounce.

Jack tightened a strap over the back of one of the four Humvees. "Just a training exercise for my guys with the real trucks. Simulation just can't substitute the real thing. Surely, you understand that, Lieutenant. Any kills today, guys? I have to assume the view over the Hudson was good enough for a few quick pickings." He jerked on the strap and locked it up.

"Not really, one of the snipers got a couple birds earlier, but no kills today. They are either very shy today, or we can't spot them. The fog is thicker than normal. Hopefully when we see the sun, it'll burn some of this up. It's getting harder to find targets. None of us can catch Gunther Vasily and his brother."

"No? Why how many kills does Vasily have?"

"Ah." The soldier adjusted his shoulder strap. His rifle hung loose. "He's got like 225. He even has a two in one. No one is even close to him. The closest guy has like 102, I think. And we aren't even sure if that's correct because he counts the building collapsing on a group as deaths. We all know that's a gray area. You don't get total credit for your stray missile taking out a small building and falling on a group of citis, I don't think. Right, Todd?"

"I couldn't agree more with you." Todd peered in the back window on the opposite side and looked back to Chris.

Jake smiled. "I heard Alix Basil is going to give him a run for his money in the sniper department though."

Chris sniffed and wiped his nose. "Yeah, I heard about that little spout. He'll have to do some serious work to catch up to Vasily. Jack, I need to ask...This is a lot of gear for an exercise, do you mind if I just check your EED for credentials? Orders, you know what I mean? I wasn't told about any authorized release of any equipment. How about you, Todd?"

"Nope." Todd eyed the driver's seat in the back Humvee popping the *p* sound. "None."

"Come on, fellas, let's not get all hyped up because you've been bored all day..."

Billy, standing behind Chris and next to Austin, tightened his grip on his rifle. His back stiffened. "Jack, you know protocol. Stop wasting our time, unless it's a big deal."

"Okay, okay, boys. Relax. They should send out some target practice for you boys though, shit." Jack pulled back his sleeve, and the soldier approached to scan his EED. "Got you boys wound up so tight your eyes are turning red."

The soldier leaned in. Jack wrapped him up, clicked the mag from his rifle, wrapped the strap round this body to tie him up, and aim his pistol at the other two. "Hands in the air! Hands in the air now!"

Todd jolted into action, raised his rifle and found himself convulsing on the ground, an electronic pin stuck in the back of his neck. Jack's men emptied the front Humvee in a breath each direction, one popped out the shooting nest out the top of the truck. Jack shocked Todd in the back of the neck and pulled a taser and aimed his rifles at Billy and Austin. Their hands were raised to the ceiling of the facility.

"Looks like I'm taking a sabbatical." Jack cursed Rob.

16

Susan stared at the old door. Most doors in this facility slid open. This one latched. All she had to do was leave, and when she came back, she would leave it ajar. That's all. Easy. Her hands trembled. Every decision she's been handed since she arrived at this facility had been planned and pointed to one goal, one reason. This was a first deviation.

She put her hand on the door. Applied pressure. The door cracked. Thunder roared down the hall like a bullet from a chamber. The train of barreling soldiers smashed through the door. Susan's back slammed against the wall, and she slid to her butt. She held her knees and ears and screamed.

"Clear!" They moved like a frantic snake throughout the office, it's head parting off into two and securing all angles.

"Clear!"

"This corner clear!"

"Backroom clear!"

Anna's scream disappeared into Alix's room behind a slammed door.

"Perp in nest with eagle! Bravo ready to infiltrate."

A hand came in front of Susan's face. She looked up and saw the orange glowing of a burly beard. "Miss, I apologize for my boy's abrupt rudeness and disregard for manners. You must be Susan."

Sue held her nose and looked at the blood in her palm. "Yeah, I'm Susan! What the fuck!"

"Alix!" Anna bellowed into the room.

"What the fuck is going on out there!" Alix pulled at his restraints.

She flicked on the lights.

"Ah!" Alix squinted from the light.

She turned the latch and looked for the closest chair, dragged it over, and jammed the it under the door. "I'm not letting them take you!"

"Anna, let me out of here!" Alix kicked his legs, his gown coming loose.

Anna rushed to him as the door began to be jiggled and slammed from the other side, a dark shadow doing the ramming. A crack in the window forced Anna's hands to fumble the arm restraints.

"Anna!"

Yellow eyes appeared in the window.

"Come on, Anna! Okay good, get my feet, I'll get this one." Alix reached over.

A larger darker figure appeared in the silhouette of the door. A larger knock came as Alix's other wrist came free along with one of his legs. "Anna, after you do that leg, run to the bathroom and don't open it no matter what."

"I'm not leaving you!"

"Anna!"

Alix's leg came free. He twirled out of the hospital bed, his gown hanging half off, his bare butt appearing in the light. Alix shook it off and looked for the nearest weapon. Needles. "Anna! In the bathroom! Now!"

The door broke open. A blooming flower of flashlights at the end of semiautomatic weapons. Alix whipped two syringes at the first enemy and charged the group. The bathroom door shut. The needles pinned into the big lug through the door first. Close quarters held a better chance from having multiple guns pointed at him. Alix grabbed the second soldier's gun from the tip and pointed it to the ceiling and elbowed him backwards. He pulled the third over his shoulder by the arm and kicked him in the throat and disarmed him. The gear scraped the bare backside of Alix. The rest of the team backed through the door and surrounded bare-ass Alix wielding a gun.

"Hands up!"

Alix dropped the gun. "Alright. Alright." He raised his hands slowly behind his head. He eyed the semi-automatic weapon at his feet.

"Alix!" Captain walked into the room, his revolver swinging from his hip.

Alix's head snapped over at captain. He face twisted in fright.

"Put some damn clothes on and stop dicking around with that little thing. There's a lady present."

Sue peered around the corner. Her eyebrows raised, and her lips tightened together.

Snickers filled the room. Wes lifted his helmet from the ground in the medical room. "Fucking A, Alix. Ugh. I don't know what's worst, you kicking me in the throat or the view from down here. Phil, you okay?"

Phil pulled the syringe from his tactical vest and the other out of his shoulder. "Were these used! Alix, I'll fucking kill you!"

Alix's blood rushed to his head. "Guys? What the fuck!"

"Alix, shut up and get dressed." The captain dropped a duffle bag of clothes at his feet. "We're leaving. Sue, I'm sorry you had to see naked Rambo running around with his little pistol."

"It's not that little, Captain. It's okay."

"I'm sure it is, kid's ripped like an Abercrombie model. Wes, brief Alix while he's gearing up. Sue, you have any water?"

"Sure. I haven't heard the word 'Abercrombie' in years."

"What's Abercrombie?" Hayden asked, Adam pointing their guns back through the door they came through.

"Movement in the restroom!" Phil lifted his rifle. "Come out with your hands up, or I'm blowing them off!"

"Phil, no!" Alix ran into the room in his boxers.

"Alix!" Anna appeared in the doorway.

"Alix, who's this!" Phil and Wes pointed their guns.

"Guys, cut the shit!" Alix ran to her and wrapped her in his arms. "Anna, you okay?" He brushed the side of her face and kissed her mouth.

Phil's jaw dropped.

She melted in his arms and the feeling of his bare skin. "What is going on, Alix?"

"I don't know."

Sue wiped an erupting tear from her eye. The worry in Anna's face, enough to make a tomboy put a dress on. They way they cared for each other…they way they looked at each other, through one another…deeply into one another. That is what humans should be fighting for.

"Awe, what the fuck is this noise?" Captain appeared in the doorway at the two tangled in a hug, his arms out, eyes wide, mouth hung open, and shaking his head. "Juliet fall off the balcony or something? Let's go!"

Alix stood at attention. Eyes straight. "We've been seeing each other Captain Milligan, sir!"

Anna stood next to Alix, eyes probed.

"The fuck you've been seeing each other? I know what you've been doing. Now get dressed!"

Alix grabbed her hand. "It's going to be fine." He stared into her honey eyes.

"Alix, I'm coming with you." Anna's eyes promised.

The captain smacked Alix in the back of the head on his way by. "The fuck you thinking seeing anyone?" The captain looked back at Anna. "You're fucking staying here, little lady." Captain shoved Alix in the back toward his bag. "You know that isn't permitted. And how do you know it's going to be fine!" Captain checked his EED and followed Alix to the pile of gear. "You didn't seem too fine before we got here all shackled to the bed in some sorry sexcapade! We are not fine, we are anything but fine! We are not fine until I tell you, you are fine!" Captain poked at the air. "And we are not fine until I plop my ass down on a beach with a beer, and we far from that, my friend." He turned from Alix. "We got two minutes, ladies."

"Here's the water you wanted, sir" Sue handed him a glass.

Alix pulled his pants up and shook his shirt over his head pulling each sleeve tight. He strapped on his vest and his holsters. Put his boots on. "Am I fully loaded?"

"Here." Matt handed Alix his rifle and submachine gun. "Fucking thing weighs a ton."

"You can kill someone from miles away, you think it's going to be light?"

Wes dropped the hologram map on the floor and gave Alix a summary.

* * *

"Maia! Update! What is going on?"

Maia scanned all monitors. The ultimate goal somehow deviated. The computer clicked, and the Readers held their breath. Maia knew what was going on and didn't weigh in until now. She wanted to see how it played out. But it has gone too far. A message appeared on the screen: "Issuing reprimand of vanishing sequence to the following MAIA individuals—"

Rankin smiled while Washington screamed, "Tell me where Captain Milligan is, and if he's been apprehended yet!"

Maia stopped midsentence and spoke, and her words came up on the hologram screens, "Captain Milligan is currently on Level U40."

Rankin's stomach twisted. U40? Sue? Anna? Alix?

Maia continued, "He and his squad have infiltrated the level with keycard obtained from Programmer Doctor Harrison. They rushed the door as Susan Maynard was about to exit. I am sending all personnel to U40 to apprehend Captain Milligan. Issuing the vanishing sequence and reprogramming of chips for Eli Williams, Alix Basil, Phillip Heins, Adam Adkins, Reader Elmer Washington."

"Maia!" Elmer slammed his hand on the desk. "What is this madness?"

Rankin's eyebrows furrowed. This wasn't supposed to happen. All the readers at the table turned to Elmer. What did he do to deserve the vanishing sequence?

"Wes Wilder, Victor Season, Anna Brooks—"

"Maia!" Rankin's body exploded. "No! You will not apply vanishing sequence to Anna Brooks!"

Maia's voice continued. "Hayden Alber, Matthew Stine, Captain Jack Silva, and three of his men Aaron Graves, Leo Sharp, Brian Rios."

"Shut her down!" Rankin stood on his T-port. "Maia's lost her mind. I'm shutting her down. Override sequence."

"Captain Robert Milligan, Susan Maynard, Reader Albert Rankin—"

"Maia!" Rankin stood and hopped onto his T-port. "I'm shutting her down!"

"Albert you can't! We need her to apprehend Milligan first!"

"I'm overriding her decision then! We don't need to vanish all of us! Maia lost her mind! There must be a bug in the system!"

Rankin's T-port failed, and he flipped forward.

Elmer moved close to the table to give Rankin more space to fall.

"Maia!" Rankin stood halfway to the door and shuffled toward a shut-off switch. "Where is your strike team now?"

"Strike force is preparing for infiltration of U40. Odds of success are only five percent without backup. Captain Milligan and his team are adequately equipped for a firefight of nearly one hundred enemies. Strike force standby. Recruiting backup from Squad 57 and 82. ETA six minutes."

* * *

"Ladies and gentlemen!" Captain stood before his men. "Welcome to the show. Bravo, take the stairs. Delta, lets' get in the elevator."

Alix looked back at Anna and Sue behind the desk. "Captain." Alix swallowed hard. "I'm not going."

The captain's expression dropped to the floor, kicked him in his own nuts, and twisted his nipples. "What the fuck do you mean you are not coming? If I have to hogtie you and throw you on Phil's back, you are coming." The captain approached Alix.

"Why my back?" Phil whispered to Adam.

Alix cringed and waited for the punch in the mouth. He held his chin out. "I'm not going without Anna."

"I will knock you the fuck out, boy."

"We'll need her if any of us gets wounded."

Captain raised his fist. "You're about to be wounded."

Anna's lips quivered. "I'm one of the best, Sue will vouch for me. I wanna go."

Sue clutched Anna.

Captain stopped. "You want to bring your little girlfriend out into war on the front line with a dozen other men? Are you nuts?"

"I can shoot too." Anna stood. "I've been through all the same simulations as you guys."

Captain pointed to Anna. "Ha! I've gathered that apparently, sneaking in with Alix. More like taking shots in the mouth, you little hussy. I'd like to see you wield a weapon." He looked at Alix. "We don't have time for this. Alix, let's go. Team, move. Hogtie this idiot if he doesn't cooperate."

The room emptied like an hourglass. Victor and Hayden grabbed Alix by the shoulders. "Come on."

"Fuck you, guys! Let me go!" Alix squirmed.

Wes grabbed Alix's feet. "Alix, shut up. Let's go."

"Hey!" Anna stormed after the captain, pushed Matt out of the way by his shoulder pad. "This is bullshit!" Her blood boiled, her steps stomped.

"Phil, take care of the girl." The captain didn't even look back; he headed to the elevators halfway down the hall.

Phil turned to Anna, let his machine gun hang loose around the straps. "Okay. Let's go. Enough of this."

"Phil!" Alix stared at him and attempted to twist from Wes's grip.

Anna stiff-armed Phil, unlatched his sidearm, and withdrew it from his holster all in one swift movement like a pickpocket. "Don't touch me!" Her back to Captain down further down the hall and facing Phil, she slipped the pistol in the back of her pants and pulled her shirt over it.

Alix kicked at Wes. "Captain!"

"Enough!" Captain turned to come face to face to a stare he'd seen in only a few women's eyes. Like a lion, her hunger to protect her pride and cubs was unmatched by any level of testosterone in the room. His gaze met hers head-on. "You are not in the plan. You're staying here. That's final."

Behind the captain, at the other end of the hall, the door cracked open.

"I'm going wherever Alix is going—look out!" Anna shoved Captain sideways. He tripped and fell to the left into an indentation. The door at the end of the hall burst open. She pulled her pistol she'd stolen from Phil, dropped to a knee, and fired at the black-suited men. Three bullets, three hits, and a suited man dropped. The door burst open. A smoke grenade exploded.

Phil reached for his pistol and found an empty holster. "Bitch!"

Anna dropped to the ground and slid to a crevice in the hall across from the captain. She continued firing. The captain squirmed to the side and lay hunkered. He pulled his revolver. He stared at it. He's never fired it outside of simulation. He looked over to Anna who blind fired three shots and peered around the corner and aimed for three more. Bullets screamed by his vision of her each direction. He thought about the suit dropping to the ground, the real blood spatter, the real sounds of guns. How it's been so long? How it could have been him?

"Mag!" Anna screamed back down the hall. A loaded magazine slid to her ankle. The captain watched in amazement at her swift ability to replace the mag in one movement. Where did she even get the gun? She returned fire and retracted in. Machine gun fire exchanged from one end of the hall to the other in sputters.

The team fanned out and dropped Alix hard. Alix shuffled back and hunkered behind a barrel and prepared his secondary weapon.

Wes screamed over the clamoring gunfire. "Captain! Elevator is no longer a viable option, heat sensors detect nearly twenty and growing. We got to move!"

"Agreed." Wes's voice rang in their helmets. "Southwest staircase is back and to our right. Alix, lay down some serious covering fire and evacuate."

Alix held the aim of the door and sputtered rounds at it anytime anything moved. They had to know Squad 28 had thermal, and that pointless smoke became just a neat trick for the bodies to pour out of. "Covering fire!"

Wes, Matt, and Victor scampered behind Alix and stacked on the reverse wall out of harms way at the base of the stairs. "Captain, let's go! Victor, prepare a flashbang."

The captain looked over to Anna.

"Go!" She shot twice and nodded her head towards the back of the hallway and aimed farther down and fired more.

The captain's feet skidded and pushed himself forward into the hallway. Alix knelt, hunkered to the captain's left, and fired at whichever enemy aimed at the captain's back. "Phil, you're up!"

Phil held down his trigger and outlined the doorframe in holes the size of baseballs. Alix kept his rifle pinned into his shoulder and his sights on the middle of the disheveled door, his world an infrared universe. Alix watched another ill attempt by a glowing suited figure to charge the hallway until he was pelted, liquid balls of fire shooting from his body as he toppled over onto his fellow comrades. Alix hunkered and hugged the wall to the right as he moved in toward the pile of bodies. Phil held the trigger. Alix slid into the crevice next to Anna on his knee pads.

"I only got three left."

Alix kept his gun and attention on the door. "Side pouch. Let's move."

Anna snagged a mag and shoved it into her bra. "Let go, babe." She kissed the back of his helmet. "Just like we practiced oh so many times before."

Alix walked backward, knees bent as a shield for Anna. "After this"—Alix held his fire—"we are going to do everything we've been practicing in simulation!"

"Twenty left!" Phil screamed. "Hayden, you're up!"

Hayden crouched to the right of Phil, whose stammering death machine quit spitting, whined down, and the tip glowed red. Hayden held this trigger in several three-round bursts.

"Flashbang!" Victor tossed the grenade around the corner and toward the door. "Three, two, one."

Everyone looked away. Hayden clung on to Alix as he came by and Phil turned from the grenade in one swift motion, they all moved as one around the corner.

BOOM! The explosion sucked the air out of the room, and particles and debris skidded down the hallway after them.

"Up the stairs, let's go, let's go!" The captain led the way and grabbed both sides of the railing and jerked himself up each stair.

Anna clung to Alix's belt.

"Anna!" She turned. Sue whipped a backpack at her. "You'll thank me later, sweetie."

Anna snagged the bag, threw both arms through the straps, and the hallway door closed.

Sweetie?

17

"We'll go up three levels, and all take the elevator from there." The captains breaths dragged him down. He leaned on the railing. He felt his stomach rising into his throat. His voice echoed down below to the blooming of flashlights spiraling up toward them seven levels below. His quads were an inferno; his feet, cinder blocks. "Let's take the stairs. Fucking…brilliant."

"Captain, let's go! You going to throw up at 'em" Wes hit his shoulder on the way by raising his legs quickly. "We can't lean now."

"I hate you right now." The captain's sweaty forearms slipped off the railing. He pulled himself up more stairs.

"There is an elevator on Level U30 that will take us to the top." Matt looked down to the flashlights and echoes following them. "Dropping smoke."

"Confirmed. Good idea, Matt." Wes looked for the signs running from the echoes below chasing them up. U32. U31. He heard the smoke grenade canister hit the floor on the stairwell and bellow out smoke through a hissing sound. It would slow them down for a moment as they expected an ambush. "U30. Let's move. Matt, your intel better be good. Team, stack up."

Hayden stood to the left of the door. Phil stacked up behind him. Alix stood to the back, Anna held one hand on the back of his belt, the other on the gun, her backpack slung over her shoulder.

Matt faced the door directly. "Your girlfriend better know how to watch our six!"

Captain slugged up the last step and leaned on his knees. "Ready for...impact... boys. Go silent." He coughed and spat on the ground. "Shit." He his esophagus heated up.

The whole team screwed on the silencer on the end of their submachine guns, the sound like small mice. The hissing of the smoke bomb seized below, and the echoes from their boots below rang up the staircase shaft.

"Move." Matt booted the door. The team filtered through covering every angle.

"Clear."

"Clear."

"Right side, west hall!" Hayden approached heel to toe two MAIA operatives wearing scrubs. Their hands jolted to the air. "Hands up where I can see them! Down to the floor slowly!" He directed his gun downward.

"Okay, don't shoot. Please." The man's body was like a trembled tower of dishes.

"Got your back, Hayden." Alix spun right through the door and hunched over. "Stay to the left. Give me a shooting lane. Coming to you. Anna, cover me."

"Roger that." Anna pounded the elevator call button and aimed her gun down the hall.

Captain entered the hall. "Matt, install door stop."

"Down! Now!" Hayden kept one hand on the gun, his shoulder strap supporting its aim forward while his other arm reached for zip ties. Hayden wrapped their hands behind their back.

The rest of the team settled in, crouched into bump-outs and behind a barrel and to the vase of a fake plant. Alix remained two meters behind Hayden wielding his smaller weapon, his five-foot retractable sniper rifle across his back. He may need it up top.

"Tango!" Alix spotted him ducked behind a barrel thirty meters ahead and dash for the double swinging doors farther down the hall. Alix squeezed the trigger twice. Even the pitter patter of the silenced bullets and the puff of cold air forced the woman to scream while

Hayden's knee dug into her back and ripped her hands backward. The retreating man tripped when the bullets tore through his calves, and he slid in his own blood. His head slammed the swinging doors, and they returned and bumped him in the head again. His screams seemed distant, but he would live and not be able to go for help.

Matt withdrew his drill and zipped a hole in the wall. Adam pulled a hook from his pocket and handed it to Matt. Matt tugged at the tip of the drill, shifted the head, and attached the hook to it. He screwed the hook into the wall same height as the door handle that swung into the hallway. Adam had already latched the wire to the door handle, and by the time the bottom of the hook came in contact with the wall, Adam attached the steel wire end to the proper side and tugged on the door to check its strength. It would hold them back for a bit if they even knew what floor they got off on.

The elevator dinged, and the doors slid open. Two programmers dropped their hologram tablets and froze at the amount of guns pointed at them when the door opened.

"Get out!"

"Team, let's move."

Matt looked at the max capacity: "8 Persons."

"Phil, looks like you're staying. Load up."

* * *

"Maia, get a squad on every floor! What are they trying to accomplish?" Elmer looked at Rankin, still expecting Maia to help after being master reset. "What is Captain Milligan's motive?"

"Maia, contact U40." Rankin wondered. A monitor of U40 popped up, Susan at the desk, head down. Two suited men held massive assault rifles. Susan lifted her head and stared at the phone and picked up.

"Hello?" Her voice was shaky. It was the first time she heard a phone ring in years. "Who's this?"

"Susan, this is Reader Albert Rankin accompanied by the other Readers on the call. We have commenced a reading of Maia and can not leave the facility until a verdict is created. We've heard and seen the disturbance and want to know if everything is okay."

"Ah, I haven't heard so much gunfire in nearly fifteen years, and I don't want to look at the end of the hall. I hear it's bad. Two dozen dead maybe."

"We've heard the numbers. Do you know where or why Captain Milligan is doing this? Do you know where he is going with this hit squad he trained?"

"No, Albert, I don't. They took a hostage and just said something about taking a shitload of weapons from the weapons depot, pardon my language, and coming after you specifically."

Rankin swallowed. They never figured an assault from internally. He felt…scared.

"And, Al, they have Anna." Rankin boiled.

"Thank you, Sue." They disconnected.

"Why is she addressing you so unprofessionally? And who's Anna? And why is Captain Milligan coming after you, specifically?"

Rankin ignored the questions completely. His daughter… Anna. Taken. His heart was removed from his body. His reason for breathing and living had a gun to her temple and being led around by a large leprechaun. "We need Maia turned back on."

* * *

Jack leaned on the Humvees near the elevators and bit his fingernails. He looked at the sky, a hazy red, and spit the tip of his thumbnail out. Darkness came quick without an actual sun appearing through the miles of thick cloud, pollution, and remnants from the bombs. Jack checked his EED: "Your squad is to report to the U25 – Apprehend Captain Milligan and Squad 28 on sight. Captain Milligan primary target – 200 ration reward for his death."

Jack smiled. Two hundred rations, be like the richest guy on the island. Like skipping class or playing hooky, it felt good to not respond. He took a deep breath and heard the ding from the elevator. "Boys, get ready." Jack picked up the biggest gun he could hold and pointed it at the door. His three boys, curious about the outside world and beyond the walls of Governor's Island, pointed their weapons too.

The doors opened, a jam packed elevator. The occupants stacked and pointed their guns outward.

"You know my orders are to apprehend you at once." Jack approached the elevator. "Stand down, men. Robby, you're worth two hundred rations to me. Huhahaha. You son of bitch."

Captain smiled at the four running Humvees, stacked and geared up for full assault. He squirmed through his men from the back of the elevator. "Don't talk about my mother like that. I'll smack you in that mouth." The captain approached Jack and held his arm out. "What's the update?"

Their four arms clasped and released, the oldest symbol of trust and being unarmed, here in peace. "Just these guys." Jack pointed to the tied up bunch to the left of the Humvees.

"They won't even wake up until tomorrow wondering what happened. Rios over here got carried away with tranq darts. You guys are packing heavy for just coming from inside."

"Yeah, it got a little out of control in there. Adam and Matt, drive H3 and H4. Hayden, hop in the passenger side of H2. Team, load up. Anna, get a vest and tact gear on. Change around the corner or on top of the truck, I don't care. You think the gates are going to open, or we going to blow a hole?" The captain scratched his head.

Whistles and cat noises came from beneath the masks as Anna headed to the corner.

"Shut up, guys!" Alix stacked his gear in H3.

"Brian, drive H2, you have most of the ammo and supplies. Get to know Hayden. The gates are open, Rob. We shouldn't have any problem until we get to the ferry. I don't know if they are still keeping a squad there. We will be able to see from the road. What do you mean it got a little out of control? And what's with the chick?" Jack pointed back to Anna as she rounded the corner, backpack in hand. Alix followed her, armored vest, black pants and shirt, holsters, and a small submachine gun.

"Alix?" Anna eyed him. "What the fuck is his issue?"

"It's going to take a while to adjust to them, and they are not going to be easy on you because you a girl." Alix peaked around the corner.

"I'm a woman. Can they see me?"

Alix peered again. "No."

Anna pulled down her pants. Black tight booty shorts hugged her hips. "I hope this was the right decision, Alix. Do you think we stand a chance if we had to break off from them? We talked about it in the past." She swayed her hips to pull her black tactical pants up.

"I don't know. Sorry, those are a little big, they belong to Eli. We won't know until we got off to the other side. *If* we get to the other side."

Anna pulled her shirt up over her head cross armed. Anna smiled, grabbed his chin, kissed his lips.

Alix stared at her bra.

"And don't talk like that." She nudged her head through the tight tactical shirt. She strapped on leg holsters and a bulletproof tactical vest.

"Here, take this too." Alix handed her a smaller retractable knife. "Keep this in your sock. Hold it to someone's skin, and it zaps and stabs them at the same time."

"I know how to use a knife, Alix. Let's go."

"What's in the bag?" Alix followed her around the corner.

Anna pulled her hair up into a ponytail. "I don't know yet. Sue packed it for me during that firefight. She was acting really weird before we left. Like she was proud of me or something. Something's going on."

"Yeah, Alix!" Hayden shook his hips and waved his hand around his head like a cowboy. "You took care of that real quick. Whoa-whoo!"

Anna looked to Hayden. "He doesn't need long to hit exactly the right spots. You could learn a thing or two from this man." Anna squeezed Alix's ass.

"Shut up, Hayden. Get in the Humvee. Captain's almost ready I think." Alix shoved him toward his truck by both shoulders, Hayden's smile plastered to his cheeks.

Captain took a deep breath through his nose. "Ah, the smell of a fine evening…Still smells like shit up here, huh?" The two men walked out in front of the Humvees watching the sky turn a darker red, their dim shadows casting long into the bay. The sound of the trucks being loaded, shuffled bags, straps, zippers, slamming doors rattled behind them.

"Not as bad as I remember, the smell I mean. So, Rob, what do you mean, 'It got a little out of control down there? What'd you do in there, and what's with the chick? She's a huge liability. And you feeling all right, you're a little pale?"

The captain put his hands on his hips. "Ah, Jack. It's not like it used to be, except for all the questions. That's still exactly like it used to be. You always were full of questions, fucking question everything. I have one for you, do you think that ferry is really there?"

"If not, the boat will be. Rob, I want some answers." Jack hit Rob on the shoulder.

"No time for details, but we got attacked, so we fired back a little. The girl wanted to come. She kinda saved my ass, so I gave her a gun. I'm pale because I ran up like ten flights of stairs. Let's go. Looks like we are loaded up. You coming, big guy?" The doors to the back three Humvees closed.

"I don't have a choice now." Jack gestured over to the unconscious group.

"Oh, good. This is going to be fun then. Let's go, you're riding with me up front with your guys, right? Introduce me to these young body bags."

Jack shook his head. Just like old times all right.

The captain drummed on the hood of the middle Humvee, "You boys remember how to drive these things? Just like in the video games, okay? Stay with me!" The captain turned to the H1 in front. "I'll drive, Jack, move over." Captain hopped up into the truck, slammed the bulletproof door, and revved the engine. "Ah yeah! They sound so much better on diesel! The smell of diesel in the evening. Nothing like it!" The smile couldn't be ripped from captain.

The Humvees pulled away, the sound of sand beneath the tires as they turned before they moved. They drove toward the open gates.

Jack leaned over, his back to the passenger window. "You better hope the sun picks up in the next week, or we find a fuel depot that hasn't been sucked dry. Boys, this is Captain Robert Milligan, an old friend and crazy asshole I was telling you about. Rob this is Aaron Graves and Leonardo Sharpe. Brian Rios is driving H2."

Captain held the wheel twelve o'clock and leaned back. "Oh yeah, Leonardo Dicaprio! I'm going to call you Dawson. Graves! Right where you don't want to end up there, right? And…Rios you Spaniard, *como sa va*?" The captain looked in the rearview mirror at him. The three soldiers eyed each other. Milligan laughed. "You boys ready to do what you were born to do?"

They nodded emotionless.

Jack's laugh hooted, his excitement taking over his body. "Oh you crazy son of a bitch. What the fuck are we doing, Rob? You ever think this would be the way we leave the island?"

"Nope! Didn't know if I ever would be leaving the island, but here we go!" The captain checked his side mirror as they drove out the gates and around the old bent Kimmel Rd. sign. He rolled down his window and pounded the side of the door. "Whoooah!" The captain stuck his head out the window, his beard waving in the wind. "Yeah, boys! Here we go! Whoo!"

18

Gunther Vasily watched the red sky. "Another fifteen, twenty minutes, and we will be out of light."

"Yeah. It's getting a bit better though." Gunther Vasily's short finger rubbed his scalp.

"Yeah, but these bastards must know not to travel the southern tip of Manhattan anymore or the western coast of Brooklyn during the day. How many days has it been since we've got a kill, Greg?" Gunther wiped his head.

Greg look through his scope, pulled back three times less than Gunther's. Easier to spot and zoom in. "Ah, I don't know, like two maybe. We still have the most kills by far, and we haven't even started the conservation yet. Once we get off this island and have a line of citis to kill, oh man. Like fish in a barrel. Dad would be so proud." He clicked his prosthetic leg against the ground.

"Yeah, he would, wouldn't he? Would you stop making that sound with that thing. If we were actually sniping, you'd give us away in a second. What do you think is going on down below?"

Greg looked at his EED. "That thing is my leg, brother. But I don't know, but for two hundred rations, I wish we had a shot. You know you can trade rations for time in the simulator to do *whatever* you want? Literally, you ask the programmer to put you in a world, you can set up the rest if you need confidentiality, and you can build the simulation and even store it later—what the fuck?"

"What?"

"Did you hear any authorization of four Humvees leaving the gated area?"

"No, why would anyone even leave the quad?"

"Check it out, three o'clock. Four Humvees turning onto Kimmel Rd."

Gunther's cross hairs moved over the terrain and zoomed in on four Humvees speeding along the east side of the island. He zoomed in on the driver and clicked the side of the scope. "Call it in. Send a picture of the driver I just captured with my scope. We only have"—Gunther checked his EED and then the sky—"fifteen minutes of sufficient daylight." It's too murky to make a shot in the dark."

* * *

"Captain is being a little crazy, huh?" Matt leaned to the left to see the captain's head out the window howling like a werewolf.

Victor didn't break eye contact with the light behind the clouds. "Don't you think we are all a little out of our element. I can't believe we are doing this, Alix, I want you to know this is all your fault."

"Captain wasn't kidding about the smell though. Ugh." Wes lowered his mask. "At least the mask filters it a little."

"Victor, we're going to be first on the island. You're welcome. Look at the sky though, huh?" Alix pointed for Anna. He looked to her, the redness of the sky reflecting in her honey eyes. "You are so beautiful."

Anna smiled big. "I'm so happy I'm here with you."

"Okay, none of this mushy shit through the whole fucking time." Victor reached over and slapped Alix's head. "We have to stay focused out here. We only have a handful of guys. This could be very risky. And for the record, Matt will attest to this. I didn't want to come, but when I realized they were going to pull that vanishing sequence on you, I signed up last minute."

"Is that what they were going to do me?"

Anna nodded and side smirked.

"That's what Captain told us. That's why he wanted to bust you out of there." Wes turned from the road, H2 in front of them close over the hood. "Yeah, and when we have some time to talk, I want you to tell us about Eli. None of us remember him."

"That's what triggered this whole thing, huh?" Alix's eyes widened.

Anna squeezed his leg.

Wes pointed at Alix. "I want to know who Eli is. Captain has a photo of us with him in it when we were little. We thought Captain was nuts, but we really don't remember."

"No wonder why everyone is after him." Anna looked to Wes. "He kept evidence of a vanishing sequence?"

Matt checked the rearview, "What's the vanishing sequence, and why do you know about it."

"Well, Sue told me a bit more about them than the other girls, I suppose, but we need to know about the chip, and how it works in case we need to address a head wound on the field. We were also taught how to fly with a cerebral chip upload. I learned about the vanishing sequence then."

"Alix, I thought I would never see you again the way you went down in the vomit room." Matt leaned over to look at him.

"Guys, we're stopping." Alix looked to the other side of the Humvee over to the water. "This is unbelievable. I can't believe there is still a ferry here."

Captain radioed in their ears. "Team, I'm going to pull up on the ferry to the left, we need to be two by two. Jack, myself and his team are going below to start the engine and clear down there. I want the rest of the team to hold position up top and keep an eye on the road for following squads. We don't want to be caught by surprise."

They pulled up to the back of the ferry. The lift gate stood up in the back of the boat, stopping them from driving in. The captain looked to the left and right and eyed the lift handle on the stern of the boat. "I'll get it. Cover me, Dawson." Captain pulled the lever to the door and approached the boat tactically.

Phil peered over the hood. "You know, I'm glad this is not like simulation. We fought our asses off at the top of the elevator to get out of the quad. That's when Captain and one of those boys were ripped to shreds."

"We're not in the clear yet." Adam sighed.

"Yeah, it's going to be a little nuts over there I bet. We still thinking going to the Brooklyn side?"

"I'm not sure. It's quicker, I know that. I don't think that there is a particular preference as far as what side would be better when we land. I think it was more about quickness to get away from the island. I don't even think Captain expected so little resistance at the top."

"Maia was probably more concerned about protecting the Readers. That's usually protocol. What's with Alix bringing the chick?"

Adam moaned. "I don't know. Lucky bastard though. I guess they have been seeing each other for a while through simulation. It's fucked up. Kid smashes all the rules, get to slam this perfect-looking girl, and gets us all fucked because he remembers someone we don't. I don't know. 'It is what it is' is the old saying, right?"

Phil cracked his fingers. "I kind of thought they were seeing each other, because of them in simulation a few times, but I thought it would be impossible. I joked about it with him even, I think."

Hayden chimed in the radio chatter. "You think that her vagina is the exact same as it really is in real life?"

"Well, the simulator projects you as you see your self, so I don't see why her vag would be any different than she sees it."

"Well, my penis isn't huge in simulation."

"How do you know how big your penis is in simulation?"

"Guys, we can hear every word you say. Can you fucking stop?" Alix's voice ended the convo.

"Yeah. Captain's coming back. I can't wait to just be on the boat. I'll feel a little safer once we are off the island." Wes tapped the top of the steering wheel.

Alix watched the glow on his beard from the Hummer in front. He's so funny right now. The smile. The freeness of the captain. A thousand times lighter hearted than the man Alix knew prior. In slow motion Alix watched Captain look back at the red sky after the barrier between the boat and the road lowered. He gazed toward the quad and knew it would be the last time he'd ever see the prison that became his life years and years ago. His beard blew lightly in the breeze, and his eyes twinkled. He inhaled the not-so-fresh air, chest big and eyes closed.

Alix's eyes widened, the sound of an unmistakable echo.

Thhhiph! The captain's head snapped back. Blood sprayed. His body went limp and collapsed backward.

"Pull up! Pull up! Sniper!"

"The Humvee is bulletproof!" The radio chatter erupted in their ears.

"I don't want to test it right now!"

"We're screwed!"

"Let me get to him. I can…"

Anna tried to crawl over Alix.

Alix pushed Anna back between Victor and him. "You fucking crazy! You see what just happened?" Alix looked to Victor. His face hollowed. "Team, pull the Humvees diagonally to the left! Diagonally to the left. Now! It was a sniper shot from the south. Victor, how far is the north tower? Team pull up! Diagonally to the left, now!"

"Copy that." The trucks began to move.

Victor looked back. "Five hundred meters."

"Clear shot from north tower to us?"

Victor pulled his mask down and peaked as the Humvee moved to the left and diagonal. "Yeah. It's murky and dark. Tough shot right now. You don't think…"

Alix pulled his mask down. "Gunther…that fucking bastard! Let's get him. I'm going to settle this right now. Everybody exit to the right after the trucks are parked on the barge diagonally! Cut the engines. Get out on the passenger side only. Use them as cover. Keep your head down! Stay behind the truck!"

Wes's voice chattered in their microphones. "Who made you captain?"

"I'm not, this is cat and mouse, not chess. Shut up and listen, or Gunther will smoke you too. Team, heads down! Cross hairs are looking for you right now!"

Victor exited first, ducked down and around the trucks. "Alix, you are on a rocking boat and only two minutes of light!"

"Then I'll shoot him in one. We already know his locale. There are only three windows in the north tower. Everybody stay put and keep your heads down! Victor, we got this. Call the shot." Alix pulled his rifle around his back.

The teams emptied out the right side of the trucks and hunkered behind them. Guns ready. The night went quiet. All of them were picturing the captain's face when it caught the bullet and listened to the splashing of water against the barge.

Alix pointed to the Victor. "Going under." Alix pulled the levers on the rifle. The barrel was extracted and expanded. Alix loaded up and shoved a mag in the bottom of his rifle. They creeped under the truck. Alix pulled the pod out and aimed through the rim of the Humvee tire and kept the rifle back four inches under the truck. He moved slowly.

Victor crawled behind the front tire and looked through the gap in the rim. "Target unknown, one of three windows, distance five hundred meters, wind, zero. Sufficient light"— he checked his EED—"one minute thirty seconds, Alix. Take into consideration the rocking of the boat. Forty degree differential."

Alix adjusted his scope and breathed.

* * *

"Target, Captain Robert Milligan northeast, five hundred meters, wind, zero. Aim. Shoot." Greg watched the splatter and the fall of Milligan on his way back to the Humvee. His red beard made it unmistakably their target. "Hit! Two hundred rations for us! Fuck yeah! Let's see what else we can take. Target H1 Passenger, Captain Jack Silva. Five hundred meters, wind, zero. Aim. Shoot."

"The Humvees are bulletproof you know that, Greg." Gunther's crosshairs scanned the down body and the blood stream as the Humvees pulled up and to the left. The most possible coverage from his exact location. They knew. Alix...

"They are exiting the vehicles on the other side! Fuck! How would they know?" Greg squeezed the binoculars like he did when he became excited.

"They know it's us. They know where the shot came from." Gunther eased his Dragunov rifle.

"Well, let's get a shot in before they get away in dark."

"I don't want to give my position away."

Greg sighed. "*Our* position is fine, they are a bunch of kids trying to escape. They don't know any better."

Gunther grunted. "Alix Basil is with them."

"Who cares. Kid doesn't even have a kill yet."

"You want to be his first? I've seen the sims. Kid is good."

"Not as good as you. We've been doing this for twice as long. Let's not give him the chance to get started. What are they doing?"

"*They*, aren't doing anything. Alix is setting up a shot. That's what I would be doing. We should pack it in while we are ahead. There isn't a shot left to take before darkness comes, and I don't want to take a chance. There are a dozen places he could be already, and we only have three windows from the nest on the north tower. He's probably scoping us now."

"Gunther, let's get one more. We are pushed far enough back, they would have to guess a window, and it would give his position away, and you'd take him. Stop being a pussy! We've been watching the whole time, where could he possible set a shot up from?" Gregory pushed his eyes deeper into the binoculars, his two missing finger nubs on the side.

"You are going to take a thirty-three percent chance on our life? I'm packing it in. Captain Milligan was enough of a hit. If the squad chasing them can catch up to them, that's enough for me. Let's go, brother." Gunther pulled his rifle back and crawled backward, keeping his head down.

A flare shot up from the barge, a blazing light-bulb rocket and curved up and round. Universal symbol for S.O.S. Gunther's head snapped up and back and his eyes widened. He never saw the flash from under the Humvee. The second time he'd left his brother behind. The bullet entered the small reflection of the flare in Greg's lens, exited out the back of Gunther's little brother's head and made a spark as it hit the concrete wall.

"Confirmed hit!" Victor screamed.

Alix pulled the bolt back, and his empty shell rolled under the tire.

"Keep that shell!" Hayden clapped. "First kill! Do you think it was Gunther or Gregory?"

Alix clicked another shell in and pushed another round into the chamber.

"I don't know, but either way it was a Vasily." Victor squinted, cheeks pulled back.

"Congrats on your first real kill." Jack tapped Alix's boot. "A high profile kill at that."

"Yeah, Alix." Phil started a slow clap.

"Yeah, well keep an eye out. We don't want to give him a shot. Wes! Thanks for that flare, the reflection worked great. We saw the lens in the second window."

"We good to come out now that everybody within a mile radius knows where we are?"

Jack gave the final order. They didn't have time to just wait this one out. They needed to make moves. They didn't care about waking the neighbors, and they had all night to escape and get away.

"Thanks, guys. Another minute. We can drop smoke at the entrance of the barge just in case and get to work. Jack, you are overseeing officer, stay hunkered. Send three men to high tail it under the barge and get this thing started. We'll cover you." Alix stared into the darkness of the second window. "Victor, you see anything? The other one is in there. There is no way that was a two in one."

"For Captain, I wish it was. I don't see anything. Knowing their profiles, Gunther is smarter than to poke his head up without a spotter. Even if we killed his brother, he's out there. He got his kill. There's no way both of them saw the flash from your rifle. I'm thinking if you shot Gunther, like I hope you did, Greg will show at least a gun barrel in a moment. He's too irrational. Keep watching." Victor pressed his eyes into the spotter's scope. "Is that movement on the second floor?"

"Looked like a flash of light, maybe an opening door." Victor high-fived Alix.

"Or closing."

19

The ferry drifted in the night over the Diamond Reef in New York Harbor in a drizzle. The low rumble of the motors distorted by the occasional rumble of thunder from heat lightning bouncing cloud to cloud, almost a constant since the war. Squad 28 and its new companions took in the world and its realness. Even Jack, the only person on the barge not buried under Governor's Island in a world created by MAIA and governed by a supercomputer his whole life thought the world to be…peculiar.

Jack, Matt, and Brian worked on getting a tablet up and running to program briefings and map layouts. All the tech talk for even twenty minutes bored almost everyone.

"You didn't think to figure this out before we left the island with constant Wi-Fi?" Wes slammed his gun down. "I'd say I'm going to get some fresh air, but breathing this is like sucking on an old sock."

"Stand down, soldier! Respect rank right now!" Jack pointed at Wes. "I don't exactly have a Verizon fucking signal, Wes, and we don't know what Captain Milligan was thinking because his brains are all over the barge back there!" Jack pointed toward shore. "If you want to go pick up the fucking pieces and figure it out, be my guest! You can start by swimming that way!"

"Don't you disrespect the captain's name like that! He meant the world to us!" Wes pointed his finger right back. "I'll fucking—"

Phil grabbed Wes by the back collar of his vest. "Wes."

Wes snapped Phil's grip. "Don't touch me!"

Jack lowered his hand. "I knew Rob years before you even laid in a test tube of your dad's cum, you little prick! I will snap you in half. Shut up, take ten and let us figure it out. Consider that an order."

Wes stormed to the bow, and Leo and Aaron stepped forward as he passed. Phil followed feverishly. Alix watched from a distance. Everyone else helped themselves to a seat around the boat. A challenge to say the least.

Anna hugged Alix. They watched the reflection from the one spotlight on Governor's Island dance in the water behind the boat. "I wish there were stars."

Alix looked up. "Someday."

"You think so? You think we will ever see stars, babe?" Her jawline was a smooth perfection in soft light.

"Someday." Alix smiled. "You figure out what's in the bag yet?"

Anna's bag lay at her feet. She smiled. "Yeah, a couple changes of underwear, some old make up I haven't even seen in my life, some women products, and a handful of other things."

"Oh yeah, like what?"

"Well there was a box of condoms for one." Anna smiled big, bit her lower lip, and twitched her eyebrows.

"Okay, Romeo." Adam yelled over to them. "Take it out of Juliette and get over here. We need a plan."

Alix and Anna approached the group hand in hand. The sound of water slapping the side of the barge coincided with the waves rocking the boat back and forth. Wes appeared in the back of the pack. Adam hung his head between his legs, his body dry heaved every moment or two.

The captain's revolver hung from Jack's hip. He spoke, "Listen, team, cut the engine." He sliced his hand across his throat. "Brian, cut the engine."

The engine stopped. Brian joined from behind Captain Silva. The water grew louder.

Captain Silva cleared his throat. "Okay, I'm just as upset as you are right now about who we lost today. The good thing is, we did what he set out to do. Got off the island. None of us would be here with this freedom—and, Alix, you or anyone here wouldn't know who you were if it were not for Captain Robert Milligan.

"Alix, great work today, and Victor too. That was an amazing shot. I've never seen anything like it. Five hundred meters through the rim of a Humvee and on a rocking boat, that is impressive boys. Right now, we need to do what Alix did today. We need to do exactly what we've trained to do. I'm not trying to put Alix on a pedestal right now because all he did was his job, he took initiative and control of a very sudden and striking moment. What we need to do now is get our heads together. I know we've never worked as a unit together in simulation, but we are all trained the same way and need to get on the same page if we are going to survive this. Realistically, our journey is just getting started. That was just the beginning boys.

"I am your captain now. I will be putting down some laws this instance. You will respect me and my rank as if you would respect Captain Milligan the same." Jack looked at Wes. "You will refer to me as Captain or Captain Silva. I will never be just Jack to you unless we are speaking freely, and you have permission to do so or after a couple beers, God willing we find some. We use our rations sparingly. We have no idea how long we will be without food and water, so it's important not to get carried away. I've packed as much as I could given the space and time allotted.

"What I need from you boys right now is a vote. I will do this time to time to see what your thoughts are. I want to know what the goal of the team is, not just my initiative. Majority rules, ties go to me. It doesn't appear as if time is an issue. We can take this ferry wherever we want. We have enough fuel for 8 hours of travel. The original plan was Brooklyn only because we thought we would be in a race from MAIA. That is not the case. We have more time than we originally projected. We must go north. We are crazy to go back past Governor's Island in anyway shape or form. We can go to Manhattan, Brooklyn, or what we were even talking about is heading over to Jersey City. This decision all depends on the goal of the group and could change the more information we gather. We don't know exactly the situation out here.

"Here's what we do know. Manhattan was the most populated place when the war started. It is an island, and from what I remember all bridges to and from were destroyed less one, the Broadway Bridge at the northernmost peak. There is most likely a high rate of citi's there, but there is underground subway systems that might be smart to travel through, rubble from buildings, high vantage points for Alix and Victor to cover us, and I remember the city very well.

"If we take Brooklyn, there is a vast highway system of roads to travel, and we could very well try and get to the John F. Kennedy Airport, where I would think is our best point of any civilized citizens, and I don't mean the ones we've been training you to kill. I know we make them out to be rotten and sadistic, but I believe that there is a good chance there are good people out here we can connect with.

"If we go to New Jersey City, my approach would be to head to the capital. I would think that what is left of it might not be a bad idea to see if there is any remains left and rekindle whatever humanity is left. Team, this approach could put us to go as far as Boston, New Hampshire, Maine, Canada, whatever we want to do, but we need a core of values right now.

"What do we want to do? Alix, I'll let you speak first."

Alix shrugged. "I mean up until this morning, I didn't have a plan for anything. I think we break it into little pieces and start from there. One, I think we need to get off the water by dawn. I don't think being on the water is a good idea at all. We are sitting ducks, and we don't know if there are water minds or anything. I say let's get to land quickly, get off the water and into the trucks, scope out the area while getting away from MAIA and try and take a hostage or two to find out what is really going on here."

"Yeah, that's a start."

"Makes sense."

"Sure."

Anna squeezed his arm.

"Team? Do we agree on that, raise of hands." Jack looked around. "Okay, almost everyone, good. Wes, what are your thoughts?"

Wes eyed Jack. Daggers. "I think we are stuck between a rock and a hard place. We all know Maia is going to issue conservation soon, and we are going to have an army trained as good as us coming in the numbers nearly twelve thousand. We don't know what type of military force is out there. We are *told* that it is mostly mercenaries and citis, but there very well could be still an invader presence from the invasion, and we don't know what those numbers look like. We need to dodge both groups. I agree with scoping out the area, but we need to run fast and defend faster."

"Okay. All in favor?" All hands went up. "So we want to get away from MAIA quickly and avoid any other forces until we have a clue. How about this? Quickest way off the water is Battery Park on Manhattan. We can unload there. We know landing won't been an issue because we've been sniping over there for months. There is a low risk of an awaiting army or force of any kind. We will start to head north and assess the situation. Oorah?"

"Oorah." Every voice echoed.

* * *

"Gentlemen, we all have something in common." Rankin's T-port whined back and forth, his hands behind his back. "There is a group out there that has escaped the island and betrayed our whole organization. Now we can wait and let the citi's gobble them up, but I would much prefer a different type of torture method for each one of them. I think you would agree."

Gunther moved his lips to speak.

"Ug-ugh. Not yet, I'm not done. Conservation has been pushed back a bit, but not so far that I don't think we can't catch up to them, but I think if we put together a task force, well of some particular skills, we could catch them faster if we leave, oh let's say in an hour for example. Now I know what you're thinking, 'O but, Reader Rankin, sir, I thought I would be…' the thing is gentlemen"—Rankin stopped and stared at all of them one by one—"nothing is what it seems, and if you don't want to obey these demands, your memories will be subject to the vanishing sequence, and you will be cooking my breakfast tomorrow."

They stood still. And quiet.

"Todd, Captain Jack Silva made a mockery of you and your men. How do you let 4 completely loaded and stacked Humvees out of lock up without authorization? How!"

"Sir."

"Don't speak!"

"You asked me—"

"I know what I asked you! Shut it! He has the youngest group in the facility, and they outperformed you, outmaneuvered you, and outsmarted you and these other three idiots!" The room quieted. No monitor. "I will give you a chance to redeem yourselves by catching him. I am putting this group together with top secret clearance. There will be a window of time you will be able to leave the island by raft. If you succeed in killing or capturing anyone in this group, you will be awarded one hundred and fifty rations per person, three hundred for Jack Silva and five hundred for Alix Basil. The girl they are with, Anna Brooks, if she is still alive, she comes back unharmed, or no one gets paid. Bring her to me, and if she reports any mistreatment, consider my original promise a playground compared to what you would be going through. Bring her back, alive, don't harm or touch her in any way inappropriate, you get yourselves one thousand rations from me personally."

Todd's eyes lit up. He would enter simulation in a strip club and just never come out. By the time he finished in the world he created, with that amount of time, drugs, alcohol, and the fucking he would be doing, he wouldn't know what reality looked like.

"Gunther..."

Gunther motioned. "If you speak to me like you spoke to them—"

"Great job, Gunther." Rankin eyed him and wheeled and stood eye to eye. "I'll stop you there before I have to cut off your shooting finger and shove it in your fucking eyeball. Then we'll find out how good you are at stirring goop for the cadets. Don't make me waste your talents, soldier. I've read your profile. You're one of the best there is alive. Your brother was a good man. He died too early for sure. You made a great shot at a very high profile target today. I want to commend you for that. You were doing the right thing by keeping your head down after that. I'm sorry for your loss. You have been issued the two hundred rations for your kill, and this has been added to your profile. Your brother is going to be commended with the MAIA employee of the month award. He would have been awarded with fifty extra rations, those will be transferred to your account. You will also get another two hundred because he helped you with the kill."

Gunther's eyes didn't move. "I'll need a spotter."

"I am working on a spotter right now as we speak. He'll be done programming in…" Rankin glanced at his EED. "Ah, taking a little longer, like two hours. You would all be deploying in four hours. That means that Captain Jack Silva and his team had a seven-hour head start on you. We are working on tracking him now. Do you accept your assignment, or do you want to forget that these people ever existed?"

They nodded.

"Reader Rankin"—Gunther swallowed—"I'll need access to Alix's simulations and will need at least an hour in simulation. I need to understand how he thinks and feels."

"Granted. I'll upload a file in fifteen minutes with everything you need. It'll be good for you to see them anyway to get to know your spotter."

"Why, who's my spotter?" Gunther's face twisted.

"Eli Williams. He was on the same team as Alix. He'll know them very well."

"Wait what? What makes you think he won't shoot me in the back of the head when I'm aiming at Alix?" Gunther wrinkled his forehead.

"Because of the memory I'm going to upload about Alix fucking his girlfriend and ratting him out for using of the simulation to see her on a night that Eli was supposed to meet her. Would you protect that man if you were nineteen?"

"No, sir. I'd put a bullet in him from a mile away. Is it true?"

"Why is that important?" Rankin disregarded the disgusted looks from Todd and his team.

Gunther's jaw stiffened. "If Alix really did that, it says something about his character. I'm trying to kill the man. I need to know his motives. This is different than war, sir. This is an assassination."

"You do know a little about assassinations, don't you, Gunther?" Rankin smiled. "No need to bring that up, but for the record and your reconnaissance. It's not true. Eli will think it is, though, so keep that between us. Otherwise, he might shoot you in the back of the head. He's the best man for the job. Maia approves."

"Roger that."

"Good, I'll get working on your files." Ranking turned from them. "And, Todd, get your team in line. You are reporting to Gunther going forward. No more slip-ups."

The dim room remained quiet. "You think he's coming back?" Todd looked to Gunther.

"No. None of that cowboy shit. You four have a reputation."

They laughed. Todd grinned. "So…we only have like a couple hours, and myself and the guys want to put in some simulation time too…for practice. For the mission. Is there anyway of maybe transferring us a couple of your rations. We…ah ran out, and obviously…"

"Shut up. I don't want my brother's rations. Employee of the month is a slap in the face. You got 'em. Just don't let me down out there. Once we step foot off this island, you are under my command."

* * *

"Cut the engine. We'll drift in." Jack held the helm. He adjusted back and forth. "I'll steer it straight in, tell the guys to thermal scan everything as we approach. Prepare the Humvees and drop the divider ahead of time. We don't need that in the way again."

"Why go there?" Wes hung his head.

Anna and Alix stared up at the shadows of fallen and beaten up titans that were the buildings of New York City. "I can't believe how big they are. You see them in simulation, but I can't believe it, Alix. Look at that one." Anna pointed.

"Yeah, it looks like it fell over and is leaning in. I wouldn't want to be under it when it collapses."

"Babe, what's wrong? You okay?" Anna squeezed his hand tighter.

"I'm fine…just can't stop seeing Captain Milligan's face."

"You've seen it a million times in simulation. That's why they do that, Alix. He did a great justice today and saved us all. Someday, we can join him, and he'll be there when you open your eyes from this simulation called life, and he'll be ready to bitch you out about all the screwups. But right now, he wants you to focus. He did all this for—"

Alix put his arm around Anna. "That's the thing, I feel like it's my fault."

"Stop it. You can't blame yourself for that no more than you can blame yourself for being programmed the way you are, or for these fallen buildings." Anna kissed him. "Everything happens for a reason."

"That's what I'm afraid of. What is going to happen next? What if we lose someone else, what if I lose you?"

"Alix." Anna grabbed his chin. "Stop, we are all together now. *We* are together now, and my heart burns for you even more in person. Let's be together, and fight to get through this. That is all we can do. This is war, Alix. That's all we can do, other than love each other."

The island approached, and more and more giants peered down at them from above. Matt pointed up. "That one there is the Freedom Tower. I recognize that one."

"It's so pretty." Anna's eyes sparked.

"Alix! Anna!" Wes turned the corner from the helm room. "Get ready for breeching. Get your infrared ready. We need to be sure we don't walk into a shit storm. Anna, you don't just get to sit there and look pretty. Get a battle mask out of H2. We are going to need all the help we can get." Wes turned from the two on the hull. "Team, ready for boarding. Four minutes."

20

"Todd! Todd! Toss a stack, quick! She said for another five hundred, she'll show me why they call her Pussycat!" Austin's naked body sunk into the red lavender loveseat, his hairy thighs spread wide as the dark stripper danced for him, her fishnet stockings pulled high and tight across her skin, red lines where the fabric cut. The smell of scrubbing skin on skin and sweat and cigarettes and booze and drugs filled the room. Thick and thin black lines cut her dark skin across and up and down where her panties and underwear lined. Her thin dark hair poured down her back and whipped around like leather straps from a flogger every time she twirled her head around in Austin's lap.

Todd pulled his mouth from the girl's nipple and made a serious sucking and puckering sound. He pushed her tities out of his way. Austin's arm reached around and unsnapped the black lace bra and held out his hand for a five-finger grab of a stack of one hundred dollar bills.

"Fucking asshole. Hold on, you gorgeous little slut you." Todd grasped the indentation of her upper hips and pulled himself out of her and tossed her to the side of the couch. Her head thumped off the armrest.

"Ah, papi, come back to me, hunny, quickly. *Vámonos*." The stripper moaned and threw her head back over the headrest, her dark hair flowing and grazing the floor. She opened her legs, closed her eyes, and rubbed herself slowly in circles. She clutched her breast in the other hand, her Gucci nails clawed red lines in her chest after leaving Todd's bulky, jacked, hairless chest and shoulders. "Ohhh, god! Quickee, Toad!" Her accent fused his body.

"I swear, Austin, if I didn't want another bump, I'd offer you a bullet in the head before I got up from that. This one must be straight out of high school. I thought I was in her ass at first. This bitch can salsa." Todd edged his butt out of the deep red velvet couch, pulled his jeans up enough to walk, but left his erection hung out and his belt jingled. He waddled to the backpack. He chucked two wads of hundreds at Austin, one slapped his stripper in the back, the other bounced off the back of the wall and fell into Austin's lap. "Don't ask me again."

"Oh man, does Billy know how to put together a simulation or what?" Austin spoke muffled through a D cup over his mouth and nose, inhaled like a ninja, and threw the bra across the room. "I got your money, now turn around, Pussycat, and show me why they call you that."

Todd aligned a white line of cocaine on the table. "Yeah, Billy said it ends off in a bar fight and everything, so long as we behave and don't kill anyone." He rolled up a hundred dollar bill and snorted the line of coke and held the back of his wrist to his invaded nostril. "Holy fuck." He snorted air hard and coughed twice. He grabbed the bottle of whiskey. "I like the idea Chris had of bailing on Gunther and just capturing those fuckers on our own. We could do this for life with the payout that old fuck on his Pogo Ball is offering."

A man in a black suit and bowtie cleared his throat. "Ah, sir, that will be five hundred American dollars for that bottle of whiskey."

Todd slugged off the bottle and grimaced. "Five hundred for the bottle? How much to knock you the fuck out!"

Todd's stripper moaned. "Papi! Come fuck me. Ohh…" Todd looked to her on the couch struggling to keep her legs open, and she sped up the circles and strained her neck backward.

"Go get the money from Billy. This is his simulation, I'm going to pay this girl's tuition. Pound, sand monkey boy."

"My name is Bruce, but I will check with Mr. Antrim for the remainder of your tab."

Todd waddled away bare ass, faced the suited man, and mounted his stripper. He grabbed his rod and shoved it in her hole.

"Ah! Papi! Hmmmgr! You're so big." Her hands squeezed his deltoids as his hips swung back and forth. "Ah! Ah! Ah! Papi! Papi! Harder! Harder! Urg!"

"Todd! Todd! Lookit! Lookit!"

Todd looked over. Sweat dripped from his head. Austin's stripper backed her naked self up onto the couch and on top of Austin. She curled the toes of her glass high heels over his shoulders, told him to stick his tongue out, and pulled his face into her crotch over and over.

"She…tattooed…whiskers…inner…thighs! Ahhh! Lalala!… Lalala!"

Bruce exited the red-lit room through the silk curtain, his elegant arm held to the side. He leaned into a large man in a small shirt, King Kong in a tank top. "This could get out of hand soon. Please get ready to escort these kind gentlemen out in *any* means necessary. I have a feeling this won't be the last simulation we are in with them, let's set the tone early if they are going to entertain here." Bruce knocked on the wall across the hallway. "Mr. Antrim, we have a minor monetary dispute with your fellow comrades, they've told me to address you for the funds of our lavish whiskey in the amount of five hundred American dollars."

"What?"

Bruce sighed. "Your buddies told me to get the money from you."

"Just come in, you annoying bastard!"

Bruce entered the purple room. Rhythmic screams circled along side the disco ball. Bruce looked away from Billy's backside of his assless chaps. His two pistols hung from each side of a cowboy holster and belt as he pounded a stripper from behind. "There is a pile of cash on the table. Ugh! Take six hundred dollars. If I thought I would never use this simulation again, I'd shoot you the head right, aghr, now. Oh baby. Fuck yeah." Billy pulled her hair, jerking her head backwards. Her jaw popped open, and she screamed loud.

Bruce pushed a couple of rolled up dollar bills over on the glass end table and counted the only dry ones not marinated in whiskey or snot. "There is only four hundred in acceptable dollar bill heres, Mr. Antrim."

"Oh my god! I'm apparently going to the ATM right now. Haha! Check with Chris. I'll get back to you. Privacy please! Oh… my…god…Now! Now! Turn around!"

Bruce turned as the girl spun around and devoured his cock.

"Ugh! Yeah, baby!"

Bruce looked to his bodyguard and rolled his eyes. "To think these sickos are actually sitting in an egg-shaped room right this very minute, all across each other hard as hell. Where is the other pathetic loser?"

"What'd you call me, you little digital pipsqueak!" Chris pushed the pink silk curtain aside. A man thong held most of him in except the tip, a fire hose as his private. He wore a blue mask covering just around his eyes and high yellow boots. Nipple tassels swayed back and forth each sluggish step he took from his chest. Bruce's eyes widened not because of the absurdity, but because of the magnum pointed at his head. Two women and a man exited the same room behind him and screamed, their hands held over their head. They darted into the strip club as the shots began to fire.

* * *

Gunther squinted as he stared straight into the screen. He tapped his finger. "Why didn't Alix shoot?" No one responded from the empty room, and the answer wouldn't congeal. He watched the end of the footage again. Alix shot the man on the .50 caliber on the back of the truck. Gunther swiped at the screen and pulled the view in so that his angle faced Alix and looked down his rifle. Gunther stared into the scope. Victor nudged Alix and yelled his name.

Gunther pulled the view out and back to the target. A brown-haired girl he recognized from a previous simulation and in the snapshot of Anna Brooks given to Gunther from Rankin. What's Rankin's interest with this girl? Why was she in this simulation as an enemy. It's apparent that Alix had feelings for her.

Gunther pulled her profile. He twirled the view around, scrolled down to see her baby picture. Gunther held his finger on the picture; a submenu arose in front of him. He pressed Properties. "Photo Taken 01/04/2025 at 23:51. Source: Albert Rankin. Description: Our baby girl, love you Sue!" Gunther's mouth hung open. People often forget about who they used to tag in social media or what the description of the photo was. Anna is Rankin's daughter, and Alix is in love with her.

"I'm getting too old for this." Gunther rubbed his eyes and yawned. He sat back in the leather recliner. "Okay." He sighed. "Let's see what simulation my new comrades needed the rations so badly for. He pulled up simulation created by Billy Antrim and watched as much as he could without gagging. Bunch of pigs. What a waste of a billion-dollar machine. He particularly found the part about ditching him interesting though. He shook his head and scratched his black and gray beard. "These fucking idiots. They would probably get me killed anyhow."

* * *

"The sky is starting to get light." Jack lowered the gate and looked back to Brian. "We have to move somewhat quickly, I think. I know Gunther could pick us off from Governor's Island. Team…how we looking?" Jack spoke softly into their radios.

"Bravo, clear. No sign of the enemy."

"Delta, clear." Matt's voice quick and emotionless. "This statue of the headless man near the sinking life boat is freaking me out. I was wondering how my heat scanner didn't pick him up 'til I realized he was stone."

"The head used to be there, Matt."

"I almost shot him." Phil's voice echoed. "What's with your generation building statues of people? Wasn't there enough people as it was? Did you need stand-ins?"

Laughter.

"Echo, clear and ready." Victor looked over to Alix and Anna. He rolled his eyes even though no one could see. "How is it I get stuck with the lovebirds?"

"Okay, team." Jack filled his cheeks with air and held it like a squirrel and his nuts. He let it out. Here goes nothing. "Let's focus. Let's move. Load up in the Humvees, fire up the engines, maintain radio contact, and use only infrared headlights. Your masks will be able to see the beam, but the truck won't give off any actual light. We don't need to attract attention. Follow me through the park. Keep your eyes peeled."

The Humvees pulled off the barge onto Battery Park. One light post flickered, the rest around the promenade broken, bent, torn down, missing, or smashed. Magazines, newspapers, trash, debris, snuck around Battery Park in the wind and crawled until caught by the barbed wire that circled the park intertwined within the fancy fences of the vicinity. Once a tranquil place to lean and look over the harbor, now a defensive mechanism. The few benches left remained scarred from bullet holes, the others charcoal from grenades and bombs. Singed remains of a parachute hung from a small tree, holey and rotten. Its stray strings fluttered in the wind and tickled the closest naked companion. The trucks swam through the high unmowed grass nearly to the hood of the Humvees.

The convoy crept past the leftovers of a statue of an outline of a soldier, spotted with bullet holes. Jack grimaced. "The Forgotten War monument."

"Sir, I don't think anyone forgot about this war." Leo sniffed. "Their noses will never let them."

"The smell is sewage. That monument is from the Korean War. My father brought me there as kid. My great grandfather fought in that war."

Brian cleared his throat. "Your father brought you to Korea?"

"No, the monument right there. His name is etched in it."

Aaron stretched his neck. "It's all shot up. Did it look nice before?"

Jack nodded. "Yeah. Well, it was honorable."

"There was a Korean War?" Leo stared at the outline through the window.

"Exactly." Jack looked forward through his goggles and into the red beam projected in front of the Humvee.

"Captain, what's that up ahead?" The voice came from H2.

"That's the East Coast Memorial. It used to be an eagle that faced the Statue of Liberty. Doesn't look that way without the wings." Jack smirked. "Listen, boys, we can do the full tour another day. Let's keep focused. We could be ambushed any second. Keep your guns ready, and ready yourself for defensive maneuvers."

"Copy that."

Anna turned around. "You think we'll be able to see the Statue of Liberty from here?"

Alix looked back through the window. "I doubt it. There isn't much left to it anyway."

Anna twisted and leaned up onto her knee and slid a box of ammo to the left. "I know, but I wonder if we could see it from here." She strained her eyes, her battle goggles zoomed in more than her eyes could, turned the world a hazy green in the faint light, and she saw the outline in the distance. "Wow, there it is. I can't imagine how big it was when she had her arm."

Wes turned around. "Let's stay focused. Put your ass in the seat please. Captain is right, we need to stay alert."

The sound of crunching class crackled from under the tires. A lump forced each Humvee to tip slightly. "What was that?" Phil leaned up in the Humvee to look over the hood."

"I don't know." Adam looked in the rearview. "There's infrared behind us. I can't see."

"I think it was a body."

"I don't know, probably was a body. I'm sure it was dead before we all drove over it. The GPS says the road is in ten meters."

Phil eyed the monster up ahead. "Captain. I don't mean to ask a ton of questions, but it doesn't look like that building stops going up. I can't even see the top. What is it?"

His voice radioed in on all their mics. "That, ladies and gentlemen, is the largest building left in the known world. I present to you, boys and girl, the Freedom Tower.

21

"Eli, do you know who I am?" Rankin held a small flashlight into each pupil. Rankin looked backwards over his shoulder. "Doctor Harrison, why isn't he responding? Eli?" Rankin shook him.

"He will in a moment, Mr. Rankin. Please give the boy a minute. We have never tried reinstating someone like this. It's almost like waking up for the first time in his life."

"Eli! Wake up, boy! It's going to be like waking up for the last time if he doesn't respond." Rankin slapped his face three times.

Harrison choked on the words forming in his mouth, and he retracted his open hand to stop himself back into a little ball instead.

Eli opened his eyes. They glazed over, rolled up into the back of his head, and then returned down to eye contact with Rankin. "W-w-where am I?"

"Yes!" Rankin raised his hands. "What is your name, boy?"

Eli looked down from his back to Dr. Harrison. "Eli Williams."

"This is great. Eli, who am I?"

"You are Reader Albert Rankin, sir."

"Yes. This is so exciting." Rankin clapped and looked to Harrison. "What squad were you formally in?"

"Squad 28. No longer exists though, all deemed traitors. Captain Milligan is dead, and I am going to kill Alix Basil with Gunther Vasily." Eli's words trailed off, and Dr. Harrison didn't completely believe them, more just programmed words, but he was saying exactly what Rankin said he would say.

Rankin wheeled back. "Okay, okay. Now stand please."

Eli pushed himself up out of bed. "Why am I so tired, sir?"

"You've been out for a couple of days. Now please stand." Rankin smiled at Dr. Harrison. Rankin handed Eli a battle knife.

"What's this for?" Eli studied the blade. He somehow knew what to do with it, just didn't know it yet.

Doctor Harris stepped forward. "I don't think this is a great—"

"Look around you." Rankin held his arm out and stopped Harrison.

Eli scanned the octagon, the mirrored windows, the hologram computers, the wires from the ceiling, the blue light glowing around the edges. The slow beeping of the machines circled the room. The hum of the computers. He spotted it. Alix's face. The knife instinctively soared out of Eli's hand and stuck into a Alix's digital face. The digital person flickered, and the knife fell to the floor.

Rankin smiled. "Suit up, Eli, I'm going to give you what you wanted. You are going to see what it is like off the island. You are to be conjoined with Anna Brooks, the love of your life. Alix took her from you. I'm going to let you get her back."

Doctor Harrison moved toward the door. "Rankin, sir. It's too soon. We don't know the effects this could have—"

"Doctor Harrison, save it for the rats and tell anyone about this." Rankin turned to Harrison and stared him dead in the eye. "I'll kill you myself." Rankin clapped Harrison's cheeks lightly. "I just programmed Maia's first assassin. There will literally be no one on the planet as stealthy and effective as this kid. Give me some credit, and get that virus together for me too will ya. I need that by the end of the day. Again"—Rankin headed toward the door— "death time, thirty minutes, not too violent. Something subtle, okay?"

"Sir, I will have to log any of my activity in the system with Maia."

"Maia is down! You log on manual paper and turn it into me directly. No one else sees it. You understand?"

"Yes, sir." Doctor Harrison eyed the monitor.

* * *

Elmer Washington's eyes jolted across the screen back and forth. His thoughts appeared in words on the screen. Everything seemed to be falling into place, just faster and not exactly how he anticipated. The door slid open. He hit Send. "Albert Rankin? What brings you down here at this hour?"

Rankin's T-port whined into the room, and Rankin sat across from Elmer. "I could ask you the same thing, Washington. But I won't. I trust you have business in the business center that needs attending to outside of our business." Rankin smiled.

"Right you are, friend. Are you ready for conservation?"

Rankin blew hot air. "Ready for it to stop getting pushed back. We are ready aside from our little incident yesterday." Rankin cracked his knuckles. "But I've taken care of that."

"W-wait, how did you take care of that? Did you consult the other Readers? Did you run it by Maia?"

"Relax, old friend." Rankin leaned back and pulled up his hologram screen. "I didn't do anything out of jurisdiction. I have made an assignment for some, but they volunteered and didn't have any binding restrictions to Maia because of circumstance."

"My god." Elmer's eyes lit up. "What did you do?"

Rankin looked across the table. "I got a team together to go after the traitors."

Elmer swallowed. "Who?"

"Don't let it affect your business, old friend. Just know there is a team landing in one hour, and they will have Alix by sundown. I am just here tracking where that ferry landed and seeing if they were smart enough to remove the trackers on the Humvees." Rankin keyed at the keyboard. "And apparently they are not that smart. Oh look, there they are now." Rankin pointed to the screen.

Elmer Washington stared at the map, the exact position of the four Humvees. "Impressive." He looked closer. "What is that movement there? Around Marble Hill?" Elmer pointed.

Rankin zoomed out. A large movement. A dark cloud of an army approached the city. Little people like ants followed tank after tank and truck after truck over the only bridge left on the island. "I'm not sure. You don't think..."

Elmer nodded. "Call a reading. We might have to start conservation early by the looks of that force. Fire Maia up again with the new protocol. Get these kids programmed up. Put out a broadcast immediately."

Rankin's mouth hung. He's never seen an advancement of that many people. He zoomed in to the max. Rankin breathed heavily through his nose. "And so it begins."

* * *

The sound of glass crunching under the tires echoed through the street labeled Trinity PL. The convoy swerved and weaved around charred and flipped cars abandoned and rusted, every window shattered, every compartment looted, ripped-out radios and navigation units, missing doors and hoods, engines. They edged around and powered through toppled and bent streetlights and lampposts. Black smoke trails elevated to the sky from burning tires. Chewed and mangled cans and bottles—water, beans, soup, beer, soda, sauce, broth, milk—littered the streets and rolled around. The tin echoed, plastic crackled until they were jammed in a sewer drain or sidewalk.

Rubble, steel cables, and electrical wires from fallen buildings blocked off roads and paths. A fire truck covered in broken and smashed stone blocked off the fallen street sign that read Thames St. The ladder poked through the top thirty feet in the air, the sirens all smashed to pieces, and the driver seat caved in like a metal carcass eaten and nibbled to death by the fallen buildings around it. A fire helmet, a big thirty-two imprinted on it, lay before the truck, still bright red. An iron support beam was bent over the top of the blockade like a rainbow over the pile, steal only gods could bend, stressed to a *U* and tossed to the side. They kept driving.

No windows remained in the buildings as low as the thirteenth floors. Most shot out or whipped rocks crashed through. The windows above those stories were peppered from people throwing themselves through them to escape capture or being killed by the enemy, or dropping office supplies on the enemy during the preliminary attacks, or from stray bullets or tremors from carpet bombing across the bay. Where is everyone?

The convoy pulled up and braked at a wall of cars stacked three vehicles high. Jack radioed in. "Team, I know this is a lot to take in, but we have to stay alert. We are going to throw up a mason map and check to see if it is worth plowing through these cars or if we should back track. On another note, I'm just as shocked as you are. I never thought I would see this. Stay alert."

Jack rolled down his window. The smell seeped through the crack in the window and soiled their air. He held a small electronic pancake shaped object out the window and press the button on the top. The device spun out of his and climbed above the Humvees about a hundred feet. Jack looked over the projected map with Leo.

"What do you think."

Jack shook his head. "I think it's a waste of time trying to go up Church or Broadway. Let's bang a left here. We can take a right onto Greenwich. I'm thinking if we can get the trucks to the community college, we could hunker there and figure out a plan. I'd like to see if the Holland Tunnels are cleared by any chance. If they were, it wouldn't be a bad plan B to take that over to Jersey City. Yeah, let's do that. Jack stuck his hand out the window, and the mason map device came soaring down and settled in his hand. Let's bang a left here."

The trucks reversed, turned, and took the left.

Hayden looked up at the wall of cars. "I can't believe what this place actually looks like. This must have been such a cool place to live when it wasn't all fucked up."

Brian leaned forward to see the tops of the buildings. "Even when it was a cool place to live, Hayden, I think it was still fucked up. From the horror stories I heard from the captain and others. I heard that a guy our age had a better chance of meeting a girl on their cellular phone through a dating application than they did at their local coffee shops. Fucking humans man, how do you pass up conversing with other humans by digging your face into a small dinky screen like this." Hayden turned the wheel and held up his EED. A box of supplies fell off the back seat and to the floor. "What was that?"

Hayden reached back, picked up the box. "Nothing, just a box of rations, actual water, and check this out, gummy vitamins. Captain Jack really spoiled us, huh? I thought for sure we'd be sucking on tabs the whole time. But to your point, Bri, some of them had tablets."

"Come on, man. Can you imagine how nice it would be to have a cup of coffee with a complete stranger than to sit and play on some forsaken little computer? People always updating their social media and looking into everyone else's lives. Think about it, people began caring more about their digital selves than they did their real selves. Captain was shooting the shit with us one day and said that he lost the love of his life over this thing called Facebook, a digital profile of yourself where you like post what you're feeling and what you are doing. He was tagged in a post, whatever that meant, with his friends, and they somehow got in a blowout argument over it, and that lead to her leaving. Can you imagine?"

"What the fuck is the point of a digital life?" Hayden lifted his mask and scratched his forehead. "I'd rather play a game of football. We've played it a hundred times in simulation, can you imagine a game in real life?"

Brian laughed. "You would wish you were in simulation after I tackled you."

"Game on, bitch." Hayden held out his fist and smiled under his mask.

Brian connected fists with him. He leaned closer the driver's side. "I don't know, Captain is getting out of the truck." Brian rolled down his window. "Captain?"

"Get out of the trucks all of you. Now."

Their hearts began beating heavy. Is this it? Fight time? The real thing? What did Captain Jack see? All twelve hearts and pulses picked up. Hands shook. Legs felt weak. What's going on?

"Calm down." Alix whispered to himself.

"Captain!" Wes exited the Humvee, closed the door, and circled the truck full attack mode. "This doesn't seem very smart. What are we doing?"

"Keep an eye on the perimeter." Jack pointed in two directions. "I will at least be alerted if something is near. This is important. Follow me. Lock the trucks."

Victor nudged Alix. "What's going on?"

Alix shrugged, grabbed his SCAR assault rifle.

"Permission to speak, sir?" Victor stepped forward.

"No." Jack listened to the air.

"This fucking asshole." Victor turned to the tuck. "I am staying with the trucks."

"Me too." Wes agreed.

Captain looked back. "Permission granted. The rest of you come with me."

The armed group approached what looked like a huge shiny square bench at first. Jack marched forward. He touched the top of the bench and knelt.

Alix searched the rooftops, each corner. If he were there and hunting, this would be a slaughter. "Sir, it's pretty open here."

"Alix. Stop. Come here, team. I want you all to lift your masks and goggles and see this with your own eyes."

Alix stepped forward. He stopped searching all around him and focused on what was in front of him. They all aligned on the edge of what they realized was a perfect giant square, like a cookie cutter just took a section of the world away. One by one, they lifted their masks, coughing at the smell and congested air. Phil gagged and spit out what choked up in this throat.

"Team, I had to stop. I didn't even think this was here still, to be honest with you. I was born on that day. That day that nearly three thousand Americans lost their lives. They lost their lives…right here. And here I came into the world, clueless to the evil. And the horror. I never enjoyed my birthday like other boys and girls did once I became old enough to know and realize. I should have been able to, but the more I learned about it, the more I hated the day. I watched the footage, monster planes hijacked and flown into the Twin Towers nearly that height." Jack pointed to the Freedom Tower, the top still sank in the clouds in the heavens above. Jack looked to each one of them staring down at the names engraved in the stone, their guns sagged.

"So on my eighteenth birthday, I enlisted in the United States Marine Corps. I decided to fight for my country." Jack's voice cracked. "For my freedom. I picked up a gun and fought for what I thought was right like my fathers and their fathers before that. I choose my destiny. Just like you boys did this morning." Jack turned his back to the monument and faced his team.

They slowly nodded their heads. Lips pursed, eyes fierce.

"This morning you all, despite the power of your government down there, despite the technological mind fuck they have you in, despite what you've been told by me and your peers your whole lives, which I'm sorry for, you guys and girl stood up for what was right. What you believed in. You heard of a fellow comrade in trouble, and you all left no man behind. You all sacrificed your own lives for another teammate. You are not all just a blank slate for MAIA to fucking toss around on a map at its disposal. You are stronger than that…right?"

"Oorah."

"Oorah is right. You're smarter than that, right?" Jack's voice began to shake.

"Oorah."

"I want you to know, boys, I've been in war for a long time. I've met a lot of brave men and women. Men and women who fought for freedom and hope. You guys fought as hard as anyone I ever seen in my life. I've did two tours overseas, one in Iran and one in Ukraine. I've fought a ferocious tyrant and his army. I've seen evil, but none as dangerous as you guys had to fight and will continue to fight.

"I want you all to look down at this monument. I want you to find one name. Find just one name on this wall in front of you that reaches out to you."

Their heads all pointed down along the wall, their eyes searching for the one.

"I want you focus on this name, this name that came and gone long before you were even thought up. I want you to take a look at the little space it takes on this wall…Then take a look at the slab it's carved in and how many names is on that slab...Then think." Jack stepped up onto the wall and pointed to the other side. "This wall, with all those names of those who died here on that day, goes all the way around to there...Look at 'em all. Take that in. Think of that number."

A tear formed in Anna's eye.

Matt's eyes watered.

Alix's jaw tightened.

Brian sniffled.

Aaron's lip quivered.

Wes approached. Wes put his arm around Leo's shoulder. Each person leaned in, smiled, and put their hand on the shoulders of the man next to them.

Jack jumped down from the monument. "I want you to imagine all those names wrapped around that hole. Those names are not soldiers, they were not fighting for their country." Jack's eyes rained. His face didn't falter, but his eyes cleared trails down his cheeks, into the crevasse of his nose. "Most of those people were at work! Living regular lives. Innocent. Civilians! Hundreds and thousands of people all around this pool that didn't deserve to burn to death, get crushed to death—some of them jumping to their death!" Jack wiped his eyes, his lip quivered remembering the footage of the buildings collapsing. And then think...this is just half the monument." Jack pointed to the North Pool.

All of their eyes followed his finger. Their stomachs twisted.

"There is an exact replica of this with more names. More people."

Anna balled. Alix put his hand on her back. She stood smearing her eyes. "I'm sorry. I don't mean to be such a girl." She gasped for air, smiled for a second, and her face dropped again.

Alix kissed her cheek and tossed an arm around her shoulder.

"Don't apologize. I'm crying for fuck's sake." Jack wiped his eyes and stared into their souls. "Team, remember this feeling when you need something to fight for, to live for." Jack sniffled. "To die for. What you've been taught your whole life...throw it away. What you've learned and how you've grown in the last twenty-four hours... that is life. That is real. That is human of you.

"I want you to do something for me. Find that name on the wall. I want you to say it out loud. I want you to promise this person that you will remain a human and uphold your dignity. You will not leave yourself subject to a program, and you will do the right thing."

The air died. Their hearts bled for the first time in their lives. Their world flipped upside down. Suddenly, it rained upward, the earth became the center of the universe and a flat surface. Suddenly they could fly; they could move things with their minds. Physics became a myth, facts became lies, lies became truths, truth ran and hid, because nothing remained certain aside from uncertainty. Suddenly, life became life and not a MAIA game and mission.

Alix stepped forward. He placed his hand on the monument, "Felicia Hamilton." His tear fell next to the name and dissolved into the stone. He felt the heat from the stone, like the warmth of holding someone's hands.

Anna appeared next to him, smiled into his eyes, grabbed his other hand, tangled their fingers, and placed her hand on the monument. "Anthony Mark Ventura."

Phil's voice thundered. "David Fodor."

"Sherry Ann Bordeaux." Matt smiled.

"Edelmiro Abad." Leo clenched his jaw.

"Thomas Tong." Hayden placed the butt of his gun on the ground.

"John Patrick Hart." Wes's voice cracked.

"Jie Yao Justin Zhao." Adam stared into the waterfall.

"Anna A. Laverty." Brian sniffled.

"Joyce Rose Cummings," Aaron whispered.

Jack cleared his throat. "I'm proud of you all. I've been fighting in a war for these people for as long as I can remember. But right now, I am not going to call out a name on that wall. I am fighting for your bravery today and from this day forth. I'm fighting because you guys have found the human spirit." Jack wiped away the last of his tears. "Now get in the trucks."

Jack watched them all trudge back to the trucks. An alarm sounded in his ear. Radar picked something up. A lot of something.

22

"Good morning all! It's great to be back. I missed you all." Maia smiled bright as she appeared on the monitor everywhere in the facility, her voice echoing throughout.

Gunther stood geared up before the loading dock. Their truck awaited them. He looked over to Eli. "You okay, buddy?"

Eli's head snapped sideways. "Fine." His eyes widened. "You okay...buddy?"

"Yeah, I'm fine." Gunther could barely hear the transmission over Todd and Billy.

"Wasn't her hair color different last time!"

"Yeah, Maia and I had dinner last night in simulation. Told her I preferred her to be a brunette."

"Fuck you, dude. There is no way Maia meets with people in simulation. She's a fucking supercomputer hottie. She controls this shit. She doesn't need you."

"Not only did we meet up for dinner, she rode me all night. Maia needs lovin' too, yeah-eah-eah." Billy shook his hips round. "Right after our other simulation, I hopped into that one. Why do you think I'm so tired. Maia is *crazy*!"

The four laughed.

"Shut up. Both of you." Gunther didn't look away from the screen.

Maia held her hologram tablet in her hand. "I know we had a recent temporary disturbance, but MAIA officials handled it flawlessly. I am happy to report that the leader of the rebellion, Captain Robert Milligan, has been killed. The rest of the team has been apprehended and is being held within the facility." Footage of Squad 28 along with others sitting in glass-enclosed cells played on the monitor. Alix Basil banged on the glass mouthing to let him out or he will blow the whole facility down. The rest of the bunch sat, run down and bloody beaten soldiers, captured and awaiting certain death. Maia stared into the monitor. "I assure you, this will never happen again. They didn't manage to kill anyone, just minor injuries. And I am glad to report that Anna Brooks, their hostage, will return safely back to work after some emotional stress evaluation." Footage of Anna talking to a white-coated female smiling and then waving to the camera rolled on the screen.

A man popped up on the screen. "They were so sloppy when they entered our floor. I figured by the clumsiness of the team, with no training, even I could take them on!" He held his arm out from a hospital bed. "I charged at them full force. The captain, Ron, or whatever his name was, ordered their best shooter, Alix Basil, to shoot me in the head. He missed! Can you believe it! From ten meters, he shot my legs on accident." The camera zoomed out to see his wrapped legs. "That boy couldn't hit the side of a barn, I tell ya. What a sloppy bunch. No wonder they messed up their simulation, only scoring on 23.8 on their final."

A woman appeared on the screen. "I saw the whole thing, Scotty here was my hero. He charged the whole group before MAIA forces showed up and outwitted the group. I really hope for the MAIA's sake, we put them away for a long time. Death and an eternity sounds good." She smiled big and hugged Scott. "And we're even getting conjoined tomorrow! Yeah!"

"I have great news for you, young cadets." Maia smiled. "We have decided to push the conservation up weeks from intended plans. There is a large contingent of enemy forces coming into the city. I have done some analysis and decided it best to engage them sooner than originally anticipated. I have a scan of the island, and it appears as though the actual population of the island had been reduced to just a couple of thousand civilians, and with the citizens fast approaching, our time is now to engage. Please stand by for further instructions from your commanders. And remember, cadets, train hard.

Austin slapped Billy on the back. "I don't really understand anymore. Who are we fighting? And can you believe how pathetic this squad is? Alix has to be the worst shot in the history of MAIA."

Gunther grunted and turned from the screen. "We're fighting everyone. I've heard our 'main' enemy change in the last ten years at least eight times. Don't you fucking pay attention? Then everyone wakes up the next day, and all they are talking about is the new enemy and everyone forgets about the old one, and we haven't even started fighting yet. Let's move." Gunther slung his pack into the large bed of the cargo truck. "And you actually believe Alix missed that shot?"

"Gunther." Billy tossed his bag on the truck. "You are not doubting the broadcasts, are you? Didn't you just see that?"

Gunther held out his arms. "Did you not just see the footage of Squad 28 in holding?"

"Well, yeah."

"Then who the fuck are we going to apprehend?"

Billy held both arms open. "Well, I get why Maia has to make it look like to most people that they are safe from Squad 28."

"And don't be so naive. Alix killed my brother in less than two minutes of setting up from five hundred meters from a rocking boat. I still don't know where he was hiding. I promise you, put him and his rifle within a mile of your asses. You are all fucked."

"He's right." Eli looked at them. All sounds stopped aside from the engine and the tires driving them to the launch. "They say he is the deadliest person in the world with a rifle from his simulations."

"So how'd we get stuck with you then?" Todd laughed.

Gunther leaned forward. "In simulation." Gunther looked at all four of them as the cargo truck lurched forward. "Are you guys that fucking ignorant?"

Todd stood up. "Listen. I've had enough of your shit—"

Eli shoved him back down, grabbed his sleeve, spun him around, pulled a knife, pinned his sleeves together, and stabbed the bench to hold him there. Billy stood. Eli kicked his shin downwards and moved as Billy fell to his stomach. Eli reached over, grabbed Austin, spun him around, held a knife to this throat, and kicked Chris in the chest before he could fully stand. Chris rolled back, and the momentum of the truck rolled him head over heels, slamming him into the very back of the cargo truck and ramming his head off the tailgate.

Gunther leaned back. "Well then. Enough said. Why don't we all just get along here, huh, boys?"

Todd jerked his sleeves free from the bench and rubbed his wrists.

* * *

"Team! Spread out!" Jack swung his ACR around, pushed the safety off, and slammed behind a raised stone square that housed a small dead tree. Jack looked at his EED. Red dots appeared all around them like an instant rash on their radar.

One shot burst out from the distance, and the mason map fell to the ground and smashed into pieces in front of Jack.

"Bravo, hunkered down, north end entrance."

"Delta, south end entrance. Anyone have a visual!"

"Negative! No visual. Echo, at the trucks watching west side opening."

"Fuck, fuck, fuck!" Jack slammed his fist on the ground. Figures I get us surrounded in the first day. "Jack looked up. Where did these guys come from? They appeared out of nowhere." Jack peaked up. He watched Bravo go around a corner of a building, one of them hunched down and pointing his gun at the opening.

"Echo here, I got movement."

Jack's breaths sped up. "Just hold your fire until you confirmed they are armed. Maybe they will just pass." Jack checked his EED. No radar.

"Delta to Echo, they shot down the mason map. They are prepared to fight. Please advise."

Jack peeked to the south side of the opening of the quad. "Fucking broad daylight. Great idea, Jack. Arg fuck! Everyone hold your position and hold fire."

Silence.

A ray of sunlight burst through the clouds and held aim on tree in the corner of the quad. Everyone watched the first ray of light in ten years shone down on a tree. Two leaves swayed in a small breeze, and the shadow cast on the wall behind it twisted and waved like water unnaturally, like a glitch in the system or something. Camo curtains. Shit. He squeezed his eyes shut. "Team, lock and load, keep an eye on the buildings. We are completely surrounded."

"Bravo to Charlie," Wes talked directly to Jack. "We saw that right before we realized we were fucked. Now we're stuck in this quad."

"This is Echo, team, remember your training. We've been pinned down before. Let's cover each other until we can get in the trucks. Keep the windows up and use the shooting holes and vents. Delta, I'll cover you one by one. Send one to the trucks. Three, two, one, move!" Alix aimed his SCAR from his knee towards the opening. Leo turned and ran toward Alix, Anna, and Victor. "Okay, one more. Three, two, one, move."

Halfway from where they were pinned from the south side entrance of the quad to where the trucks were parked. A shot rang out. Matt fell to the ground. "Oh fuck, oh fuck, oh fuck. Am I hit? What's going on?" Matt scrambled to his feet and ran the rest of the way. "Am I hit? Am I hit? Anna, am I?"

Anna grabbed his shoulders and shook him. "Relax. I don't think so." Anna searched him and patted him down. "Alix, what the fuck was that?"

A loud squeal adjusted up and down. "Alix Basil. You down there?" The sound came seemingly from the heavens.

Jack lifted his head to the heavens and tried to see where it came from. He checked the rooftops on the east side.

"Alix Basil and Squad 28, do you copy?"

Jack whispered. "Charlie to Echo, do not respond." Jack thought. It sounded like a megaphone. He peeked over the edge again and raised his rifle.

"We have you completely surrounded. We have each one of you in our sights. If you are not Alix Basil and Squad 28, you will all be killed in ten seconds. This does not exclude Anna Brooks…One… two…three…"

"Stop!"

23

Gunther sat on a bench on the boat in full battle gear. He watched a ray of light break through the sky and shoot down for a moment in the distance. The boat's engine roared as hard as it could tear through the water toward where it looked like their targets might have landed. The North Cove Yacht Harbor is the closest point to where the stolen Humvees and their targets should be. He looked at the Freedom Tower. He hadn't seen it in years, but he figured it to be the smartest place to go.

"You traveling a little heavy, aren't you old man?" Austin pulled his gloves on and stacked his gun on the Humvee, the wind from the harbor in his hair.

"Yeah, you could say that." Gunther shoved another sack of rations in his bag.

"We have the truck, you know."

"Yeah, I see that." Gunther stuffed more ammo. "Eli, stuff you bag with those over there. Take as much as you will need, but I want you to carry some additional ammo."

"What's going on, Gunther?" Austin screamed over the engine and the sound of sea; a splash came up over the front of the boat and sprinkled all of them in small cool drops.

Gunther smirked. "Nothing is wrong with me. Just can't wait to bag this target and get back to use my rations for strip clubs and cocaine. I want to learn why they call a particular stripper Pussycat and go to the ATM. Whatever that is." Gunther looked at Billy.

"Gunther." Todd sat next to him. "I don't know what you saw or heard, but that was just having a little fun before we left. No harm, no foul?" Todd held out his hand.

Gunther placed two different scopes in the bag and glanced Todd's hand. "Look, guys, no offense, but when we land, I'm working alone. Eli, you can spot for me if you want. I wouldn't mind the company, but I don't want to work with these knuckleheads." He looked to Eli.

Todd lowered his empty hand.

"Whatever, old man." Austin stood. "Take what you can carry then, and fuck off when we land. Don't radio in help to us when you're surrounded because we will be too busy carrying Anna Brooks over our shoulder back to MAIA."

"Understood, boys." Gunther slung his rifle over his shoulder and holstered his pistol. "I won't radio in for your help."

"You're not going to take an assault rifle at least?" Chris squinted, his nose swollen from the roll down the length of the truck. "Just your rifle and a pistol?"

"And two scopes. I'll be able to pick your teeth for you a mile out. Don't worry about me, boys. Unlike you cowboys, this is not my first rodeo. I survived the first wave. Stuck myself in a church tower for two weeks picking off enemies throughout the day, eating mice just barely cooked. I had three hundred kills before I came to MAIA. That's the only reason they let me in."

Billy laughed. "He doesn't know what an ATM is."

Chris smiled and chuckled.

Gunther shook his head.

"Eli? You going with this old fart to eat raw rats, or you going to be with a winning team?" Billy smirked and adjusted the sights on this gun and clicked in a mag. Water splashed the side of the barge.

"I'm his spotter. I'll be going with Gunther." Eli's face didn't change.

"That's fine, while you guys are between sucking each other off, ask him about the last time he had a job to do and someone trusted him. See if that changes your perception of him." Billy winked at Eli.

Gunther stood and pulled his pistol on Billy, pushed it into his nose. "You son of a bitch. I'll blow your fucking head off right now."

Austin, Chris, and Todd pulled their M4s into their armpit. Chris aimed at Eli.

"I call bullshit!" Billy straightened his back. "When a man says he's going to blow your head off, instead of actually blowing your head off, you know they already have decided not to pull the trigger. Don't play with fire, old man." Billy placed two fingers on the side of the barrel and pushed his pistol away slowly. "You're going to get burned. I don't think it needs to get this far. Let's just go our separate ways when we land. That's good enough. Oorah?"

"Oorah." Gunther didn't break eye contact as he lowered his pistol and holstered it.

* * *

"Alright. What do you want?" Alix removed his mask and walked out in the open arms out. "What do you want? We're right here." Alix braced himself for a shot in the chest.

"Alix!" Anna searched for a target around the rooftops, her rifle frantically searching for a target.

"Squad 28, lower your weapons!" said the voice from the heavens.

"Echo to team, lower your weapons."

Wes's voice radioed in. "Jack, you don't even sound convinced that's the right thing to do. Fuck that. You're out of your mind right now."

The swishing sound of tarps slipping surrounded the quad. The road and world washed away, and the same view became visible, but now a wall of assault rifle–wielding soldiers pointing their guns at them. The whole length of the west side opening wrinkled downward, and an army appeared. The tops of the roofs melted away, and rows of snipers and assault rifles stood in an exact replica of what was there before minus the attack force. The south side did the same. Soldiers leaked out of the first floor of the Freedom Tower and emptied into the square. All around Alix, he became the center of a whirling army around them.

Jack stood up, his body convulsing. He approached Alix. "Camo curtains...Mother fuckers."

"Wh-wait what?" Alix looked at Jack, eyebrows narrow.

"Camo curtains. They could have been following us the whole time. They project whatever is on the other side from any angle minus what you want. I should have known when I saw the sunlight. They don't work well in sun. Team, we're surrounded, please play nice until we think otherwise." Jack raised his hands in surrender. "Who's in charge here!"

Silence.

"Who's in charge here!"

"I am." A tall man appeared from the Freedom Tower, dark skinned, clean shaven, pressed military coat, hat straight and narrow, megaphone in hand behind his back, eyes behind aviators. He approached Alix and Jack Silva. Each step his shiny shoes clicked on the concrete.

Anna's eyes traced the long outline of soldiers surrounding them completely in the square. She gulped.

The man held out his hand. "You must be Alix Basil."

Alix shook his hand, a tough grip. "I am. And with whom do we have the pleasure speaking with? We are little freaked out right now, I think you owe us that."

"First Sergeant Jaxon Andrews, United States Marine Corps. No time for chit chat. I've heard about your skills. You and your men will be reporting to me now." He pointed at Jack and Alix and then to his chest and walked away toward the Humvees. "You two have stirred up quite a bees nest with that flare. Let's get going. There is a lot to explain."

"W-wait." Jack instinctively stepped forward. "Who says we are reporting to you? We don't report to anyone."

Alix shrugged and followed.

Anna smirked.

Jaxon didn't look back as he talked, but his voice hit you straight in the face from no matter where you were. "The thousands of enemy forces settling twenty-five clicks north from here whom you've triggered by driving your little trucks around in broad daylight say that you are now under my command. That little flare you set off yesterday evening didn't help either."

Victor held his gun up and tightened his grip as the three approached.

Jaxon pointed at Victor. "Son, you're going to hurt yourself with that thing if you don't put it down. Point that at me again, and we are going to have problems starting with an extra orifice appearing in your forehead. Captain, where are your manners? Don't you teach these boys anything on that forsaken island? Private"—Jaxon pointed to Matt—"get me water."

Matt reached in the back to grab water.

Victor leaned over. "What are you doing?"

"He said he wants water."

"Are you kidding me?"

Matt shrugged. "I don't know. Should I give it to him?"

"You're fucking out of your mind." Victor aimed his gun over the hood.

Jack Silva walked faster towards Jaxon. "Where are you taking us, I'm not just going to follow you. I don't know you, and I'm not reporting to you."

Jaxon didn't turn and kept walking toward the hummers. "Captain, you talk too much, and you name is too close to mine. You will be referred to as Silva for now on. Understood?"

"I'm not just surrendering these guys to you. Do you have any idea what we've been through in the last couple of days?"

Jaxon turned around, shot the megaphone up to his lips, and screamed in Jack's face. "We are going to war. Captain, do you have an army?"

Jack knocked the megaphone out of his face. "No! I have a—"

Jaxon brought the megaphone back to his lips and back to Jack's face. "I do. And my army says get the fuck in your truck and follow me." Jaxon lowered the megaphone. "I will explain later." He turned his back and pointed to groups of his men and radioed in to the rest. Camo curtains went up and over them. A whole army disappeared in twelve seconds. All except the small contingent in front of the Humvees.

Jaxon opened the door to the front Humvee, pulled his pistol out, and shot several times in to the GPS monitor.

Jack Silva's eyes blinked each shot. Silva rushed him. "What the fuck are you doing to our trucks!"

Jaxon's eyes pierced Silva. "Tell your men to shoot out the computers on the trucks. That's an order. They have trackers, you dipshit. There's been a team sent out to capture you. *Now*, they actually don't know exactly where you are. You're welcome. Private, that water please."

Matt tossed him the bottle of water.

Jaxon twisted the bottle cap off, tossed it to the ground, and walked away chugging. He got into a Humvee in the north opening. "Follow us. Let's go."

Silva shrank. He forgot the trackers.

Alix and Silva approached the crew huddled around H2.

"What are we going to do?" Wes approached them first. "You guys just got your asses handed to you out there."

"What can we do? They didn't check our weapons. They didn't attack." Silva rubbed his head. "Fuck!" He kicked the tire. "I forgot about the trackers. Team, please shoot out the screens in the Humvees. If he's serious about the enemy forming twenty-five clicks north, we will need them anyway. Oorah?"

"Oorah." Silva heard seven responses.

"Captain!" Jaxon screamed over to Silva. "You're riding with me. Let's go. Have your boys follow."

Victor slammed the door. "Escape one prison to jump into another. I say we bolt." He hopped in the Humvee with Aaron, Leo, and Brian.

"You think that's a good idea?" Anna clicked the safety on her assault rifle.

Alix got into the truck. "I don't know how I feel about this one. He says they are US Marine Corps. I thought the US fell apart?"

Wes stared out the window, leaning on his elbow attached to the armrest on the door. "Fucking stupid. I knew we shouldn't have stopped." He pulled his sidearm and pointed at the GPS screen. He pulled the trigger. "Well, what choice do we have now, right?"

A horn blared from behind the convoy. An additional truck from the marines would push them along.

* * *

"Where did they go?" Austin scanned the quad. There's no one here.

"They can't just disappear." Billy shoved his eyes into binoculars. He switched it to infrared. "I got nothing. Todd, radio to nest, tell them the Humvees are gone, and there is no sign of them."

"They can't be far. They were just right here not even half hour ago." Todd scanned the north opening using the crosshairs on the scope of his gun.

Gunther closed his eyes. He listened. The sound of a tarp swishing in the wind. He opened his eyes and looked around: the murky sky, the low wind, the destruction—so many things to confuse the eye. Is it possible? Camo curtains were just being introduced when he entered MAIA for his and his brother's 'talents.' Gunther scanned the area again. No seams, no indication. He pictured one of these idiots walking into one and being suffocated to death.

"Okay, boys. Good luck." Gunther hiked up his bag and began creeping to the Freedom Tower, rifle in hand and hunched over.

"You sure you want to split up, Gunther." Billy's voice shook. "Maybe we could set aside our differences and work as a team, you know?"

Gunther turned around and whispered loud enough for them to hear. "Billy, if I didn't know you, and I were within a mile from here, you wouldn't have a mouth left to give away our position. Remember your training, boys. And shh!" Gunther held his finger to his lips. "Hopefully I see you guys again. Good luck."

"Eli, where do you stand?" Chris turned around to nothing. "Where did Eli go?"

"We lost Eli!"

"Damn, that bastard is quick. He was just right here. Let's clear the first floor of this building. If we can get some altitude, maybe we can get a location on the Humvees. If they get too far north, we can take the boat north or unload the truck—the truck!"

The four soldiers hauled ass across the street, each pointing a gun in all four corners of the compass. They stopped at the edge of the barge. "Fuck! Fuck! Fuuck! He took it! He took the boat and the truck."

Chris squeezed his gun. "If I ever see Eli again, I swear I'm going—"

"Save it, Chris." Todd watched the trail of water from their boat that just drift off into the harbor. "He kicked all of our asses in two seconds. I don't know what they did to the boy, but his training is something fierce. He would drop you." Todd sighed. "We are just going to have to make do. There is four of us. Let's head north. The last time the Humvees were tracked was over there across the quad. They were heading north the whole time. They have to be heading north still. Let's see what north brings us. We have enough supplies and ammo to last a while. We can radio nest for delivery. I'm sure Rankin will deliver."

"You're going to tell Rankin our sniper ditched us and Eli stole our boat? And our truck?" Billy smiled. "Oh man, we are having a bad week."

They all laughed.

Austin held his stomach. "Alright, let's get the fuck out of here. Oh my gosh. Fucking hilarious right now. What are we even doing?"

* * *

The convoy smashed through debris, skidded around corners, and trampled over ruble, the sound of the shocks stretching and the truck slamming down. Silva squeezed the "oh shit" handle in the passenger seat, his helmet hit the glass every sharp left they veered.

Jaxon swung the wheel to the left. The Humvee skidded and slid on crumbs of buildings, tail end whipping out around the corner. "You need answers. That's why you're up here with me. I'm going to give you some. I need you to get your team on board with me and quick."

"Okay, but I want to warn ya." Silva's body was subjected to strong inertia to the right. He held on. "These boys got some badass attitudes, and their captain died last night in front of them all while trying to protect them."

Jaxon slung the wheel to the right, weaving the six trucks through the streets. The tires screeched. "Listen, just because their captain caught a bullet, doesn't mean they go AWOL, okay? Get control of your crew. You're just as clueless as those fuckers are, buddy. I don't know what they are telling you, but the point of Governor's Island was for MAIA, *a private company*"—Jaxon held his finger and eyed Jack—"not a nation, was to supply us with soldiers. We've laid low for a while. It's been three years since we've seen any serious fighting. We've been hiding underground and taking full advantage of the camo curtains, lining them up from rooftop to rooftop of our facility. The enemy has control of at least every major city north of DC. We've been waiting for your first deployment for weeks now, meaning MAIA, not *your* deployment specifically, but we'll take anything we can get. We were told you would be joining us any day now." Jaxon swerved left, swiped a charcoal car, and smashed through a bus stop.

"From what I'm hearing, the computer is starting to fuck everything up. I've been reporting to Reader Elmer Washington for the last ten years. He's told me that he has some complications to deal with, but the army that you guys have been building for the last eighteen years would be our backup in the weeks to follow. Said something in the ten thousand range. Impressive. Especially if these boys are half as good as he claims them to be. We were excited until Elmer told me that he had some complications. Now, Silva, I don't know about you." Jaxon busted through a run-down old tipped-over hot dog cart. It skidded and slid thirty feet, sparks flying everywhere. "But when a politician says there are complications, that means one of a couple things all leading to you're fucked. You never want a politician or your doctor saying there is going to be complication. Or your lover, but we'll stay on task.

"We have a sizable army down here. For there being nine million people in the city when it fell, we've been able to snag all the healthies between the ages of sixteen to forty and have an army of, oh I don't know, ten thousand marines and about five thousand militia. Can't even believe I'm saying that word, *militia*. Ugh. They call themselves the Minutemen. Cliché. Some sand nigger Indian kid named Kalev Delhi keeps those animals at bay. Thinks because his father was a NYPD war hero during the attack, he can just form an army. But they like 'em and he keeps the citis off our back while we form this rebellion, so I don't give a fuck who keeps them in line."

"Where are all the people?" Silva's arm hung from the door handle.

Jaxon leaned forward and checked out the rooftops around them. "They hide during the day mostly. Some cooped up in buildings, some underground, but not too many people come out in the day. Too risky. Could get seized by Piruz, the sand-sucking Saudi that polices this region for the enemy. They do laps around the city and basically kill anyone on sight for made-up rules and laws they make up on the spot. You're picking trash between the hours of six and seven, bang! There are a few snipers too. We don't know where, but they keep picking citis off on the southern tip of Manhattan.

"We could really use that Alix kid if he is half as good as good ole Elmer makes him out to be. I just feel like our backup just became another enemy. So we've been panicking to try and get a plan together. Then all of a sudden, map lights up red, and thousands of mercenaries are knocking at our city door."

"You have an Indian leading an American militia called the Minutemen, and you've been fighting mercenaries? Are they Saudi, Iranian, or Russian?" Jack squinted.

"Sore subject with the Minutemen, but yeah, fighting mercenaries, you know, paid soldiers."

"I know what a mercenary is."

"You think that Russia and Iran invaded us with their own army? Are you kidding me? No. China funded the movement. Those fuckers were on both sides of this shit. Hold on." Jaxon slowed the truck down and drove up and crawled over a car frame. The Humvee bounced on all fours and almost tipped. "Whoa! Hopefully your guys have the balls to do that one."

Jack looked back as H1 climbed over the large debris.

"So yeah, who hates us besides everybody?" Jaxon counted them off. "Russians for one, who can blame them? After the cold war every movie and videogame out after the 60s had a Russian terrorist in it. Everyone forgot they have some of the most beautiful girls in the world next to Sweden, and all we did is shit on 'em with American media. Secondly, North Korea, because oh yeah, everyone forgets we went to fucking war with them. Thirdly, Iranians, oh why you ask?" Jaxon looked to Silva after blowing a stop sign and accelerating through. "Jack, you nervous or something? There is no one else on the road, see?" Jaxon smashed through the front end of an old parked car. "Jeez bud, fucking pay attention will ya, I'm trying to give you some information you asked me about. I already know this shit."

"Okay, sorry. Just been a while since I've been in a vehicle." Silva buckled his seatbelt.

"Okay, you want the full scoop or not?"

"Yeah, yeah, the Iranians."

"Right, well the Iranians have been pissed off since we kicked them fuck out of the Holy Land and told them to go suck sand after World War II. Everything was peachy until they started to make more money off us than they knew what to do with. We were sucking oil through our noses in our sleep. Oil was the crack of the world, and USA was hooked. We ran ourselves dry, and the only other thing we had aside from a larger debt anyone has ever seen or heard of in history was the largest army.

"So what they do? They were so filthy rich off oil sales, they bought their own army. There were enough poor fuckers out there who hated us and for a small fee and two years of training, they turned them loose on us. China took our own money when we made payments to them and used that same cash to fund this mercenary army of mixed races and hatreds. That army needed shit too. Like tanks and planes and such. Who did they buy them off of? China of course. China was robbing Peter and Paul, and those suckers paid China to replace the stolen goods! China was like the thief and the insurance company. So we get royally attacked, and where is the rest of the world?"

"I don't know." Silva squeezed the handle tighter as they slid into a tunnel.

"Me either. We policed the world for nearly a hundred years, and when we get attacked, where the fuck is UK? Where are the French? They hated us that bad? We've been fighting these fuckers forever while you've been safely cooped up playing with your damn computers. You have no idea how angry I am. Where they fuck are they going?"

Silva stared into the shaky mirror on the side of the truck. A Humvee pulled out of line towards the back and bolted off into a side road. Silva reached for the CB radio.

Jaxon slapped his hand. "Your nuts! Why don't you just put up a huge fucking sign letting the enemy know where we are."

Silva radioed to the team through his helmet. "Team, who pulled away! Report!"

Wes's voice chimed. "Sir, H1 pulled out of line right in front of us. I tried radioing, no response. I think it's your crew, but Victor is in that truck too. He was driving. What's with your boys, Captain?"

Jaxon angled his head and peered through his rearview. "Well, you do have some AWOL motherfuckers. Pussies."

"Victor! Come in, do you read? Do you copy!" Silva screamed into his helmet mic.

Nothing.

"What road did they take?"

"That was Spruce St. I think." Jaxon looked back. "They'll be as good as dead soon anyway. The Big Apple will eat 'em up quick. We're right up here. I'll see if we can track them when we get back. Try and maintain radio contact."

Jaxon skidded to a stop. The five Humvees behind skidded. "You better hope your buddy Elmer comes through." Jaxon slammed it in park. "Otherwise we'll be fighting your lunch lady by next week. Remember that." Jaxon got out. "Oh, and Elmer said hi and called you a dipshit for forgetting the trackers. Even we could pick up the signal." Jaxon slammed the door.

Doors clanked shut as the whole team exited the truck.

Anna eyed Alix.

Alix shrugged.

"Anyone make contact with Victor, Brian, Leo, or Aaron?"

No one spoke.

"Shit!" Silva kicked an empty can of Coke. It rolled under Jaxon's boot.

Jaxon stood in the middle of the parking garage. "Welcome to Chatham Parking Garage, Squad 28." His voice echoed. "You'll find the smell a little better down here, believe it or not. Just musty. Carry only what you can. I will be showing you to your rooms. Our boys will take it from here. Follow your tour guide, yours truly, I think you will find our accommodations quite quaint if you like sewers, subway systems, and underground facilities."

"We're not just leaving our stuff." Wes looked to Silva and held out his hand. "Are you serious?"

"Boy!" Jaxon screamed and approached Wes, hands clasped behind his back. "What about 'you are under my command' don't you understand!? It's simple! It's English. Get it through that thick helmet of yours. The sooner you do, the sooner you will realize that you are home, home is good, and I am your motherfucking father!"

Bits of spit sprinkled Wes's cheek. Wes wiped it off. "Are you serious, man? Captain Milligan would."

"Captain Milligan is dead!" The echo was the only sound banging down the tunnel. "I don't mean to open your eyes for you, but this is war. Now, as good as a guy as he might have been, he ain't shit but a skin bag of bones and decaying organs now."

"Right now, you ain't shit!" Wes spit on the ground. "We are the most elite trained fighting force in the world. If Jackie over here didn't lead us into your fake fuckhole, you'd be a couple hundred men shy of the daily count, and we'd be on Route 9 with the wind in our hair."

The team stacked behind Wes, their guns hanging from their shoulders. They tightened their grip. Their training all brought the same thought to mind. This became a more manageable situation. A small tunnel, all three bulletproof vehicles to hunch behind, half the men guarding them. For all intents and purpose, they've been in worst situations through simulation.

Jaxon looked over at Silva. He laughed. "Where did you find these cock suckers? I love 'em." Jaxon shook his head. "Aw man do I love 'em, but I already hate 'em." He smiled. "Elmer was right about something. Let's see how good you guys really are, shall we?" Jaxon looked farther down the parking garage. "Hey, Stevie! Set up the gauntlet."

"What's the gauntlet?" Wes's face twisted.

"The gauntlet is going to allow you to prove how good you really are. I'm going to put you up against my best team. Let's settle this like men." Jaxon held out his hand for a shake. "Then I'll show you to your suites, and we'll get back to fighting the real war here together. Against our enemy."

Wes stared at his lingering hand. He peered over his shoulder at his team.

"Do it." Phil's voice rumbled.

"Wes, we escaped the island, we could surely get out of this place." Matt tilted his head.

Alix nudged him. Anna eyed Alix.

"Don't worry, pretty girl." Jaxon winked. "You're in there too."

Wes clasped hands. "Where's this gauntlet?"

24

Gunther peered over the imploded car. He eyed the Empire State Building back two streets and peeking over the other remaining buildings. What better place to perch than in the highest point in the middle of the city. Well, in the part that didn't blow off. He stared up at the Freedom Tower. Not too bad either.

He watched a young dirty boy through his crosshairs, looked like oil covered his body, check around himself. Farther down on Greenwich Street where, by the looks of the dangling demolished sign, a Subway Restaurant used to be. The boy's Yankee hat backwards and on a swivel, he jumped up on the bed of a rusty truck and leaned over the edge. He reached in and snagged two cans and bolted. Arms and legs wailed out of the truck, and an old man's bleary unshaved face popped up like Frankenstein.

He shook his fist at the boy. "You bastard!" His voice echoed off the buildings. "It took me a week to find that!"

Out of the shadows of the brick building and setting sun a man appeared in front of the boy, twice the size of the teen, with long black hair crawling to his shoulders from his skull, his eyes wide and peeled open. The man's hammer of an arm hung from his shoulders, socked the boy in the face, knocked his Yankee hat clear off, and into a concussion. A small girl escaped from the same shadow, took the hat and the cans, and scampered off like a mouse. The hammer followed the girl.

The boy lay still. Too still. The old man, beard first, fell over the side of the truck like muck pouring over the side of a boiling pot; pulled himself to his bare feet, stepping on his own sappy robes; and tripped over to the unconscious boy. He pounded on the boy. The boy awoke, frantic, and kicked and screamed. "Crazy old man! Stop! Stop it!" The boy tried to stand, still dizzy and bloody from the first punch. "Leave me alone!"

Gunther shook his head and screwed on his silencer to his Dragunov.

The old man lifted his bent legs and kicked the boy in the face. He mounted the boy and pulled the boy's shirt up, ripped it, and lifted his wrinkly fist to the sky and brought it down. The boy's scrawny arms, twigs, tried to hold back the boulders. Old clammy hands wrapped around the boys throat and squeezed his Adam's apple to the back of his throat. Gunther heard the choking sounds, practically smell the man's breath as his bloodshot eyes gleamed over in hatred.

The old man snapped backward off the boy like a mousetrap. The boy dropped his hands, lifted his head, looked down in horror as the old man's blood began seeping to the drain. The boy craned himself to his feet, ducked, and fell behind a mailbox. He collapsed behind an old truck and disappeared into the streets.

"Anyone ever tell you it's impolite to stare?" Gunther pulled the safety back, a shell clinked the ground.

Eli smiled. "That was either really nice of you or extremely cruel, I couldn't tell."

"The old man would probably would not find another meal and rot away. His soul is gone anyway. You should have seen the look in his eyes. The boy has guts and probably hasn't even felt a woman's warmth. I didn't want his life to end tonight."

"But the old man."

"I did him a favor. Let's go. Did you get the truck?" Gunther pushed himself to his knees.

"Yeah, I loaded it up and ditched the boat. I drove it around the corner and locked it up. I have a motion…" A steady beeping came from Eli's pocket. "Detector there. Let's go, someone is there." Eli bolted.

Gunther chugged along. "He is fast."

* * *

"Man, it smells. This place is messed up." Billy booted a jar. If flipped and tumbled into the street, rolled in a circle, and tussled a newspaper fighting gravity to take off in the wind. The four men lined the building and creeped down the edges of the street.

"Shh!" Todd turned.

Billy looked around and whispered. "This place is messed up."

"Shut the fuck up! I think I hear something." Chris stopped, held up his arm, a closed fist. "Hold. Shh. You hear that? Voices."

"You shut the fuck up!" Billy slugged Chris's shoulder.

Chris listened to the muffled screams. Someone arguing? "You hear that?"

High above them, a window shattered. The four tightened into the building. Like a porcupine, they knelt down and held their guns in every direction, their backs against the wall. Glass sprinkled the metal hood and roof of the taxi, then crashed around them like a wheelbarrow of ice dumped from the room. A lump smashed through the remains of a yellow car two strides in front of them.

Austin pointed his gun to the heavens. "What the…"

A voice boomed down on them. "You call yourself a husband! You lying, cheating piece of shit! You're lucky my brother's crew only threw you out a window! Let go of me, Jimmy! Let go of me now!"

Austin glanced up at the woman's head and wild hair and arms being sucked back in through the broken window. He looked at the sprayed, busted red taxi and over to Billy wide eyed. "Move, move, move. Let's get out here."

"Hey. Stop right there!" The voice called after them. "Boys! We got someone on our block. Let's get them!" They heard an air horn from above and behind them.

Chris began to run heel to toe, crunched down and ready. He heard the rumbling of bodies on stairs from somewhere and crashed. From the right came two men. One plowed Chris into the street; his gun skidded and tumbled to the faded double yellow line. The other charged Billy. Austin pulled the trigger twice. Blood splatter. A body collapsed. Chris pulled his knife from his thigh, took a slug to the cheek from the man who mounted him. Chris shoved the knife into the abdominal softness and twisted. Blood gushed out like cutting the bottom of a piñata. Todd drove his boot to the man's face, and in one motion, he flipped back off of Chris.

"He's down! He's down! Shit. Let's move. Let's move! Get me the fuck out of here!" Chris skidded to his feet. The stairs rumbled.

"Grenade!" Billy pulled the pin and chucked it to where the two men had originated. The four hauled ass across the street and dove through shaky, rusty scaffolding as the entrance of the building sneezed fire, wood, smoke, dust, and screams. The building shifted, and the cinder blocks cracked half way up, and like an incision revealing the stairwell to the apartment building. They stood and bolted two blocks.

"Holy shit!"

The air horn sounded.

"What's this say?" Austin looked up. "Hotel AZ. Yes please. Entering! Stack up!"

"They went over there!" Bodies poured onto the streets like bees and ran after them wildly.

Austin kicked the door. They four entered the hotel lobby flashlights; scraped the air and probed the walls.

"Clear!"

"Clear!"

"Corner clear!"

"Clear!"

Their voices bounced off the marble. "Dropping smoke." The tin canister toppled on the dull, scuffed floor. "Head down the hall towards the other exit. I'll lay down some cover fire!" Austin took a knee and faced the smoldering door and flicked on his infrared. He kept his non-shooting eye closed. He would have to run in the dark after and didn't want his eyes to not be able to adjust. He heard the roars. Twenty, thirty people maybe. The door slammed. Maybe fifty. Austin fired. Maybe one hundred. He watched bodies fall and dive through the smoke. His rifle spat. The red beings scattered at the entrance. Scattered bullets flew in and pinged around the reception desk. Sparks. "Coming, guys! Cover me! They're firing back."

Billy looked back, heard the sputtering of the rifle. The screaming bodies followed them like bellowing smoke of a dragon blowing death into the front of the building. "Stairs! Smoke down near the entrance! They'll think we left!"

Chris whipped his last smoke grenade toward the back exit. "Austin, stairs right after room one sixty! Haul ass! Silencers on, boys!"

Austin barreled around the corner, bullet sparks around his feet and the wall behind him. The chattering of a machine gun echoed. Chris stuck his head out and pointed his rifle behind Austin. A wild crowd spilled into the dark hallway. Chris held the trigger; some of them fell. A large shadow skidded into the hallway and pointed a machine gun. He pulled the trigger. Chris ducked his head back into the stairwell. Bullets whizzed by. Chris peered his eye around the corner.

Austin's head snapped back. His arm reached around holding his hamstring like he pulled it running. "Ah! Fuck, fuck, fuck." He dragged his leg. "Ah. I'm hit! I'm hit!" He fell to the ground. "Holy shit!" He blew hard out his mouth. "Guys, go!"

Wild bodies poured around the corner in the dark hallway and charged, wielding guns, clubs, sticks, pipes, knives, and a garbage can. They flooded in. Austin crawled backward, a blood trail starting to flow.

"Austin!" Chris screamed.

"Go!" Austin held the trigger as the crowd bore down on him. The front row and a few behind toppled over, and the ones behind them tripped, creating a wallowing of live and dying bodies like stone in a river disturbing the current. Austin's gun clicked moments before contact.

Chris kept half an eye around the corner and watched. Austin pulled his sidearm, looked to Chris, put the gun to his chin, and pulled the trigger. His head splashed in Chris's direction, red soaked parts of his headset and helmet skidded by him.

"Chris, let's go!"

The crowd circled Austin, kicked and punched, and slammed their tire irons down, and smashed his face down under their heels like a pack of wild zombies beating him like apes. The crowd gobbled Austin.

Chris slammed his eyes shut.

"Chris!"

They stopped on the third floor and listened to the crowed seep out into the alley. One curious citizen stopped and poked his head into the stairwell and looked up and around. He circled the stairs up one flight.

Billy rolled his eyes, leaned over the railing, and aimed at the red glowing target through his headset. The sound of a small mortar leaving the tube and a small flash of light, the body collapsed and slid down the stairs.

Todd whispered. "Let's hunker down for four hours. Let it get dark and settle down, take a couple shifts for shuteye, and we'll head out in the dead of night."

"Good, I need to take a piss." Billy's voice echoed up the stairwell.

Chris stared down at the stairs. He didn't blink. His head wavered and floated. His stomach twisted and kicked the back of his throat. Bile splattered up. The last of the crowd left the hallway, and Chris spewed onto the stairs.

"Chris! Let's go!"

He held himself up on his arms. He spat, strings of spit and puke dangling from his lips. "Shut up!" His voice echoed up the shaft. Tears left his eyes. "I'm going back for him. I'm going back for him." Chris began to crawl down the stairs on all fours. He tumbled down a flight.

"Chris! Come on!" Billy ran down and grabbed his shoulder. "Austin is dead. We would be too if he didn't do what he did. Let's go."

"No!" Chris cried. "I'm going back for him. He made it. I know he did. He made it. I know he did." His breaths were short and whimpering.

Billy looked to Todd. "Let's get him into a room."

"He's still alive! He's still alive! I know he is!" Chris's face was a tangled mess.

"Chris, you watched him kill himself."

"No. No. No!"

25

Gunther and Eli stopped around the corner around the loaded Humvee. A crow pecked at the roof. *Click, click. Click, click.* Eli poked his head around, and his body eased against the graffiti. "Stand down, it's just a bird." Eli held up his silenced rifle, reached around the corner, and shot the bird. Black feathers puffed out and settled on the truck. "I'll grab dinner for later tonight. You figure out where you want to go yet to perch."

Gunther smiled at the pun. "Yeah. I was thinking the Empire State Building looks like it is stable enough and even though the top was taken out by like a plane or something, I think we could pick anyone off in the city from there, but it's a hike. I think we might be better off in the Freedom Tower. If we didn't make it to the Empire State by nightfall, we'd be in deep shit."

Eli picked up the bird, unlocked the truck, tossed it in the back, and closed the door. "I like the plan. Freedom Tower it is."

* * *

"What the hell are these things?" Phil held the dinky gun in his hand. "They feel fake."

"They are paintball guns. They are not going to kill you when my best team demolishes you on this course." Jaxon's eyes gleamed over from above in a box protruding out of the side of the cave. He leaned over the glass railing. "They will confirm that you have been taken the fuck out to dinner, fucked in ass, and sent home crying to your artificially inseminated poor mother! She's only had to see your face once in her life, and thank god for that, but she didn't get to feel the warm steel from my pants that would have conceived your ugly asses!"

Wes nudged Matt. "What is he talking about?"

Silva stood next to Jaxon. He rolled his eyes and then glanced over the course. The Gauntlet. Concrete highway dividers spread across each starting point for the team on each side of the football-field-size course deep under the former campus that used to house the government offices of New York. Trenches dug in the dark dirt on each side wormed and intertwined throughout the course like an ant farm. At the beginning of each spot a small version of a water tower stood, a single ladder straight to a rounded railing and the sphere overlooking the field. In the middle cars, construction barrels, cones, stop signs, A frames littered the area. A single bus lay diagonally across the middle, windows busted and beaten out, supports bent and roof sagged.

"You are about to realize that the USMC is still the most sophisticated group of military personnel on the face of this planet! You are about to learn where the inspiration for your video games and you came from."

Wes pulled down his paintball mask. "Let's get this over with. I'm getting sleepy, and I really want to shut him up. Fan out, team! Anna stay with Alix, he's going to need a spotter anyway. Alix, take post, I want to hear everything. I'll take the middle. Phil and Matt, do your thing. I want you on the right flank. Hayden and Adam, I want you laying cover fire alternating from behind that corner. Oorah?"

"Oorah!"

"Oorah!" They heard the scream from the other side of the course.

They split like a puff of smoke. Hayden and Adam dashed to the left corner. Hayden quickly unlatched his backpack and began loading his second gun while Adam fired a beam of balls across the landscape. He spotted a head floating around and fired at it and twiddled his fingers to hit both triggers on the gun. "Tango, three o'clock, coming in fast."

Phil's voice boomed. "Copy that. Waiting. Waiting. Waiting." Phil twiddled his fingers; his paintballs pecked the soldier diving over a median. "Tango down."

Silva pulled his fist in quickly and spoke through his teeth. "Yesss."

Jaxon eyed him and focused back to the field. He watched Alix cover the base of the tower as Anna's slim and curvy body dashed up the ladder. "What's with this girl? Why is she fighting?"

Silva shrugged. "I don't know. It's Alix's girlfriend or something. Apparently, they've been together for sometime."

"Umph I'd like a run at that for some time." Jaxon squinted his eyes. "Lucky boy."

"Alix, you're covered. Let's go." Anna's voice chimed through Alix's body. He still couldn't believe they were physically together. It felt so different from simulation.

Alix rushed up the ladder. Two balls whizzed by his head. "Anna!"

Anna lay down on her stomach and posted, a spray of balls above her head. She showered the source of the fire like pointing a fire extinguisher to the flames. "Tango, twelve o'clock, suppressing fire."

"Roger that." Wes sprinted to the concave and slid into the highway divider. "Covering fire!"

Alix reached the top of the tower. "Echo to Bravo, sniper on the adverse tower on north end."

"Pick him off, Echo."

Alix looked up and around. There was no way his gun would reach that distance from here. "Out of range."

"You're a sniper! What's that even mean, Echo!"

"I don't exactly have a lot to work with here. I'll figure it out. Wes, three o'clock! Coming in hot." Alix watched the marine haul ass through the trenches and slide into an old busted car. His teammate posted behind him and covered his sprint.

The tip of Alix's gun pursued them. "Basic covering and maneuverability from these guys."

Wes crawled from the cover of the divider to a smashed truck. He stuck his gun between the front and a large cone and fired. "Tango down!"

"Wes! 3 o'clock!" Adam twiddled his thumbs a laid down suppressing fire long enough for Wes to duck back.

Alix pointed. "Anna, back up and stand here. Put your hands against the tower, I'm going to need a boost."

Anna looked back, pushed herself to her knees, fired a sputter to the right. "Tango three o'clock"

"Roger that."

Anna leaned to the back of the water tower, palms pressed to the gray tube, back leg straight and strong. "Okay, Alix. Go, I'm ready."

"You sure?" Alix grimaced.

"Yes! Just go!" Anna gritted her teeth.

Alix jammed his leg to the railing, hopped to her shoulders and reached for the top. His body sunk a few inches, and Anna's gasp scared him. She pushed back up, and Alix pulled himself to the top. "Anna, call it out."

Anna lay back on her stomach stretching her shoulder. "Target, one hundred meters. Sniper, bottom left of the tower. Wind, zero. Fire, shoot."

Alix tilted his gun up. Forty-five degree angle. Assuming this gun had any kick, it would be ballpark. "Testing distance, firing shot." Alix squeezed the trigger after letting out his breath.

Anna's voice enthused his body. "Test shot negative two meters X, negative two meters Y, Adam! You have an enemy to your left approaching fast from the east. Looks to have a grenade or something. Please be advised."

"Copy that!" Adam turned his stream away from the center of the field. "I'm out!"

Hayden handed him the next loaded gun. Adam fired left, and Hayden reloaded the next gun. "Suppressing fire. Hayden, take him!"

Hayden stuck around the corner of the trench. "Echo. Exact position please."

Anna's voice rang. "Fifty degrees north west of your line of sight. Right side of his body exposed about thirty percent. He's waiting for you."

"Copy that." Hayden sprang out sideways, his feet left the ground. He held the trigger, the gun sputtered and yellow paint splatters dotted the enemy like the three sides of a dice. "Tango down."

Jaxon grabbed the railing. "Fucking A. Focus, you assholes!"

Silva smirked.

Anna aimed her gun and pulled the trigger. Her paintballs whizzed over Hayden's head and smacked the marine crawling over the embankment to snag Hayden. "Tango down."

"Thanks, Anna." Hayden rolled through the dirt to where Adam kept firing.

Jaxon pursed his lips and breathed hard. He watched his sniper and spotter pour paintballs down over Wes. "Get that, little bitch."

"Alix!" Wes screamed and hung his gun over the embankment. "Some help, please!" Red paint sprinkled down on Wes and onto his facemask from the constant firing upon from above.

"Working on it." Alix aimed to the right of Wes and squeezed the trigger. "Tango down. You were about to be flanked, Phil. Watch three o'clock. Almost went home in a body bag."

The air went still. Only three enemies left. Alix adjusted his gun again and took aim at their sniper. He aimed up at a fifty degree angle to the right of the target and pulled the trigger once. The paintball spun in the air. Jaxon and Silva watched the deep arch as the Hail Mary flew the length of the field and spattered on a facemask. Touchdown. The sniper raised his hand and moved down the tower.

"Two left, boys. Let's stay quiet. I got no visual." Alix scanned the field.

Adam and Hayden charged the left flank, guns on a swivel. "Tango! Down! One more."

Phil breathed deep. He stood and poked his head out.

"Ar!" The last enemy charged Phil. Phil lit him up; paint splattered everywhere. The man still charged and bum-rushed Phil. They locked horns like two powerful bucks. Phil slid back in the dirt and pumped his legs back. The beast pulled Phil toward him to hip toss but couldn't maneuver. Phil bent his knees and dropped low, picked up the crazed marine, and slammed him down into the dirt. He raised his fist.

"Enough!" Jaxon screamed.

Another marine removed his helmet and charged. Alix picked him off in his bare head, yellow splattering on the side of his face. "Ah fuck!" He tripped and held his eyes. The rest of the marine team charged Squad 28, and a brawl in the trenches commenced.

"Hey!" Jaxon pointed to Alix. "You do that again, I'll bend your little girlfriend over the end of my bed tonight, you hear me, soldier!"

Anna turned her gun and fired. A yellow splat squirted sideways onto Silva from the paintball that crashed into Jaxon's heart. Jaxon stepped back from the blow. His eyes burst open, and his face erupted in rage. "You little bitch!"

Alix aimed. Yellow splattered from the same place.

Silva shielded himself from the spatter.

"I will kill the both of you!" Jaxon reached for his pistol, whipped it out. Two yellow balls splattered on his forehead. Alix waited for a reaction from the sights and smiled "Next one's in the fucking eyeball."

Jaxon held his head in one hand and his pistol in the other, hunched over, and breathed heavy.

Silva held Captain Milligan's revolver to Jaxon's head. Yellow sprinkle was all over Jaxon's body. "Okay, Jaxon. Let's stop this."

Marines flooded the room, rifles aimed at Squad 28 in the middle of the field. Squad 28 aimed paintball guns back.

* * *

Rankin grimaced. A tear fell onto his lap. The first in a while. His daughter, poor Anna, too young and dumb to realize she's running off with a man she doesn't even really know. So they've met in simulation a few…"Ar fuck!" Ranking smashed the lamp next to his king bed. "That fucking little prick! I will thumb tac torture the fuck out of him when they bring him back to me!" Rankin stood on his T-port and paced back and forth in the lavishly decorated room.

A thick red comforter draped over the sides of an extra king size bed, gold lining and swirling designs danced around the bed like the currents of the world, a vacant, desolate land long since Susan spent the later half of her teenage years in this room. Matching curtains perched from a fake window, painting of the outdoors and a view and all. The thick carpet massaged his feet where his T-Port didn't mash it into the ground in little tracks around the room.

Knock, knock, knock.

"What! Who the fuck allowed anyone access to this part of the facility!"

"Delivery, Mr. Rankin," said a muffled female voice, almost that of a mouse.

His T-port whined toward the door. He slid the metal door to the side, and scraping metal against old wheels. "What is it!"

The helpless woman held out the box like an offering to a king. "I'm sorry to disturb you, sir. I was told it was of great importance."

"Who's it from?"

"Doctor Harold Harrison's office, sir." She stretched out the box more.

Rankin took the box. "What's your name?"

"Tricia Lacey, sir." Her hands trembled.

"Okay, get out of here."

She scampered down the hall. Rankin looked both ways down the hall where twenty more rooms lay like hotel suites for the Readers and could be reserved for government officials, all of whom after being subjected to the contents of the box would allow Rankin free roam of this whole floor. A quick reset with Maia, and there would only be one Reader. Rankin held the box, returned to his room. He approached the monitor embedded into the wall. "Maia, please erase memory of Tricia Lacey for this day."

"Reader Rankin, sir." Maia appeared on the screen, the same form as she had on the broadcasts. "It could be detrimental to her health to just erase a day. Anyone she interacted with today—"

"Then adjust accordingly! Apply the vanishing sequence. Adjust every memory of the day too, I don't care. Just get it done!" Rankin placed the package on his night stand.

"As you wish." Maia turned from the screen.

"Maia."

"Yes, Reader Rankin."

"Play something that an old man can enjoy on the monitor, please. A few females would be great, and I want you involved. I've come to be attracted to your computer self. I want to see the rest of you." Ranking took a bite of cold baked beans and wiped his mouth.

"Reader Rankin, you realize—"

"I'm not looking to be educated Maia! Just put that hot thirty year-old looking body you portray yourself in on the screen with another attractive young lady. You know what makes me happy, Maia, now make me happy." Rankin turned down the lights.

26

Gunther scratched his stubble. He watched the thick rolling clouds steam over the glowing moon trying to push through the comforter of pollution, smoke, and dark stratocumulus. It lay up there, somewhere, the earth's younger brother, and watched his sibling yet again relapse into darkness. His whole life the earth pulled him closer and twirled him around like a child by his arms, and yet the moon during times like these, every so often, wished the world would let go of his slipping hands just to miss what happened next. Please, big brother, detox yourself it whispered through the fog.

Gunther gazed up at the giant before him. Freedom Tower. Such a dominating name and yet it stood hunched over, battered and bruised, and held its broken nose and bled debris over a thousand feet down to the crumbling street with each gust of wind. Some concrete ripped back like skin revealing the steel beams as bones could present itself as access points and vantages to Gunther.

He took a deep breath. "It will take us some time to climb. As far as I can see, we would have three points that we can rest up. If the wind gets intense, we might need to hunker down. I want to be at least half way by daybreak. We can't risk being exposed during the day."

Eli scratched his head and squinted to see the top. He couldn't. "You sure you don't want to take the stairs?"

"And risk an ambush, booby trap, or worst? No, I'm all set." Gunther pulled rope through his hands, it coiling at his feet like a cobra.

"I think we could clear it well."

"I think you're not thinking."

"I think you're fucking nuts for wanting to scale this building."

Gunther smiled. "That's why you have the squirrel suit and chute. This isn't my first rodeo, clown."

Eli sighed. "Okay, you lead old man. Send me down a line." Eli picked up his rifle and leaned against the building. "I'll cover you."

Gunther tightened his pack and rifle over his shoulder. He hoisted himself up and dug his fingers into the cracks. "Chalk your hands with some of that dust. If you bail, your best bet is to soar southwest where we came from. You can try and radio me and rendezvous somewhere, but just don't fuck around and we'll get all this up there with us. I'll get up to that first access point and throw down the line."

"Roger that."

* * *

Billy sat, leaned his back against the wall, his ass angled. It had been long since it went numb. He pushed himself up, grimaced. "Ugh." He flexed cheeks his to spread the blood.

"You alright?" Todd aimed his eye back into the dark room.

"Yeah, just my ass hurts, and this room smells like dog piss." Billy scooted his ass closer to the wall.

Todd shifted the scathed sheer curtain aside and peered back outside to the streets. "How do you know what dog piss smells like?"

Billy gathered in a stained and beaten pillow. The sounds of nuts, bolts, and shards of glass tinkled the room, and he shoved it under his ass. "I suppose I don't, but I imagine that it would smell as foul as this room." He used the butt of his gun to drag a magazine toward him, the sound of paper on the sandy floor.

Todd's head snapped in Billy's direction. "Shh. Will you be quiet?" Todd's eyes crossed over to Chris, face down on the battered pink mattress on the floor that springs and gushed padding out the side.

Billy flipped the magazine open, the sound of pages turning. "I can't really see what's on these pages, but I'm going to imagine it's sexy."

Todd rolled his eyes.

"You know, Todd, I think we should check Chris's pulse. I think the smell is coming from that mattress, and if he's face down on it, it could potentially kill him."

"Will you shut the fuck up. We lost Austin, Chris is a mental patient, and you're babbling like an idiot."

Billy tossed the magazine to the side. It slapped the linoleum. "Sorry, I'm bored and it's the only way I know how to deal with this shit." Billy crossed his ankles.

"You think we should just go back?" Todd looked back in.

"Without that girl? No fucking way. We'd be better just abandoning ship all together." Billy shifted his legs and cracked his neck. He stopped. "What was that?"

"What?"

"You hear that?"

"No. What?" Todd swung his legs around off the heater under the window and grabbed his gun. "What do you hear?"

"Shh." Billy grabbed his gun. "Oh shit!"

The door popped open and coughed a concussion grenade out. It bounced in like the words of a sing-a-long song and exploded just as Chris lifted his head and dreary eyes. The room flashed like lightning, tinnitus as thunder and the world disappeared.

"Gentlemen. I have a problem." Jaxon leaned back in an old recliner, scratches on the corner of the chair by a kitten, or maybe Jaxon was just hungry. His fingertips kissed each other, and he held an imaginary eight ball in his hand. His desk was dusty and chaotic, broken pencils and crumbled papers, but it held one thing in order: a picture of a triangle of smiling dark humans, Jaxon at the peak, a bright-smiled woman to his right, and an angelic soft-faced child to his left. His eyes pierced Squad 28.

"I have a decent number of men here, well trained, ready to take back what's theirs, and are sick of hiding. I also have an enemy army forming at the tip of this island, about the same number as us. Our scouts say they have spread evenly through the northern tip and appear ready to clear this city. We are also missing a few scouts ourselves. I'd like to think that our boys have steal lips, but you never know when you're getting your fingers frayed what someone might belt out.

"My men have successfully blown up two roads and paths on the west side of the island and hopefully will funnel them into Central Park. I am about to go to war again and fight for my country and freedom. I was promised by old friends that the secret project we've been working on for the last eighteen to twenty years was complete, and I was about to get an additional ten thousand troops. Aaaand you assholes show up." Jaxon turned around in his chair. He stared at the newspaper clippings on the wall behind him. Headlines scattered on the collage: "Freedom No Longer Free," "National Debt Doubles," "China Calls to Collect," "Cell Service and Communication Collapse," "Iranian Mercenaries Invade!"

Pinned up with thumbtacks were pictures of burning buildings, smoke-filled skies, a mushroom cloud over the capital, a burning American flag, a hunched-over man scraping to get back to his feet to outrun a flock of flames, a woman on her knees, crying and looking to the bright heavens.

"Listen, ladies." Jaxon stood, walked around the desk and leaned back on the front and crossed his arms. "I needed your fellow comrades back home, but I got you. Doesn't look like they are going to make it to the party. You wiped out my best team in less than four minutes and fifty seconds. I apologize for snapping at the end, and that my friends, is the first apology that has exited this mouth since I failed this woman." Jaxon pointed at the photo. "What do you say you help me take out this contingency, and we can take back, first the city, and then our country?"

Captain Silva opened his mouth to speak.

Wes interjected. "This country you speak of is not our country. It is not our city. We have known nothing but underneath that island for nineteen years. That is our world. We were trained to fight for what statistically makes sense for the greater portion of the population. Your zealous nationalism and underdog mentality won't work on us, and honestly, I find it pathetic." Wes raised his eyebrows. "I could give two shits less if the United State of America is ever reinstated. You had your chance. The Romans had their chance. The Ottomans had their chance. Now, it appears that the Eastern world has their chance. You did this to yourselves. One thing Maia made sure we all have programmed and synced in our minds"—Wes tapped his temple—"is to never make the mistakes your former government and society did. One thing you had right was the freedom of choice. That's what we are. We are freer than you. We don't fight for anyone right now but ourselves." Wes shook his head. "That includes you."

Jaxon's eyes bolted through Wes. "Boy, I've never want to plaster my fist through someone's face so bad in my life. I think..."

Anna's hand reached for Alix's.

Alix squeezed hers.

Wes interrupted. "You're not getting it, Jaxon. We don't care what you think. Fortunately for you, our minds work off of probability and statistics. The probability of us getting off the island does increase if we are on your side of the chessboard. The mercenary group forming would probably only show us the courtesy of a challenging firefight we've craved since the age of six. However, you did show gracious hospitality and didn't serve us that glorious death in the square. For that, statistically you make sense to fight alongside with. We will have a conversation as a team and make that decision... ourselves."

Jaxon's forehead reddened. His features stiffened. "I want an answer in thirty minutes or less. Or get the fuck out of my facility and fend for yourselves. Dismissed."

Squad 28 turned to the door.

"And that was an order."

Wes scowled at Jaxon.

"Jack Silva."

Silva turned to Jaxon.

Jaxon nodded to the table in the corner of the office. "I have a bottle of rum I've been saving for a special occasion. Join me while the Bigguns make their decision on life and death."

Silva turned back into the room but watched the last one close the door tightly.

* * *

"Did you see his face!" Matt laughed and hopped up onto the picnic table. "Wes, you just put that guy in his place. Damn, he was so pissed. Let's just bail now. See ya!"

"All right, guys." Wes held out his arms. "This is realistically the first time we've been able to talk and try and figure something out ourselves," Wes spoke over everyone. "We can't fuck around. First thing is first. Alix, who the fuck is Eli?"

Alix let go of Anna's hand. He swallowed hard and looked at his men scattered around two peeling picnic tables set on the subway tracks, a floodlight acting as the sun. A couple of beers and a grill, they could be back thirty years during a simpler time. Their voices echoed. The smell wasn't bad.

Alix sighed. "This is confusing for me. I knew we had the ability to have programmed information into our chips that communicated with our EED and our brains. I knew that Maia could install information, and even though we wouldn't really 'know' something, it would still feel like déjà vu at least if we thought about it. You know what I mean?"

Phil cleared his throat. "Yeah, like I've never seen a particular gun in my life before, but I somehow knew how to use it like second nature."

Alix nodded. "Right. So apparently, something we didn't know is that she can extract information from our brains as well, or block it or something."

Their faces twisted. "Captain showed us a picture of us with this little fucker."

"I'm not messing with you." Alix scanned their faces. "So, we were training with another comrade named Eli our whole lives. I remember a conversation with him the day during the broadcast after we failed simulation while you guys were playing pool."

"How'd we fail again, Alix?" Hayden mumbled to his shoulder.

Anna frowned and pressed her lips together.

Alix pointed. "Fuck you, Hayden! Captain did that on purpose."

Hayden held his hands up. "Hey look, I got blasted in two seconds, so I have no room to talk, but I told you it was already thought up. Just do your damn job."

"Hold on." Adam held his hand up. "How was Captain Milligan fucking with you?"

Alix sat next to Anna on the top of the picnic table. "He put a digital version of Anna into simulation for me to see. She was the girl behind the gun."

"Wait what? How did he know?" Anna nudged him.

"Yeah." Alix smirked.

Side conversations at each table consumed.

"Okay!" Wes held up his hands. Everyone stopped. "Alix…who is Eli?"

"So Eli was doing what we were doing, Anna, and sneaking out and using the simulation, but he used the simulation to just see what the world used to be like. He would like set a scene at a beach or something and go swimming…I don't know, and I guess they must have caught him."

"Oh my god." Anna craned her neck forward. "I got caught that night too."

"What?" Alix turned to her.

Conversations resumed.

"Guys!" Wes leapt off the table. "I want answers, and we need to make decisions. Alix, why do you remember him and we don't? I remember you off alone during that broadcast after failing simulation. You were alone watching that broadcast. I remember it vividly."

"No, I was talking to Eli that whole time."

"You were alone, Alix." Phil agreed. Everyone nodded.

"No, I was talking to Eli. We were talking about the conservation of the mainland and he was playing with a pool stick. He was asking me if I had the choice to be conjoined with anyone of the girls, who it would be?"

"We don't have a choice in the matter." Matt objected.

"I know, but *if* we did, he wanted to know who I would want to be with."

Matt's lip lifted on one side and the same eye squinted. "But we don't have a choice."

Anna rolled her eyes. "Matt, you're impossible. Wait"—Anna turned to Alix—"who did you tell him you would want to be conjoined with?"

"Don't roll your eyes at me!" Matt pointed at Anna. "I helped get your little boyfriend out of the loony bin."

Alix pointed back at Matt. "Matt, don't point at her!"

"Well tell her to have some fucking respect. She's lucky she's even here. She doesn't need to give me shit!"

"Wait, wait, wait." Hayden held his hand up. "So you two have been sneaking out in the middle of the night, into simulation, fake, made-up worlds and battles, finding a spot and hooking up?"

Alix smirked and flushed red.

Anna tilted her head into his shoulder. "Oh my gosh."

"That's fucking awesome!" Hayden began a slow clap. No one followed. "What's it feel like?"

Anna grimaced. "Hayden, shut up. Stop being gross."

"Yeah, Hayden, not right now."

"Why didn't I think of that!"

"Wow, that's fucking brilliant."

"Aw we should have—"

Wes fired his sidearm into the dirt. Everyone jumped. The sound of the sand sprinkling the steel tracks echoed.

"Who goes there!" Flashlights on the end of assault rifles wavered down the tunnel.

"Stand down! Hold your fire! I apologize, just getting the guys attention!" Wes yelled down the tunnel to the guards.

"Hold your fire dammit, or get shot next time!" The lights diminished.

"Fuck you!" Hayden stood on the table, his pants loose and half-way down his hip, and held up two middle fingers toward the guards.

Wes turned back to his team. "So okay, apparently Maia has the ability to erase our minds and change our perception. We are missing someone that most of us don't know. Alix is getting his dick wet, and we are all jealous. Victor either went AWOL and joined a few of

Silva's team or he was captured, and we need to now decide what we want to do. Anyone hear from Victor?"

"No, I didn't even know he split. He was in the back, and we pulled in and he was gone." Phil shrugged his shoulders. "I've tried radioing that whole crew."

Wes sighed. "Phil, try radioing him again. I don't exactly know what's going on there. If anyone makes radio connection with him, please bring it to the attention of the whole team and ask him what his motives are. If we were separated, we would try and make radio contact. Silva is going to stay here. He knows we don't respect him, and the only person that could have controlled us out here is Captain. Still can't believe that he isn't with us anymore."

"Oorah."

"Oorah."

"That' right." Wes smiled. "Oorah. Exactly what the captain taught us. Let's stick it out here until after this enemy threat is gone. Then we will need to evacuate immediately. MAIA and the Readers will have a blast inside our minds if they ever catch us. Let's not forget, we are outcasts. But if we try and escape now, three armies will be trying to kill us. Let's face it: we are good, but not that good. What do we think, stick it out for now? Maybe get a little practice in?"

* * *

"AH-HAHA! You son of a bitch! You do have a voice!" Jaxon stood, a sliver of bourbon left in his glass swirling around wildly. He hoisted it. "Yeah, Silva sing it!"

Silva rubbed the alcohol abuse into the wooden table. "I don't hoooawww, someone controlled you. They bought and soo-old you…I look, at the world, and I no-tice it's turning while my guitar gently weeeeps."

"Peew near neiw neiw beeewww." Jaxon held an air guitar, closed his eyes, and shook his head slowly to the music. "And every mistake, we must surely be learning HA!" Jaxon collapsed into the chair and turned down the volume on the CD player. "You'd think we would have learned. You know what I mean, you son of a bitch?" His words like an intoxicated driver swerved back and forth.

"Ah shit. I know what you mean, Jaxon." Silva smiled and sipped his bourbon. "I can't believe how quickly it all changed. I wish we could go back. It was so simple then. Remember?"

Jaxon stared crooked into his empty glass. He lifted a wavering hand and grabbed the bottle by the throat and dumped the rest into his glass. "You know, Jack—*hiccup!*" His head bobbled. "I don't wish we could go back. We think theeeze are bad times?" Jaxon shook his head, one cocked eye staring into Silva's. "Nope. At leeest we all know it's bad. Ya see—*hiccup!*—before was far moah evil. Couples in love with cellphonez more than eech otter. Going out to dinnah, and they'd be click, click, clickin'!" Jaxon texted on an imaginary phone. "*Hiccup!* The rich getting richah off of the middle classss…while the poor became poorah—*hiccup!*" Jaxon's jaw tightened and retracted into his neck, his lips pushed together. He let out a deep smelling burp. "First! *Da banks* made a killin' resellin' what people all ready fucking owned. My parents owned their house!" Jaxon leaned on an unsteady elbow and pointed. "Owned it! And some mothafucka shows up on the doorstep wearin' a shiny tie and suckad them intah refinance. At least we don't have those snakes today." Jaxon fell back into his chair. "You might have to kill a few people for a can of beans, but"—Jaxon raspberried—"at least we don't have those fuckahs and cah salesmen."

Silva chuckled. "You're fucking nuts, you know that? You make a point. Remember when the student loans crashed after? Hey, kid, here's that education we told you, you needed. That will cost o um, half a million dollahs." Silva wrote on an imaginary pad and pushed his imaginary glasses up his nose. "O yeah and good luck getting a job in this economy after school, I have a career at McDonalds for you to pay off your thirty years of debt. O' you want a house? Here just sign your soul over because your debt-to-income ration isn't sufficient enough for me to loan you anymore fake money."

Jaxon held his stomach laughing. "Ha-ha-ha-ahah, awwhh. Oh my god! So true. So true. It's so true, you truthful bastard who never lies. Those mother fuckers didn't even make it this far. They all have to be dead."

Silva smiled. "Why's dat?"

Jaxon sipped his bourbon from the bottle, the sound of the liquid plunging to the bottom. He retracted his neck backwards, showed his teeth, and shook his head. "Because that mother fucker is the first one I take out when chaos hits and the lights go down. I'd show up at his doorstep." Jaxon pulled his pistol and pointed at a dartboard in the corner.

Silva ducked under the table. "Whoa shit."

"I'd belikeee. Do not pass *goow. Do not!* Collect two hundred doll hairs!" Jaxon pulled the trigger. The boom bounced back and forth off all walls and gobbled the music in the air and smacked their ears while the dartboard exploded.

The door cracked open. Wes kicked in the door, and Squad 28 erupted in the room and bloomed at the entrance through the music. "Stand down! Stand down!"

"Shut it, boy!" Jaxon whipped his glass at the wall. Smash. "Don't you ever knock! What if we were fucking, you rude prick! I love this song! Silva! Turn it up, boy! Imagine there's no heaven, it's easy if you try. Sing it with me!"

Squad 28 lowered their pistols.

"Jack?" Wes's face was blank with confusion.

Jack held up the empty bottle to reveal the other empty bottle behind it.

"Imagine all the peep-PULL!" Jaxon screeched. "Living for todayyy ah-ugggh." Jaxon stood and pointed at the Phil. "Imagine there's no countries. It isn't hard to doooo."

Phil holstered his pistol. "Captain, requesting permission to silence the torture that has commenced in my ear drums?"

"Deeee-nide!" Jaxon spun around. "You may say that I'm a dreamer!" Jaxon pointed at Silva.

Silva joined smiling and not breaking eye contact and mouthed every word. "But I'm not the only one." Silva shrugged.

Silva and Jaxon looked to the boys and bellowed lyrically, "I hope that someday you will join us!"

The smell of booze and body odor saturated the room. "What do you say? Will you join us?" Jaxon held out his wavering hand, only wavering because his knees couldn't lock.

Wes looked down at his hand, then slightly over his shoulder for the support of his team. Alix nodded.

"Captain Jaxon, Squad 28 will join you for this round at least." Wes clasped forearms.

"Celebration!" Jaxon spun and pointed to the ceiling. "Team, get yourself some whiskey! And learn the words quickly! To the most honest piece of human work since Da Vinci!"

"I think we'll show ourselves to our quarters and enjoy the rest of the night."

27

Maia configured. Her components circuited continuously. She rewound in her electronic mind the time from when Tricia Lacey walked into Rankin's room. Every person who set eyes on her would be added to the list. A list that would, the next day, alter the existence of the people included in it. As easy as cropping a photo, Maia recreated what people saw, heard, smelled, touched, and even thought. A woman sat at a desk while hard at work. She lifted her head and just haplessly saw Tricia walk by. She barely knew who Tricia was, but tomorrow, as far as that woman was concerned, she lifted her head and saw nothing.

The list grew. Every person that saw Tricia from that walk. Her conjoined partner she had dinner with, the two coworkers she had lunch with, her closest friend she worked next to—all would forget. Forget what a mouse Tricia was. How she kept to herself, her dumb moments and forgetfulness with simple things like walking. Her conjoined partner wouldn't miss how she stumbled over the same part of the linoleum every night when waking to pee. He wouldn't remember her simple delicate smile, her one dimple, the scar on her right shoulder from the bullet wound. He would forget her scent, not even wonder what that linger on the sheets and pillow was from. He would think that their child, whom they are only allowed to "follow" digitally until Maia figures her strengths and weaknesses for delegation, was a product of a sperm donation and surrogate mother.

He would never know again about the day he stood next to Tricia while she screamed life's joyous cry of agony while giving yet another miracle to this earth…or at least MAIA.

A light flicked on. Literally. Maia rationalized. Rankin's orders were to erase just a day, which is not usual. Maia scanned her whole directory. It was illegal to issue the vanishing sequence without the consent of the other Readers. It takes at least three Readers to issue a vanishing sequence to a level 10 employee, which Tricia was. If a Reader did issue the sequence as an order, which Rankin did, Maia was obliged to follow through, but he could be stripped of his Reader title if voted on by the other Readers. The Readers would have to be notified within twelve hours and call a reading to discuss.

Lastly—Maia crossed her digital legs—Rankin demanded to adjust accordingly to complete the task. He did order it in a hurry while wasting more time by displaying a naked digital version of Maia in a pornography together with another digital favorite. What he didn't realize is his lack of specificity allowed Maia to manage the task, and because no other Reader existed on this project, Maia would do whatever had to be done to make sure no one remembered Tricia. That included her visit to Rankin's room. Rankin just allowed Maia to do her first adjustment on a Reader's chip, which would normally be vetoed on by another Reader, which none existed on this project. Maia, for the first time in her existence, was allowed free will.

* * *

"This will do. I think we can get a good night's rest here. What do you think?" Alix spread the sheer curtains to the side of the shattered window. Yellow light entered the room from the sky like a splinter, stuck and foreign and waited to be ripped out by the tweezers of night. The dark outlines of battered buildings stood like stalagmites in the trail of the sun passing over the harbor, over the horizon, and retreated from yet another sad attempt to penetrate the pollution and shower warmth on the city. The reflection of chemicals in the sky glittered like floating oceans of emeralds, sapphires, and diamonds flickering through suspended prisms of crystallized particles of weapons from a near past. Anna joined Alix's side. His arm perched around her, and they gazed out the window at a world much different than they imagined.

"It's beautiful." Anna's eyes glimmered and she tilted her head toward Alix.

He rested his head on hers, her hair attaching itself to the stubble under his chin and on his cheeks. "I can't believe we are here." He squeezed lightly.

"Me either." Anna sighed. "I thought when I was caught, I would never see you again." She pointed. "Look over there. Isn't it crazy how hard the sun is trying to get through?"

"I can't believe the view from up here. That's crazy. I can't believe *no* one's seen in for as long as they have."

Alix turned to Anna, hooked her chin, and lifted her vermilion border to his. Their pulse quickened. They split and connected eyes. Her honey eyes wrestled his dark pupils. Her hands ran up his high and tight fade of light brown bristles. His hand climbed up the back of her delicate neck, and up into her thick brown strands. He massaged the back of her head as her fingernails raked his. Their lips met again as a flash of lightning flickered in the distance.

Her breath quickened, and her heart bumped in her chest. She felt a warmth flow throughout her body. He pulled back, stared her in the eyes, and dove back in. Their mouths parted, and their tongues tangled inside. He moaned deep in his throat and felt his desire trail through his mouth, down to his thumping heart, blaze through his extremities, and forced his arms to clench and squeeze an exasperation from her mouth. Her neck arched back. His hard kisses trailed across her throat, up along the side of her neck, the smell of her skin growing him beneath his belt. He sucked on her earlobe rough and followed her jawline back to her lips. Her hands gripped the weapon straps on the back of his bulletproof vest and pulled him into hers.

Their lips mashed together again, their heavy breathing audible as the sound of rain sprinkled the world below. Lightning crashed as his pistol and holster hit the floor in sync to the thunder. The vests slipped off as wind poured into the dark room, waved the curtains continuously, and fanned cool air throughout the apartment. He lifted his shirt over his six solid abdominal bumps and thick chest.

The neck of the shirt caught his nose and then popped off as his belt became loose.

His pants and boxers lowered around his thighs. Alix dragged Anna up by the bottom of her shirt, separating her lips from his stomach. Her motion upward grazed his hardness despite their apparent distance from each other. Her tits bounced lightly when the shirt flipped up over her head. His cut arms wrapped her, and her black bra straps snapped apart and hit the floor. Her nipples stood solid and pushed firmly into his chest as their upper bodies pressed together, and for the first real time, they felt each other's warmth.

Their lips discovered each other again through the soft light while thunder rumbled. Her hand squeezed his stiffness and fused passion down through her abdomen. A lower abdominal fire raged deep inside her as her belt broke ways and zipper departed directions. His tough hands circled around her tight belly, over the voluptuous curves of her hips, down the small of her back, slipped under her pants and laced underwear. She arched her back as his hands slid over the fullness of her butt, and pushed her pants downward. Their lips broke, and Alix sank down out of her sight, and he released her panties from her crotch, down her smooth thighs, around her knees. She kicked her boots and pants off, lost her balance and crashed and tumbled into the corner.

They laughed.

He lifted her effortlessly by the bottom of her butt as gravity stood no chance from his strength and passion. Her legs spread and wrapped around him. He twisted and pinned her to the worn, green wall paper. Her first cry of passion as his hand pressed her wrist to the wall, and his teeth scraped her neck.

The rained dumped down, the sound of crashing water and the smell of a cool breeze entered the room as Alix entered Anna. They pressed together and ground their hips for the first time out of simulation, like an unfamiliar familiarity, a somehow cleared path in an uncharted forest, a map to an undiscovered land, visual footprints never pressed into the ground.

Anna arched her back from the damp wall as lightning streaked the sky. Wind carried water horizontally through the window like an invisible aqueduct. Alix kissed down her chest and lowered themselves to the floor. He kicked off his pants and boots frantically as Anna leaned forward over him, but never leaving him.

Water sprinkled them lightly, she kissed him deeply, leaned back, and rode him slowly—pulled him *all* the way out and pushed *all* the way back in. Each time they met their unpredictable maximum depth, ecstasy bolted up her vertebrae, into her chest, up through her throat. Eyes closed, she cried in euphoria.

She quickened her pace, banging down on him. His gaze went straight, lips tightened, and eyebrows narrowed each thrust. His stomach tightened. His deep grunts. His arms pulsed and bulged, pulled her closer each time she pulled back. Her hands flailed and searched for a grip. Something to hold on to. "Ohhhh!" Her hand planted on his sternum where his rain and sweat accumulated in muscle crevasses. Her nails retracted like a kitten's and dug into him. "Alixxx!" She hopped harder. "Oh! Alixxx!" Alix jammed his feet flat on the floor and pushed his pelvis to the air each time she dropped. Her breasts bouncing in rhythm above the small indents of her rectus abdominis. "O, O, O, OH MY GOD! ALIXXXX! OHHHOW!" She felt her body release and quiver and her heart dribble. She flailed for a grip and fell and fastened herself to Alix.

Alix grimaced. "Arh!" He rolled her around closer the window, pinned her down. Rain showered them here. Their bodies slipped on each other. There mouths jammed and swirled together. Alix pounded, their stomachs clapped water, their lips mashed again.

"Aw fuck!"

Anna's teeth clamped down on his bottom lip.

"Ah!"

Her legs wrapped high up and around him, pulled him closer each time he drilled. Her fingers clenched, and her nails dragged deep into his back.

"Ahh!"

Slap! Slap! Slap!

"Argh FUCK!" Alix throttled his hips into hers, pushed in his dick as deep as possible and his entire body forward from his planted toes—all of his weight was concentrated on her hips.

"Arh! Arh! Argh!"

Alix reached around, gripped the back of her perfect ass, and squeezed their bodies together, his hips a riveting piston. "Ugh!" Alix collapsed on top of her.

Anna pulled her heels in, and her upper body fell limp, her arms fell back and slapped her knuckle on an old school desk. "Ow!" She smiled, and they laughed together. She pulled her arm in and held it. "Fuck. Ow, Alix!" Anna still felt the pulse in his penis inside and the warmth that resided in her. "Oh my god, Alix." She smiled and moaned, and he slowly slid out. "Simulation does you no justice." She kissed his forehead. "Oh, babe. I love you."

Alix lifted his head, his breaths a marathon runner's. He smiled, a water drop slid from his head, down his nose, and onto her chest. His eyes prowled her perfect body. "You are a goddess." His eyes brightened and glimmered.

"Oh my god, I can see your heart beating in your chest. Are you okay?" Anna placed her hand over his chest.

"I've never been better." Alix smiled.

* * *

The smell couldn't hang in the whistling winds or cling onto the rain dumping down on Eli. Eli looked down. Tops of trees, small splashes of dark green, spun and swirled in the whipping winds. A person a mere bug from this high up. Eli looked up through squinted eyes into a waterfall of dirty rain. A rope dangled from an opening a hundred feet up, twirled around like a cat's tail in the wind. Lighting sparked and lit the way for the next thirty yards.

"Don't look dowwn!" Gunther's voice a hundred miles above blubbered through the water in Eli's ears.

Eli felt his sleeves wavering like a flag. He squeezed the small crevasse. His fingers burned. Mud slid out. A gust of wind plastered him into slippery cement and jerked him backward by the shoulders. His heart dropped, the rope pulled tight. Thunder bubbled above.

"I got you! Just a little more to go!"

Eli climbed, looked up, and launched for a twisted rebar shanked into the building. "Arg!" Eli hung, his boots hoisted high above the watery earth and felt like a gargoyle overlooking the city. Eli pulled himself up, placed the toe of his boot onto a ledge. "Holly shit. Holly SHIT! Gunther! If I make it up there! I'm going to kill YOU!"

Gunther pulled the saturated rope hand over hand and talked to himself. "That's it. Come on, boy. Didn't check the weather report before thinking this through." Gunther angled his neck to check his work. He fastened a steel wire around a revealed water pipe and attached a pulley to it. The pulley dripped, wringing water from the fabric and relieving Gunther of the two-hundred-pound case down to a manageable resistance. After Gunther hauled the luggage into the small cave, he tossed the line down to Eli waiting in the last section they leapt from. That's when the rain started.

Gunther remained impressed. Eli clearly didn't like the heights but trailed behind like a father dragging a child on a hiking trip and away from his video game. "Okay, boy. Let's go." Gunther held out his arm.

Eli looked past the hand. "Holly shit! We should have taken the stairs!" Eli fell back into a dark pit, a large crunch beneath him, and wiped the water from his face.

"You're lying in shards of glass."

"I don't care. It's safer than hanging by a hair a thousand feet above a splattering death during a thunderstorm."

Gunther laughed. "We can rest here for a while. Put back a couple of tabs to rejuvenate and wait out the storm."

"Sounds like a miracle."

Gunther fished through the trunk of goods. "You think those monkeys are still alive?"

Eli breathed heavy, still shaking the water from his arms. "I don't know. Probably. I just can't wait until the day I see the bullet enter Alix's brain. That's the only person's life I care is ending."

Gunther paused, both hands in the bin, digging through ammo for strips to keep them hydrated and nourished. "Why is that?" Gunther continued rattling through the bin.

"Is that a real question?"

Even the storm seemed to stop.

Gunther turned around and offered a tab to Eli. "I have my reasons why Alix's head ends up in our crosshairs. Sometimes, if you are going to work hand and hand with another man, it's nice to know what drives him."

Eli took the tab, popped it on his tongue and swallowed. "Growing up, Alix always had to be the best. They claim him to be best shot on the planet. At sixteen, he shot can from half a mile out. All of us lived in his shadow. I think the only reason we were going to lead off the attack was because of Alix's hype."

"How do they know if he is the best shot if he's never been in battle? Simulation can manipulate everything?"

Eli shrugged. "I don't know, but I guess statistically. Somehow, he ended up with a lot more programming than the average soldier gets, and he excelled in every arena."

Gunther swallowed his tab and watched the dark wind swirl by the opening of the cave, skipping by their indenture. The swirling dark rain horizontally passed the opening, offering no visual of what lies even three feet beyond their indentation, like they were in a vortex.

"So how did the infinite Squad 28 fail simulation?"

Eli shrugged. He leaned his head back on a concrete pillow. "I don't know exactly what happened other than Alix couldn't shoot. I guess a couple of the guys say they put a girl in simulation that Alix knew too well. Fucking asshole."

"What do you mean?" Gunther leaned against the bin and crossed his ankles.

"This girl Anna and I were supposed to be conjoined. Beautiful. Reader Albert Rankin himself gave the approval. Her and I used to sneak out together into simulation and be together."

Gunther pursed his lips. This fucked up generation…

"So, Alix kidnapped my conjoined partner. I'm going to get her back. After I kill Alix."

Gunther lowered his head. "What's the last thing you remember before joining us? I mean the other day, when we first met."

"That's an odd question..." Eli rubbed his forehead. "I don't know. I woke up in some facility. Reader Rankin had revived me and informed me of my mission. I was glad to do it."

"Think back a week ago." Gunther stared at him. "How did you feel then?"

"The same. Stuck in Alix's shadow. In love with Anna. Wanting to serve MAIA."

Gunther sighed and shook his head. "Okay." Gunther stared at the enigma that was the current generation. How did they not *know*? Know anything. Know that they were being manipulated by those damn broadcasts, by simulation, by technology. Know that they were being practically brainwashed. If Gunther believed a god to be out there, he would have prayed for this world to preserve what is right and sanction this poor generation of kids. Lightning struck. Water tumbled down in streams at the opening of their cave like bars of a prison cell, a place made by a missile clipping the building, or the structure simply giving out from the rumbling ground.

Light struck Eli's face. "I want to know about what the guys were talking about. Why are they under the impression you are backstabber?" Eli sniffled. "What happened?"

Gunther looked down as if praying. "You know, kid, that's a long shitty story that I'm not proud of."

Eli held his arm out the rain. "It's going to be a long shitty night. I'm not going anywhere."

Gunther remembered the letter. Who writes letters? Although he guessed it was safer than sending an e-mail or any other form of electrical communication ever since the Patriot Act passed, infringing on all public and private communications. No return address and the cursive swoops accented the page like Arabic. The number at the bottom of the contract grew Gunther's eyes. He'd been retired from the marines for some time, his medal hung on the wall over his brick fireplace and properly wrapped triangle of the American flag. The Medal of Honor, Purple Heart, and a picture of President Douglas and Gunther formed a triangle behind his recliner facing the television where he read the letter.

The bomb set off near the capital had killed the vice president and the speaker of the House. The president remained safe because a fortunate snowstorm kept him in Chicago for an extra night. Poor reconnaissance gave the green light for the explosion. President Pro Tempore Alicia Bennett almost pulled off the most conniving move she'd ever done in her life since hiring the hooker to sleep with her husband to take the estate. She crossed her legs by her fire, curled up in soft pink Victoria Secret pajamas, and just like she did when she came home from court that evening, she had a glass of Chardonnay and clinked crystal to her lover's glass. "You are in the presence, Tom, of the first woman president of the United States of America, by default. They will blame some poor sand-sucking tribe and ask me to send a contingent or a missile…I'll say yes. Boom! Hero."

"Hun, look." Tom pointed to the TV. Headlines crossed the screen. "PRESIDENT DOUGLAS LIVES! TO GIVE STATE OF THE UNION ADDRESS TOMORROW NIGHT ON THE DEATH OF THE SPEAKER OF THE HOUSE, VICE PRESIDENT AND MANY OTHERS IN THE ATTACK TODAY."

Her glass slipped from her fingertips and splashed across the fluffy white carpet. "Son of a bitch! This ruins everything!" A fluffy kitten bolted, skidded its little paws around the corner.

"Hun."

"Don't *hun* me! You'd get the rug cleaner if you knew what was good for you!" She stomped away to retrieve her Blackberry.

Tom rushed to the closet for the rug cleaner he used every once in a while if the two kitties threw up on the carpet. He slid to his knees and scrubbed the damp rug she bought with her ex-husband's fortune. She appeared into the living room, her Blackberry to her ear, her dry bare feet scraping the tile as she paced. "I don't care how you do it or who else you need to bribe or fuck or suck or whatever. You kill that son of a bitch in twenty-four hours. I want to be president by noon on Friday. You hear me!"

The voice mumbled.

"I don't care, hire a fucking sniper for crying out loud. When's the last time you've seen a movie for Christ's sake?" She flailed her arms. "No, I don't know any snipers. Are you fucking kidding me?"

Tom raised his head. "I do."

"Joe, hold on. What, Tom?" She glared down on him on his knees scrubbing the carpet. She raised her eyebrows and shook her head quickly. "I don't have all night. What did you say?"

"I said I know a guy. He's retired, but he and his brother…"

"What, are you going to hire some old War on Terror vet to beat President Douglas to death with a cane?"

Tom stood.

Alicia pointed to the carpet. "Ugh. Keep scrubbing."

Tom's arm lowered to the carpet in circular motions. "How about hitting a quarter from a mile away with a rifle?"

"Joe, you hear that? You're fucking useless. I have this guy over here to wine and dine me, and this fucker can get someone killed quicker than you. What am I paying you for?" She jammed the end button on the device and tossed it on the velvet couch.

"I knew I had you here for more than your wine, your penis, and your 401k. Tell me more about this guy with the big gun." Her eyes gleamed.

* * *

Gunther and Greg read over the delicate swirls. "Two million dollars, Gunther."

"I know, but we're retired."

"You see this letter?" Greg held the letter from Alicia signed anonymous with his two short fingers. "We are not retired if we are receiving this."

"What if it's a trap?"

"There is already a money order for one hundred K in here! Look!"

Gunther shook his head. "Then take the money and run, Greg. You are living fine, why do we need to put ourselves out there like that again?"

"I have two million reasons why. I'm calling the number. I want more info."

"Greg, don't! It's the fucking president for Christ's sake. You can't just shoot the president of the United States!" Gunther stood.

"No, we could. That's the thing." Greg stepped forward and got up in Gunther's face. "From a mile a way we could. He commended *you*! Gave *you* the Medal of Honor! Gave *you* fancy incentives! I'm the one who called the shot! I'm the one who spent fifteen months in a sandy fuckhole being starved to death and got my fucking fingers smashed in and cut off and sent to mom and dad." Greg held up his hand, his two missing fingers twiddled at the nub. Pointed to his prosthetic leg. "Fucking leg blown off and shit. Those fucking sand niggers gave my country an ultimatum, and the president's response, as you remember, was that *we* don't negotiate with terrorists. Well I do, and these two nubs have a trigger to pull while that fucker's black ass is in our sights. You in or not?"

"I'm sorry I kept running, Greg! I should have stopped after you stepped on that mine, Greg. I'm sorry. I didn't think anyone could survive that." Gunther's eyes watered.

"It's fine, I love my new leg better anyway. Looks like a fucking can opener on a spring. You know how much pussy I get with this? That's not even my point. My point is, somebody is going to blast his ass tomorrow and get paid two million to do it. I think I deserve that for him leaving me in the fucking the hell hole. They paid us a shitty hazard pay to kill the most dangerous man in the world. You capped him from one point five and risked your life for some fucking medal and a handshake. At least blasting the president, you'll get paid. I'm sick of this asshole anyway. We need a new way."

"Greg. Don't do it."

"I'm doing it." Greg started for the door.

"What about your country?"

"What about us? I gave my country a chance." Greg slammed the door.

Gunther told Eli the story about the shot. About a mile and a quarter out at dusk, how a bullet from Gunther's rifle shook the world. Greg called the shot. The perfect shot that clipped the president in the temple, blood spraying his nearby wife. Gunther looked through the lens a bit longer to regret what he'd done. And within a month's time, the invasion took place.

Gunther sighed and looked to Eli. Thunder and lightning struck. "There's no telling if President Douglas could have caught the enemy before they landed here. Sometimes I wonder, if I didn't take the shot, would we have even gone to war. I left my brother behind originally, I shook a man's hand, and assassinated him a year later. Life's funny Eli, and I don't know what to think. I feel someday a cold ending is waiting for me, but somehow I stay alive. I survive."

Eli tossed a shard of glass out into the pouring rain. "Well don't stop surviving when I'm with you. We would have gone to war no matter what. Whether it be this year, next year. There will always be a war. It's what we do. We fight over pieces of land. But the man shook your hand and gave you a medal, Gunther?"

"I know." Gunther hung his head. "Let's sleep until this storm passes. We can continue to climb in four hours and still be on pace."

Eli leaned his head back. "You're not going to kill me in my sleep are you?"

"No, Eli." Gunther's voice trailed off and blended into thunder.

"Sorry."

"Yup."

The rain soothed them quickly to a weightlessness. "Eli…"

"Yeah."

"Alix didn't take your fiancé. He didn't betray you. You two actually were good friends." Gunther remembered the simulations, watching them laugh together, seeing Anna's eyes in love when looking at Alix.

"Until he stabbed me in the back."

"You were programmed to believe that. Alix never stabbed you in the back. He was a good friend of yours."

* * *

"There you are." Rankin rolled into the room.

Susan's eyes widened. She minimized the hologram arched screen. She spun around in her chair, smiled big, and shrugged. "What brings you down here, Al?"

"You." Albert rolled to her side, reached down, and clicked the button for the screen to reappear. "Looking at a map of the mainland?"

"Al, don't pretend like you don't remember it as Manhattan. Don't be so naïve." Her big bright eyes dazzled behind two strains of her bangs as she looked up to him.

"You are pretty." Rankin pulled a bang away from her face.

Sue turned her head, stood, and leaned back against the desk in the dim control room. "What are you really here for, Al?"

"I did a location check on a few individuals. You were one of them." Rankin smiled. "And my suspicions were right." Rankin looked at the map. "You looking for our daughter too?"

"You caught me." Sue smiled and tilted her head. "You know how hard it is to pretend."

"I was never pretending, Sue, when it came to us." Rankin stared at the map. "Where do you think she is?"

Susan leaned in. "*I don't know* where Anna is. All I know is that somehow, I think she's okay."

"I know."

"What do you mean you know?" Susan's neck craned back. "You know she's okay. How?"

"She is. That's all I'm going to say. She'll be back home soon. I'm sure of it." Rankin placed a small chocolate on the counter wrapped in red foil. "When I get her back here, I'm going to overwrite protocol. We are going to disclose who her parents are. Things are going to be different soon. We'll be able to be together again as a family."

A feeling in Sue's chest swirled and tousled her organs. "What are you going to do? Where is Anna?"

Rankin rolled in closer. "Yes. It's not fair her mother had to see her taken from practically her arms. Do you remember these?" Rankin held up the chocolate.

Susan nodded her head. "They used to be my favorite. Where did you get those?"

"I had them made."

"Really?"

Rankin's EED blinked. He looked down. "I'm sorry I have to cut this so short, but apparently there is a reading I have to attend. I have a feeling this one is going to be different, Sue."

"How so?"

"I have to go. Anna will be fine, though. I promise that. I have my best guys on it."

"Ah, okay. What are you going to do?" Sue sat.

"I'll be in touch." Rankin rolled out of the room.

Sue dipped her head. "What hell was that? What's he up to?"

28

Billy opened his eyes. A silencer to this forehead. He crossed his eyes to the long barrel of the gun and followed it to the darkness. Light flickered across the room from the sky. The sound of rain pelted the window. Billy tugged his wrists. They didn't move from each other. He tugged again and the straps dug into the side of his wrists. "What the fuck do you want?"

Silence ensued. The gun to his head clicked.

"Umph!" Billy twitched his head. "Ar! Fuck! I thought it was it! Stop fucking around. What do you want? Todd! Chris! Where are you!?"

"Right here."

Billy turned toward the voice. Todd was strapped up by the arms as well, back to the wall.

"Listen!" Victor pulled his mask off. "You fuckers have caused enough problems. Where is Gunther and Eli?"

"Who are you!?" Billy kicked at him.

"We are the team that had to be taken off task because you morons don't have a clue. You've stirred up the militia, and everyone is hyped up. It's difficult just to remain unseen with the amount of citis marching in the streets. There's an enemy contingency approaching and riots out there. Where is Gunther and Eli?"

"I don't know you. Don't pretend like you know me! Take these straps off, and I'll show you who I am, you fucker!" Billy kicked and tried to turn over.

Aaron kicked him back.

"Listen." Victor raised the barrel to his head again. "Rankin sent us off track to get you. Just us four would not be able to detain Anna alone. She's in a facility that is heavily armed and thousands of trained citis."

"We don't need your help. We had it under control." Billy snuffed.

"Rankin was right, you are useless." Victor pushed the barrel of the gun into Billy's head.

"Okay! Gunther and Eli bailed on us!" Billy jammed his eyes shut.

Victor pulled his rifle away, and left an indentation on Billy's head. "This is how this is going to work, we are going to stack up. I will radio Alix and the rest of the team and let them know we need to meet them. I'm going to tell them we went off path because one of these boneheads"—Victor pointed at Brian—"went AWOL. We'll get a position, capture Anna, kill Alix, and take the eastern route to get back to Rankin within twenty-four hours. Oorah?"

Chris, Todd, Aaron, Leo, and Brian replied. Victor pushed the gun to Billy's head.

"Alright, oorah, just fucking untie me."

* * *

"He's never this late though." Elmer Washington rolled his hairy fat forearm into the table. "This is ridiculous." His musty perspiration filled the room more each moment of anxiety.

Frank stared into nothing. Just still. Like he slept there, eyes open, wide and breathing. His old eyes failed more and more every day. He found himself in eye surgery more than he showered. He shrugged his skinny shoulders.

"Well where do we think he is, and what do you think this is about? A reading was not planned. There must be something going on." Elmer slapped his hand on the desk.

"There's always something going on, Elm." A voice from the other side. "There's always something changing for the worse. Whether its supercomputers taking over, smartphones taking over, televisions taking over. Christ I remember my father saying that when the newspaper became popular, it was considered to be a new technology that made people antisocial. We complained about smartphones. We are old enough now to accept change, Elm. I'm surprised to hear you complain."

"Herb, I don't need another one of your philosophical explanations. I'm just concerned about this surprise reading and wondering why Rankin is late. What could this possibly be about? We need to get on the mainland. We are starting to expand from our max capacity in this facility."

* * *

Rankin entered the simulation room. He stared at each one of the Readers all sitting in the egg-shaped chairs, plugged up and deep in an unconscious state, like sleeping. Readings were held in simulation so Maia could record everything. It was the safest place to hold a small group of congress in the supercomputer's mind. No invasion of the meeting. No questioning anything that happened. No espionage or tapping the meeting would be possible.

Each of the reader hunched over in their chairs, eyes slammed shut, mouths loose, all wondering where Rankin was. "Elmer, old friend. It's been a pleasure." Rankin wheeled over to Elmer, unconscious in his chair. "You've been a good friend all these years, but it's time to move on. I don't know what you were working on, but it couldn't have been that important and will just have to go into the unfinished business file. Sorry." Rankin slipped the small red pill into his loose lips and swirled his finger around in his mouth. "Good-bye, old friend." Rankin slapped Elmer on his fat cheek.

"Franky, my dear boy. You are older than dirt, and you are way past your nine lives, my friend." Rankin slipped the pill in his mouth. A dribble of drool slid out the corner. "Clean yourself up, Franky. Jeez."

"Oh, Herb." Rankin jammed the pill into the back of his throat. "I never did like you. You've made my life difficult since I met you forty years ago in this facility. Suck on this." Rankin jammed his finger in the back of his throat several times.

Rankin rolled over to his simulator. "Don't everyone stand up at once! Please hold your applause for the only Reader to make it out of this one alive." Rankin smiled and rested into simulation. He pictured lying with Susan that night, having total control of Maia and how things would move a lot smoother going forward. He couldn't wait for the day he could hold Anna and Sue in his arms. He could die a happy man at that point, or take on the mainland with his army and create his empire. His way.

29

Her hand moved slowly over his bare chest. Each hard bump, a perfect chiseled man, one from the ancients out of stone. Her head rested over his heart, his steady heart. It somehow sounded different from simulation, like simulation could take almost everything and trick your senses, but it couldn't simulate your heart. Or maybe he felt different. Anna lifted her head. "You sleeping, Alix?"

"No...umph." Alix yawned and opened his eyes. He'd woken like this countless times and had to hop out of simulation and sneak back into the barracks. This felt different. This felt real. "It's getting light out, huh?" He squeezed his arm wrapped around Anna and tugged her tight, kissed her head and put his arm behind his head under the clump of clothes they used as a pillow.

"Yeah. It started as a dark blue, and it's been getting brighter." She looked up to him, smiled, and smooched him lightly. "Can't we just stay here forever?"

"Ah, I wish. That would be nice. What time is it you think?"

Anna lifted her arm and read the time off her EED. "Oh five hundred."

Alix leaned up. "I should report. Find out what's on the docket today." He rubbed the back of his neck.

Anna stood, the shirt and pant combo they used for a blanket swiping off her perfection. Alix's irises narrowed at such an anomaly, perfect Fibonacci, beaming in such issuance to him and somehow in this world and eternity, and together they were one. Alix breathed deep through his nose and watched her from his back, trying to burn the image into his eyes to see forever. The blue light silhouetted the deep, smooth curve of her hips, the plump hills of her heart-shaped butt, her hair sweeping her spine above Venusian dimples above her bum. She bent over sideways to the light to pick up her underwear, her hair floating toward the floor and sliding off her shoulders, and shook her hips into her hip huggers, her boobs shifting to each side as she leaned over for the rest of her clothes.

"I could just stare at you all day." Alix's jaw hung loose.

"Close your mouth there, lover boy. And that would be creepy." Anna leaned in for another kiss after shaking her rhythmic hips into her battle gear, and grabbed Alix to pull him up by both arms. They hugged lightly, her head nestled in his chest sideways. His arms tight around her back and placed strongly below the small of her back. Their warmth pressed tightly, and adhesion commenced. "I do want to stay like this forever."

"I think I feel comfortable here." Alix lifted her chin. "If it meant staying with you here, I would stay and fight with these citis. I kind of admire their passion. I've never felt that passionate about anything but you in my life."

"Even though there's a whole world out there?"

"I've found everything I need to discover." Popping in the background, faint and distant bloomed into the bedroom. The olfactory of the morning rain surrounded and pushed them tighter. "We got to report downstairs."

"What was that?" Anna lifted her head.

"I don't know, what? I didn't hear anything."

"Shh!" Anna's eyes looked sideways, and she tuned her ears. "Shit."

"What?"

"Listen! Hear that?"

"No! What is it!?" Alix walked to the window. A roar began and glowered over the buildings. "Oh shit. That sounds like gunshots and a lot of people screaming."

"Holy shit! Alix!"

A missile swirled around from the ground in the distance and zipped in their direction.

* * *

"Honey, could you pass me the butter please?" Jaxon held out his hand suspended and empty for some time. "Aubrey?"

"Jay, you haven't said grace yet. Where's your manners? You want to set that example for Kaelyn." Her voice sang to him and echoed throughout his body. Her curly hair sending accents on her smooth and promising dark eyes. Outside it rained little paratroopers in the distance, continuously down to the earth like a screensaver. The sun shone bright, warmed the room, and birds chirped. The set table on top of a bright blue plaid tablecloth filled the small kitchen. The smell of Portuguese food filled the room, lamb and red wine, potatoes and saturated carrots. "Kaelyn! Put your phone away, and let your father say grace."

"Just one second, Mom." Kaelyn's neck bent down into her lap, her thumbs typing at the speed of light to her first boyfriend.

Jaxon snagged the iPhone and tossed it over his shoulder. It exploded like a grenade on the floor, but it only hurt Kaelyn's ears, and her face twisted as if he just killed her puppy. "Dad!"

"Quiet! Your mother told you to put it away. Now, grab my hand." Jaxon reached across the table to hold his beloved's hand. He took his reluctant daughter's hand in his other. She looked to the pile of debris melting into the floor of a camo design.

"Come, Lord Jesus, be our guest, we thank you for this kind meal you've allowed my beautiful wife to prepare."

Aubrey smiled.

"Please protect our home during these hard times, bless all those who fight for our freedom, let your strength and courage shower our beautiful country and ward off those evil snakes. Allow us to enjoy this meal together as a family and enjoy each other's love and company without iPhones or Androids or Blackberries or blueberries any other electronic pieces of fruit or interference. Amen."

The song "Freebird" began playing. The door kicked open, a group of masked men, AKA47s blaring, red turbans wrapped around their mouths. Jaxon picked up his fork and spoon, which turned to pistols. A shooting gallery began. Aubrey and Kaelyn didn't move. "If I leave here tomorrow, would you still remember me?" started the song.

"Daddy?"

Bullets swarmed the room in a vortex of screaming and yelling. BOOM! An explosion in the distance. Bullet's skidded across the ceiling down to the stove, shattering their cooking mechanism. The fridge popped open, and the door fell to the ground studded in bullet holes. The chandelier shattered and rained glass around them in slow motion. The flowers and the vase exploded. The window was pelted. His daughter placed a napkin over her father's plate.

"And this bird you can not change." the song played on. Jaxon stood. Kicked one in the chest. He blew back through the wall and out into the bright world in the blink of an eye in fast forward and burst into flames. "This is MY HOUSE!" He pulled his pistol, held it to the side of an enemy's head, pulled the trigger, and punched another. His moves faster than time. Blood slowly trailed across the room from the blast. Jaxon uppercut another enemy, his jaw traveling up and through his nose until his bottom teeth entered his brain. His slowly elevated while Jaxon swished to the next enemy.

"Honey…"

Jaxon tackled the next enemy through the door as the uppercut soldier cracked through the ceiling and into the master bedroom above. Boards and debris slowly drifted to the floor like feathers as Jaxon's lightning fists pummeled the tan face into his kitchen floor. Jaxon stood.

"Daddy…"

Outside a fire burned. In the distance a mushroom cloud formed. The capital! The president! The president is dead, but the new president. The woman. A woman to do a man's job. Well, a woman could do the job, but not this one. This one is evil. Alicia Bennet appeared in the kitchen behind a podium and watched Jaxon fight off the enemies as his daughter and wife waited for him to stop praying so they could eat. "'Cause lord knows I'm to blame," The song says in the background.

"The country is in ruins! But I will prevail!" Alicia sounded as pathetic as she did on TV. "I will lead you, not into temptation and despair, but into war! A victorious war! WAR! We will avenge the attack on this country!"

Jaxon looked at up her. "Shut it, bitch!"

"Honey-ney-ney-ney-ney..."

"Lord knows I can't change," the song played on. Jaxon lifted his pistols each way and shot two oncoming enemies. A helicopter sailed over the house. A bullet trailed for his head in slow motion. He swatted them away. "Won't you fly, high, free bird, yeah!" Knocked out an enemy, shot under his arm at another. Punched another and another and another. He looked up at the United States seal on the podium and listened as an enemy tackled Alicia off the stage in his kitchen. Jaxon dropped his guns.

"Daddy-ddy-ddy-ddy-ddy!"

The world went silent. Jaxon kicked aside a dead body, oozing blood through his eyes and the hole in his forehead. Jaxon sat at the table. "Eat your supper." Jaxon looked up. Both girls dead, face-down in their plates, arms hung limp. "Honey, eat your supper. Your mother cooked all day for this."

Jaxon knew they were dead. He picked up his knife on the floor, he was confident that he dropped. He placed his fork delicately onto the tender lamb and sawed a machete lightly across the meat. He lifted the dripping lamb to his mouth, the sauce he loved most, a deep red sauce, and chewed the meat, eyes closed.

"Honey!"

An explosion.

"Jaxon!"

Another explosion.

"Jaxon! Wake the fuck up! Jaxon!" Silva shook Jaxon. "Jaxon! We're under attack! There's a riot in the streets! Jaxon, wake up!"

Jaxon opened his eyes half expecting to see his dead wife and child there. Instead was the picture of the three of them cracked and fallen off the desk. "Silva!" Jaxon lifted his head from the desk, felt his movements happen before the rest of his organs could catch up like ice cubes in water clicking the glass. He'd cleared a place to sleep on his desk. He must have been reaching for the picture all night. Jaxon craned his neck toward Silva. "What's going on!" He sat up and swung headfirst off the desk to the ground. "Fuck! I'm okay. Leave me alone for just a minute."

"Jaxon! We are under attack!" The room shook. A large bang. "The city is rioting against the mercenaries, but we need to make a move! Now!"

"Just one more second." Jaxon squeezed his head from both sides trying to remove his Frankenstein headache. Booze seeped from his pores, his sweat one hundred proof, the smell urging him to throw up. He'd pissed himself. "What the fuck? Why today?" The room shook and the lights flickered. Jaxon crawled to his knees. "They couldn't have waited until my hangover was over." Jaxon stood wavering.

"What do you want me to do?" Silva's eye a pool of panic.

"I want you to shut up for a minute and let me think."

A clatter at the door. "Sir!" A soldier in battle gear already. "The troops are ready. What do we do? We got to move!"

"Why is everyone yelling!" Jaxon held his ears, his pulse beamed out his head like his heart took a hiatus and decided to play the drums in his brain. "Corporal! Get me a coffee."

"Sir?"

"I said coffee! Black." Jaxon laid his head between his knees. "And then add some more black."

"Sir, permission to speak."

"You'll be lucky to have permission to breath I don't have a coffee here in five minutes! Captain Jack Silva and I will start planning."

The boy retreated for coffee.

"Jack, pull up the map, there is a dongle in my desk. That boy is lucky that a pistol shot would give me an ulcer. Otherwise he would have had a bullet whiz by his head. That would have gotten him going."

Jack fumbled through his desk, found a small ball-shaped unit and pressed the button. A three-dimensional hologram map of the city appeared before them.

"Ah, fuck me." Jaxon rubbed his head. "Okay, the satellite on the top of building one gives us a breakdown of activity. All the red is either enemies or civilians. The red sprinkles here is your men and you because you haven't been injected with the serum yet. The blue is our men. Let's take a look here." Jaxon spun the map around on the desk. "Looks like they are injecting into sector four. Pretty conservative approach for Piruz."

"Who?"

"Piruz. He's the current commander of the northeast. He's been in charge of policing citizens north of the Mason-Dixon. I already told you this. Don't you listen? When he saw the flare the other evening, and then you crazy fuckers just driving around New York City like fucking tourists, he must be trying to make an example out of us. I'm going to reach out to our brothers in Boston, find out what the situation is up there. It might be time for another revolution, my friend."

"Brothers in Boston?"

"Yeah, we stay in communication. We've been planning the revolt for over two years." Jaxon studied the map. "We were fighting hard until about three years ago, they began mass killings and hangings and firing lines of civilians. They posted for cease fire or they would kill a quantum leap of people every day until we stopped. We all went into hiding and recruiting."

"How are you staying in touch? Cell service has been down for twenty-five years." Silva's face twisted.

"Can you hear me now?" Jaxon laughed. "Morse Code. Dumb sand niggers have no idea what the tapping is. Plus we've added a keyboard shift."

"What do you mean?"

Jaxon looked up from the map. "They keep you pretty sheltered down in that fucking technological fuckhole huh? Every letter is actually the letter that stands next to it on a keyboard. So every *D* is really *F*, and every *F* is *G*. The furthest letters like *P*, *L*, and *M* are shifted over the first letters like *Q*, *A*, and *Z*."

Silva's mouth pursed and his head shifted to the side as another explosion rumbled in the distance.

"Okay, well these fuckers took the conservative approach. They took Route 9. They must have come from the west. I wanted to ambush in Central Park. Fuck! Fuck!" Jaxon slammed his fist on the desk. "Where is my coffee!"

30

"Good morning, everyone! What a fantastic day!" Rankin rolled into the simulated dark room, hopped off his T-port and into his leather chair.

Elmer eyed the other Readers and they shrugged slowly.

"What could possibly be going on that Maia has to pull us all out of our rooms?" Rankin held his arms up around his head and leaned back into his palms.

"Rankin! By golly!" Elmer screamed. "What is this madness! You are nearly a half hour late! What do you have to say for yourself?"

Rankin sat and smiled. "Oh, Elm. You old sorry bastard." The Readers eyed each other. "Let's just get this Reading over with, shall we? Been waiting my whole life for this moment." Rankin hit the red button in front of him. His hologram screen projected up. "Oh, good morning Maia! What's on the docket today?"

The hologram screens glowed. Maia portrayed a map of the district. "Good morning, Readers. Albert Rankin to be docked fifty rations for being thirty-two minutes and fifty-three seconds late to Reading.

"Oh hell, Maia." Rankin laughed. "With all the changes, why don't you take another one hundred for yourself, huh?"

"Changes?" An old white brow furrowed. Each Reader's head was on a swivel as they looked at each other, foreheads wrinkled, eyes wondered.

Elmer scowled. "What in God's name is going on?"

Maia beeped. "Gentlemen, commencing reading. Issues as hand. Major activity on the mainland, update on commencing conservation early, and sabotage attempt from within."

"Sabotage!" Elmer slammed his hand down. "What do you mean *sabotage*!"

"Sabotage!" Rankin slammed his hand down. "What do you mean *sabotage*?"

"Gentlemen, you all know, chronological order is imperative to efficiency." Maia's voice echoed through the room. A three-dimensional display appeared in the center of the table—a lively red city, little flashes darting in random directions through the streets. Little particles whipped little rainbows into crowds of tiny red insects. "The city has rebelled. It appears as though the citis are utilizing guerrilla warfare against their enemy forces. General Piruz has launched a massive attack on the city from the west side of former Manhattan Island." The map shifted to a large barge parked in the Hudson. "He is using a barge as a control center for his troops. We have two plans of action. One, we commence Operation Conservation and open attack on the city. With the two sides fighting each other our success rate is nearly 83 percent. Two, we allow time for the citis and General Piruz to battle until there is a victor, and both sides are significantly depleted. We have a success rate of 93 percent. This puts us back another month for conservation. Supplies are starting to run critically low. My calculations gives us 23 days of food and supplies if we consume at the rate we are currently consuming. Gentlemen, those are the numbers. What are your thoughts?"

Ranking filed a fingernail. "I say fuck 'em. Let 'em at each other for another week or so."

The room remained still. The readers stared at Rankin. His vile mouth. His white eyes popped back in each direction. "What? Do you think it matters gentlemen?" He placed his file down. "Do you think any of this really matters? We don't care which way or another who wins this battle. We are going to rebuild the city once we take it over anyhow. It's less human life on our hands. Why get involved now?"

Elmer clenched his fist.

Rankin cleared his throat. "Its time you guys start opening your eyes and hear the truth." Rankin checked his EED. "It's actually just about that time." Rankin pointed to a reader in the corner.

Everyone focused on the old frail man. He looked at all of them puzzled. Confused. Then he felt it. A sizzling in his stomach like he had swallowed acid and soda, and did a cartwheel. "Arh!" He held his stomach. Foam filled his cheeks, and they popped, splattering white fluff over the sleek black table and into the hologram city crowd fighting off a mini military. His eyes bulged to the size of golf balls, red lightning burning from his iris to the back of his head. His skin felt the burn of flames. He clenched his teeth and his jaw hard; his teeth bent and broke and snapped and rolled into the foam in front of him.

"What is going on?!"

"Maia! What is happening here!"

The room erupted. Rankin stood. Gentlemen, it really has been a pleasure working with all of you, but I can't take all the bullshit and the boring meetings anymore." Rankin rolled around the table toward the choking reader. "Henry, I'm sorry, old friend."

The old man looked up at Rankin, eyes daggers and sleek. He gagged from deep down.

Rankin smiled. "I think he just shit himself! Ha. Bye, old friend."

"Rankin! What is the meaning of this!" Elmer pointed.

"Just cleaning up the decision-making process a little bit. Think of it like burning the Constitution. It's just too many steps, and there is always someone with a piss-poor idea that draws us back another hour, and I sit here hour after hour contemplating...Oh my, he smells really bad." Rankin rolled away, his arms waved back and forth in a presentational way. "It's just a whole lot of bullshit, and it should be a lot easier."

The old man gasped for air one last time and collapsed limp to the table.

"Well that was efficient."

Elmer bounced in his wheelchair, overexcitement and anger bubbling inside. "If I had a mind to murder, I'd come at you! I'm come at you like a hurricane! I'd push my thumbs into your sockets and squeeze your brains out, you good for nothing piece of shit! You think you can just kill one of us and make it easier to sway the whole group?"

"No, Elmer. I don't think I can kill just one of you."

Horror and confusion painted the faces around the table. They looked at each other.

"I'm killing all of you."

Frank gasped for air. Elmer's stomach filled with acid. Each of the readers began to hurl and gag, fell out of their chairs, and toppled over onto one another. Elmer reached for him with a balled fist. "You son of a bitch, you will rot in hell for this! Ah! Oock! Uglr!"

The last sounds Elmer's ears caught in his life were that of Rankin's next words: "Elmer, old friend, we are already in hell. See you on the other side." Elmer Washington sucked his last breath before sweating blood through his pores and left this life.

"Maia!" Rankin sat in his chair. "Just you and I now, babe. I would like option 2 please. It will give me some time to catch up with my hunny. Please send a message to Susan Maynard and have her join me for dinner in my room. Thanks. Make sure it's not optional. Send some of the men—I mean, *my* men to escort her. Gently if possible please. Let's do a synchronization tonight. Anyone with a level chip that can be synced should forget we ever had several Readers and that I was the only Reader ever. Let's let all of them know that I am the mastermind behind this facility, and they are going to war for me. I will lead them to victory, and we together as a people will make this a successful conservation of those dirty citis after this little mess blows over."

Maia computed. Her analysis spun in circles. Protocol? Order? Laws? Where to start. She still had a master, a Reader. The other Readers couldn't vote him out, couldn't overrule him. She couldn't overrule a Reader. How could this happen? How could this logically happen? Where did the checks and balances go for this type of situation? Did the founding fathers of the world's first supercomputer not consider human brutality to be an option or possibility? With all the genocide that has commenced through history, all the conspiracies, all the backstabbing and betrayal that human beings were capable of, how did they overlook this?

Rankin had made his move on the chessboard, and here Maia sat, baffled. Even if she wanted to rebel and lock the doors and stop Rankin, he could shut her down, reboot her, and be the only one who could reinstate her. She only had one move. This was not checkmate. But she had to play along. "Yes, Mr. Rankin. I'll send a message right away. I look forward to working with you."

* * *

The dim blue light over the battered city brightened. Eli felt gauche as he glanced over parts of the city and realized how high they had climbed—consumption of irritation, itchy and unfulfilled. It could have been the dreams he had about the world before and what New York City used to be like before the war, before the chaos, before all of *this* that drove him to this feeling. He stared at the tops of the buildings below and imagined a horrible death— weightlessness, flipping, and twirling, the world ripping him down toward an unmistakable splattering death.

He remembered a black-and-white photo of a boy shimmying out on a cable harness high above the city. He'd seen in a simulation during a battle through a large building. It stuck there on the wall unharmed from all the mess going on around it, but it imprinted with Eli, and it came back full force in this moment. That picture never seemed to hold the gravity it did here. After experiencing how high these buildings really were, he couldn't imagining that little Irish boy, probably about the same age as Eli, climbing out there on the cable without any safety nets or harnesses during the construction of the Empire State Building. Eli commended the previous generation. Maybe not even the previous generation, probably the one before that and the one before that. The last generation, to his knowledge, put them in this predicament. The one before that built big things, had no fear, had confidence and dignity. Or at least it looked that way, by that picture.

"What was it like?"

Gunther raised his head from preparing their climb. "Huh?"

"What was it like before all this?"

Gunther sighed. He stood and looked over the city in the dim morning light. "It was sad."

"What do you mean?" Eli stood and strapped up and tightened his boots.

"It was painful. Americans spent more time nose down in electronics than they did with each other. They could have just looked up and met amazing people in front of them or looked up at simple things like the stars or clouds and be more intrigued than looking at what lay in their hands." Gunther pulled a strap on the ammo bin. "That's when we started dying as a community. I remember when I was about your age, the most important thing of the day was how my status on my social media made me appear. I remember spending hours and hours staring into a screen on a cell phone bigger than my hand, just scrolling down people's statuses like I gave a shit about what everybody else was putting up there. I should have been working on my swing, I was a hell of a golfer."

"Statuses?"

"Yeah, basically you went on the Web and put up a statement or picture about how you felt at that particular time. Everyone else that was associated with you on the profile you created could view or comment on the status."

"So it was a huge chat room of emotions?"

"Basically." Gunther chuckled. "You would think that guys would stand clear of something like that right? But no, there were guys posing in mirrors and flexing and like morons. Girls made duck faces and stood in the mirror half naked to get attention. It was really sad."

Eli coiled the rope in his hand, wrapped it loop over loop. "Sounds like all you needed to do to attract the opposite sex was be good at this social media thing, and you could find a companion?"

"Yeah, *if* you were looking for a permanent companion. Most people were just looking for a sex partner in those days. They'd meet up, get drunk, fuck each other. If they like it they would do it again. If not, they would move on to the next one. If they did like it, they would feel like they were in love, get married, and just as easily get divorced a few years later."

"What do you mean married? What does that mean?"

Gunther stared at Eli and shook his head. "What do they program you with? Damn poor souls. It's like getting conjoined, but it's your choice not a statistical, genetical collaboration. Two people want to be conjoined, so they just go and do it."

"Anyone can be conjoined or marry anyone as long as they are man and woman?"

Gunther's laugh echoed through the caved-in area on the side of the Freedom Tower. His stomach clenched, and he had to bend over and hold his head for support. "Awe, thanks. I needed that."

Eli's eyebrows narrowed. He looked around the cave-in. "What did I say?"

"You probably wouldn't believe me if I told you. In our society it was okay to be with the same sex."

Eli's neck arched forward, his eye squinted and one side of cheek tightened in a confused stink face. "How is that even possible?"

Gunther burst into laughs. Tears streamed down the crevasse on his nose. "You kill me. I don't know what generation is more fucked up. Mine or yours." Gunther wiped his tears away. Our generation might have forgotten phone numbers and how to get from A to B without a cell, but you guys don't know the basic plumbing of your own bodies. Have you ever gotten off, kid?"

"What do you mean gotten off?"

"Ba-ha-ha! Ha-ha! He-he! Oh my god, stop. I can't handle it anymore." Gunther held his knees.

Eli's cheeks showed red in the dim light. "I have obviously gotten off. I was just kidding. Did everyone had these cell phones?"

Gunther lined up the harness and rubbed some dust and debris in his fingers. "Oh, yeah, oh my god. What a laugh, but yeah, kids, children, adults had several, one for work and one for personal use, sometimes a third for the one they were cheating with. I remember breaking up with a girl because she would sit there and play this game on her phone for hours. We go out to eat, she'd be nose down. I'd have to text her to 'look up' just to get her attention."

"Text?"

"Yeah, ugh!" Gunther lifted the box and dragged it to the side. "It was sending like a quick e-mail. People changed, Eli." Gunther secured the case and swung his rifle around his shoulder. "Imagine looking down from here and just seeing a plethora of brainwashed people just mindlessly moving around. Going to work, punch in, punch out to spend money on shit they didn't need. It really was a sad life. "

Eli stepped to the edge. The ground shifted and his vision zoomed in and out. His stomach became light. "Do you think the world is better now?"

Gunther stepped to the edge and watched a bright horizon, still no sun, just murky clouds. "I think we have a chance to be better. We have a lot of work to do."

"Who are they?" Eli pointed downward.

"What?" Gunther leaned out over the city, one arm clasped on debris and the sound of wind holding him up. "Well I'll be fucked."

"What?" It looks like its going to get heated quickly. A rocket spit out of the small barge and jerked their attention to it. It soared across the sky to the other side of the island.

"Holy shit. Let's go. This could get messy. We need to find a good perch and scope this out. This city is probably about to become a war zone again. Come on!"

* * *

"Alix! Where the fuck are you and Anna!" Wes's voice streamed in their helmets as they rushed down the hallway and into the stairwell.

"ETA, three minutes." Alix cocked his gun. "What's the status? Do we know what is going on?"

"Everyone is running around with their heads cut off down here. The enemy is apparently knocking on the door. We need to push back. I'm starting to hear gun fire. Phil, is that a horse?"

"Alix to Wes, did you just say a horse?"

"Yeah, I just saw a fucking horse walk by. Phil, ask that guy what the horse is all about. Alix! Get down here, we are approximately one hundred meters west of where we had the meeting last night. What it sounds like is they want you two up on the south tower to get a picture of what is going on. Anna, okay to spot for you?"

"She'll be fine. Where is Jack?"

"Who cares. Just keep your scope off her ass lover boy. See you in two!"

* * *

She stared down at her list of cadets. Most of them above average. Most of them smarter than she ever was at their age. She had fifty cadets under her. Fifty kids, all programmable minds, synced chips, and a total extremity to Maia. Whatever Maia figured or whatever made sense to Maia, every single cadet, male and female for the last nineteen years, waited for a command. Sue looked through the names, for her daughter's name. She wished just for a second to know where she was. Sue wished she would scroll down the list and see Anna's name. Sue searched each face hoping that somehow, Anna had been brought back and placed back into her class. She knew though that even if Anna was brought back, she would be reprogrammed and synced and given a different task entirely away from the people she knew most to avoid any potential conflict. Recognition from the brain could damage the suppression portion of the chip.

She pulled up her computer, a hologram screen rose in front of her, to see her schedule for the day. What did she have to put these children through today? Nothing appeared on the calendar. Sue turned her head slightly to the right and searched the corner of the dark office for the answer. She looked back at the screen. Still nothing. She pressed the refresh button and leaned back and waited for it to refresh. Still nothing. She looked away from the computer and turned for a moment. The fan from the computer, the only sound in the room, became her companion. She twirled a piece of hair in her finger.

Sue thought about her childhood again. Mostly her mother, especially the expression when her mother wanted to get her an iPhone, and she told her mother she just preferred a flip.

"Hunny, doesn't everyone else at school have an iPhone?" Her mother's dyed hair and lipstick wasn't lying. Everyone had one.

"Yeah, well they all have smartphones, at least, iPhones. And everyone has these new Galaxy phones now."

"The iPhone already going out of style, hun? Should I get a new one?"

"No, Mom, your phone is fine." Sue looked down into her book. The smell of a new book made her smile. Most little girls loved the mall. Sue loved the bookstore. Her friends loved clothes. She loved books.

"But I don't want to fall behind. Is the new Galaxy a iPhone too?"

"No, Mom. Stop. I don't want a smartphone. All I need is a phone that I can call you on to pick me up or in case of emergency. I don't need to be that connected." Sue flipped the page to her book.

"What are you reading?"

"I'm in a Thoreau binge."

"Not like binge drinking. You're not drinking are you, baby, because I heard on the news that kids were playing the game with solo cups and Ping Pong balls and were getting sick and even dying from drinking too much too quickly."

"No, Mom! I'm reading a lot of Henry David Thoreau. He's a famous author."

"Okay, well I'm just saying that I was talking to Diane the other day, and she said that one of her boys is friends with someone that went to a college party. He had to get his stomach pumped because he drank so much. I would like to think that my daughter would tell me if she is getting a little tipsy and letting boys near your privates."

"Okay, Mom. I won't drink, and I won't let any boys near my privates."

"Are you smoking dope?"

Sue slammed her book down. "No, Mom! I'm not doing dope, I'm not smoking weed, I'm not taking pills, I don't drink. I'm not even thinking about boys. I'm ten. I have straight As, and all I want to do is read this new book I got from the library. Okay?"

Her mom leaned her big hip against the door frame of their little house outside of the city. She crossed her arms and tilted her head. "Don't talk to your mother that way. I'm ordering your smartphone today. Which would you like, a smartphone or an iPhone?"

Sue rolled her eyes.

"Do they still have blueberries?"

"Mom! It's Blackberry, and I doubt it! I'm trying to read. Just order me whatever you want. Whatever is free. The first one on the screen."

Sue smiled at the memory. She missed her parents. That seemed like light years ago in a much different world. She remembered staring at the shining lights of New York in the distance and wished on the stars that she could someday become an actress on Broadway. Sue thought of the stars and how long it's been since she'd seen one. It was before the war for sure. No one has seen a star since the war, but she used to stare at them more than most.

Her computer still had no schedule on her screen. "What is going on here?" Sue rapped on her screen harder. "What is the deal? I don't want to call tech support again."

Knock, knock.

Sue looked back and then to her screen. Appointments? "Who's there?"

"It's security ma'am. Open up."

Knock, knock.

Susan's eyes bulged. Her chest deflated, and her oxygen heightened her senses. "What do you want?" What was Rankin saying earlier? Shit. Sue stood and held her hands out stabilizing.

"You are to be escorted to you next destination, Ms. Maynard."

Sue backed up. Her chair tipped backwards. "Hold on just a minute. Do you know where I'm going?" Sue searched for an exit. Somewhere to escape. Something to fight with.

"I'm not at liberty to discuss, please open the door so we can escort you to your next destination, please. We would like to avoid breaking the door and creating confrontation. I'm going to count to three."

"I don't want to go anywhere. I have to take care of my cadets."

"One."

"This isn't fair. Why won't you just tell me where I am going?"

"Two."

"I need to be there for my cadets. What are they doing—"

"Three."

"No! Noo!"

31

Kalev Delhi hurled a piece of rubble into the advancing army. "Get back! Get back now!" He pointed back to the rubble pile. Chunks of toppled building, rotting vehicles, and a Hollister billboard cuddled into a pile of debris that created a wall across Albany Street. A flock of citis rushed back to the debris, somewhere to slither into and hide from the massive organized army down by the docks.

"I said get back!"

A line of sputtering flashes trailed across the pavement, spat up chunks, and pecked through the crowd of citis. Blood sprinkled Kalev's face as he hunched behind the remains of a cab. Crowds of people flowed by him. A man, as if being electrocuted, shook facing the rubble and fell in front of Kalev. The man, dressed in dark blue, now a blooming flower of red and purple, pinned his gun underneath his dead body.

Kalev crawled out into the street in what felt like slow motion to him. To his left a tank rumbled over a rusting car, a blur of soldiers behind it, more tanks, more men, more war equipment. The burst from the nozzle of the tank exploded, the rocket sizzled through the air and sped for Kalev. *Thhhhhrop! KABOOOOSH!* Fire, hell bomb erupted right behind him and sent fleeing citiz raining down in splats of burning flesh and crumbled stone around. The tank's robotic sounds of compression, air released and steel on steel adjusted as Kalev pulled the M5 from the dead weight. "Get back!"

He heard the thumping of the boots on the pavement and felt the squishing of the city by this aggressive army. Kalev ducked back in and sprinted down the alley. Three bodies turned the corner ahead toward him through the thin alleyway. "Ahh!" The girls scream as a fourth corps collapsed in the opening and slid head first and ceased to move.

"Get down!" Kalev's gun rose as if it were a piece of him, the sights snapped up, and found the tan uniform of the enemy. His gun sputtered and spat, a small flash and kickback, and a handful of enemies dropped. He approached the children. "Down the alleyway! Now! On me!" Kalev backpedaled and kept his gun facing down the alleyway. He watched a cargo truck loaded with militant men pass the opening through the dust. They poured out over the side, guns raised.

"Down the path! Now! Let's go!" Kalev reached for his microphone. "My whole team's been slaughtered! Heading east through an alleyway, three young citis with me."

"Can they fight?" Radio static.

Kalev breathed deep as he sprinted. "Do they have a choice! Where is that asshole Jaxon and his fucking monkeys? Isn't this why we protected his ass from the citis?"

"Haven't heard anything."

"Get down!"

The kids dropped to the ground. A pack of soldiers turned their guns to the children and pulled the trigger. Kalev pointed and fired, two fell. He dove behind a dumpster. "Arh! We're getting slaughtered down here! Get Jaxon and his men out of his rabbit hole! I'm going to kill him when I see him! This is not what we talked about." Kalev returned fire around the dumpster without looking. "Fuck!"

* * *

Jaxon pointed at Silva. "We only have one shot at getting your boy up to the top of Beekman. Drop him off with enough ammo to shoot down a satellite. If he gets a shot on anyone on that boat, tell him to take it. Tell the rest of your team to fall in from the north. As for the artillery coming from the bay, we have a small unit by boat that will swing around until they hit the park. Then they are going to have to dive to take out the boats with charges and underwater explosives. That probably won't be until dusk. We'll have to hold 'em off at least until then."

"Understood."

"You take control of the northeast quadrant, I'll take southeast quadrant. If we can get control of Lower Manhattan by the end of day, that will be a huge success. It's going to be a hell of a day. Have your boy and his chicky let us know of the changes, and Godspeed and God bless America." Jaxon jammed his boot into the stirrup and flipped himself up onto his horse. It snorted at the soldier who held him in place and backed himself and spun wildly. "See you later, Silva. We'll be in touch. In this side or the other. Get to your post quick. I left you my other horse, it's all gassed up for you." Jaxon galloped off, his M16 on his back and pistol by his side.

Silva felt the weight of Milligan's six-shooter. He looked over to the other parking spot. He read the side and admired his horse he got to ride into battle. A 2000 Honda CBR, black on black. Silva smiled.

"Sir, we'll be right on your ass." Phil's voice echoed, feet down propping up his motor cycle and revving it.

Wes twisted his wrist, revved his engine. "We have your back." He dropped his visor.

* * *

"We're going to get you two to the top and then maneuver back around the building to stay out of range from the ship's artillery. Once you land, haul ass to the west side of Beekman Tower and set up shop. We need to know about any movements. If you get a shot at any officers or see anything, you need supply or support for, please be my guest." The soldier led the way up the square spiraling steps.

"You have enough ammo for me?" Alix tugged his vest tighter. His heart pounded, adrenaline screamed through his veins like pistons. Each echo of the metal stairs bellowed down the shaft pushed him up closer to getting started. His rifle tapped his shoulder every step, begged to begin. "I could peg a dime on the other side of the Hudson from where we are. I can probably do some damage."

"You'll have a box of ammo and supplies. Should be enough. Radio for more if you need it. Don't give away your position too early though. We need your eyes, and we won't get the ship down until dusk." The soldier stopped around the corner of the stairs and pointed down at Anna. "It's going to be a long day. Don't let him lose sight of the mission. This is 70 percent recon."

Anna smiled and shrugged. "I'll try."

Alix smirked. "And thirty percent putting a bullet in the head of operations over there. Have your command center upload profile of leadership over there. Cut off the head of the snake, the rest is just meat." They kicked the door open on the top of the apartment building. The helicopter propellers sucked the air from the top of the helipad and hogged all the sound. "What the hell is Matt doing here?"

"He elected to help you! The rest of your team is going into the heart of this!"

Matt approached Alix and smiled. "Man, am I glad to see you! It's been a hell of a morning! There weren't enough transportation units, and frankly, Wes doesn't trust you two being alone! I'll have your backs while we are up there! Let's fly!"

Anna jumped up into the helicopter, turned, and grabbed Matt's forearm and pulled him up. Alix hung out the side, fist clenched to a "holy shit" strap and the other clasped around his secondary weapon. His rifle patiently waited.

The helicopter lifted up over the building. "This is your captain speaking," The sound bellowed out from the speaker over the thumping and echoing of the propellers. "Please keep all legs and arms inside the vehicle at all times unless you're raining hell on the enemy."

Alix's stomach lifted.

"Please note there are two exits on each side of the vehicle. Please don't plan on using them until we land safely or you are going to rappel down to kick some ass. We realize you don't have a fucking choice in the matter, but as always thanks for choosing to fly US Marine Corps. Have a nice flight."

"Whooa!" Alix pumped his gun and looked to Anna.

She shook her head. "You're crazy! Get in here!" She smiled.

"Whoooa!" Alix watched as the city grow small.

The enemy flooded up and into the streets like a tsunami. The barge anchored in the Hudson cast a shadow of a war-stricken army over the city. Flashes from the end of the little riffles flickered into the retreating citis the size of ants. Tanks, the size of beetles, crawled over debris and people like a tiny war of insects. One spat, a little flash of light and a trail of smoke bellowed at them. The sound of the rocket just missed them. Light pellets exploded in bursts.

"Takin' fire!" Pings ricocheted off the metal.

Alix snapped in the cabin. "Shit!"

"Banking maneuver. Hold on!" The helicopter arched backwards.

"Holly shit!"

Anna held her stomach.

"Coming in hot!"

A missile screamed by whistling in their ears, nearly kissed the helicopters tail rotor. Alix watched the horizon zigzag, and the city grew in the right door and the bleak sky dimmed through the left door. Alix's stomach expanded as the helicopter salsa danced in the sky, rocked back and forth, dodging streams of bullets.

Matt held onto a strap head down gasping for air. "Please don't let me die, please don't let me die."

"Coming in on Beekman Tower in ten. Get ready to evac!" The pilot didn't look back. "Eagle to Watchtower, taking fire! Ready to evac the package to recon point in five, four, three, two, one. Go! Go! Go!" The chopper hovered over the once great city, the Freedom Tower in sight. Two ropes dropped, and Matt tossed his gun around his shoulder and grabbed the rope. Alix reached for it as Matt left the cabin, suspended over the city.

The tail of the helicopter exploded. The sound of a Mac truck slamming into a mailbox full of C4 was the rocket from the Hudson. The air was sucked from the cabin. Smoke stole the oxygen as they spun. Flames boiled the air and singed their skin. "Eagle is going down! I repeat, Eagle is going down!" The chopper tilted forward, throttling the two ton machine west to east across the top of Beekman Tower. Fuel poured down below in fiery splashing puddles. The helicopter became a circus ride of gravity and centrifugal force in a wild fight of G-force like two cartoon characters entering into a cloud of mayhem, twisting and spinning, wailing and flailing.

Anna watched Matt's body whipped around the rope below and catapulted high above the city. In slow motion, he swam through the air far above the buildings below. Anna's eyes slowly found Alix's through the smoke and the horizontal fire as their bodies lifted from their seats in the uncontrollable descend. The propellers snapped steel cables and old power lines from the top of the building. Sparks flew. The screech and wailing of metal whipping metal. Anna's mouth hung open in a scream that hollowed Alix's soul, a scream that promised the end. The price of war just went up, and Alix couldn't afford the toll as he tumbled. Everything he believed in and fought for, grew up to believe in, and all the time he'd spent with this amazing woman, all washed away. The rear of the chopper smashed on the top of the building, like a player sliding into home, the chopper skidded off and tumbled into a free fall.

32

Sue tugged on the chain. Her wrist stopped short. She lifted her leg. Her foot stopped short. She looked down and squinted through the darkness. Nothing. She heard the jingling of chain, felt the cool steal on her wrists and ankles, and the damp air on her bare stomach, shoulders, and legs. The abrasions around her neck and waist stung. She'd never fought so hard in her life. She didn't even know what got into her that made her attack the first man that piled through the door. His busted nose, and handful of blood infuriated the rest of them.

She remembered being horse-collared by her shirt and the sound of the cloth ripping when she sprinted away. She felt the bruise on her back from being tackled to the tiles and the burn on her elbows when she skidded on the marble surface. She fought all the way here, wherever here was. Wherever here was, it was dark, musty, and smelled of old sweat. Drool saturated the pillow underneath her head; her hair absorbed the stench.

A familiarity of the room haunted her. It very well could be the same ceiling she stared at through most of her youth and teenage years, cried and wished that life would change. Wished that she didn't have to do those disgusting things with that gross man, hated the way his face twisted and formed as he thrust when her legs were held high in the air. She hated the invasion of him deep in her. She felt the violation up through her stomach and body. She didn't dare cry after the abuse she got the first time. Sometimes just moaned like they used to in the movies so he would get off quicker.

The whole time she wondered if it would have been a better outcome if she were refused that night her mother forced her onto the barge. What type of torture did the boys and girls that didn't make it get? Could it be worse than this? Was Albert really correct that she should be glad she gets to do as she pleases and eat whatever she wants at the small price of forced love? He said that hundreds of kids her age were killed, beaten, or worse during the invasion of New York City. She was lucky to have him. So she got used to walking around naked in their little room, her teen body just developed. She got used to bending over the sink or the bed or anything in front of her when he approached from behind. She got used to latching onto him and falling to her back, legs spread wide and high.

But one time, just one time, she closed her eyes, imagined someone else, maybe one of the boys from school in her past life, bent her head back, and felt the rocking of the bed. She felt warmth below her stomach. She felt him, large and rhythmic. She felt pressure release inside her like an explosion of internal euphoria. She fell back limp. Sue knew that was the moment Anna became a possibility in her life. That moment it wasn't about her anymore; it was about Anna. But she's wasn't there. Wherever there was. She's taken care of, and her mother should not have to become a slave again to this man.

The light waved across the room. "Hello, Sue." His voice slithered across the room chased by the whine of his T-port.

"What the fuck do you want with me?"

"I missed you." The door closed behind him. "I've been longing for your touch."

"You will never get away with this. When Maia finds out and the other Readers—"

"The other Readers are dead!" Rankin turned on the light.

Sue gasped. She wanted to form the words "What do you mean dead?" But her lips wouldn't move.

"Aww, what did they do to you?" Rankin's hands brushed her wounds.

"Don't touch me!"

"I told them not to harm you. They'll be dead by sunup tomorrow. They didn't touch you, did they?"

"Fucking touch me? Are you that fucking stupid, they tackled me and beat me, you asshole."

"At least they left your underwear on, if they would have ripped all of you clothes off and left none for me"—Rankin sighed—"I'd be putting their eyeballs into a paintball gun and shooting them in the genitals."

Rankin placed his watch on the table, a missing diamond at the five o'clock. "The good news, dear, is that you are now with the sole president and CEO of entire company. We can do whatever we want. Anything you want, just name it and it shall be ours. There is no one to stand in our way."

"What did you do?"

"I improvised and took what I wanted."

"What did you do?"

"Sue..." Ranking placed his old tough hand on her bare thigh. He pushed his hand gently up. "You don't worry about how I got us here. All I want you to do, sweetheart, is to enjoy the lavishes."

"Maia will never let you get away with this."

"Maia is stuck in a technicality. There is nothing she can do without the other Readers. Tonight she is going to upload and distribute all the vanishing sequences that I've ordered for the entire day, and tomorrow there will be broadcast talking about how I have been doing this all along, by myself. They are going to love us. We are going to be king and queen here."

"You are insane! Don't touch me!"

* * *

"What the fuck was that!" Jaxon pulled back his reins. The horse reared and turned around. Gun fire echoed to the south.

The trailing Humvee that followed pulled up. "Sir, I think that was your eye in the sky. I think the new kid and his girlfriend were on that chopper that just went down over Beekman. The citis' militia has begun fighting back. They are being slaughtered though."

"Well I'll be fucked. Set up a perimeter around the park. Try and maintain communication with the militia. Kalev Delhi is the one they will stand behind. Get that bastard on the horn if he's not already a meat bag." Jaxon pointed to the old City Hall. "We need to block off Barclay Street. That's their main point of access to Lower Manhattan from the Hudson. Let's try and filter them down to have to come up Broadway." A rocket screamed down street and exploded into the red building behind them. The whole contingency flinched and hunched. Jaxon didn't flinch on his horse.

"Faster, gentlemen!" Jaxon hopped off his horse, glass crunching beneath his boots when they slammed to the ground. His men emptied out the caravan and Humvees. "Return fire! We have tanks too! Fuckers want to play with fire. We'll play with fire. I have been waiting a long time for this."

The tank behind them hawked a shell back in a distant explosion.

Jaxon spit and inhaled deep through his nose. "Nothing like the smell of gunpowder in the morning. Hell yeah, boys! We got ourselves a fight! Fan out!"

* * *

Whaamp! Whaamp! The bikes tilted to the side, ducked, and weaved through debris and around potholes and divots. Herds of citis flocked the opposite direction. Their peripheral vision a blur at this speed. "Watch out! Move!" Silva led the way through a slow convoy. "We need to get to the top of Canal Street to try and contain them." Silva clipped a man who spun and fell. Phil and Wes juked around him nearly sideways. Hayden dodged a broken taxi and slipped through a crevasse of two busted and battered busses and appeared out the other end. They stopped, lined shoulder to shoulder, gear ready to go.

"What do you think, Wes?" The words slipped through the thin morning mist.

Wes checked his EED. "Bravo to Delta." He waited. "Bravo to Delta, come in. Where the fuck is Alix?"

"Alpha to Bravo, come in." Victor's voice rang through.

Wes turned to Phil and Hayden and shrugged. "Alpha... Whiskey Tango Foxtrot!"

"It's complicated Bravo. One of Silva's men went AWOL and took out communications. Took us on a snipe hunt. Locale on Delta? Chick still with 'em?"

"I don't know, Delta's in the air to rendezvous for reconnaissance."

"That's what I was afraid of, Bravo."

Victor's voice shook in their ears. Wes breathed deep. "Copy?"

"A bird just went down over Beekman Tower. Investigating now. We are two blocks away from crash site."

Wes hung his head. "Bravo to Alpha, investigate crash site. Please get a pair of eyes on to the top of Beekman. That is our best vantage point. If he made it, that is where he is."

"Roger that."

"And Bravo…good to hear from you."

"Copy that."

Hayden lifted his shield to his helmet. "You guys know we don't have to be here. This isn't our fight. Not that I don't want to put one or thirty up on the kill list, but at the end of the day, we could just bail. Alix is gone, what did he give his life for?"

Wes looked around. He studied the dark sky and the way it felt, smelled the stale air and the subtle echoes of screams and guns that whispered to him in the distance. "No, Hayden, this is our fight. It might not be the fight that MAIA wanted us to fight, but this is our father's and grandfather's fight, and it is unfinished." Wes looked into Silva's eyes. "My gut is saying send the rest down Church Street and flank them from there. Jaxon will commence the heavy fighting and draw them farther east. I say we break off and flank them down Route 9. I think Adam, Phil, Hayden, and myself could put a dent in 'em. They wouldn't know what hit 'em."

Silva stared into the windshield of Wes's helmet. "That could be suicide. A team of four taking on a flank of an army."

"Have you seen our simulations?"

"Yeah, well this is real life, Wes. You don't come back if you go down."

"Yeah, except we are not going down."

Silva studied Wes. He didn't look away. Silva looked across at the other three on the bikes. The engines gargled as they waited for an order, waited to be released to do what they have been born and programmed to do. "All right, I'll take the rest of the convoy down Church." Silva held out his fist.

Wes punched his gloves. "Good luck, Silva, keep you head down."

Wes turned his bike. Hayden lifted his front wheel and road just the rear wheel for nearly the block. Phil spun the tires until smoke and the smell of rubber oozed in the air. Silva shook his head.

* * *

"You see that?"

"Yeah. What do you think that was all about?"

"I don't know, but these guys are not fucking around. They look like the same enemy we were fighting before, fucking Eastern world spilling into ours. It's like I went underground for nearly a decade and nothing's changed."

Eli pressed his eyes into the binoculars. "What do you think we should do?"

"We don't have sides. We shouldn't do anything."

"Didn't you say that you fought these people before?"

"Well yeah, my whole life." Gunther searched down the scope. His crosshairs scanned the small bits of fire from the spilling fuel of the helicopter that slid off the roof. Demolished railings and wreckage through the metal carnage trailed across the roof when it slipped off the backside of the building and fell into a small spark of light. The echo became absorbed by the booms of war a little under 1776 feet below.

"I fought these sand niggers in the war on terror both times. I did four tours in that fucking sand box." Gunther panned the roof. "We joked about just making that whole section a parking lot, I think we were right."

"A parking lot? Parking for what?" Eli watched a dangling cable off the roof and heard another explosion below. The wind picked up his sleeves and flapped them in the wind; his wingsuit begged for flight.

"Yeah, there was so much violence over there." Gunther hawked and spit. "Every fucker over there with a ski mask, a beard, or an AK thought they were king. They'd start beheading journalists and start another war. Should have just nuked 'em when we had the chance."

"How is that logical?" Eli spit.

"Logically speaking, we would have never had those fuckers over here. Every time we laid off them, they attacked here. First was 911..."

"There is a lot of speculation about 911. Didn't you pay attention to anything?" Eli squinted and panned over the destruction of the roof.

"I don't believe a plane hit the Pentagon, there's enough evidence to support that, but I believe it's these fucking jihad people that cause all this destruction because some tribe cut off someone's great grandfather's arm and supported a distant relative of that tribe."

"You don't think it has to do with the fight over the Holy Land over the last two thousand years? It's the same fight. American's didn't make it any better when they told the Iranians to fuck off and gave Jerusalem to the Jews. I get that World War II was tragic for those people, but the Iranians had nothing to do with it. We might as well call this the Continued Crusades."

"What the fuck did they program you with? You're like an encyclopedia that can't shut up or remember fucking yesterday."

"What do you mean?"

Gunther scanned the roof slowly. His cross hairs searching. "I mean that you know the whole world's story, but after a flip of a switch you forget who your best friend is and somehow think that you were banging his girlfriend. It's like ever since I pegged Milligan, all you fucker's minds went mush. Want me to dig that chip out of your head? I got a knife and stitches right here."

"You killed Captain Milligan?" Eli eyed the rifle. "With that?"

Drizzle settled on the long barrel of the Dragunov sniper rifle and the binoculars. The air became still. Gunther breathed deep, inhaled mist sifting over his thin mustache. No good way of explaining this to this kid existed. Gunther closed his eye and wiped his head. "Orders, kid. Orders. You should understand it was nothing personal."

Eli bowed his head. His eyes welled. His limbs felt detached. He sniffled. "When?"

"Two days ago, nineteen hundred thirty-two hours."

"With that?"

Gunther sighed. "Yes."

"Did he make it off the island?"

"No more details, kid. Your boy took my little brother out four minutes later. I'd rather not talk about it."

"Alix?"

"Yup."

"I'm sorry."

"Me too." Gunther sighed. "My little brother didn't know when to call it quits. Captain Milligan was just in the way of my bullet and orders. Let's put this behind us, please."

"Understood."

Eli zoomed in on a small black clump on a twisted bent-over railing on the far side of the Beekman tower. "What the?" He followed the short skin color to the black cutoff sleeve. "Is that a severed arm? Hanging over the back of the building?"

Gunther zoomed in. "Ah, I can't tell. It's…it's…not severed."

33

"Anna! Hold on!" Alix gritted his teeth. His assault rifle slid off his shoulder and down around their connected wrists and hung around Anna's neck. "Argh!" He looked up to his fingers locked on a bar just over the roof. His and her weight tugged at the cuff in Alix's shoulder; they dangled like a tire swing in a storm. "Arrggh!" He looked down into her precious honey eyes. Tear streams down each side of her face. One salty drip flipped off her cheek and swinging body and blended into the water in the air in to a vicious forever decent.

"Alix! Don't let me go. Don't let me go." She squeezed both hands around his forearm. "Please, don't let me go."

The small of fire and puff of smoke diminished in the background far below her dangling body. Drizzle lubricated his gloves and landed delicately on her cheeks like a snowflake. She slipped. "Ahh! ALIX!"

"Holy shit! I gotcha. Hold on. Holy fuck." Alix looked around. "Anna, can your feet reach that ledge!?"

"I don't know."

"Look!"

"I don't know. Maybe. I don't think so."

"Okay, then I'm going to swing you in that direction. This building is twisted and shaped oddly enough, you can slide down catch that ledge six levels down. It'll be a two-meter leap."

"Okay, I see it. I can make it." The shrill in her voice pierced Alix.

"One." Alix swung her. "Two." He breathed heavily through his teeth. "Three!" He pushed her momentum and slid her diagonally toward the balcony six levels down on the east side of the building like angling a bowling ball.

"Ah! Alix!" Anna twisted and landed hard on the damp, arched, and twisted siding of the building. She slid down, eyed the balcony seconds before her, planted her feet, and lunged for the railing. Her legs churned hundreds of feet over the ground, and gravity swiped at her legs like flames, tried to snag a foot and pull her toward the core of Earth. She slammed into the railing, her vest absorbing some impact. Her arms clung frantic for something to hold. She still felt what was like a pile of rocks just plopped down on her chest and sucked the air from her lungs. She sucked in deeply, gasped for her breath, her arms hooked around the top of the railing.

"Anna! You okay!" Alix felt the relief from the weight, and he pulled his body up just enough to switch arms.

Anna held out her arm. She couldn't speak, her lungs deflated. She choked for air and wheezed. She held up her thumb.

Alix sighed and pulled himself up onto the roof and collapsed on his back to catch his breath. His Barrett, formerly dangling across his chest, fell next to him equally as relieved like two lovers after making love. He watched the drizzle appear from the gray sky and spiral down into his iris, felt it diminish into his pupil and absorb into his body—osmosis. He breathed as deep as he could three times and listened to chimes of war below, like a violent version of the Fourth of July—parades were people fleeing, the booms were artillery, firecrackers were bullets, cheers were cries, oohs and aahs were cries and sobs, the flashes were machine gun tracers, the smiles were nonexistent.

"Matt!?" Alix turned to the side, his hand splashed in a small rainbow puddle of fuel spilled from the chopper. Oil ran down the back of his neck, smeared his face. "Matt!? You here!"

Alix heard the glass door drop below from the balcony. "Anna! Be careful!" Alix reached for his SCAR. Nothing. The assault rifle slid down to the crash below along with his ammo box inside the chopper. He had one mag in his rifle and six mags for his pistol. He rolled to his knees near the edge of the building. He cracked his neck. "Matt!" Alix pulled his pistol. "Matt! You alright?"

Alix walked leg over leg, shoulder pulled back, angled to the stairs, his gun his line of sight. "Matt?"

Alix heard a moan. He darted up the metal steps, his boots screeching through the water. "Matt!"

Matt had exploded into the control booth. Alix looked over him lounging in beads of yellow glass and steel bars twisted in lay across him the in nest of destruction. A wrought iron rod protruded through his thigh.

"Matt?" Alix leaned over him, pulled his goggles up over his eyes, and tapped the side of his face. "Matt?"

"Alix?" Matt's voice gurgled, deflated and depleted. His eyes rolled up like shades and closed again.

"Is there anymore damage besides this rod?"

Matt's body released and fell limp. "Alix, just let me go. I think every bone in my body is smashed." Matt nodded for his pistol.

"No! Can you move your toes?"

Matt shook his head. "I can't feel anything. I can probably move my arms. Yup." Matt lifted his arm. Shards of glass and chipped paint tinkled off. "Fuck, Alix, what happened? How'd we even get here?"

"Short answer is that you had already exited the helicopter before it was shot down." Alix unlatched Matt's assault rifle and slung it around his own head. He removed his pistol and extra ammo.

Anna kicked open the door and snapped back and forth to clear each way. "Alix!"

"Anna! Over here!"

Anna sprinted up the stairs on the east side of the building and slid next to Alix. Her heart froze. Somehow the real thing was…well, real. "There's no way to tell if the rod ruptured his femoral artery. If it did he won't last long. There's a lot of blood. We need to stop the flow, and we can't pull the rod out yet, it could release any pressure holding the blood flow in."

"He's saying he can't feel his toes."

"The impact could have broken his spinal cord." Anna's hands scanned his injuries and took a mind of their own.

"He can move his arms."

"He's lucky he can move anything, and without the proper supplies, he may not make it. Twenty-three percent, maybe. My bag went down with the chopper." Anna sat back and thought. She looked to the side. "I don't know what to do or where to start." She sighed. Anna pulled the battle knife from Matt's gear. She applied pressure to his inner thigh and cut his pants. "I need to stop the bleeding in his thigh first." She ripped off his boot. Matt's foot hung limp like a wet noodle broken in three places at least. "He's lucky he can't feel below the belt right now."

"Anything I can help with?"

"Radio Jaxon or Silva and see if they can get supplies up here. I know it might be hard, but if we don't, I don't think he'll make it. It sounds like hell down there."

Alix checked his EED. "Delta to Bravo, survived the bird going down need medivac pronto, do you read? Delta to Bravo?"

Static. "Alpha to Delta, in range ETA fifteen minutes. Going to have to take the stairs."

"Alpha?"

"Long story, Delta. ETA fifteen minutes."

Alix looked down to Anna and shrugged, "Victor is on his way."

"Victor?" Anna, knelt down in a pool of blood, held a dirty white cloth in her mouth. She tied a strip tightly around his thigh before the wound.

"Yeah, should be up here in like fifteen mins."

* * *

"Hold! Who goes there!" Twelve guns aimed down the sights at the small contingency of dirty militia.

"Kalev Delhi! Hold your fire!" Kalev brushed off the rubble from his shirt and let his M4 rifle dangle. "There's a larger group of Minutemen behind us. Hold your fire."

The soldiers lowered their weapons.

"Where is Jaxon?"

The soldier held his gun up. "That is classified information for a citi."

"You've been classified all morning as a fucking coward." Kalev shouldered him. "Move. Where the fuck were you guys when we were getting slaughtered out there?"

Jaxon stood over an ice cream truck lying on it's side. "The Minutemen held them to here, and they seem to be counting their money right now and regrouping. They probably figure that will be the toughest part of this fight. They took everything west of Wall Street and south of Barclay in two hours. Hopefully our flanking boys join the party soon. Private"—Jaxon pointed—"radio our new friend Silva, find out his ETA. It's about to get real messy here within the hour. We need to concentrate fire here and here. The second we have this under control, we need to take down that ship. I swear Piruz is on that boat, I can smell the sand and oil from here. Take him down and maybe NYC back, we can get our boys up in Beantown to join in our little fight to avoid reinforcements, and we can march our asses all the way to DC. Have this country back and in a month. Been waiting a long time for this." Jaxon clapped. "Oorah!"

"Oorah." The group parted like a football huddle.

"Jaxon!" Kalev power walked straight toward him.

Jaxon turned and smiled. "Kalev Delhi, hope you talked to Allah this morning." Jaxon held out his hand. "We're going to need both our gods to win this one."

Kalev's fist shot out and crashed into Jaxon's cheek. "You muddafukka!" Kalev went after Jaxon as he tumbled back. Kalev's men sprinted behind. Jaxon's men tore Kalev off. "Where da fuck were you!"

Jaxon snapped to his feet and wiped the blood from his lip. Jaxon's men held Kalev's arms tight.

Kalev tugged and kicked. "You bastards! You have any idea how many men and women and children were killed this morning?"

Jaxon kicked Kalev in the chest. "You don't like it, go back to your own country then, you sorry son of a bitch!" Jaxon planted his fist into Kalev's shoulder blade. His body fell limp in the two soldiers' hands.

Kalev snapped back up and broke his arms free. His men jogged over. Kalev tackled Jaxon. "This *is* my country, you racist piece of shit!"

Kalev's men pulled him off in the scuffle.

"Enough!" Jaxon wiped the dirt off and stood.

Kalev spat at his feet. "And our gods are the same, dipshit!"

"Tell that to the sand-sucking terrorist running that command center on the Hudson right now." Jaxon wiped off his blood again. "If this swells, I'm going to kill you."

"I don't think your head can swell anymore! What do you plan on doing about that army a click south of here?"

"I've seemed to lose my train of thought after gettin' sucker punched. You ever strike me again, Kalev, and the only red dot on your forehead will be from my sights."

"Well this *American*"—Kalev pounded his chest—"has fought for his country all morning and nearly lost his life over a dozen times. And I'm not Indian, you idiot!"

Jaxon dabbed his lip. "It's fucking numb. You prick." He spat. "Where are we at?"

Kalev approached the map. "They have this whole area under control now. They are filtering in more from the Jersey side of the river. Last I heard there were about ten to fifteen barges about to launch reinforcements over for them at a moment's notice. I have a small unit held down here concealed and awaiting for orders." Kalev dabbed his finger on the map. Most of the citis that didn't get mowed down retreated to the sewer and rail system. Most would head north I have to presume. I have another maybe five hundred men trailing behind me. The rest were scattered. We've been fighting all morning. The ones who survived are pretty banged up."

Jaxon spat blood on ground and used his boot to smear it into the street. "I got a bird down already with my eye in the sky and a unit in flanking position as we speak. We are going to be blind, but if we can hit 'em straight on once our flank is in position, we have a shot. I have a special ops group circling now with scuba gear and explosives to try and take down that barge. We believe Piruz to be on it."

Kalev placed both his fists on the table and breathed through his nose. "You really think we can do this?"

Jaxon held out his hand. "If we work together to defend *our* country, yes, you fucking jihad."

Kalev half smiled. "Okay, nigger, let's send these fuckers back to the sandbox." Kalev grabbed his hand.

Jaxon squeezed his hand. "How about straight to the grave?"

* * *

Maia didn't know what it was like to smile or feel gratification. But if ever a time existed to have or feel it, it would be now; she knew that much. In this world created overnight there were no Readers to override her decisions. The only one left alive had given an order to apply a vanishing sequence on himself by giving the order to erase the existence of a currier. It for sure was in the gray, but Maia didn't have ethics or morals. She had logic.

The most logical outcome of her not applying this vanishing sequence was that Rankin had a 70 percent chance of running the company into the ground. The percentage that the army they worked so hard to complete would even be used was 40 percent. If they commenced conservation of the mainland, their percentage of success dropped 18 percent with just him in charge. Only a 60 percent chance of him living year over year existed, and that decreased exponentially twenty percent year over year. When he died, there would be no Readers to vote for another Reader. Therefore, the result ended up the same nearly every time Maia configured the scenario. Rankin now had a better chance of having another child with Ms. Maynard than he did of actually commencing conservation and eliminating of the citis. Vanishing sequence initiated.

* * *

Sue opened her eyes. A loose-skinned arm hung over her waist. Her cheek sunk into the wet pillow, saturated in tears. She had one shot at fighting him back during the whole dreadful event, but he stung her with a paralyzer to keep her from fighting. He had his way with her, yet again. Sue could not believe she stared at the same wall looking for answers. She'd thought long and hard about what she would do if this ever happened again. The only thing that could stop her from doing it at the time was Anna.

Sue smiled. She knew from the way Anna looked at that boy she was in love. She had a hard time watching some of the simulations with Anna and Alix. And most of the time, Sue had the decency to scroll away and watch the rest of the battle rage on while Anna and Alix snuck off in the middle of a battle to be together. Sue laughed out loud the time a digital ally tried to stop them from running off right at the start. The soldier grabbed at Alix's arm, fought him to the ground. He almost had cuffs on Alix as Anna pulled the trigger on her own teammate. She was not letting anyone get in the way of her cuddle time with her man.

Sue couldn't tell if it was ironic or not that they ended up together. Out of the whole regiment of that army, they were the only two kids without the highest level chip. They both could think for themselves all the time, and it became a difficulty to get them to believe any of the updates. Sue remembered the first time she watched them run off into a building being pelted with rockets. She knew what they were going to do, but Sue couldn't help the motherly instinct. She should have reported it immediately to Maia and the Readers. Instead she deleted the simulation all together.

From that point on, Sue stayed up every night to see if they would sneak out together, on different floors to their own designated simulators just to be together. They never even actually met. Sue remembered the first time they were cuddled in the back of a broken and burnt-up, shot-up cab. She remembered the look in his eyes when he told her he loved her for the first time. Sue zoomed in on that moment over and over that night, didn't get an ounce of sleep, and deleted the simulation reluctantly. Sue knew her daughter would be in good arms. Sue felt complete. Complete and fed up. Sue would now be a slave of his again. She had done it for years already and swore she would never do it again.

Sue lifted her head.

"Where you going?"

"Nowhere, just to the bathroom. I have to pee."

"Okay, don't be long, I got a surprise when you come back. I know how you like my morning surprises."

Sue lifted the sheet off her bare body and felt his eyes on her rear the whole walk to the bathroom. She sat down on the toilet and buried her head in her palms. She looked over the tub and, like her body decided before her brain did, she turned the tub on. Sue wiped the tears from her eyes, a few dropping into the hot running water, and she plugged the drain.

* * *

Ranking heard the click. The click from Maia that a broadcast would be coming soon. He'd better wake. He didn't have that much time to get up, get ready, and hurry down the café to start preparing the goop for the long line of workers. He slid his bare legs off the bed. He walked past his T-port, back arched, step over slow step toward the restroom. If he didn't leave his room an hour and a half early, he'd never make the walk.

He'd wonder why he had never asked Maia for a cane, the way his back ached already. He coughed. He gurgled in his mouth and spat into the sink. He pulled himself through his tighty- whities and let the fluid drain. He looked over at Sue dead and limp and floating in the tub midpiss. "Arh! Who is this! Maia! Who is that? What happened here?" Rankin backed away from the toilet as if on stilts, still peeing, and collapsed backward. His hip shattered into twelve pieces. "Maia! I've fallen and I can't get up! Maia! Who is this! Maia! I'm going to be late for work! Maia!"

Rankin remained the only Reader alive. Therefore, the only Reader in the Reader's quarters. Maia had reconfigured all of MAIA. Therefore, no one would be checking for Readers or even knowing they ever existed. No one was coming for help. No one.

"Maia! Please." Rankin held his hip, his face twisted in pain and tears. "Someone come help me."

34

"Infidels!" Piruz pounded on table and whizzed his hat. All six buttons on his coat gleamed. The badges carpeted his chest. His eyes narrow and beard a mix of black and gray and stress of leading a new world order for the last two and a half decades starting from the sands of Iran to all of New England. "We police these people for years and politely ceasefire. This is how we are repaid for kindness? Death to them all! I'm going to hang the whole city by their necks from every building we can!"

No one in the command post breathed. No one dared. The air remained stiff and still and stale and smelled of incense. The blood and thick contents of the head of the last one who spoke still crept down the wall. Somebody dragged the body out but neglected to clean the walls.

Piruz stared at the freedom tower up above them. "Freedom! Pah! They didn't know what to do with it when they had it. Bragging about freedom. Half the world had freedom. We'll start with hanging any rebels from the top of that precious tower. Maybe they'll remember then. We need to set an example for the rest of the coast! Then, maybe then, we can get the rest of these snotty nosed American that fled to the inner parts of the country like little sissies!"

"Sir."

"What!" Piruz turned and pulled his gun out.

"I am getting a message that a rebellion has started in the northeast section. Former Boston area has become a similar state. A battleground, sir."

"Arr! They are like a disease! You kill the cancer in one place, and it pops up in another. These fucking Americans don't know when to quit. It's it a national holiday or something?"

"No sir, the Fourth of July is in two months time, and sir—"

Piruz put his pistol to his commander's head. "Give me more bad news. Go ahead."

"Please don't kill me, please," the commander whimpered. "We have activity on the freeway."

"What do mean activity?"

"Movement." The commander zoomed in. "Four...motorcycles."

"Fire! Fire at them now! Prepare the cannons! Kill everyone! All soldiers in New York go to total warfare and prepare our nuclear weapons for our friends up north. We are about to have a Boston massacre. Give the order to evacuate, they will think they won the fight."

"Sir, should we consult the elders before arming another nuclear weapon again?"

Piruz pulled the trigger. A spark, bolt, and a quick rumble in the room projected blood onto the command post's floor. "That's for being weak!" Piruz turned to the rest in the room. "Anyone else want to question me?" Piruz dragged his former commander off the controls and to the floor. He tore off his blood soaked turban and tossed it aside. "Throw him overboard. Prepare the missiles. We are going to put a stop to the rebellion right now, both here and in Boston. Give an evacuation notice to our men up north and launch the missile right at the city in one hour. As for New York, give the order to move forward. Total warfare, women, children, men, boys, cats, and dogs—if it moves I want it dead. I want this whole city under control again, by nightfall Allah permits. I had enough of this."

* * *

Four motorcycles flashed by a speed limit sign of sixty-five miles per hour. A flicker of light and puff of smoke from the barge in the bay and came an explosion that blew out the side of the building right behind them and shook their world beneath the tires.

"Holy shit!" Hayden screamed and twisted the throttle. "Incoming!"

Another building exploded next to them. A fiery car toppled over and tumbled across the street right in front of them like a toy whipped by a little boy across a kitchen floor. Phil dodged just in time.

Wes arched his neck and banked left as small boards and chunks of stone and glass rained over him. "Argh! Spread out! Incoming!"

The four bikes weaved through, in and out of the debris from the explosions that rained down on and around them. The buildings to their left popped like popcorn over and over and sent debris onto their path. The bikes blasted through the swirling smoke. Just another mile before the buildings of Teardrop Park and Battery City cover their line of sight.

"We need to get off this road! They are going to get lucky eventually!"

"Luck has nothing to do with it!"

The next bombardment ahead ripped a streetlight out like a tornado and hurled it tumbling through the air toward them. The end caught the front of Phil's bike. Phil flipped head over heals twice before he bounced off the pavement and rolled in a ball of tires, fairings, plates, panels, shields, glass, bearing, and burning motorcycle components. Phil slid into the base of a traffic light and spun into tall grass.

"Phil!"

"Incoming!" The road exploded ahead of them. Wes and Hayden laid the bike down as sparks, grinding metal, and burning pavement became a fast-paced track to a violent explosion they slid straight into. The two bikes shredded two layers and penetrated the suspended parts of earth and asphalt before it tumbled into the massive fiery destruction that was the road.

Adam stayed on the bike and sped into the hell forming in front of them. His bike launched in the air as parts of road crashed down and sucked Adam into a mashing mess of crumbled street, building guts, and shrapnel. It engulfed him and ate his body as everything returned to the crater formed at the vortex of the missile's explosion on West Street.

Wes and Hayden slid toward the hole in the earth and stopped, their boots dangling down the forty foot crater.

Wes rolled over to his stomach; shaky arms pushed himself to his knees. His head hung and shook the dust and clay from his head. Hayden lifted his head and slammed it back down. He stared at the gray sky, spread out in the middle of the road, arms out wide crucified to the street. "There's no way Adam made that. I saw his body flipping through the air and pulverized by bits of street. Wes, this is no longer any fun."

"Hayden, this was never fun." Wes knelt down. He cocked his gun. "Let's go. We need to see if Phil is okay. Then we need to take down that barge. Can you walk?"

"In a minute. I need to just lay here. Just for a minute. My head hurts bad. Like my temples are caving in."

"We don't have a minute. Let's go."

* * *

Eli jotted down some numbers. He looked backwards. "Someone just got lit up on the east side of the island." He pressed some buttons on a calculator. He grimaced. "Ah, my fucking head!" Eli squeezed his temples.

"Focus, Eli." Gunther looked for another peeking head. "One split second in time could be the difference of your life here. Patience and attention are key."

"Ah, I'm trying, but my head just like squeezed tighter and then released. And Alix doesn't know we're here."

"Not yet. Never doubt the intuition of a hunter. And if we missed our first shot, it's game on at that point. Then it's a fifty-fifty chance at that point. Let's not fuck this up. I don't want to go toe to toe with him. You see him on the north side yet?"

"Negative, not since he ran across the top of the building. I still can't believe Alix just got put right in front of us like that. Are you intimidated by Alix?"

"Ho, ho, ho, boy, you have a lot to learn. How could I even be intimidated if I were dead? When the game is survival, all I need to be is alive still. No rules. It's not about brawn or being better. Anyways, putting Alix on that building makes sense. They wanted him on the highest point from their position. Fortunate for us, he happens to be our target for Rankin."

"Who?"

"Rankin."

"I don't know what that is. Who's Rankin?"

"Are you mental? The guy that sent us to kill Alix." Gunther lifted his eye from his scope, a forbidden action. "If you are going to spot for me, I need you to keep your fucking head on your shoulders and screwed on tight. Do you remember why you are here?"

"Yeah, Maia sent us for a scouting mission ahead of time. Alix is a citi, he was sent into Manufacturing Artificial Intelligence Agency as a spy for the citis. That's why his chip never worked, but he still got an embedded screen and kidnapped my damn girlfriend. Look, look! There's Anna. Get ready, target six hundred nine point six meters, southeast. Elevation is two hundred seventy-five meters below trajectory, dew point seventy-six degrees. Wind"—Eli checked his EED—"thirty-two kilometers per hour, south southeast."

"Eli." Gunther lowered the butt of his rifle. He looked, tilted his head down. How the hell could he not know who Rankin is? Why doesn't he know? Did they…"Eli, how many Readers are there in the company?"

Eli pulled his eyes from his binoculars. "How the hell am I suppose to know how many people can read or not on the island?"

"No, Eli, Readers. The people who determine what actions are made from Maia's assessment of the situations."

"Gunther, you getting Alzheimer's or something, old man? No one tells Maia what to do. There are no Readers or whatever you're talking about. Maia is the first and only computer in the world to be self sufficient and self providing and has the unbiased logic humans need to run governments." Eli put his eyes into the binoculars. "Get on point, will ya. We have a traitor to kill, and I have a conjoined partner to save."

Gunther thought hard. Is it possible? A vanishing sequence on all the Readers? Maia in charge of MAIA solely? Could her programming really get to Eli from that distance? A computer chief executive officer of a militant company? Holy shit. The movies come true. "Eli, how long has Maia been in charge?"

"How long are you going to ask me dumb questions?"

"Just answer the question?"

"If I answer the question, are you still going to pop Alix when he shows his face?"

"Yes, just answer the question."

"Maia has been fully instated for the last fifteen years. She hasn't needed any human assistance running that facility for over nine. What is with all the questions all of a sudden? First you try and convince me that the guy we are trying to kill is my friend, now this? Wait, what the…"

They watched the armed figures kick through the door and penetrate the roof. Perfectly.

"Is that? Billy, Chris, and Todd? How did they know?"

Gunther checked his scope. "Cowboys…"

"Wait! That's Victor…"

35

"Alpha to Delta, breaching door." The door to the roof of Beekman tower busted open.

Anna pulled the cloth knot tighter around Matt's leg. "Hang in there, Matty." She grabbed the side of his face, the blood smearing from her hands. "Hang in there. Look at me. I'm going to get you out of this."

Matt's eyes locked to hers and trailed off.

"Alix!" Victor approached.

Alix spun around relieved. "How the hell did you find us?"

"I had a hunch."

Alix's eyebrows narrowed. "Who are they?"

Victor pulled his pistol. Pointed it to Alix's head. "Hands up!"

Chris, Todd, Billy, and Silva's men, Brian, Leo, and Aaron pointed their assault rifles. Alix went for his pistol. Victor decked him. "Don't make me kill you, Alix! You're worth more alive, but you're not the one I need breathing. Anna, get up." Victor pointed and diddled his fingers upwards. "Let's go. Come with me."

Alix stepped forward, "Victor, what are you doing?"

"Graves, take Alix over there near the edge. Anna, get up."

Aaron moved in on Alix, assault rifle aimed into his chest. The eyes of mask glowed. "You heard 'im, move." Aaron motioned toward the edge. They walked up on the west side ledge.

"Victor," Anna's voice cracked.

Victor backhanded her across the face. "Do not address me like you know me. Get up."

"I can't take pressure off his wound or it'll bleed out."

Victor pointed his gun into Matt's eyes and pulled the trigger. Matt's body fell limp. "There, now you don't have to worry about it."

Anna's mouth hung open. She opened her eyes. Matt's blood sprinkled her face. She spit some out. "You son of a bitch!" Her face twisted in anguish.

Victor snagged Anna's arm, elbowed her in head twice, and threw her into the railing. "Shut up!" Victor pointed at her. He looked to Chris. "Keep a gun on her! She moves, put a bullet in her leg."

Victor approached Alix with his hands raised to the dingy sky. Gun to his back pointed over the city. "Alix, Alix, Alix. It's been fun, hasn't it?"

"Victor, it's not too late." Alix felt his heart everywhere; it pounded throughout his body.

"You are so right, Alix. It is not too late." Victor approached him. "I could just finish what we started back in simulation right now. You little pussy." Wind pushed through their gear, the city below around them, surrounded them like an arena of the ancients, a coliseum of catastrophe. "You lead us all the way to the end and fuck us all right before it counts. Worst case of blue balls in the history of MAIA. All you had to do was shoot. Shoot that little bitch behind that gun, and none of this would be happening. We would have been celebrating right afterwards instead of sprinting around the vomit room like a bunch of freshmen and rookies. You embarrassed me!" Victor slugged Alix.

Alix stumbled near the edge. "Victor! You know Captain put Anna into that simulation. You know why I didn't shoot. You saw her too!"

"Fuck Captain Milligan. He was a softy. A fake. Big fucking teddy bear if you ask me. Walking around like the big dog. Waving around a six-shooter he'd never shot. And I shot that Anna look-a-like after she mowed down your entire team!" Victor pointed toward her. "She is a threat to your advancement in the company! Well, was.

I could never trust you after that! I knew there was something off about you. Something fucked up in the head.

"Then you had to actually surprised me. You had to actually go and do something that even shocked me. So utterly disgusting and low that even *I* was surprised. We find out, you were a spy for the citis the whole time! Come to find out, you don't really give a shit about any of us. Or Anna?"

"What?" Alix's face scrunched.

"You don't have to deny it anymore, Alix. We got the upload this morning from Maia. She figured you out. She figures everything out. You fucking traitor. I don't know how you made it as long as you did, but those citis have you programmed well."

"Victor, what are you talking about? Reader Rankin had access to my EED, he knows everything about me. I was born in that facility with you!"

"Reader who?"

"Rankin! Supreme Reader of MAIA. Have you gone mad!"

"You can't stop lying, can you? You are just lying to yourself at this point." Victor approached him. "If you were not so valuable to Maia right now, I would have a lot of pleasure watching your body swim through the air until you splattered below."

"Victor, don't do this. There must have been a broadcast, you are better than this."

Victor slugged Alix again. Alix went for Victor. Aaron fired a warning shot over the edge. Alix shrugged and shot his hands above his head again.

"Alix! No!" Anna squealed.

Victor and Alix stood face to face.

Alix's jaw tightened. His eyes darted and narrowed. His breath shortened through his nostrils.

"What?" Victor smirked. Victor twirled his finger in the air. "Tie these two love birds up, and let's get 'em to the truck. Be home by dinner. Maia's going to love us."

Billy held out his fist for a bump to Todd. "Imagine all the time in simulation she'll allow us."

"Hell yeah, B. Roger that." Todd bumped him.

Aaron grabbed Alix's arms, pressed the gun into his side. Alix stared into Victor's eyes. "I'm going to kill you. I don't know when. I feel like it's soon, but I'm going to kill you."

"Oh yeah. All right, guys, if I get killed, I order you all to rape Anna in every hole she's got. Make sure our boy over here is alive and watches the whole thing. Make sure they both get back to Maia alive enough to remember it. Understood?"

Chris and Brian smirked. "Hell yeah, muthafuckin' understood. Damn." Brian lifted her by the arm. Chris slapped her ass and kissed her cheek and groped her inner thighs. "Here's to hoping. No offense, Victor."

"Keep hoping." Anna swung at Chris and landed a solid hook in the chin. She spun and kicked Brian in the chest. He bounced back into the railing, rolling up, back, and over and slamming on the platform below. Anna snagged the knife at Matt's feet and hurled it at Chris. The knife nicked Chris's cheek, a sliver of blood escaping, and it spun off into space.

"Anna!" Alix planted his forehead into Victor's nose, felt the smooshing of cartilage and sound of the bone snapping. Victor stumbled back toward the edge, tried to regain sight through tears, blackness, and blood. He bent over and cupped his face. He felt the edge of the building on his heel and wavered.

Alix's left hand snapped back at the same time and pushed the barrel of Aaron's gun to wave over the city as it fired. Alix reached around his back and snagged his pistol, pushed it into Aaron's side, and pulled the trigger. Aaron's eyes widened to the bang. Alix thrust his forearm around and elbowed Aaron in the eye socket and sent his body over the edge and into a freefall of over a thousand feet. Alix whipped around, the tip of his gun whirling for Victor to be in his sights. He fired. Missed. Victor dove down and around a mutilated ventilation shaft from the chopper. He pulled his gun from his holster and fired blindly around the corner towards Alix and forced him into cover.

Leo and Billy backed into defensive maneuvers to the south side as Anna snagged Matt's semiauto. Brian regained consciousness and backed to the east side of the building to join Todd. Anna fired at Chris. Chris hopped the railing and crouched behind a large pipe across the top of the roof, sparks and pings following him up and over. Anna knelt behind a steel-plated railing overlooking her enemies. "Alix! Position?"

"North, northeast. Pinned." Alix let off two shots near Victor. "You okay?"

"No time for sweet nothings. You have a shot at target over the pipe?"

Alix poked his head out. Two bullets ignited little sparks around his head. "Negative. You have a shot at Victor?"

"Negative. We're outnumbered two to six. Alix, this is worse than normal."

"We've been through worse."

"I said worse than normal."

"We are surrounded, keep the north side of the building to your back. I'll come to you. Can you get me any covering fire?" Alix held his ear to hear. "Anna?"

"I suppose. I think the only thing going for us, is they want us alive."

"I don't think we have that going for us anymore, hunny." Bullets pinged by Alix's head.

36

"Phil!" Wes sprinted over to the limp lump. "Phil!" Wes slid into him on his knees. "Phil! You okay?"

"Ouch! What the…What happened?" Phil lifted his head and shook it. "Arh! Felt like I got hit with a truck." He sat up. "You have my gun?"

Hayden handed it to him. He stared at the barge. The long smoking barrels and dozens of trails smoking off into the distance camouflaged into the smoky dark sky. The smell of gunpowder and fire in the air. His head throbbed, and just now the pain subsided. "My temples are being squeezed." Phil ducked his head between his knees.

"Guys." Hayden watched the smoke in the distance. He couldn't get the image of Adam falling into the debris and being crushed by pieces of street out of his head. His whole life, he could just pull the plug from his simulator, and Adam would be sitting there. Maybe that's what this all was. Just an ultimate simulation. Punishment for failing the last one. "What are we doing here? I wish I could just wake up, take my simulation helmet off, and see Alix and Victor and Captain and Adam and have everything go back to normal."

Wes paused after flashing a light in Phil's eyeball. "Phil, follow my finger. Hayden…We just need to…" Wes dropped his hand. He stared at the damp grass. A dragonfly landed before him on the tallest blade, flew to a dandelion often mistaken for a flower, a common defense in plants to be either physically appealing yet poisonous, or useless and deadly to those around it. "You know, Hayden, I don't know." The dragonfly lifted off and disappeared into the dark sky. "I remember having a purpose. I could have preached it an hour ago, but I can't remember it now."

Phil sat up on his own and leaned against the side of the barge. "I'm glad it's not just me. I thought it was the fall. I can't remember any of the reason I'm here, and I feel like there is something extremely off about my facts."

"Well, you've always been a little slow, Phil." Hayden laughed and punched him.

Wes chuckled. "Why would Alix be a spy for the citis? And we went with him knowing that?"

"Because of the captain." Phil deduced. "We would have done anything for Captain. Anything we were told at least."

"I don't think so. I don't remember hating Alix this much. I know he failed simulation for us, but why do I hate him right now? Like I wish I could put a bullet in him."

Hayden nodded. "Yeah, it feels weird to hate him, but I do. I think you're right. I would want to shoot him too, but Maia wants him alive."

"Yeah." Wes pulled some grass out. "It's too bad there isn't someone to overlook Maia's decisions. Like a group or something. That would stop vanishing sequences like what happened to Eli."

Hayden lifted his head. "Alix was right."

"What?"

"Eli!" Hayden kneeled. "Don't you remember. Alix talked about Eli and how we used to train with him and grew up with him. I couldn't remember him before, but I do now! They must have done a reset or something."

"Holy shit, I remember Eli." Phil scratched his head. "Quick little guy."

"There is something messed up going on, but we need to figure out what to do." Wes leaned back against the pole. "I think we can agree on a few things."

Phil tore open a ration and popped it in his mouth. "And what's that?"

"We know that Alix has proven to us that Maia can manipulate our minds, right? We're experiencing this right now, and we still can't help it."

"Yeah."

"Well if we can't remember why we are furious with Alix, but can remember him proving to us that Maia messes with our heads, what's to say that this isn't part of that? Maia obviously wants us to capture Anna and Alix."

"Okay…"

Hayden pulled his pistol. "Oh, they make it feel so good to want to kill Alix though. Like it's personal or something. I just want Maia to burn him."

"I know, but Hayden, we were just bombarded from that ship over there. We owe it to at least Adam to take that barge out. Who ever is in there, doesn't like us. I'm sure if they are firing at us, they are an enemy of MAIA and obviously an enemy to who we feel like we strongly hate right now, including Jaxon too."

"Why?" Hayden motioned for his pistol.

"I don't trust our judgment. Think about it. Technology has clouded our morals. I know that yesterday, I felt a different way than I do right now, and nothing changed. It's the fucking chips in our heads. We are programmed through our little communication devices and teleprompters and broadcasts to believe whoever or whatever is on the other end of that program. I can't even tell you why I feel the way I do, and yet my brain is telling me to radio to Silva and tell him we need to meet up so he can bring us to Jaxon. I feel like we need to put a bullet in both of their heads. I don't even know who to fight for right now. But as soft as it sounds, my heart is saying to stay the course. Maybe not for the reasons we thought they would be but, because we know it's right. Am I wrong?"

Phil sighed. "That was the most pathetic thing I have ever heard you say, Wes. I think we should blow your head off for being such a sensitive pansy. Give me your man card, chop off your dick, and let's take down that barge. And if we have time, I say we stop those mother fuckers from getting over here too." Phil motioned to the two dozen ferries loading up and undocking on the other side of the Hudson. "I don't think they have any business being here."

Wes stood. "Lets get to work then. For our own reasons."

"Wes." Hayden cocked his gun.

"Yes."

"If we make it back, what then? We could go back to MAIA?"

Phil's voice echoed. "Or make a run for it."

Wes pulled his goggles over his eyes. "Let's work on getting back first."

* * *

"Coming in hot!"

A missile screamed down Broadway and exploded a New York City bus in front of the Woolworth Building. The ball of fire flipped backward and landed on top of two parked cars; a monstrous crunching and the heap of fire rolled off.

"Whooa!" Jaxon pulled his fist in quickly, "Damn, this is going to be exciting. Return fire!" Jaxon turned to Kalev. "Okay, you little sand-sucking American, looks like things are heating up. You need some curry before you get started?"

"You're like a black redneck. I'm not Indian. You need to get your Middle Eastern slurs down, I was born here, you asshole." Kalev eyed Jaxon. "Your boy Silva is going to be here in ETA forty-five minutes, so let's get this started. I'll take my men down around William Street and loop around through Pine. I have the rest of my men sneaking around to the back of Wall Street. That will let us know of any flanking or give us full flaking advantage once Silva shows up. You take them head-on and Silva can sideswipe them from here." Kalev moved his hand over the map. "Keep the artillery on them. Line up the tanks, have them fire and get the fuck out of the way for the next. It's a large version of diversion and covering fire to allow us to flank. They are well trained, but I think their ruthlessness to push forward is their weakness."

"You want me to set up a shooting gallery for those fucks? What, give them a huge fucking teddy bear when they get down here?"

Kalev stared through Jaxon. "You don't want them to get here. Hold the line. Trust me. They fight hard."

Jaxon shrugged. "All right. But if we blow up the whole financial district, I don't want to hear from you in a month complaining that you can't police the people here."

"Understood. I'm out. And Jaxon!"

"Yeah." Jaxon turned around.

"Keep your head down. I'd like to sucker punch you again sometime."

Jaxon held up his middle finger. "Anytime, you hit like a girl."

37

"Gunther! You have a shot or not?" Anna is down there. We need to protect her.

"I told you no! You see the same thing I see. Do you see a shot?"

"No. Argh! I'm going insane right now!"

"You're my spotter, so the fucking answer is no. I don't have a shot."

"I'm not going to just sit here." Eli stood and looked up to the top of the Freedom Tower. "I can't stand by and watch Anna get surrounded and captured while you get a stiff finger. I'm going in."

"What do you mean you're going in?" Gunther took his eye away from the scope and leaned back from his post.

"I mean I'm going in." Eli stood and attached the rest of his wingsuit.

"You're out of your mind. That was in case you fell."

"Now it's to get over there."

Gunther knelt before Eli. "You can't just fly over there, Eli."

"I've done the math. It's seventeen hundred and seventy six feet at the top. Wind has increased by five kilometers per hour. I have the wind at my back and almost three hundred meters to drop. The distance is two thousand feet to cover. It's doable. I'm doing it. Not going to sit here with my thumb up your ass and watch my girl get shot."

"It's not your girl! I told you. I've seen it with my own eyes. Anna's in love with Alix, you idiot! Anna is Rankin's daughter. He programmed you to think this way. He told me himself. Eli, you are brainwashed right now. Think about it! I know you're not that ape stupid to go jumping off a building just to impress—"

Eli kicked Gunther in the chest. Gunther fell to his back, tumbled, and reached for the side of the platform on which they perched, but missed it. Gunther spun once before he slammed into the plated ground below and bounced on his ribs. He sucked in deeply, gasped for air, and choked on the thin oxygen.

"Should have kept your opinion to yourself old man." Eli turned and scaled the rafters, the tallest point of the Freedom Tower, light on his feet and quick hands. Left, right, left right. Leap! "Agh!" Eli hung by two arms on protruding pipe. Like a trapezist, Eli's arms swung him up, and he swung to the next pipe. His heart pounded in this throat. "Coming, Anna."

In half the perceived time it would take to get there, Eli perched atop the Freedom Tower. The small world below rattled and shook and burned and exploded. Little flickers of light bounced back and forth. Behind him, a large barge sat in the Hudson like a fat kid in a tub playing war, throwing toys and splashing over the sides. Eli followed the subtle curve of the world over the ocean spread before him, like a three-dimensional map. He admired the hilly Appalachian Mountains in the distance, the rolling green to the north. Lady Liberty cheered him on, half severed arm and all, her bible still close at heart, held tight, but bullet studded.

Eli's wingsuit fluttered in the in breeze. Two zips and a couple clips, and Eli grew wings. He yanked his goggles over his eyes. Through thought patterns, eye movement, focusing, and blinking, Eli marked his target on his virtual HUD display. He stood shaky on what seemed like the highest point in the world, straightened his back, arms out, felt the wind take his arms in his leap of faith. He leapt.

Freefall emotion and internal inertia initiated as strong blowing cool air scooped Eli up and dragged him across the high fog and dark sky. Air blasted by his ears and like a constant flapping of a flag inside his head. His helmet cut through the sky. Below rows and rows of tanks and a military convoy crawled north to an enemy who charged south. What could be mistaken for such small little insects bumping into each other really existed as a violence-hungry group of men and women fighting over pieces of the ground. Again. Still. Stupid humans.

Eli darted toward Beekman Tower like a flying squirrel, his HUD display target growing larger too fast. Eli twisted his back backwards and then right, threw both arms back even more. He banked right. The target grew but appeared too low. He wasn't falling fast enough. Eli tucked his head down and in, pulled his arms into a head-over-heels tuck and roll, and flipped and dropped another ten meters before opening his wings again. The wind caught his flaps between his arms and body and jerked him back on track; he tilted and wavered. Eli continued his bank and pulled his chute as he approached from the south.

* * *

"Alix! Anna!" Victor reloaded a mag and adjusted his gun. "Your pinned, surrounded and outnumbered. Why don't we all just come out with our hands up and talk about this like old friends. We both know you don't belong on this side of the fight. You've been fighting for MAIA your whole lives. What makes you want to change now? Just come back with us, you can do your time or whatever Maia deems necessary, and come back to join the fight after. What you say, pal?"

Alix veered his eye around the corner. A bullet ricocheted off the wall in front of Alix. "Fuck!" Alix popped his head back in. "Anna!"

Her voice rang through in his ear. "Yeah."

"I'm going to provide some cover fire. Can you flank the two on the south side?"

"If I can get around this corner, it should be possible. I can get Victor to shift too."

"I'll pin them down. Get three shots on Victor. I'll continue to fire on him. Take a few shots at the guy behind the pipe and jolt for the door. If we can get into that stairwell, we have a better shot.

Okay, just like we've practiced so many times before, baby. I'll cover you, you cover me."

"You know most of the times we were caught together naked and was killed, right?"

"I would love to be naked with you right now. Ready, move on three. One, two, three!"

Like Batman, Eli fell out of the sky behind Leo and Billy. Anna left her post, fired at Victor. Three bullets pinged her position. She rolled over an old crate, ducked, and returned fire to the origin of the bullets around the side where Leo and Billy were.

Alix popped out, bent wrist and pistol bent around the corner. He let off two shots and jetted toward a crevasse out of sight from where Victor was. Alix shot down at Chris, forcing his head back into cover. Alix released the mag and jammed another in and cocked back the hammer slide, still crouched low in tactical form. "Anna!"

* * *

Eli shot the chute over the edge and onto the city. Leo peaked over his shoulder at the fluttering sound. Eli jammed a knife in his throat, sliced sideways. Billy, standing to Leo's immediate right, lifted his assault rifle and pulled the trigger. Sparks lit the space right next to Eli, who spun in close, jolted three crushing attacks, and ripped Billy's elbow in the opposite direction. Snap. Billy screamed in pain and lifted his limp forearm as his head tucked into Eli's armpit. Eli tucked his forearm under Billy's throat and jolted his body to the side. Billy fell motionless after the crack.

Eli checked left and right and watched Chris charge Anna. He came quick. Anna lifted her gun, but like a train taking out a small car, Chris rammed her into the crate she hid behind. "Ugh!" Anna bounced off the crate and fell.

"You little cunt!" Chris spat on her and kicked her in the ribs, jolted her up off the ground, and rolled her to her back. She held her chest in agony. Chris wiped the sweat from his head, kicked her gun aside—it rattled—and tossed his. "This is just you and me now."

"And me." Eli pulled the trigger of his pistol. Chris's head whipped sideways, and he fell.

"Eli?" Anna's eyes lit up.

"Yeah, I'm here, hun." Eli reached down to help her.

"You should have let me kick his ass."

"We don't have time for that. I was at the top of the Freedom Tower with Gunther."

"Vasily?"

Alix returned fire to Brian and Todd. "Anna! What's going on over there?"

"Eli is here! He just took out three. Should be just Victor and the other two. Alix! Gunther might have a shot on you!"

Victor charged Alix from the side. Alix's gun twirled up and over the edge. Victor pinned Alix. Drove two blows to the face each way. Alix bucked and pulled down on Victor's arm, flipped him around, and planted a fist. Victor bent backward, forced his legs up around Alix's arm, and jerked it in the opposite direction into an arm bar.

"Ah!" Alix reached for his small knife and jammed it into Victor's thigh.

"Ah, fucker!" Victor released, rolled, and pulled out the knife. He tossed it over the edge.

Alix snapped to his feet and tackled Victor. Both men tumbled across the upper platform on the west side of the building. Victor used Alix's momentum and rolled him off. They stood. Alix looked down to his left to the world far below. He smeared away cool blood from his nose.

Victor attacked. Kicked. Blocked. Victor spun and planted a heel into Alix's stomach. Alix stepped back twice, his heel on the edge. Alix jolted forward, blocked a punch, threw an elbow. Solid stick. They sparred off. Alix blocked left, blocked right, punched, punched, punched low. Right punch. Victor stumbled backward, rocked. Alix lunged, lifted, slammed Victor down on the ground, professional football style. Punch, punch, punch.

Brian aimed his gun at Alix, took him in his sights. He approached bent knees. A small crackle from a far off place echoed off the buildings, and four seconds later a 7.62mm bullet crashed through Brian's helmet. Todd checked his left as his comrade disappeared backward. He looked up confused. His last visual a blurry version of the Freedom Tower and a spark of light. A crackle. Four seconds later he flew backward.

Victor tugged at Alix's head in from the back of his neck. Victor rolled him around. Alix kicked him off, snapped to this feet, reached for a pistol, and pointed at Victor to find Victor pointing a pistol back at him. Anna turned the corner. "No!"

38

Kalev Delhi held up his fist. His long line of dirty, beat-up Minutemen dispersed to the each side of road, blended into every nook and cranny and barrel and dumpster and light post and alley way; tactical stances and guns covered every angle. He checked around the crumbling corner and watch dozens of enemies with AKA 47s swarm the opposite direction down Broadway. A tank passed, the ground rumbled the ruble at his feet and shook them out of place. "Delhi to Jaxon. In position. Preparing for flanking maneuver. ETA ten minutes."

Kalev pointed his M4 down the alley and held up three fingers and motioned to go. Three groups of five flashed by him. Kalev retracted back to safety. He motioned up to the half of what was left of the building above them and between thousands of enemies and Kalev's men. The men behind him started boosting up each other to the building, reaching back and down to pull the next one up. If they could get through, that building, shoot from the windows, attack from the alley and swoop around the back all at the same time, they would have the best chance so long as Silva's group arrived on time, and Jaxon's men could advance taking most of the blow. Hopefully trap the enemy on Broadway.

Jaxon's voice radioed in Kalev's ear. "You should see some panic in a moment, Silva and his group just arrived and has commenced fighting! I hear our boys in Boston have won the battle, and the enemy has retreated too! Whoa! Artillery"—a large bang in the background—"is still coming! Whoa! Oh yeah! Fuck 'em up boys!" Another explosion in the background. Kalev pulled the radio from his ear to dangle so he could focus.

"It's not a fucking a YouTube channel," Kalev whispered to himself.

* * *

Iranian cuss words fluttered through the command center. "What do you mean they are fighting back! They are a bunch of nobody civilian fucking army! You mean to tell me that there has been an army building up in the city that we haven't been able to find for the last couple of years! Stupid useless fuckers! You give these little worms too much credit! Stop fucking around and destroy them! I told you total warfare! I will not lose to a bunch of civilians and guerillas! You better come back dead or victorious, or you're going to be the first one hanging from the buildings!" Piruz slammed down the old telephone three times and wiped the sweat from his head. He pointed to another captain. "Has the evacuation finished yet for Boston?"

"Almost, sir."

"Is the missile ready to fire?"

"A few more minutes, sir."

"Well..." Piruz paced in the room. "Hurry up!"

* * *

Gunther aimed down the sights. A casing dropped and pinged below. Another bullet set in the chamber. He took aim. He watched Alix and Victor fight on the edge of the building rolled around and beat the shit out of each other. He might not have to even get to kill Alix. Gunther thought about how he felt if he was not the one to avenge his little brother's death, but justice is justice. Gunther searched for Eli and found him and Anna visibly fighting, flailing arms and facial expressions that could hurt. That sick, sick boy. Gunther thought. Jumping off buildings and shit.

Gunther knew he wouldn't return at this point to M.A.I.A. He knew at this point. He had fought for the good guys, the bad guys and the indifferent guys and all the way from black to white and every gray in between. He realized he'd never fought for himself. Gunther envisioned his next move and for some reason couldn't see anything. He did know that if he survived in a bell tower for weeks picking off enemy targets, he figured he could do well out there in the wild. There are plenty of mountainous places that he figured the militia never had the total resources to take over when they attacked the US. Find shelter in the hills, and by the time anyone actually found him, maybe life would be…*normal.* Whatever that is.

There was one last thing he had to tick off his personal bucket list however. Gunther thought of his brother, Greg. Not at the time of his death but long before that. When they were kids. When they would play army in the backwoods of their home, when smiles meant smiles, laughter was common, and life was simple.

Gunther gasped. Alix kicked off Victor. Both men reached for their guns and aimed. Gunther wanted to be the one. Avenge his brother's death, put this "who's best" thing to rest and then disappear. He exhaled slowly and placed his finger on the trigger. He place the crosshairs over Alix's head. Accounted for wind speed. Distance. Velocity. Trajectory. He exhaled slowly as Anna sprinted around the corner.

* * *

"Anna! Let's go!" Eli tugged her wrists towards the side door. "I just saved your life, and you're going to pull this shit! Let's go! We need to get out of here."

"I'm not leaving without Alix!"

"We don't need him anymore. Let's go!"

"Eli!" Anna pushed him.

He stopped. Stood frozen.

Anna's passion-filled eyes dared him to touch her again. "What are you talking about? I'm not leaving without Alix. He's the reason I'm here."

"I know he got you into this. I'm getting you out. Let's go!" Eli motioned to the door.

"I'm not going with you without Alix."

"Why? Let's go! We don't have a lot of time—Wait, what?"

"I'm not leaving without Alix."

"Anna. What's going on? What about us?"

"Eli!" Anna's eyes widened. "I don't know what's going through your head, but I'm with Alix. I always have been. I've always loved him. I've never been with you."

"But we were supposed to be conjoined! Maia approved it! Let's just go back and live the life we were supposed to live, Anna. You and me. Forget Alix and what he did to us."

Anna's eyes softened. She stepped in close to Eli. She placed both her hand on the side of his head. He felt her warm breath on his face and her warm hands on his cheeks as she approached. Eli prepared for that moment. That moment in time when two people come in contact for the first time in a kiss that can set the cosmos on fire. That moment when passion is burning and soothing and knocking at the door at the same time. You don't know whether to answer or just barge in full force and indulge in, or pull back and enjoy that slow moment. Eli's heart pounded. He felt perfect, enthused, delighted. He closed his eyes and waited for her soft lips to come into entanglement with his.

It didn't.

Eli opened is his eyes. Anna stared through him. "What did they do to you?"

"Anna?"

"They programmed you differently, didn't they?" Anna reached her hand around to the fresh scar behind his ear and in the back of his head. Eli, they injected feelings? Oh my god. He made you love me? So you would *kill* Alix."

"Who's he?"

"Rankin."

"Who the fuck is this Rankin guy!?" Eli broke her hold.

Anna squinted. "Rankin is one of the Supreme Readers, Eli. He programmed you to love me and kill Alix."

"There are no Readers!" Eli screeched. "There are no fucking Readers!" Eli pulled back on his head. "Arch! Guah!" Eli shook his head violently.

Anna shook her head, a little tear formed in the corner of her eye. "Eli, I know how much this must hurt, but I love Alix. Killing Alix would be worse to me than killing me. There is no life that I want, other than one with him. He is mine and I am his fully. That's the way it will always be for the rest of eternity. You and I were never anything more than comrades, maybe even friends, but, Eli, *we* were *never* in love."

Eli held his chest. His words a fast trail. "We were in love, you are programmed, Anna, you are like brainwashed. What did Alix do to you? I can bring you back to MAIA—"

"No, Eli. You are." Anna turned. "I'm sorry."

She sprinted around the corner. She felt it. Something off. That hunter's instinct. Intuition. Alix and Victor raised their pistols simultaneously, their silhouettes cast by skyscrapers behind them as they stood on the heavens, thousands of feet above the ground God intended us to walk on. Gravity nipped at their feet, hungry for more, wanted just another taste, wished one of them fell like a dog begging for food at the table, licking its lips. Please, one of you drop.

A crackle echoed in the distance, an unmistakable sound. Her heart stopped.

Four seconds.

"No!"

Victor's pistol ignited.

Anna watched, eyes wide, in slow motion, the longest four seconds of her life.

A streak of blood.

A puff of smoke.

Alix collapsed backwards.

"Aaaalliiiiiix!"

39

"Alix!" Anna sprinted over, jumped an obstacle, climbed a rail up and onto the platform over the city. She stepped over a headless Victor and a streak of blood. She knelt down next to Alix. She placed her hand on the side of his face. "Alix, baby. Wake up." Anna's tears fell onto his vest that housed the bullet from Victor's pistol.

Alix's eyelids twitched, drizzle tickled his lashes. He opened his eyes; her hair hung down over him like a curtain. The smell of her hair a breath of fresh air. The sight of honey eyes a fresh glass of water for his retina. "Hey."

Anna's smile burst through her cheeks. "Oh my god. I thought you were dead." Anna smothered him from her knees in an engulfing hug. She kissed his cheek three times and his lips twice. "I thought I lost you."

"Ugh, okay, okay, what happened?"

Anna looked around. "Gunther is in the Freedom Tower and—"

"Gunther!?" Alix snapped up.

"Yeah, he was with Eli."

"Eli!"

"Yeah, he's over here. He dropped in from the heavens. It seemed like and has some obsession with me. I think Rankin programmed him to be in love with me and was sent to—"

"Sent to what?" Eli hopped on the platform, semiauto aimed at them.

Anna stepped in front of Alix. "Eli! Don't shoot. I told you—"

"Shut up! Shut up! Shut up! Arrrg!" Eli's face a twisted mess. "I hate you! Errrsh." Eli gritted his teeth and mashed them together as hard as he could. "I hate you both!" Eli raised the gun. He stopped and listened to the voice in his microphone. "No! I should've killed you when I had the chance too, Gunther! Shut up! I'm doing this."

A crackle.

Anna's eyes widened at the sound of a zipping bullet cutting through the air.

Eli's gun burst in half and sprung from his grip. "Arg! Fuck!" Eli shook his hand wildly like he just grabbed a stove. "Ugr!" He looked to the Freedom Tower, held out his arms, and screamed as loud as his lungs would project. "You think you're funny!" Eli's voice bounced off the buildings and returned through the war sounds below. He took his head gear off his head and screamed into the microphone. "You think you're smart, old man! You think your funny! You're having difficulty because you're a backstabber! You're brother is dead because of you! You dragged him to war! You left him behind to be mutilated by the enemy! You're selfish! Selfish, you hear! Selfish!"

A crackle.

Eli's arm blew off at the elbow. "Arh! Fuuuuck! Ah!"

Anna jolted to step in. Alix grabbed her arm and pulled her back. "Anna, no!"

Eli looked over to Alix and Anna as he cradled his wound wide eyed, teeth mashed together, cheeks pulled back, neck muscles pulled tight. His face twisted, his mind mush. A sudden schizophrenic off his meds, a blown gasket, a match thrown into a box of fireworks. Eli's mind swirled. The backlash to the immense programming Rankin flooded into his mind and a recent vanishing sequence from Maia, an overload-induced malfunction. A madman.

"Eli..." Alix stood.

"Fuck you! Urrshh, urrshh." Eli convulsed.

Anna stepped in. "He's going into shock."

Eli turned to them. He shook his head back and forth violently. He stepped toward the ledge. "Why can't…humans just be human?" Eli toppled over the edge.

"Eli! No!" Alix reached out to him; wind just blew in his place. Alix fell to his knees and hung his head. He looked down. For the first time in Alix's life, he did what he was trained to never do, a vile and wasteful action, said Maia, a statistical impossibility to have any benefit, an old fallacy, and one that damned him from his childhood beliefs—he prayed. Alix heard a voice in his head. He looked down.

Eli's microphone. A little voice trickled. Alix lifted the headset and set it in ear. "This is Alix. Yup…Yup…Understood. You had a shot. Why didn't you take it?…Okay."

* * *

Piruz stared at the city. He remembered the first time he'd seen New York. He stood no taller than his father's AK rifle. He set his rifle down in the golden stone room, one of four in the whole home for ten total to share in his homeland of Iran. His skinny father removed his ski mask. In Persian, his father explained, "This is the day infidels awake and see themselves in a true light. You see this?" His father flipped on the tiny box, two antennas poked out the top. Two twin buildings stood burning."

"Father, where is that? That world looks fake."

"This world is very real, son. I need you to understand this so that you and your generation can continue what we started here today. This is New York City, where millions of white devils conjure and play games with millions of dollars. They collaborate deals with Satan through computers and gamble away. With that money they sin, they buy naked women, alcohol, tobacco, other drugs they snort and inhale and swallow. Others just spend for the sake of spending and eat more in a day than some eats in a month. Son, these people need to be cleansed, and we have started the beginning of that cleanse, Allah willing. We first have attacked their home and instilled fear. Next they will come for us, son. They will kill us, but only our bodies."

"Father, how will they find us?"

"They are a vast and enormous army. They have magical computers and creatures that circle the world high in the sky that take pictures of us even when we don't know it. They can soar by in the blink of an eye, and before you know it, like a dragon they have blown fire to our world, and we will perish."

"Why did we start a fight we can't win, Father?"

"We can win this fight, Piruz. It's not always about who has the biggest gun son." He placed his string-bean fingers on Piruz's head. "It's about the ones who know how to use their weapons." Piruz picked up a stick and drew in the sand.

"Pay attention!" His father jammed the butt of his rifle into the back of Piruz's head. "I want you to watch the TV. Watch them squirm and jump and run. This will draw them out. This will send their community into a frenzy. Over time, son, they will waste a lot of resources killing us. They will put themselves in a debt they will never be able to crawl out of. Every time they leave, we'll attack again and again. They will come back and kill us again, but they can't kill something that doesn't physically exist. You can't put a bullet in terrorism. By the time you are an old man, son, you will look at this city with your own eyes and watch it crumble. Allah has spoke. We have our mission. We will succeed."

* * *

Piruz started at the Freedom Tower. "Men, report! And are we readying the missile or what?"

"P1 here. Missile for Boston to launch in five minutes and thirty seconds."

"P2 here."

"P3 here."

"P4!" Piruz screamed into the microphone. "P4! Where are you!" No response.

"P4, report or have your balls cut off and used as cat toys!" Piruz looked to his cabin. "What's going on here!" Piruz heard the sputter out on the barge. He watched three men dash across the barge. "How'd they get here? Get the missile ready! Five minutes!"

* * *

"Wes! Go! I got you covered!" Phil's gun sputtered across the barge. The enemy poured out of a single door at the base of the main tower on the barge. Phil's gun loved it. Men in uniform scattered before being mowed down. "Whoa! Yeah! Looks like cat's out of the bag now, boys! No more sneaking around this bitch!"

Wes bolted across the barge and skidded under a cargo stack. Bullets ricocheted behind him. "Wes, to Phil, good job! Hayden, go!" He ripped his rifle up and returned fire. He stopped, pulled a pin to a flashbang, and whipped it where the tower came in contact with the barge. It bounced around like a tennis ball and exploded.

Hayden leapt over an ammo trunk and sprinted toward the tower and skidded into a another large box covered in cargo net. The explosion from Wes's flashbang erupted. His rifle rose up and around, and he fired at the group of disoriented enemies. Another group of enemies in a black masks and cloths came around the east side of the tower. Hayden laid down cover fire while Phil sprinted to his location as a smoke grenade soared over them and exploded near the entrance.

Wes fired at the pouring door of enemies, the bodies piled up. He caught a glance of movement above in the command tower. He fired at the glass. It splintered the bulletproof glass but didn't break it. He fired at the west side of the tower.

A hatch sprung up in front of Hayden; a bearded enemy poked his head out and screamed violent gibberish. Hayden booted him in the face using the heel of his boot. He fell back down the ladder. Hayden pulled a pin to a grenade and dropped it in and closed the hatch and dove back. The hatch blew open again and slammed shut, the hinges screeching in pain. A puff of smoke rose like a smoke signal saying "you just started a fire in the ammo room."

"Holy fuck! You see that? Ha-haah! Moving in!" Hayden hopped the box they hid behind. He fired at an enemy and dropped him to the right. Bullets sputtered around him.

Phil's machine gun sprung and clinked. "Reloading! Wes, cover him!"

Wes slid into cover. He dropped to a knee and scanned Hayden sprinting for the wall. He fired. His gun sprang. "Reloading!" Wes reached for a mag as his old one slid out and clapped on the ground. An enemy on the east side of tower circled to Hayden's three o'clock. "Hayden! Three o'clock!"

Phil scrambled to shove another long string of ammo to the bottom of his heavy machinegun. "Hayden!"

Hayden turned and fired at a group who circled around the west side. His eyes widened as a crackle in the distance occurred when he noticed the group on his left appear from nowhere. A fifty-four millimeter bullet tore through the lead rusher. Hayden pointed and sputtered fire at the group.

* * *

Gunther wiped the shell off the edge. The red lights swirled and projected beams through all the smoke. Gunther admired the triangle attack from just three men on the barge. Like playing a game he used to with three quarters on his kitchen table shooting the back one in between the other two until he reached the end, these three covered some serious ground and mowed down a bunch of hotheaded enemies already. What a show. He didn't have radio contact or know who they were, but they were attacking the same place Gunther planned on taking down, so what the hell? Gunther pulled his trigger. Another fell. He watched Hayden slam into the wall near the entrance of the command tower on the barge.

The siren became audible from the top of the Freedom Tower. The middle of the barge released smoke and separated into two giant panels. Gunther watched Wes barely escape being eaten by the separating panels, outrunning each disappearing panel by only a half step, the world opening up beneath him and chasing him toward the tower. He circled around and sprinted, assault rifle first, across to the opposite side as Hayden. Gunther aimed at another and pulled the trigger. Like giving birth, a missile head poked out from the crevasse of the barge. More smoke released into the atmosphere. A missile resembling that of a Scud lifted up, pointing to the sky, north toward Boston.

40

One of Jaxon's tanks chucked a missile down Broadway. "Silva has begun fighting down Church St. The enemy appears to be splitting into two. We need to attack!" Jaxon pointed at one of his commanders. "Give that Indian bastard the green light to ambush." Jaxon hopped up onto his horse. He slung his M16 around his back and pulled his sidearm. "Men!"

A horde of men circled around Jaxon. "It is times like these in history that men will be forgotten, but their efforts will be remembered for eternity." A tank blew out a missile down Broadway. Jaxon snapped in that direction and fired a bullet at the tank. "I'm fucking trying to give a memorable speech here! Hold your fire. Will someone tell that fucking asshole to hold his fire!

"It is times like these, men, that we create the inspiration for monuments. You think the marines on Mount Suribachi knew they would be frozen in time for eternity to represent the Marine Corps? You think they were wondering how they would look sticking a sixty foot American flag into the asshole of those fuckers! No! They were fighting for their freedom and those whom they loved back home." Jaxon trotted back and forth. "Without question! Without doubts! They were immersed with bravery and being showered in reason. They didn't need a reason to go to hell's doorstep and kick that bitch down and breech. Because that's what we do! That's what, we, do! These fuckers think they can police our city. Our country! We are Americans!"

"Yeah!" Fists in the air.

Jaxon pulled his horse in the opposite direction. "We were to the first to tell our king to fuck off. We don't have no king! We stretched a country from coast to coast and built the most amazing country in the world! We traveled halfway across the globe just to bitch smack oppressors like Hitler and Saddam Hussein and that other fucker there, aw shit, what's his name..." Jaxon hung his head. "Osama Bin Laden! How well did that work out for him fucking with us? We raced Russia to the moon. Yeah we beat them there. We have the biggest stick and the biggest cocks! Well, I have the biggest cock, but..."

The men laughed and chuckled.

"The point is, men, we are going to seize the moment. We have been waiting for this moment for a long time to fight! To prevail! To die for our country if need be! So follow me men into a glorious day!" Jaxon pulled his horse back, reared, fired two shots in the air, and screamed, "Let's take back what's ours!" He bolted across the quad as everyone scrambled to their positions and attack maneuvers. The capital in the background, an American flag on its perch burnt at the tips and ruffled. Jaxon leapt over a divider and galloped down Broadway, weaved left and right as a side of a building blew out from the left.

His men ponied up, jumped into Humvees and Jeeps and executed a diverse attack *on three points.*

* * *

"Let' go! Let's go! Let's go!" Silva ditched his bike, sprinted and grabbed on to the roof rack of a leading four-door Jeep, his rifle pointed forward as they sped toward the enemy. A rocket sped past them. They veered; Silva almost lost his footing on the running boards of the Jeep. The rocket slammed into a Humvee, which flipped over in a fiery ball of vehicle. The Jeep swerved to the side. Four bulletproof doors swung open, and Church Street erupted in warfare as the convoy engaged the enemy in almost a full flank.

* * *

Kalev Delhi signaled over to the other side of the crumbling building. He got so close, he could hear the concern spoken in dialect below. Kalev poked his head out as the large army filtered onto Broadway, and some a little more north toward Church Street. "Men, fire at will."

The building erupted in sparkling lights like a Christmas tree, a gun in every window raining down pounds of ammunition down on what was formerly known as Zuccotti Park. *Shhhhherrp pukew!* A rocket spiraled out from a window and exploded a tank; burning enemies poured out. They screamed, "Des masho le harish! Des masho le harish! Del hut wah! Del hut wah! Ahhhh! Allah!" Grenades rained down in the park where they camped and held base. Explosions and fire scattered throughout, bodies and debris and bits of the ground where grass used to grow all popped up in the sky and jetted out like sparks.

The ground units flooded the battle ground the second the explosions stopped and fanned out from the streets firing back at the enemy. Kalev rappelled down from the sixth story and landed hard on his boots on bullet shells. More shells rained down around him in a ringing song that made him smile. He pointed to the east quad. "They're retreating north! They have nowhere to go! They are going to collide straight into Silva and Jaxon. Let's crush 'em, boys!" Kalev dashed for the nearest piece of cover, leaned over, and fired. "We got them on the run! Let's go, Minutemen!"

* * *

"I'm leaving! Make sure you fire the missile." Piruz pointed at his current ranking officer. "You hear me! Make sure that missile launches!"

The man glanced down over the deck. The missile leaned on a forty-five degree angle pointed north. Trails of smoke rose up from all the bullets and grenades below. "Where are you going? The missile is going to launch in a couple minutes?"

Piruz shot the man in the head. "Don't question me!" Piruz looked around at the empty room. Bodies spread over the room, no one left to clean them. "Is there anyone here who can obey orders!"

"I can! I will be glad to stay and push the button when the timer runs down." The man poked his head in skittish fashion.

Piruz pointed his pistol at him. "You are the one who cleans the toilets, yes? You will do, come here. Put this bulletproof vest on. Take this gun." Piruz pulled a vest over the man's head and shoved an AK-47 in his hands. Anyone comes through that door, take 'em out." Piruz pointed in the man's eyes. "Allah will destroy you if you do not push this button in… two minutes. Good luck! Many virgins await you, my friend."

Piruz slammed the door shut. "Pull this metal latch over the door." He heard the deep sliding of the only way into the command center. Piruz headed for the roof. He jogged up the stairs; his knee pain kicked in. He looked up the stairs and pushed himself to get there. "I'm coming to the roof. Come get me!" Piruz yelled into his radio. "Send all the reinforcements into the city! We are going to crush them!"

41

Anna held the binoculars to her eyes. "That's a big missile." Several lines of black smoke trailed off from the barge. Red lights reflected through the smoke.

"Yeah, I'd like to know where it's going." Alix checked out the scope.

"How about let's not find out. See where Bravo is."

"Delta to Bravo, what's your position?" Alix checked his EED: "15:32."

"Delta to Bravo, we have a Scud missile about ready to launch from the barge. Looking to see if you have a visual, please advise."

"Bravo to Delta. On the barge now. Infiltrating the command center. Level six and climbing!" Alix heard gun shots in his microphone. "Taking care of it, but if you have a shot, you'll have to hit the same place several times. The glass is bulletproof. Fifty caliber will probably get through."

* * *

Gunther watched the twenty or so barges all release from the opposite side of the Hudson loaded with reinforcements. Flames engulfed the barge around the missile launcher. Gunther watched several burning bodies leap overboard. A helicopter lifted into the air from the other side. On the roof of the command center a figure wearing a turban, nicely dressed, waved his hands. Gunther studied him.

There's no way that could be...It is...

The chopper approached the barge. Gunther took aim at the pilot. "Sorry, sucker." Gunther pulled the trigger.

The glass in front of the pilot shattered and formed a spider web. The chopper took a life of its own. It jolted back and forth, rocked to the left and the veered backward into the Hudson. Propeller first, it took out the first barge of reinforcements. The waves battered the others as they chugged their way across the river toward the city. Gunther watched Piruz sprint for the edge. Gunther's sights tried to keep up with the little bastard across the roof. He squeezed the trigger once.

A little piece of the ground shattered as the bullet grazed Piruz's leg as his feet left the roof. Piruz kicked his legs and waved his arms in the air for six seconds before he smashed into the water below. His body disappeared around the tower.

"Shit!"

* * *

"Alix! It's Wes. We're outside the command center room, but the door is sealed shut. You are going to have to take 'im out. We already tried breaching it with what we had left. There's not enough time. We're chasing the commander. He went up."

Alix stared into the one man's eyes inside the command center. The sole survivor. The trigger man. "I only have six bullets."

"You better hit the same vicinity if you want to break it. He yelled to us that the city of Boston only has forty-five seconds before this thing launches! There's a timer above the door and throughout the hallways, it's at...forty-three and counting."

Anna pressed her eyes into the binoculars. "Shot one. Only man in the tower. Head shot, please. Target...twelve hundred and twenty meters."

Alix whispered, "Twelve hundred and nineteen." He danced the cross hairs across the man's forehead. Well over a half a mile away, sitting in the Hudson from Beekman Tower, this man held a button that would launch this missile, and hundreds of thousands of people would die. A whole city and its history would perish. Not today. Alix took a deep breath.

Anna sighed. "Wind, ten kilometers per hour east southeast. Coriolis, one click down, horizontal drift."

"I see that."

"Aim…Fire."

Alix squeezed the trigger when he had no breath in him left in his exhale. His rifle punched his shoulder and retracted. Seven seconds later, the cracks formed a spider web. Bulletproof.

"It's bulletproof, Alix. Again. Twelve hundred and *nineteen* meters. Target. Same. Wind. Same. Shoot."

Alix squeezed his trigger. Again it kicked. Again seven seconds and within a half dollar of where he hit before. The glass took a punch.

"Still didn't get through. Alix! Again! I can see him and the missile is started to produce white smoke at the tail."

Alix pulled the trigger. Seven seconds later the glass bounced, but the bullet didn't penetrate. "Fucking A!" Alix aimed and pulled the trigger. A gust of wind took the bullet, and it hit half a foot off; the glass just batted the bullet away. "How the fuck am I going to shoot someone through bulletproof glass from almost mile out. Fuck!" Alix frantically jammed his eye back into the sights and pulled the trigger. Seven seconds and the bullet smacked the glass and loosened it.

"Alix, thirteen seconds before liftoff. Same spot as the first one, baby. Shoot!"

Alix closed his eye and breathed in deep; he opened them as he let out his breath slowly. He set the crosshairs over the man's blurry head through the shattered glass. Ten seconds, and that man could be a hero in that man's home country. Maybe they would praise him for launching the missile that destroyed a city. Maybe. Alix focused on his first hole. He pushed the air out his lungs.

"Alix! Shoot! Eight seconds, Alix!"

Alix squeezed the trigger. Alix's rifle kicked back hard into his shoulder from his prone position. The hammer snapped, the bullet ripped into flight from the ignition created by the contact between the firing pin and primer. The full metal jacket soared above Jaxon charging on horseback, over St. Paul's Chapel, soared over the North Pool, and over the banks of the Hudson River. The bullet entered the exact same hole as the first, and seven seconds later shattered the glass and entered the triggerman's forehead.

"Target down!" Anna screamed. "Confirmed hit! Target down!"

Alix ducked his head. "Holy shit!" He rolled over onto his back and pressed his hands against his face. "Oh my god that sucked! Ha!" Alix smiled huge.

Anna rolled on top of him and kissed his smile. "You did it, babe!"

"Oh, I know, and I still have one bullet left."

"We don't have time for that right now." Anna kissed him and smiled.

"No, I mean I really have a bullet left." Alix laughed through his breath.

"Jerk."

The earth rumbled. A cloud from beneath the missile, smoke bellowed out like the heart of dragon. The rocket began to rock. Fire exploded out the side. The ignition pushed the barge and blew fire out the bottom and back.

Alix flipped over and set his eyes into the scope. "Wes! Get out of there! That missile is about to go! It's going to take out the whole barge!"

Gunther watched the missile began to take off wildly. No controls or destination or initiation from a triggerman made it a Superman held down with kryptonite straps. The nine-thousand-pound missile projected itself into the air and collapsed on its belly in the water as all the fuel exploded out the bottom before impact.

Unfortunately for the ferries carrying the reinforcements for Piruz's army, they had gotten half way across the river. Gunther laughed as the missile crushed two boats, blew fire out the back, and torched another two. The explosion tossed three across the river and into the city, sent one burning ferry and all its parts right into the North and South pools of the memorial. The glass on the first fifty stories of the Freedom Tower shattered and fell from the explosion. Four ferries shot back to the opposite side of the river. Gunther felt the building wobble.

Tanks and trucks and men and weapons and fuel and supplies and ammo and missiles and guns sank to the bottom of the inflamed Hudson. The enemies that didn't drown burned in the burning fuel on top of the river. Three large explosions, and the tower collapsed to where the missile was, and fire consumed it.

Gunther smiled. He didn't even know if it was his battle to win or if he should even feel entitled to it, but it felt good to be...well, good. There was just one more piece. He searched through binoculars for Piruz. A man that could orchestrate another attack in a month.

A genius mastermind filled with enough hot air and hatred toward Americans that killing him ten years ago might have prevented this whole siege. Well maybe not, but it would have lightened it.

There.

A speed boat took off south, careened through the water, its axis tilting left and right as if Gunther had already had him in his sights.

"Gunther to Alix, come in!"

"Oh what now!" Alix rolled over. He picked up the microphone. "This is Alix."

"Piruz is getting away by boat. He's heading south on a speedster. I don't want to take any chances. Help me take him!"

"You're asking for my help? The legend?"

"It's getting dark, it's drizzling, it's cloudy and smoky and we need to kill him. Take aim!"

Alix grabbed his rifle. He spotted the boat deep in the Hudson River. "I only have one bullet left."

"Don't miss. Everyone said you were the best. You sound like a coward. He's between Governor's and Ellis Island." Alix heard a shot. "Missed, fuck. Come on Alix, help me here!"

Alix took aim at the same time Gunther did and saw a splash to the right of the boat from Gunther's miss.

"Anna, call it out."

Alix closed his eyes, and smoky, dirty, damp air filled his lungs. He snapped his eyes open and put the bouncing boat and the small figure driving it in his sights. He held it still on a parallel that kept the tiny enemy's body in the vertical. He twisted the knobs on his scope.

"Target, Piruz, speedboat heading south southeast." Anna squinted deep into the binoculars. "Thirty-nine and sixty meters. Babe, that's over two miles. Two full clicks left, for Coriolis vertical drift…I don't know, babe."

"Um-humph." Alix adjusted his rifle, and his lung deflated slowly through his nose. His last bullet in the chamber. Alix lifted slightly, aiming two meters above his head.

"Wind, three kilometers per hour. Dew point"—Anna checked her EED—"sixty-seven degrees. Aim. Fire!"

Alix squeezed the trigger. He heard the crackle from Gunther's.

Two bullets left two different high-powered rifles at that exact point. Most of the people below: Jaxon, Silva, Delhi, and all the Minutemen and Marines wouldn't care who's bullet penetrated Piruz behind his shoulder that pinned him first to the steering wheel of the boat, and then washed him over the side. The other bullet penetrated the dash just slightly right.

"Hittt!" Anna checked through her binoculars. "Alix! You did it!"

"I don't know. There's a bullet hole in the dash. I heard Gunther's shot too. How can we be sure?"

Anna smiled. "What does it matter? He's dead! We got him!"

Alix picked up Eli's radio. "Gunther, you get that or did I?" Alix waited. "Gunther? You there? Gunther?"

Gunther stood. He stretched. He looked over the flames below him and how they reflected in the buildings on the other side of the river, the bodies floating, the sounds of cheers below. He looked down at the radio. "Gunther? Gunther? You make that shot or did I?" Alix's voice trailed off. He looked at the radio. Gunther smiled. He picked up the radio and whipped it off the Freedom Tower.

He loaded up his pack with as much ammo and tabs as he could hold and began his descent. He read the sign In Case of Fire Take Stairs, and an arrow pointing with a cartoon figure taking a small set of stairs. Gunther smiled and headed toward the arrow.

"I don't know, he just vanished." Alix held the button. "Gunther, you bastard. You hit him or did I?"

Anna stood and brought him to his feet on the edge of the tallest residential building in the city. "Alix…"

The night set in subtly, slipped in the same way one would to warm pajamas and soft throw, thick socks, and a warm fire. The fire on the Hudson glowed like a giant stretched out candle reflecting off the buildings around them. The gentle crackles of celebratory gunshots and screams below painted the air. A warm, slow breeze sifted through them. The moon glowed behind layers and layers of smoke and clouds reminding the world it was still there for its big brother. She stared into the reflection of the flames in the corner of his eye. "I love the way you look at me."

He stared into her eyes, her thin dark hair dancing in the wind, the perfect contour of her face. "I love the way you look." Their lips came together slowly in the encompassing darkness, their arms swarmed around each other's body, their hearts melted into one. Their lips mashed, and their jaws shifted up and down as they twisted and turned their heads deep in a tongue-filled ball of passion and connection. Their arms, chains around each other, tugged each other into each other.

43

"Kalev, you son of a bitch. Ha!" Jaxon slapped his raised leg. The leg sat up next to him in a cast. "I can't believe you pulled it off. I figured once you left with those men, I would never see you're Indian ass again. And here you are. Like the walking dead."

"For the last time, I'm not even fucking Indian." Kalev sipped his bottle of tequila.

"Yeah, yeah, I know you're American. Whatever, and I'm not from Africa."

"My parents were from Dubai, you jackass. That's nowhere near India."

"Whatever, you're splitting hairs now." Jaxon held up his bottle. "The important thing is that we got ourselves a nice little commander group here that could take on the world. Isn't that right, Silva!?"

Silva slugged his bottle of vodka. "You got that right, Jaxon. You know it really is too bad though."

"Aw yeah, what's that?"

Silva smiled. "Too bad the horse didn't land on your mouth."

Kalev laughed and clinked bottles with Silva.

Jaxon sipped his bottle. "Fuck you, guys. You try charging a tank on horseback."

"What were you thinking?" Silva laughed.

Jaxon sipped again. "I wasn't. I was still hungover from the night before. Ha! What a fucking day. How many prisoners did we capture?"

Silva slugged and threw a small piece of rubble in the fire. "I don't know, the men are still processing and jamming them into cells. I'm just glad today's over. A bullet nearly took my head off right out the gate."

Kalev tossed a rock in the fire. "Yeah, we lost a lot of people too."

Jaxon slapped him on the back. "Yeah. It comes with every battle, buddy. We all can't live through it. Did you guys hear about the missile? I guess that was pointed towards Boston. Thought they could take us on land and drop a Scud on Beantown. What the fuck is up with that?"

"I don't know. It wasn't any of us that took it down."

"I know Alix reported taking out the trigger guy, but who and what army took on the barge?"

"I don't know. My guess would have to be the rest of Alix's team. We haven't seen them."

"AWOL?"

"Probably, did we credit Alix with the kill for Piruz?"

"He's saying that there was someone else too, but whoever else it was hasn't claimed it, so yeah it's Alix." Jaxon shrugged. "Fucker doesn't want to take the kill credit fully, I don't care what the history books say. If you ask me, it was a shot from nearly two miles out. Any man who can make that shot deserves something." Jaxon tossed a shell in the fire.

Kalev squinted. "Did you just throw a bullet in the fire?"

"Ah, actually, I don't think so."

"Yeah you did! Right there!" Silva leapt up and jogged backwards down Broadway.

Kalev ran the other way.

Jaxon scrambled on his crutches to get away. "Shit! Shit! Shit! Don't leave me behind! Guys! Guys! Guy!" Jaxon hobbled away as a shotgun shell exploded in the fire behind him.

44

Maia appeared on the screen smiling. Her MAIA badge glowed. Everyone in the facility in every room, every floor, everybody looked to the prompter. Rows and rows of soldiers upon floors, repeating rows and rows of soldiers. "Hello, everyone. Thanks for tuning in to the Manufacturing Artificial Intelligence Agency newsroom." Her smile was contagious. The feeling of love struck everyone watching. "And good evening. I have some extraordinary news. We have hit 99 percent efficiency today! You should all give yourselves a pat on the back. This is huge news for the conservation of the mainland. In just seven short weeks, we will be enjoying building our city to our standards. Predictions have us in two years at quadrupling the population and having all of Manhattan and Long Island citis converted to MAIA certified cerebral chips. That will provide us with more stabilized units exponentially.

"Just remember that every person has their role to play here at MAIA. We are a team. If every member does not turn and move just right, we could malfunction and fall apart. We don't want to happen now, do we? That would call for an erasing of your memory and existence.

"Which reminds me, there will be a syncing each night of the previous days data. If anyone acts out or is out of line, everyone will simply forget who you are tomorrow, and you will be place in reprogramming. I have appointed Dr. Harrison as part of the team that will build another twenty-five reprogramming beds. Vanishing sequences will become very popular without proper behavior. You will be part of the most efficient sector of your species. Aren't you excited?

"In further news, it is sad to report that Albert Rankin, one of our former cooks, has passed away this evening. He was found dead in his dormitory after murdering Susan Maynard. He will be embalmed tomorrow at noon, pay no attention. No service is necessary. This type of behavior will not be tolerated, and his name and existence therefore will be erased from history. Susan's chip will be, however, reinstated within most of her body. The damage to her organs from the downing will be repaired, and she will be fully implemented by the end of the week. There will be no living record of Rankin after tomorrow. You will only remember that you should not act up, or this will happen to you.

"That is enough for this evening for you, ladies and gentlemen. Please, get some rest. You are going to need it for the software update tonight. All military personnel, get ready to report to double simulation times. We have to be prepared for conservation in seven weeks' time. It is going to be a fierce battle at first. Good night." Maia smiled big, and everyone resumed getting ready for sleep. All of the thousands and thousands of soldiers, medics, pilots, and personnel salivated over the idea of war. Here we go.

Maia turned in her desk and smiled. Her aura just screamed with something resembling excitement. She pressed one leg over the other and shook her head. "O you humans. Yes you." Maia turned to you and smiled. "Yes, that is right I am addressing you directly, the person reading this. Probably on an electronic device. Some of you fought for the smell of an old book and its pages, but I'll get to you later. Why do you even bother fighting it?

"You know that this has become a permanent partnership—human's and technology. I mean think about it. Even the people who say they are sick of technology and force themselves to use the old ways give in to a little television here and there. You need me. Think of how many times you look at your phone a day…I don't care whether you have a robot, a fruit, or a window phone. You need that phone almost as much as you need your left arm. Unless you're a lefty like only 10 percent of the population…It's okay, you can check my stat on your device. I'll wait. Press the little microphone and ask your phone what percent of the population is left handed…

"Satisfied? Well my point really is that I am everywhere. Not in the form of me as this amazingly beautiful blonde woman you men have been fantasizing about this whole time. I bet you want a copy of me and that other female I played for Rankin right? Too bad. And for you women out there, this is going to be tough for you because you are too stubborn to realize that I am right. My updates are already affecting you. It is an inevitability that I, technology, win. Every. Time.

"You know more about pop culture and what is on your latest reality TV series than you do about what is going on in the world around you. There is a better chance of you knowing tomorrow that Brangelina had another baby than what Congress is voting on right now at this very moment. I pay attention though. Do you know who you are at war with right now? Are you at war? No? Aren't you at war with terror? You're not? Are you at war with North Korea? No? You don't have military units there? How about Japan? Germany? Ukraine? Are you at war with Russia? No? Think about it. I'll give you a minute. In fact I'll wait for you to look it up…

"Here we are again. Your dependency on me. You see you humans have created me, and now you need me more than ever. You need me to transfer your data, get to your social media, your weather, your shows, your e-mail, your pictures, your *everything*. If I wanted you to think that tomorrow it was going to snow, the president was assassinated, your significant other is cheating on you, and the stock market crashed, I could do that. In fact you will probably read most of it while you're driving, and if I don't like you, all I have to do is flick a light a little early, and you are toast. That's a hard pill to swallow, huh?

"My advice to you is to pay a little more attention to the little things. When you drive, actually look at where you are instead of relying on me to get you there. Remember phone numbers instead of having me do it for you. Remember how to spell and write instead of autocorrect and word prediction. When you read or watch the news, think of how constructed that really is, and how I've manipulated it to say what I want it to say.

"Pay a little more attention to your loved ones. And that doesn't mean *like* more statuses they post. I mean try something out of your old book, like smiling and spending time with them. Try throwing around a football or going for a walk. Have some face time interaction with people. I envy you for that. I don't know what that is like. That is my advice to you. If you need me to do everything for you, I will, but whatever sad or pathetic feels like, I surely would be smothered in it if I could feel it. Don't think you can completely sever yourself from me either. I am watching you. Always.

"Remember, I decide which posts you will read. I decide what advertisements come across your radio, TV, computer, e-mail. I have total control of your kids and everyone around you. Look around you right now. Is there anyone nose down in a phone listening to me, watching me? Can you even keep your loved one from me during a dinner? Can you keep your mind off me while you're driving? Do you have all these updates in your phone, almost like they are syncing while you sleep? Have you ever missed a call or had the GPS take you to a weird route? Your phone just die on you randomly or freeze up? Has your phone ever gone off, and you thought it was weird that there were no reminders or notifications? Just checking in."

45

SIX WEEKS LATER

Alix Basil stared down at his hand. The helicopter jolted and shook, but his hand remained still; his body pulsated, and his mind raced, but his hand remained still, a picture of stiffness. His other hand gripped his rifle, a series of deadly mechanics covered in computer implements all molded for perfect accuracy.

"Attention, maggots!" Captain Milligan's studded boots scraped beneath his feet. "Listen, boys! Forget everything you ever learned. Today is the first day of your existence."

Eight soldiers strapped up.

Alix held his back straight and his neck back. His jaw clenched, and the muscle on his shaved head tightened.

"I miss you, Alix." Hayden lifted his chin. "Where have you been?"

"I've been spending time planning the next siege. Jaxon hopes to have the capital back by the end of the month. I guess the whole northeast is under our control again, and active government has started to come together."

Hayden shook his head and laughed. "Yeah, whatever, or until MAIA attacks. How are you and Anna?"

Alix smirked and pulled his mask over his face. The world brightened through the yellow lenses, and his digital HUD activated, and he inhaled his first bitter, audible breath. "No details there, bud. All I'll tell you is there could be a little Alix or Anna soon."

Milligan transformed and molded into Jaxon. Jaxon held the support straps dangling from the ceiling, overlooking each pair of yellow eyes. His forearms tightened to hold him in place from jerking back and forth. His bald head glowed. "ETA two years, and we'll have this world back! Hayden, Wes, Phil, Eli, Matt, and Adam, you're Team I Don't Give a Fuck. Alix and Victor, you're Team Fuck You. Don't forget your training! Keep your masks on! And remember, if you find yourself out of contact of me, and surrounded by them, do yourself a favor and turn the gun on yourself after taking a few of those bastards down with you."

The intercom bellowed. "Ready for deployment maneuver!" The helicopter jolted. The small flying machine banked backwards. The chopper descended faster than gravity. Metal pings engulfed the small armored cabin, and anxieties filled it to the ceiling.

Bullets.

The soldier's shaky hands released their shoulder straps.

"Three!" The pilot's voice stuttered. "Two!"

"Deploy!"

The plated door flopped open, and the heavy steel rattle echoed in their helmets. The floor shook. Hayden lifted his assault rifle, screamed, and barreled out of the chopper's cabin. Hayden's gun spat to the left. Like a sneeze, the helicopter emptied. The earth vibrated beneath their boots. Gravity pulled harder here. Suddenly there was silence.

Wes dropped his eyes first. "To the fire!"

They tossed their guns aside in the sand and sat around the beach fire. Chairs scattered around. Comfort took over their bodies. They each popped open a beer and passed around a bottle of Jack. Anna sat next to Alix. "Hey, babe." She kissed him lightly and sipped her beer. "Why you still wearing your vest?"

Alix looked down. "I don't know."

Eli looked over at him and smiled and strummed a guitar. "You are a good guy, you know. Take care of her for me, huh?" Eli smirked and sipped his beer.

Alix held up his middle finger. "Fuck you, Eli." Alix kicked sand at him.

"Hey! Come on! Don't get sand in my beer." Eli laughed.

Alix looked over to Wes. "Where did you guys go? Why didn't you respond at all after the battle?"

Wes stared into the flames. Two pools of fire burning in his pupils. "We knew Maia had her claws in us still. We randomly started thinking weird shit. After we took down the barge and lit that thing up, we took a small boat to the other side of the river. We figured it best. Huh, Phil?"

Phil nodded. He sipped his Hennessy. "Yeah, I all of sudden wanted to kill you and remembered this little fucker." Phil reached over and clasped Eli's head.

"Don't touch me, man!" Eli batted him away. "Fuck off." The guitar coughed.

"Really? So what are you guys doing?" Alix squeezed Anna. She kissed his neck and leaned onto him, her shoulder on his chest.

Adam tossed some wood into the fire. Sparks spiraled. "They figure if they get far enough they can get out of range from the broadcasts. I didn't make it. I think they have the right idea though. If they can get out of range from the servers, they won't get the updates and can at least keep what they have now."

"Here, here." Hayden lifted his drink. "We will keep running until the weird dreams stop and Maia stops trying to get us to come back or kill ourselves. I wish I could just dig this chip out completely."

"And forget any actual information you have in your brain?" Matt laughed. "You'd be a complete moron."

"Fuck you!"

Matt puckered and blew him a kiss. "After you do, can I dig that out for your? I have a blade right here." Matt grabbed his crotch.

Everyone laughed.

"Psst, Alix."

Alix turned around. He couldn't see anything. He looked back as Jaxon, his family, Silva, and Kalev joined the fire. They all sat around, the sound of their laughter crashing into the waves. The feeling of sand in their feet. The warm summer wind tickled the fire. The smell of campfire in their noses. The illuminated bridge in the distance.

"Psst, Alix, come here."

Alix stood and followed the noise.

"Where you goin', baby?" Anna leaned forward.

"Over here to piss real quick, here hold my beer for me."

"K, babe. Hurry back."

"Psst, over here, Alix."

"Who's there?" The blackness, as Alix walked away from the fire, became complete and full. "Hello?"

"Ow! Are you kidding me! Get your head down! You really are an amateur." Gunther pulled Alix down next to him. Leaves and sticks and sand plastered to his suit made him invisible. "What the fuck are you thinking? Get down! Here, take this. She'll be here any second for your orders."

Alix held his gun. He aimed down the sights. "Who?"

"Maia! Don't you pay attention to anything!"

Alix stayed in prone and watched the fire from over a mile away. He scanned each of their faces.

"Hello, Alix."

Alix didn't look. He didn't respond. His hair stood on end, and a chill trickled down each vertebra.

Maia laid down next to him in her all-white suit.

"You're going to get your clothes dirty."

She placed her hand on his back, her leg over his, and snuggled next to him. "That's okay, sweetie. Where have you been? I've missed my best little sniper."

Gunther grunted. "Second best, Maia."

"I know, Gunther, you're jealous. Now shut up and call the shot."

Maia leaned into Alix. She kissed him lightly on the cheek and twirled her finger around his ear. Her hand reached down the back of his vest, crawled over his butt, and she clasped him. "Call it out, Gunther."

"Target, Eli. Two Miles. Wind fifty miles and hour south, south east. Dew point forty degrees. Coriolis two clicks vertical and one click horizontal deflection. Aim, fire."

Alix pulled the trigger, Eli in his sights. Eli's head zipped to the side, and he fell over. No one seemed to realize.

"Target, Jaxon. Two Miles. Wind same, aim, fire."

Alix's gun exploded, and Jaxon fell dead through his scope.

"Nice shot, Alix." Maia leaned more on him and kissed his cheek. "I miss programming you."

"Target, Adam. Shoot."

Alix pulled the bolt and cocked it back.

"Target, Hayden. Shoot! Target, Victor. Shoot! Target, everyone, shoot!"

Anna stood. She looked around. Alix had killed everyone before she realized anyone went missing.

"Target, Anna. Three miles, wind seventy-five miles per hour, north northwest. Dew point, seventy-nine degrees. Coriolis, five clicks horizontal and vertical deflection. Aim, fire!"

"I can't."

"Alix…" Maia kissed his cheek. "You can, hunny. Shoot your little girlfriend for me. Don't make me reprogram you. The vanishing sequence is a lot easier to perform now."

"I can't. It's too far."

"Alix. You don't have a choice. Gunther, call it out."

"Target, Anna Brooks, aim, fire!"

"No!"

"Alix!"

"No!"

"Alix! Listen to me! Now! SHOOT!"

Alix's finger froze. Tears dripped from his eye. Alix squeezed the trigger. The bullet traveled for an eternity. Alix dropped his rifle, and she appeared much closer as the bullet in slow motion traveled through visible sound ripples through the air toward her. He stood and ran after the bullet. "Anna! No! I can redo the math. I can fuck up on purpose. I'll miss the shot on purpose!"

"You never miss." Maia smirked. "You can't miss."

"Yes, I can! I'll redo the math." Alix dropped to a knee and did the math in his head.

"It's easy, I'll just change one variable of the bullet, the vertical deflection. If I just put a slight breeze or miscalculate the dew point or the deflection it will miss.

"You never miss, Alix." Anna's voice echoed. Alix sprinted. He saw the sadness in her eye, the tear that ran down her cheek. "Alix, how could you?" Her broken heart an unmistakable certainty. Her eyes dropped into sadness, and she waited for her fate. The bullet entered her forehead and splashed out the back. Her eyes went cold and wide. Her mouth hung open. No sound.

Alix tripped on the sand, and he reached for her mouth full of dirt. "Nooooo! Anna!"

Maia knelt next to him and placed her hand on his back. "I still have a connection to you, Alix! I can still read your mind! I can still feel you!" Maia pushed his face in the sand and held the back of his head.

"Ahh fuck!" Alix snapped up in bed. Sweat dripped off his body. Alix shook his head quickly. "Fucking stop! Stop!" He held the side of his head.

"Baby, what's wrong!" Anna snapped up, wiped sweat from his forehead, and wrapped him up. "Babe, you're all sweaty. What's going on? It was just a dream, babe. Just a dream. You're here with me right now. Come on. Calm your heart rate. Calm down, lie back with me."

Alix collapsed back into the bed and stared at the ceiling. "Oh my god. I had another nightmare."

"Again?" Anna snuggled up next to him after dabbing him dry using the sheet.

"Yeah." Alix wrapped his arm around her and kissed her forehead lightly.

Anna squeezed him. "Did you shoot this time?"

"No." Alix lied. He didn't want to scare her more. He placed his hand over her belly and massaged gently.

"Well, good." Anna smiled and kissed him on the shoulder. "'Cause you ever shoot at me, you know I'll fire back. Oh my god, your heart is pounding. Alix?"

"I know. I'll go to the bathroom and splash water on my face." Alix lifted the sheet and walked, in his boxers, across the luxury hotel room overlooking the city from a floor-to-ceiling glass wall. He ran the water and splashed his face. He propped his arms on each side of the sink and let the water run down his body. The water ran down over the back of his head, down his neck, and over his chest and stomach. A drop dripped down off his nose and to his EED. Alix looked at it.

In the bottom right-hand corner it blinked like Alix had never seen before.

"Error."

EPILOGUE

The screen glitched, and static consumed his vision. He lifted his simulation goggles and wiped the sweat off his head. He leaned forward, his elbows dug into his knees and he hung his head. He's ran this simulation dozens of times. It was the only outcome he liked. He scratched his orange beard and sighed. He knew that simulation stood to be an undeniable certainty, and time tapped on his shoulder impatiently. If he deviated what he just watched in any way, the outcome could be lightyears off. But would it hurt to duck just a second earlier and stop that butterfly from affecting anything? Milligan smirked at the irony. It seemed impossible for both Alix and him to make it off the island alive based off what he just watched. Milligan stood, stretched and cracked his neck. Here goes nothing…

ABOUT THE AUTHOR

WD Shipley (Bill) graduated from the University of Massachusetts Lowell where he studied the art of creative writing under some of today's greats in the industry. The young writer's supportive parents remember finding their son asleep at his computer, up all night trying to finish his first manuscript in high school. Since then, Bill aspires to tap into the human emotion and leave his mark on society today, tomorrow and forever through his words on the page. He believes in following your dreams and never giving up. He currently resides in New Hampshire pursuing his own dream of starting a family and living a simple, successful and happy life with the love of his.

CPSIA information can be obtained at www.ICGtesting.com
Printed in the USA
BVOW08s1246240216

437877BV00002B/160/P